Great News Town

By Sue Merrell

ISBN 978-1-257-85991-7
Cover design by Ryan Wallace

For more information go to http://greatnewstown.blogspot.com

DEDICATION

Great News Town is a work of fiction. The characters do not represent actual people, living or dead. Some of the events, however, were inspired by a series of murders that occurred in Will County, Illinois, during the summer of 1983 when I was assistant city editor at the *Joliet Herald-News*. Although it's been almost 30 years, I still remember the horror of that summer, as I am sure the friends and families of the victims do. I'd like to dedicate this book to some of the people who were murdered that summer. Death is not anonymous.

In memory of:

Zita Blum

Honora Lahmann

Kenneth Chancellor

Terri Lynn Johnson

George Kiehl

Cathleen Norwood

Richard Paulin

Steven Mayer

Denis Foley

Anthony Hackett

Anna Ryan

Pamela Ryan

Barbara Dunbar

Marilyn Baers

Chapter 1

Dust swirled through the budding cornfields, a harbinger of the horror that would invade Cade County that summer. But for Old Ben, it only meant a car was coming.

"Natalie," he thought, rocking on the porch of the white farmhouse where he had been born eighty-five years earlier. He wasn't clairvoyant, just observant. He could tell by the height of the corn it was late June, and the slant of the sun told him it was about six in the evening. His cousin, Shirley Conley, who lived on the next farm over, had passed his house half an hour ago, and her teenage daughter, Natalie, usually came home a little later.

Surveying the western horizon, as Ben did for hours at a time, he could see the line of trees, far to the right, where the Jordan River meandered a few miles north of his farm. The Victorian house his grandfather had built was straight ahead about half a mile. Off to the left a little was Richland Baptist Church -- from his porch he could see just the grove of trees around the church and sometimes, when the sun was just right, the glimmer of the cross at the top of the old steeple. Farther to the left were the three squat silos of the Thompson place. Beyond these familiar landmarks, Ben liked to say, "It's so flat you can see all the way to Iowa."

The view from Ben's front porch hadn't changed much in his lifetime, but it was a different story looking east out his back door. Twenty years ago the Interstate slashed through his farm, taking his barn and his pond and any hope of keeping his little herd of cattle. If there could be a single spot where the past meets the future, where the rural expanse of northern Illinois gives way to the creeping tentacles of Chicago, it would be here on Ben's farm.

To the west, a grid of dirt roads cuts the farmland into nice even sections, every mile in each direction. Sometimes the gravel ribbons bear the names of settlers like Gouch, Murray, Thompson, or Ben's Grandfather Davis, and sometimes they use the numbered convention favored farther east -- 128th Street, 132nd Street, 144th Street. On the other side of the Interstate, dirt roads meld into asphalt thoroughfares, houses sprout as thickly as corn once grew, and apartment buildings replace silos as the rulers of the skyline. They call it civilization, but it isn't always so civilized.

As Ben watched the cloud of dust, he realized two vehicles were coming, driving fast and much too close together. Foolish kids. He was on his feet and headed down the walk to shout at them when Natalie's old Ford swerved into his gravel drive and the truck that was following sped past, barely navigating the curve along the Interstate just beyond Ben's place.

Natalie jumped out, speaking what sounded like some foreign language. "MBL376, MBL 376" she repeated over and over, walking in circles. Suddenly she used a finger to write the number in the dust on her car's trunk.

"Did you see that?" she screamed, turning to Ben. "He had a gun! He shot at me! He pulled in behind me back by the church and got right up on my bumper and shot at me!"

"Are you sure it wasn't a firecracker?" Ben said, unbelieving.

"No. It was a gun and he was shooting at me! He's a crazy man!

She went around to examine her car for bullet holes but found none.

"I don't know what I did. He was shooting at me for no reason, "Natalie shouted. "What kind of truck was that? The police will ask. Would you say black or green? It was so dusty."

Ben began to laugh.

"You're pretty dusty, yourself " he said and reached out a gnarled hand to brush her shoulder. "Want some lemonade?"

"No, thanks, what I really want is . . ."

A loud clap of something that sounded like ground-shaking thunder interrupted. The old man and the girl looked up at the sky. Not a cloud.

"Wow, was that thunder?" Natalie wondered out loud.

"I don't think so," Ben muttered. He prided himself on understanding the signs of nature, and that wasn't one.

"I'd better go home and tell Dad about the crazy man," Natalie said, sliding behind the wheel of her car. "He'll call the police. Thanks anyway, Ben."

Old Ben watched as she disappeared around the curve, then turned his eyes skyward as a second clap of the strange thunder resounded.

Chapter 2

At the Jordan swimming pool, Josie Braun surveyed the sky. It didn't look like rain, but it sure sounded like thunder.

"Come on Kevin," she hollered to the boy paddling toward the side. "We need to go. It's going to rain."

"Just a little longer," Kevin hollered back and started paddling in the other direction. With her short, blond pixie haircut and petite figure, Josie looked a little like a boy herself instead of a single mother and city editor of the local newspaper. She gathered Kevin's towel and flip-flops and met him at the other end of the pool.

"Let's go, *now!*"

"Aww, not yet" came the response as the boy paddled away again. One of the other parents laughed. Then the lifeguard's whistle squealed.

"Everybody out. Dinner break," the guard yelled and blew the ear-piercing whistle again.

"Wha'd he say?" Kevin asked, pausing halfway across the pool to tread water.

"He said your mother is leaving without you!" Josie responded and turned away. She could hear complaining children exiting the pool and rushing toward the locker room or concession stand. Another whistle. "No running," the guard warned.

"Can I have a snow-cone?" Kevin said, coming up wet and dripping at her side.

"No, I have chicken marinating in the fridge. Dinner in thirty minutes. I promise."

"I'll be hungry again by then," Kevin whined. "Just a Coke, *please?*"

"No, Kevin." She draped the towel over his shoulders and handed him his flip-flops as they parted at the door to the men's dressing room. She smiled; every day was so much the same.

Minutes later, Josie could see this night would be different. A crowd was gathered outside the grocery store, where a huge plate glass window had shattered.

"Oh, it wasn't thunder," a woman said. "It must have been an earthquake."

"We don't have earthquakes in Illinois," a man guffawed.

"Well, I heard there was one in Missouri once that moved the Mississippi River," another man said.

The buzz continued inside.

"I thought a car was coming through the window," the cashier said. "I started to run."

"Sounded like a shotgun going off," said a woman in line.

Josie wasn't sure what had happened, but she was sure going to find out.

Chapter 3

Second shift was well underway in the tractor plant, and the low drone of machinery masked the loud noise that caused such a commotion elsewhere in Jordan. In the office, however, plant manager Carl Anderson heard it. He jumped to the window and looked toward the intersection, because it sounded like a car crash. He remembered all too well when a carload of teens collided with a semi three summers ago. He was still at the window when Tracy Morton knocked on the open door of his office.

"Mr. Anderson?" the shapely nineteen-year-old in too-tight jeans said in a loud, showy voice. Then, with a smile, she asked more quietly, "May I come in?"

"Of course," Carl said, closing the blinds on the glass window that separated his office from the plant. Tracy slipped in and closed the door.

"I wasn't sure you could get away," Carl said, stepping closer.

"I wasn't sure you'd still be here," she replied.

By now the two were standing almost face-to-face. Though her blond hair had three-inch dark roots, there was a freshness in Tracy's face that Carl mistook for innocence.

"I wanted to apologize for yesterday," Carl began.

"Why?" Tracy asked flirtatiously.

"Well, I wanted you to know that I don't do this sort of thing. I mean not usually."

"That's not what I hear," Tracy teased and turned away.

"What do you hear?" Carl followed her.

"Women talk."

"Men talk," Carl countered.

Tracy gathered the papers and books from the credenza along the wall and handed an armload to Carl.

"Do you really need all this stuff?" she asked.

"Listen, you've got to understand . . . "

"Oh, I understand," she cut in as she continued to stack books and papers in Carl's outstretched arms.

"I find you very attractive but . . . "

"But what?"

"Well, it could get messy. I just don't want . . . "

"Are you afraid of a little mess, Mr. Anderson?" Tracy giggled as she added a large black folder to the top of the teetering stack in his arms.

"You're too young to realize . . . " Carl was saying when Tracy pulled off her T-shirt and tossed it on the top of the nose-high stack. He stared, unbelieving, at her perky breasts as she hoisted herself up onto the now bare credenza.

"You really ought to get a sofa in here."

Carl set his load of books in a chair and reached for Tracy, laughing. He held her tight and kissed her hungrily, his hands roaming her bare back, inhaling her sweet scent. The forbidden fruit excited him; he felt nineteen again instead of forty-five and balding. Vigor coursed through his body as it had the night before, when they had gotten carried away in the back of his car after the company softball game.

She was right; he'd had other indiscretions. Other passionate moments with other female employees. But never one as eager, never one this young.

Insistent beeping interrupted his thoughts.

"Ignore it," Tracy breathed and began unbuttoning his shirt.

"I can't," he said, lifting the beeper off his belt and glancing at the message. He jerked and pulled away. "Hey, listen, it's a fire. I've gotta go."

"What?" Tracy sat up indignantly. "You've got to be kidding. I'm on fire!"

"And so am I," Carl paused for another embrace, "but I'm one of the lieutenants in the department."

The phone rang and he reached for it. .

"Yes, yes, I got the message, I don't know, as soon as I can, I'll let you know," Carl's one-sided conversation continued even when Tracy slipped off the credenza and began rubbing against him. He pushed her away. "Well, the boys will just have to understand. I'm sorry; I can't control these things. I'll call you when I can. I will. I love you, too."

When Carl hung up, he turned to find Tracy huddled in the corner, her arms folded protectively over her bare chest. Suddenly, she felt naked and her cheeks burned pink with the slap of his words.

"I'm sorry," he said, and turned to leave. She grabbed a book from the stack and threw it against the closing door.

Chapter 4

When Josie pulled into the driveway of her little split-level house on the west side of town, her neighbors were gathered outside talking about the "loud boom." It had been strong enough to knock pictures off the wall and break dishes. The phone was ringing as she opened her front door

"There's been an explosion at the refinery," said Hoss, the chief copy editor at the *Jordan Daily News*. "A cat cracker or some such thing took off like a rocket and landed in the middle of the highway a mile away, taking out the power lines on the way."

"Shit," Josie breathed as she set her groceries on the counter.

"You owe me a dollar," Kevin snipped.

"No power north of 157," Hoss continued, making a smacking sound in the phone as he sucked on his cigarette. "They've closed the highway, traffic's backed up to the Interstate. Maggie headed out there but hit a roadblock."

"Maggie?"

"She was here."

"Shit, she's too old to be tramping around at a fire."

"That's two," Kevin squealed delightedly. "You owe me two dollars."

"Not now, Kevin." Josie pushed her son away and turned back to the phone. "Call Mack. No, I'll call him. I'll bet he can rent a plane at the university. I'll be right in."

Josie made a couple of peanut butter sandwiches as she called photographers and reporters. Gray-haired Mack Stanton lived near the university, where flying was one of the courses offered. The *Daily News* had rented a plane there before and Josie was sure Mack could find a pilot eager to fly him over the fire for some photos. Then she called Stanley Pajeniewski--Page for short, though there was nothing short about the six-foot-seven photographer. If anyone could walk through fire, it was Page.

"Pack some toys in a backpack, Kevin, we're going to the office." she yelled down to the toy-strewn family room.

"You owe me," he whined, sitting stubbornly in front of the television.

No answer at Nick's. He'd show up. Juan answered on the first ring.

"Yes, Yes, I'll be right there," he said eagerly. Calling him was the right thing to do, but still Josie hesitated. Juan was their summer intern. He needed the experience, of course, but taking him along tonight probably would be a strain for the other reporters. Maybe he could answer phones.

At Duke's house, his wife, Sharon, answered. "He's not here," she said rather stiffly. Duke was the most experienced writer on the staff; Sharon and Josie had known each other for years. Something was wrong, but Josie didn't have time to find out what.

"Well, when he comes in, have him call me at the office."

Josie peeked into the family room. "I need your help, Tiger."

"But you said two bad words," Kevin said, plowing a circle in the beige carpet with his toy tractor. The seven-year-old was a miniature version of Josie: the same cap of blond hair, Caribbean blue eyes and turned-up nose. Josie grabbed a sleeping bag off the closet shelf, tossed an empty backpack to Kevin and turned off the television.

"Hey," Kevin protested. Josie waved two dollar bills in his face.

"You're right. I shouldn't talk that way".

Chapter 5

Jordan was a blue-collar town of about 80,000 people, forty miles southwest of Chicago. Though enveloped now in faceless suburbs, it was an historical town, founded where the Jordan River flowed into the DesPlaines. In the 1800s it was a key port on the I &M canal that connected the Mississippi and Illinois Rivers to Lake Michigan. The canal was replaced with the Illinois Waterway in the 1900s and Jordan's four drawbridges still saluted a steady traffic of grain and petroleum barges.

The *Jordan Daily News* occupied a sprawling one-story white building on the western edge of town, just across the road from Caterman Tractor Company, the town's major employer. Part of a successful national newspaper chain, the *Daily News* was furnished more like a flashy savings and loan than a no-nonsense newsroom. Charcoal gray desks, burnt orange file cabinets and matching chairs were perfectly coordinated with the gray and orange tweed carpet. But the clutter of newspapers, reference books and mountains of mail revealed the true nature of the place.

At seven-thirty in the evening, an hour after the explosion at the Union Oil Refinery, an army of blank-faced computer terminals stood over the empty desks of the newsroom.

"Pow, pow, take that. Oh, ow, you got me." The fighting words came from beneath a red sleeping bag stretched between two chairs to create a tent in the middle of the newsroom. Juan looked questioningly at Josie.

"It's my son, Kevin," she said, pulling back a corner of the tent. "Kevin, this is Mr. Hernandez. Can you say hello?"

"Hello," Kevin mumbled without looking up. He had a *Star Wars* character in one hand doing battle with another perched awkwardly on the seat of a little metal tractor. Josie returned his tent covering and motioned for Juan to follow her to a map as colorful as a patchwork quilt hanging on the wall. The refinery was about eight miles north of Jordan, closer to the little bedroom community of Vollinger.

"Here, I want you to go with Page," Josie said as she stood on tiptoe to point to the location. "Now, this road is closed, and all the major entrances are blocked," she continued, pointing. "But back here, on the other side of the Interstate, there are lots of old dirt roads. I'll bet one of them leads to a back gate."

"Oh, yeah, we'll get through," Juan said eagerly. Page looked doubtful. "Keep an eye on him," Josie told Page without a hint of apology and reached for the ringing phone.

"Becky! I knew we could count on you. Hit the hospital. And find Teasdale. We need to know what the death toll is."

Zach Teasdale was the county's publicity-hungry coroner. Becky Judd, a determined young black reporter, would have no trouble getting a comment from him. Hundreds of people worked at the refinery. With a fire this big, certainly someone was hurt or worse.

Nick Davidson, still wearing a red and white baseball uniform, came in as Juan and Page left. His team had been playing a team from the sheriff's department when the game was called because the competitors' beepers kept going off.

"I figured it was something big," Nick said, his pale blue eyes dancing.

"I want you to go around it on the Interstate and try to enter from the east," Josie said, pointing to the map. "The city papers and TV stations will come in that way. You can hold your own with them, even in a baseball uniform."

"Eh, maybe I can slide in," Nick joked, grabbing a notebook from his desk. With wavy, brown hair and a lean, athletic figure, Nick was heartbreaker handsome and it gave an air of confidence to everything he tried. His face seemed sculpted by the hand of God with a deep, thumb-size dimple in each cheek and a little nick in his chin like the flick of a pinky finger.

As suddenly as it had come to life, the newsroom was quiet again. Like most modern offices, it was one big room with bookshelves and file cabinets providing separation between the desks. A wall of windows, unhampered by any covering, looked out onto the street.

Hoss sat at the end of a row of dark computer terminals, editing copy on a silvery bright screen. Nicknamed after the bountiful brother on his childhood western, *Bonanza,* he wore a T-shirt and jeans. Sweat dotted his brow and left his dark blond curly hair in little wet ringlets around his face. His jeans rode low, under a big belly that protruded sometimes from beneath his shirt, and if he didn't tug on his jeans frequently, his cheeks peeked out in the back. Josie thought he looked like a giant baby, and in many ways he was: A forty-eight-year-old man who had never left home or married and loved to work the odd hours when the newsroom was quiet. But he also loved to break the rules, smoking at his desk, drinking Cokes and munching candy bars -- all strictly forbidden in the newsroom. He didn't see it as breaking the rules, of course, because these behaviors were perfectly acceptable until the computer system was installed a few years earlier.

"You know that has to go," Josie said as Hoss puffed loudly on his cigarette and surveyed a fan of white pages on his desk.

"Yeah, I know," he said, not even looking up. "We'll need more space."

"Yeah, I'll call Donnellson," Josie said. The production manager would have to approve a new lace-up. "You think four pages will cover it?"

"Better make it eight, Peter Pan."

In Hoss's nickname-for-everything vocabulary, Josie was Peter Pan, the spunky little leader of their "Neverland" newsroom, a Cathy Rigby-like woman with boyish looks and attitude. She was so different from the city-editor stereotype, old journalists like her bald predecessor, Martin Jameson.

Josie went to her desk and swirled the gigantic black Rolodex, flipping past Davidson, Daniels, DEC Financial Services, Demer Museum. Then one card, printed in red, jumped out at her. "D-E-C-I-D-E." It was one of several encouraging words she had planted around her desk a year ago when she moved into the city editor's job.

"Bet Martin never needed cheat sheets," Josie thought. Gruff, cigar-chomping Martin, who had hired her fresh out of college ten years before, was the only city editor she'd ever known. She could never be like him, barking orders without so much as a pause for breath. Maybe that's why she always felt a little inadequate in the role.

"Never say please," he had told her. "Go with the gut, and if you're wrong, never apologize."

Of course, Martin never expected Josie to succeed him when he made her his assistant five years ago. He simply liked her organization skills and her rewrite ability. He didn't know cancer would make his final decision.

Josie flipped a few more cards to Donnellson and dialed. When the production manager answered, she tried to speak with Martin's no-apology certainty.

"Just wanted to let you know, I'm adding eight pages to tomorrow's paper."

Chapter 6

"Are you little Scotty Miller?" Maggie said to the young officer directing traffic at a roadblock. "Why, I can remember when your father joined the sheriff's department. I knew him before you were a glimmer in his eye."

"Yessem," the skinny young officer replied. "But you still can't go through here."

At sixty-eight, Maggie Sheffield was the oldest reporter on the *Daily News* staff and had just celebrated her fiftieth year at the paper. She had started right out of high school taking obits. Her writing style was a bit stilted and she shunned computers, still composing her stories on a typewriter. But there was hardly anyone in Cade County she didn't know.

"Daniel Franklin, good to see you." She turned to the second officer, a fifty-ish black man.

"Good to see you, Maggie."

"So, what's going on up there? I understand there's some debris blocking the road."

"That's what I understand."

"Was anyone injured?"

"You'll have to ask the sheriff, Maggie. I can't say."

"Oh, I know you can't say officially, but you can let me know how bad it is. Any motorists injured?"

"No motorists," Dan replied, a telling hesitation in his voice. "If you want to know more, you'll have to talk to the sheriff."

"Oh, I see. Well, it didn't hit a house did it?"

"There was some damage to property."

"Oh, my." Maggie watched as Scotty directed another car to the detour and then turned back to Dan. "Say, I was sure sorry to hear about your wife."

"Thanks, Maggie."

"How many kids do you have, is it four or five?"

"Five."

"Oh, yes! Well, your oldest must be as big as Scotty here."

"Almost."

"My, my, time flies. So, how many you say were injured, then?"

"Listen, Maggie, you didn't hear this from me, but they've called the coroner and every ambulance in three counties."

"Oh, my Lord! Well, thanks, Daniel. Good luck with your kids. Hope you don't have to work too late tonight."

"Looks like an all-nighter. Scotty here is missing his own bachelor party."

"Don't say! When's the wedding?"

"Saturday," the freckled-faced officer said, beaming.

Chapter 7

Page's brown van was iced in beige dust by the time he and Juan pulled in next to a restored Chevrolet Impala parked along the banks of the Jordan River about a mile south of the fire. The couple inside had forgotten about the flames on the horizon and was fanning those inside the car.

Juan jumped out of the van and headed toward the riverbank, speaking loudly to no one in particular.

"Wow, look at that. You can see the fire from here. There must be flames a hundred feet high. I wonder how much fuel they're burning up. Bet I could run my car on that fuel for a year."

The driver of the Impala, a burly man of about thirty with slicked-back, dark hair, stuck his head out the window.

"Hey, man, ya mind?"

"Huh? Oh, sorry," Juan said as if noticing them for the first time. He stretched his neck from one side to the other, surveying the car.

"Sweet, man. '63?"

" '62," came the response.

"Sweet! 283?"

"327"

"No way! My ol' man hab-im-one-a-dos." Juan purposely slurred his words together with a melodic street rhythm. Then cocking his head toward the hood, "Cud-I?"

In an instant, Richard Angelo jumped out and popped the hood to show off his pride and joy. It was almost nine, but it was just a few days after the summer solstice, the longest day of the year, and enough light remained for oooing and ahhhing.

Inside the car, Kathy Woods smoothed her blouse and straightened her just-so coif in the rearview mirror. Then she glanced over and saw Page sitting silently behind the wheel of the van and got a little suspicious.

"Richie?" she wailed, but the duo under the hood didn't budge. Page smiled and she nervously honked the horn.

"Hey, whaaa?" Richard stepped around to the side window. "Keep it warm for me, baby." He returned to Juan, whispered something, and soon the two were laughing like old friends. The hood came down and Juan approached the window.

"Sorry to interrupt." He smiled at Kathy and raised his eyebrow in an approving leer that made her blush. Then he turned to Richard. "Man, these roads all look the same to me."

"Take the one by the round barn, across the river and down on your left a ways," Richard said, pointing toward the fire. "There's a gate but it's just a loop of wire over the post. You can open it easy."

"Thanks, man." Juan jumped back into the van with a wink at Kathy, who was leaning out the opened window, her low-cut blouse showing just enough cleavage.

"Nice guy," Richard said as he opened the car door and nuzzled up to Kathy. "You know his cousin went to the same high school in the city as my dad?"

"No kidding?" Kathy said, looking after the van.

As Juan had suspected, Richard was a veteran of make-out spots on these dark dirt roads and knew just where to enter the refinery property from this side. Juan and Page were there in minutes. The winding dirt driveway led right into the heart of the confusion, where no one noticed them. That close, however, the heat and smoke were suffocating.

Juan started with a huddle of employees in the parking lot. Simple questions at first. What happened? How did it start? The tales came pouring out.

"I'm not even supposed to work this shift. I was substituting for my brother."

"The whole building collapsed, just fell over. I don't know how I got out."

"There were so many people trapped."

"They'd already called the fire department before the explosion because somebody reported the leak."

"Yeah, it was one of them high-pressure tanks. You could hear the hiss, you know?"

Page shot photos of firefighters silhouetted against the flames. Smutty faces filled with horror and fatigue. Ambulances everywhere.

Then a security guard spotted them.

"You crazy?" he bellowed. "How the hell . . . " Get out. Hey, Steve, help me get this guy."

Page sprinted to the van and slung his camera into the back seat, where it rested with two others. Each guard grabbed an elbow and Page surveyed the smoky scene looking for Juan. Josie's words came back to him and he could just imagine the kid's body being hauled out like so many others. Then he picked out the intern talking to one of the firemen. He could stall for a few minutes.

"I got rights," Page said quietly, and dug in his substantial heels.

"Not here ya don't" one of the guards said. There was a loud popping sound and everyone looked up as another piece of building fell into the flames. "Come on, before you're toast." The guards pulled at Page.

"We'll go, we'll go!" Juan said, running up behind the guards. "Show us the fastest way out! Holy Mother! You should get all these employees out of here before somebody gets hurt." Juan motioned to the huddle of people watching from the parking lot.

The guard looked around. "Okay, everybody, in your cars and out of here." Turning to Page, he added, "I'm going to ride along with you two just to make sure you don't get sidetracked."

Page's soulful eyes spoke volumes.

"Sounds good to me," Juan said and pulled back the side door on the van. He jumped in, tossing newspapers from the floor over the cameras in the back seat and feigning a coughing spell. "Get me outa here!"

Page shrugged and walked around to the driver's side while the guard closed the slider and slipped into the other front seat. "Hey, kid, you gonna be okay?" the guard said, looking back at Juan in concern.

"Yeah, man," Juan replied, holding the newspapers in place over the cameras. "Let's go."

Page smiled and followed the line of cars. Just outside the front gate, television vans were lined up like the ambulances inside. Among them was Nick's bright red convertible.

"Hey, Page," Nick hollered when he recognized the hulking photographer and his dust-covered van.

Page stopped and the guard got out. "Go home boys," the guard said.

Juan peeked over the back of the seat. "Hi, Nick. Whadja get?"

Nick peered at their darkly smudged faces. "Jeez, where you two been?"

"Ahem, Nick" Page said in his low-key manner, "Isn't that your car?"

The cloth top on the little red car suddenly burst into flames , ignited by a shower of sparks from the building that had just toppled.

"Oh, shit!" Nick ran to his car as the television cameras turned to the fire in their midst.

"What can we do?" Juan said, eyes wide.

Page slipped the van into gear. "Man said to go home."

Chapter 8

Nick, swatting flames with his baseball jersey, was shown live on the ten o'clock news, but Duke was too drunk to recognize his buddy or the news story glowing behind him. Duke couldn't see much farther than the bottle of bourbon on the table. Sharon had gone to bed. She never stayed up with him anymore. He added another swig to the already strong drink in his glass and guzzled it down.

On the south side of town, in a run-down neighborhood known as Shabbytown, Hannah and Zoe Otis were sitting on their doily and cat-covered divan watching the same newscast. An old upright piano stood in the corner where the elderly black sisters had taught half the kids in the neighborhood to play. Hand-stitched signs hung nearby with sayings to remind the young students of the notes on the musical staff.

"Every Good Boy Does Fine." "Good Boys Do Fine Always."

"I can't imagine such an awful fire. Those poor families," said Zoe, the more slightly built of the two, as she stroked a large white cat.

"Imagine the laundry," the more rotund Hannah countered. " Why, last year when you dropped the ashes from the wood stove, I thought I'd never get it all cleaned up. Soot everywhere."

Zoe straightened up indignantly. "It wasn't my fault; the handle broke."

"Yes, dear, I know, but if you'd just be a little more careful..."

The doorbell rang and cats went scurrying every direction. The sisters looked at each other questioningly.

"Oh, dear," Zoe said, a little fearful.

"At this hour," Hannah sputtered. The braver one, she opened the door as far as the chain lock would allow. She peeked through the crack, "Yes?"

Chapter 9

Two men emerged from the shadows and pushed in through the doorway as soon as Becky inserted her passkey.

"Hey!" the leggy, black reporter shouted as her notebook skittered across the floor. "Hey, thanks a lot!"

The men started left but, seeing no lights, turned around and buzzed back past Becky, almost knocking her down and stepping on the opened notebook. "Up yours!" she shouted after them. The shorter one turned and tipped an invisible hat.

Thin as a model and twice as striking, six-foot-tall Becky wasn't easy to ignore. Though not pretty in a delicate, feminine sense, her features were as bold and demanding as her personality. Her nose was broad, her lips thick and sensuous, her skin dark with all the richness of her African heritage.

"Big city guys," Becky thought. She didn't recognize these two but guessed they were from one of the Chicago papers come to use the "facilities." The unwritten policy of Associated Press newspapers is to help their brethren when called upon, and when a big story breaks, welcome rivals into their buildings. Josie was expecting them.

"Running tight, aren't you?" Josie said loudly as she met them in the hall. The city's morning papers would be going to press soon.

"Midnight deadline," the bigger one said gruffly and pushed past toward the dark room like a seasick passenger rushing for the railing.

"Hi. Ted Simpson, *Tribune*," the smaller one said, offering his hand and card.

Josie didn't take it.

"Wouldn't you two be time ahead just to drive home?" she asked. "You could have made it in forty-five minutes from the refinery if you'd headed the other way."

"Well, we plan to file a quick one and get back out there," Ted said, trying to look past her to scope out the newsroom. The unstated purpose, of course, was to see what the hometown paper might have to steal. In reporting, it's not the more experienced or higher paid writer who gets the story; it's the one who has the sources. The hometown staff puts in thousands of hours, day after day, visiting the police stations, having coffee with firefighters, covering fundraisers and city council meetings. When the world blows up, they know whom to ask and the firefighters know whom to talk to.

Natty Ted Simpson could exchange cards with Union Oil's PR flack, rushed in from California to deal with the media, and a fire chief whose hands aren't even sooty would give him a carefully worded, sanitized statement, but the blood-and-guts story would be here in the hometown paper.

The *Jordan Daily News* was an afternoon paper, however. Even the earliest editions wouldn't be in readers' hands until noon, hours after Chicago's morning papers were flying out of news boxes all over the metropolitan area. Josie wanted to protect their best stuff so it would appear in the *Daily News* first.

"What kind of count do you have?" Simpson asked. Josie knew the coroner had just held a press conference, and she suspected Simpson had figures as good as theirs, but an answer might keep him away from Juan.

"What's the latest, Beck?" she said to Becky who was making faces behind Ted's back.

"Well let's see," Becky said, making a great show of opening her notebook to a page with Ted's shoeprint. "Looks like nine dead, mostly the company's firefighters, at least twenty injured, a couple of other employees missing."

Josie had heard the same figures on the news at ten, straight from the coroner's mouth.

"Yeah, that's what we got," Simpson said. "Got a terminal I can use?"

Becky again made signs behind Ted's back. She formed a circle with her forefinger and thumb to indicate she already had talked with the widow of the dead security chief and had visited Coroner Teasdale's makeshift morgue in a refrigerated truck. That was the kind of embarrassing detail he'd left out of the press conference, and the big city guys would never question how many bodies a small town hospital morgue could hold.

Josie smiled. "Sure, take your pick," she told Ted, gesturing toward the mostly empty room, where only Hoss and Juan sat at terminals. Maggie was writing on an electric typewriter behind the door of the library.

"Our reporter hasn't made it back yet," Josie said nonchalantly. "Our intern has been taking tips over the phone."

Juan looked up but didn't disagree. He understood the game.

"You work at the *Tribune?*" he asked. "Gee, maybe next summer I can work there. You got a name I could use?"

"Sure, kid," Ted said condescendingly, and flipped a card across the room. Juan jumped at it and beamed. Oh, it was too perfect!

The big one came out of the dark room and pulled Ted aside. Josie's heart was beating fast. Surely Page had heard her warning and hidden the good stuff. Mack emerged from the photo lab, his bag slung over his shoulder.

"Well, that's enough for this old man," the distinguished-looking Mack said, and winked at Josie. The *Tribune* probably had sent a plane to take aerial photos. They wouldn't have any use for Mack's film.

Then Page stepped out as well with a photo bag over his shoulder.

"Me, too," he said and then hollered back. "Last one cleans up the lab. You can handle that, eh, Trib?"

"Huh? Listen I . . . " The gruff *Tribune* photographer was stunned as Page and Mack disappeared out the back door. Josie was surprised, too. This was not the turf-protecting posturing everyone expected. There was nothing to do but play along.

"Sounds like you've got the lab to yourself, Tribune," she said with a weary sigh, "but don't take too long, I want to get the office closed up by midnight."

Ted and the photographer exchanged glances.

"Well, that's enough for me." Hoss turned off his terminal and picked up the tiny cooler where he stashed his illegal snacks. "Gonna catch a coupla hours of shut-eye and be back by five a.m."

"Hey, wait for me," Juan said, joining the exodus.

"Shit," the *Tribune* photographer said, tossing an envelope onto the desk. "It'll take me an hour to clean that developing machine."

"Whoa, that long?" Josie sighed looking at her watch. "Better hurry."

It was all she could do to keep from laughing out loud. She stepped into the library to warn Maggie and check on Kevin, who was curled up in his sleeping bag in the corner. Kevin clutched the cold, hard tractor as though it was a treasured stuffed animal, and Josie pulled it out of his hands so it wouldn't leave a mark on his cheek.

Chapter 10

Across town, Carl Anderson opened another door to check on his son. The high school basketball player was so tall his feet stretched over the end of the bed and poked out of the sheet. Carl pulled the sheet over his toes, and even in the darkened room he could see the sooty mark his fingers left on the white fabric. He was overcome. He rushed from the room, tears streaking down his blackened cheeks, and bolted out the back door into the cool, grassy yard. His sobs came noisily now and he gasped for air as he fell to his knees. Karen watched from the kitchen window. She knew he was like this after a bad fire. Inconsolable. It was better to let him have his privacy and preserve his manly dignity.

Carl wasn't a perfect man; Karen knew that. Somewhere deep inside, she suspected he hadn't always been faithful. But he was a good provider, he was a loving father, and he had been her best friend since high school. She wished he would quit this volunteer fire department. It was too dangerous. It had been years since anyone on the Jordan department had been killed, but still she worried. And when he saw other people die, it left him like this. Yet, watching him sobbing on his knees, she felt an overwhelming love. She admired his strength, but she loved his weakness. It was an unbeatable combination.

She had a smile on her face a few minutes later when he tramped through the back door, and she held out a cold beer like a trophy.

"Fire out?" she asked innocently.

"Oh, it won't be out for days," Carl said, as he steadied himself with a blackened hand on the gleaming white doorframe. He slipped off his boots, reached for the beer and took a long pull. "They flew in a team of experts from Texas. We were just the interim squad."

He stepped into the bathroom off the back entry and splashed his face with water, sudsed up and rinsed. She watched him, grimacing at the gray splatters on her floor and wall. Then, he grabbed a towel, leaving as much dirt there as in the sink.

He held out his arms to her and she stepped in with only the slightest concern about getting her pink robe soiled. After a few moments of silence he spoke, still holding her tight to his chest.

"I'm going to do better," he said, looking over her shoulder into the spotless kitchen. "I promise. No more long nights, no more missing the boys' games, no more fires."

"Really?" She pushed away to look at his face.

Tears welled up in his bloodshot eyes, but he wouldn't let them fall.

"It's okay," she said, hugging him close so he wouldn't have to look at her. "It will all be okay."

Chapter 11

Johnny Morton was fuming. He had spent the evening on the balcony of his north side apartment, sipping beers and watching the fire on the horizon. The flames seemed to mirror his anger. Every now and then he would toss an empty bottle a few feet across the dining area and listen for the comforting clink of another bottle in the trash can.

When Tracy Morton slipped her key into the lock and turned on the light, a beer bottle whizzed past her head and shattered against the wall.

"What the hell was that for?" she screamed.

"Sorry," Johnny slurred. "I missed!"

Tracy noticed the empty crib in the living room.

"Where's the baby?"

"What's it to you?" Johnny shot back. "You're never here for him."

She rushed to the balcony to confront her husband.

"Where is he? What have you done with Justin?"

"Justin," he mimicked in a prissy voice. "What kind of sissy name is Justin? The kid woulda faced a life of teasing."

"Woulda? What do you mean woulda?" Tracy was in Johnny's face now. "What did you do with my baby, you miserable drunk?"

"Your baby?" Johnny pushed her hard, so she fell across the living room. "If he's your baby why aren't you here taking care of him?"

Tracy crawled away from Johnny sobbing. "I'm calling the police."

"Go ahead, bitch. I'm calling Family Services. You're an unfit mother."

"Unfit? How can you say that? I'm just trying to earn a living."

"I earn a living. Your job is to care for our son."

"I left him with you." Tracy reached for the bedroom door and Johnny grabbed her.

"Shhh," he whispered loudly. "You'll wake him."

Tracy opened the door slowly and saw her infant son lying in the middle of their double bed, a pillow beside him on one side and on the other the imprint of where Johnny had lain to get the baby to sleep.

"See what I mean? What kind of mother would leave a baby with a miserable drunk like me?"

29

Tracy looked closer to be sure the infant was breathing and smelled that sweet baby smell. Her heart melted.

"Awww, look at him. Isn't he perfect?"

None of this had been the way she'd planned. Not getting pregnant. Not marrying Johnny. Most of the time she hated how her life had turned out. But watching the baby sleep quieted the anger in her chest.

"Look at Justin," she repeated, turning to Johnny.

"Shhh," he hissed. "I promised him that from now on we'd call him J.D. So the kids won't laugh at him."

"Oh, silly." Tracy nudged Johnny and he laughed.

"Well, it worked," he said, draping a heavy arm over Tracy's shoulders and pulling her so close that his beer breath made her gag. "He went right to sleep."

Johnny squeezed her a little too hard but when Tracy looked up, he was beaming. What a man of contradictions! She wasn't sure whether to fear him or love him, but she knew how to control him.

" Now where are *we* going to sleep?" she purred.

Chapter 12

By the time the sun came up Wednesday morning, the staff of the *Jordan Daily News* was toasting its success.

Reporters can't douse flames or soothe burns. They have no control over the horrors they witness. But if they can overcome fear and physical obstacles and wrestle the monster to the page before the sun comes up, it's a victory – not just for the newspaper staff but for all those sleeping soundly who will find the facts at their fingertips and all those victims whose suffering won't go unnoticed.

"Well, you'd better send a helicopter to haul in that great, big 'W' from the Hollywood sign in California," Hoss said with mock seriousness, "because it's a winner, a big win."

Everyone around the table in the break room cheered, raising paper cups of coffee, doughnuts, and a few diet drinks in salute. The mood was more manic than carefree, the euphoria people feel when there's more adrenalin than blood in their veins.

Juan, his clothes still smelling of smoke, was jabbering with bravado to mask the uneasiness of his first fire. The challenge of capturing what he'd seen energized him. Becky had more experience, so she knew she would be haunted every time a Sara Lee Frozen Pie truck passed her on the Interstate. It would be years before she would forget the indignity of human beings zipped into black plastic and stacked into that makeshift morgue. It made her mad that people could die just doing their jobs, so she fought back the only way she could -- giving each and every victim one more day of life, one more moment of dignity, on the pages of the *Jordan Daily News*.

"I still can hear that *Tribune* photographer complaining in the next room!" Josie laughed.

"How did you guys ever come up with that idea?" Becky asked.

"Well, I couldn't get anything done with him hanging around, so I figured I'd just take my film with me and go get dinner," Page replied in an aw-shucks tone that was barely audible. "The comment about cleaning up was an afterthought."

"Well, you guys added a page to the unwritten policy, that's for sure," Hoss said.

Josie looked around the room at all the eager young faces. Hoss, forty-eight, easily was the oldest, and at thirty-four, she was the old lady of the bunch. Maggie and Mack were older, of course, but they wisely had gone home for a little sleep not long after midnight. Duke, who was pushing forty, had never appeared. Perhaps that was why. All-night journalism was a young person's game. They'd all been up for twenty-four hours, working almost continually, and yet their enthusiasm and energy just seemed to grow.

Josie wondered briefly if Ted Simpson and the nameless photographer were cheering somewhere now or licking their wounds. She suspected in a staff as large as the Tribune's there would be little of this camaraderie. They probably put in their regular shift and abided by union regulations regarding overtime and such.

The *Jordan Daily News* was different. The staff was mostly young. The good ones would go on to bigger papers, and a stint here would be a fine addition to their resumes. Everyone knew Jordan was a great news town, one of those places that seemed to attract more than its share of big news stories. Part of that, of course, was due to its proximity to the city. It was big enough to attract criminals and yet small enough for crime still to be news. It was smack in the heart of America, where Midwest sensibilities ruled. But there was something intangible too, some quirk of fate that meant when a plane crashed, one or more of the passengers would be from Jordan; when a hostage was taken in some foreign land, he would be a hometown boy; and when a refinery blew up, the smoke would settle here.

"Say, everyone," Josie said, "before Ham gets in and tells us what we did wrong . . ." she waited for the grumbling that always followed such remarks, "I just want to say what a great job everyone did."

She lifted her doughnut to Page. "Page's pictures, Juan's wonderful interviews, Nick's quality reporting under great personal strain . . ."

Everyone added a "hear, hear" before she continued.

"Becky . . . touching and truthful as always, and to Maggie and Mack, who couldn't be here because they're old enough to require a few hours sleep,"

Again, shouts of affirmation from the room.

"It's a great paper; we can all be proud," she finished, taking a big bite from her doughnut.

Hoss rose to his feet. "Let me add that I just put the front page together at a record-breaking six a.m., and in honor of our Polish picture snapper and our new school's-out-so-I'd-better-get-a-job writer..." Hoss paused for dramatic effect, "I'm christening it Page Juan."

Laughter erupted and Juan, never one to miss a cue, jumped up and did a little Mexican hat dance, Spanish-sounding expletives rolling off his tongue. Josie knew his Hispanic name was part of the reason he had been hired. Even at smaller dailies like the *Jordan Daily News*, there were many applicants for the sole summer internship. A candidate with a cosmopolitan name like Juan Hernandez had an edge. But she also knew that Juan's Hispanic roots were about as thin as his lanky arms. Maybe his father's father had come from Mexico, but Juan's pale ivory skin, thin nose and square jaw were much more Anglo. He knew, however, which card to play, and tonight he had a full house.

Soon, everyone was dancing around the break table conga style, creating a commotion that could be heard all the way back in the newsroom where Hammond Reginald, the dour managing editor, was opening his sealed office door. It was well before his usual arrival time. Perhaps in his ivory tower knowledge of what it took to put a paper together, he thought a couple of hours would be enough to get a jump on such a major news event. At least it would be enough to deflate the egos of his staff.

Hammond never had been a reporter. He'd never attended a city council meeting and hadn't the first notion of what one might find in a police report. Certainly he'd never watched as a lifeless child was loaded into an ambulance or asked a wailing mother if she could spare a photograph. But he was an excellent speller and could spot a dangling participle without his reading glasses. Though these skills might have been better used in a classroom, Hammond had taken a job on the copy desk of a big city daily right out of college. He could have lived out his days happily managing nothing more than pieces of paper if Ginny, his frail wife, hadn't begged him to leave the city for a small town. So, with no more knowledge about how to inspire people than he had of how to worm a straight answer out of a city councilman, Hammond was named managing editor of the *Jordan Daily News*, strictly because he had twenty years of experience at a paper ten times its size.

Rob Greene, the impish backshop supervisor, stuck his head through the break room doorway.

"Hey, Rob, join us," Nick said, standing up to offer his seat.

"No, no," Rob shook his head. "Just thought you'd like to know something ain't kosher."

Curses passed through the room and everyone stood at once. It was newsroom code that Ham had arrived.

"Oh, shit!" Josie said, and as soon as she uttered the word she imagined her son dunning everyone in the room for a dollar. Then she remembered -- Kevin still was asleep in the library.

"Well, good," Hoss said as if he could read her mind. "I've been eager to show Ham the front page layout, and I want to show him those two photo pages we added and give him a budget of all the stories we have. It might take us a half hour or more, behind closed doors."

"Thanks," Josie breathed. "I'll owe ya one."

"I'll put it on your tab, Peter Pan."

Chapter 13

Everyone dispersed, some to their desks to finish last-minute tasks, some home to bed after a more-than-double day. After Hoss slipped into Ham's office and shut the door, Josie gathered up Kevin and helped him clean up and change clothes in the small ladies' room. She smoothed early morning grouchiness with a promise of McDonald's breakfast on the way to Ranch Rudy, a nearby day-care center with a Western theme. On the way out she spied the full ashtray on Hoss's desk and slipped it into a spare plastic bag. It disappeared along with Kevin, sleeping bag and poseable super heroes. It was the least she could do.

When she pulled in at Ranch Rudy, she noticed Dan Franklin, a sheriff's deputy, bringing in his two youngest. He looked as tired as Josie, yet he was not about to let his children know it.

"Is it animal?"

"Daddy, I already told you it was mineral. It can't be both animal and mineral."

"It can't? Well, is it yellow?"

"No, silly."

"It can be brown *and* yellow!"

"Yeah, but it isn't."

"Okay, you remember what you spied and we'll finish the game on the way home tonight."

The boy, about Kevin's age, took his little sister by the hand and ran into the building; Dan Franklin waited to see them inside the door.

"Look what I got, Mr. Franklin," Kevin said as he ran by, showing off the toy that came with his McDonald's breakfast. His ever-present tractor was under the other arm.

"That kid," Josie thought. "He sure isn't shy." Then she closed her eyes and said a sentence prayer, as mothers have since the beginning of time. "Keep him safe, Lord." It's the best a mother can do when her children are out of sight.

Chapter 14

The newsroom had come to life by the time Josie returned at eight. The rest of the copy editors filled the terminals. Eager Juan was back at his desk, with a clean shirt and a freshly showered look, ready to tackle two days in a row if needed. Maggie was at the front desk, regaling the receptionist, Helen, and women's editor, Dottie, with tales of the previous night.

The elusive Duke was typing away at his desk as though he had been there all along. He was a handsome man with thick eyebrows, a matching mustache and dark, close-cropped curly hair with just a touch of gray. Looking over Duke's shoulder was his twin, a larger than life cardboard cutout of the confident reporter holding his notebook and looking serious for the camera, a remnant of some *Daily News* marketing campaign. "Gotcha covered!" the cartoon bubble shouted.

"So, what's up?" Josie asked, approaching Duke's desk.

"Well, I thought I'd whip out a column about famous fires, compare the methods used last night to the Great Chicago Fire of 1871, and the damage totals, lives lost, that sort of thing." Duke said. There was no excitement in his voice; it probably had been Ham's idea.

"That's good, that's good," Josie said, "but first I need you to do all the regular cop checks. Nick and Juan already have put in twenty-four hours."

"You mean burglaries and dino droppings?"

Josie smiled. Creative cursing was Duke's specialty. "Anyone can say bullshit and damn. A writer should be a little more colorful," he had told her once.

"Yes, I need you to make the calls right away, in case there's anything that should get into today's paper, and type up all the rest as briefs for tomorrow. Then, I'll need you to catch the noon Rotary meeting. Lt. Gov. Helms is speaking. I was going to send Juan but . . . "

"I know, I know, but he's a real reporter now," Duke said, his voice rising. "He's got a page one byline. He gets the rest of the day off."

"Duke!" Josie cut him off because Juan was looking. "Let's take a break."

"Is something wrong?" Josie asked when they were safely ensconced in the empty break room. "It's not like you to miss a big news event like this."

"And it's not like me to complain when I'm a little under the weather," Duke responded, "but I don't appreciate getting punished like a bad child."

"You're not being punished. Cop checks are very important. You should know that better than anyone. Right now you're the freshest body I've got. You can write the historical column this afternoon, after you finish a short piece on the Rotary. I know you can whip it all out without breaking a sweat. And you'll come back with stories the others would have missed. I wish I'd had you to count on last night. I think you would have enjoyed it. But I'm certainly not punishing you by asking you to do what needs to be done today."

"Have Maggie do the Rotary thing. She's fresh enough to gab it up with Dottie already this morning."

"She's still on that Jacobs trial."

"Okay," Duke said, with more defeat than acceptance in his voice. "Guess I'd better get busy." He stormed out of the room, the metal toes of his fancy Texan boots making a staccato rhythm as he disappeared down the hall.

Josie shook her head.

Ormand "Duke" Dukakis once had been her hero. When she joined the *Daily News* a decade ago, he already was a legend. His stories had won several Illinois Press Association awards. He had a way of getting people to open up to him, of telling a story people could identify with. He'd become a columnist in addition to a reporter, so twice a week his photo ran with his slightly offbeat angle on some happening. He could turn a dogfight into an exciting story. He could make people care about a sewer bond issue. And he had become such close friends with the local cops that they trusted him with tips they wouldn't give anyone else.

Somewhere along the line, however, his ego had become as big as the cardboard cutout behind his desk. He'd heard it all before, so he'd stopped listening.

Suddenly, Josie looked up and saw Ham standing in the doorway.

"I need a word with you," he said and headed back to his office, assuming Josie would follow like an obedient dog. She did.

Ham closed his door and began a litany of complaints. Juan and Page should not have been encouraged to enter the refinery property and endanger their lives. Juan never should have been assigned at all; he was too inexperienced. A friend at the *Tribune* had called and said *The News* staff had been less than hospitable. And he thought he had seen a full ashtray on Hoss's desk when he came in.

"It was a long night," Josie said with her head down.

"But rules . . . " Josie didn't need to hear the rest of the sentence. He didn't say Page's photos should be submitted for Pulitzers. He didn't say Juan had done an excellent job for such a novice. He didn't commend every one of the staffers for putting the rest of their lives on hold for the good of the *Daily News*.

"And I don't want to see inordinate overtime over this," Ham finished.

"I'll take care of it, sir" Josie said, like a private reporting to a general. If she hadn't been so tired, she might have spoken up, but probably not. Still, she left the office with her head high. The paper would be coming out soon and she was proud.

Chapter 15

Triumphs in journalism are short-lived.

Thursday morning the phones at the *Daily News* were abuzz, not with compliments on the great coverage of the fire or concern for the dead firefighters' families, but complaints that the wrong crossword puzzle appeared in Wednesday's paper.

"You people never get anything right," one elderly gentleman told Josie. "I'm canceling my subscription."

Helen was keeping track of the callers --seventeen so far-- and sending each a copy of the correct puzzle (with the answers to the previous day's puzzle) and *101 Best Puzzles,* a booklet *The News* provided whenever it made a mistake on the daily games page.

"We'd be time and money ahead to rip out those two photo pages from the fire and fill 'em with puzzles," Hoss was saying, when Josie looked up and saw Kurt coming up the walk.

She hated the rush it gave her. They had been divorced for more than a year and her heart still jumped into her throat when she saw him. It was a different feeling from when they were courting, that flutter of anticipation, and yet it was similar. Would she ever be able to look at Kurt and simply see the director of the downtown development board, or would he always be Kurt, the man she used to love, the father of her son, the man who had ripped out her heart?

He came in the back door, as though he still worked there. Josie could hear him chatting with the security guard, and then with Dick in Sports. He worked his way across the newsroom with a handshake here, a pat on the back there, and always the right word. Kurt sure had a way. He even introduced himself to Juan.

"Hey, you must be the summer intern. Good to meet you. I'm Kurt Walsh. Used to be on the cop beat here myself," he said. "Now, I'm stompin' for downtown Jordan." He handed Juan a card. "Stop by and see me sometime. I can give you lots of good stories."

Kurt looked up and gave Josie a silent nod. There was no reason to cross the room to greet her. This wasn't family business. He stopped and hugged Dottie and complimented her colorful new scarf. Then he turned to Helen and, after a few pleasantries, nodded toward Hammond's office.

"The old man around?"

Helen buzzed the boss and soon Hammond was standing in the doorway with his hand outstretched.

"Kurt, come in, come in."

This couldn't be good. Josie was willing to bet Kurt wasn't here to invite Ham to a golf outing. The two men had chatted behind the closed door for about five minutes when Josie's phone rang.

"Can you and William step in a minute? And bring a copy of today's paper, will you?"

Josie's heart went into overdrive. When Hammond used Hoss's real name, it was never a good sign.

"See, here's what I mean," Kurt said, grabbing the fresh-off-the press Thursday edition from Josie. "'Two bodies pulled from rubble, death toll climbs to 11.' Yesterday it was 'Explosion kills 9.' How many days are we going to have to put up with this sensationalism?"

"What?" Josie exclaimed. She was flabbergasted, and Hammond wasn't saying a word.

"Thirteen fire departments showed up to help out with this fire, departments from all over the county," Kurt said, punctuating his points by poking the newspaper. "They did an excellent job. The Union Oil people are lauding the cooperation they received. All but one of the dead are employees who knew the risks. The fire was contained. Very little . . ."

"Wait a minute," Josie interrupted. "Are you saying those firefighters deserved to die because they worked for a refinery?"

"They make top dollar, babe." Kurt slipped too easily into the familiar when he was angry. "Double what the average city fireman makes. And most of the time they sit around playing cards. These guys knew what they were getting into. And most of them don't even live in Jordan."

Josie was seething. "Kurt, I don't understand what you are saying. You don't think we should mention the deaths in the headline?"

"No, I don't. Certainly not two days in a row. And if I know your thirst for blood, tomorrow's will be 'County mourns loss of 12.' That one guy isn't expected to make it, I hear."

"Excuse me," Hoss broke in. "Josie doesn't write the headlines. If you've got a problem with the headlines, deal with me."

"Now, I'm sure we can handle this without raising our voices," Hammond said and gestured toward chairs clustered around a table in the corner. When each person had taken a seat and a calming breath, Hammond continued.

"Kurt has a point here. We all know the power of seventy-two-point type, and we have to realize that not all of our readers will read the whole story."

"Exactly. Which is why I put the death toll in the headline," Hoss said with deliberate calmness. "It's the most important point."

"And that's where we differ," Kurt said with a conciliatory smile. "I think the most important thing is that the community came together to deal with this crisis and did a damn good job. We can put a positive spin on this story instead of sensationalizing the negative."

"News isn't positive or negative, " Josie pleaded. "People died here. Lots of people. We can't pretend it didn't happen."

"I'm not asking you to pretend anything, just see the good as well as the bad," Kurt said.

"Here's what we're going to do," Hammond said, his signal that any debate was over. "Kurt, I stand behind our coverage to this point. This has been a catastrophe of national proportions. But I agree the daily repetition can be a bit overwhelming. Josie, assign a story on the cooperation between all the local fire departments and Union Oil. Tell Duke to do it as his column this week -- he always does a nice job -- and we'll run it page one tomorrow. Above the fold. And Hoss, I don't care if all twenty of the injured succumb overnight, no more death tolls in seventy-two-point type."

There was a moment of silence while Kurt gloated and Josie tried to assess what really was being said.

"Sir," she said finally, making clear her acceptance of the chain of command. "The funerals are Saturday. We were planning to cover."

"Fine, but not on page one. Find something nice happening. We've had enough bad news this week. I think we'd all like to see a little more good news, right Kurt?" "That's right," Kurt said with a victor's smile. He stood and offered his hand. "Thanks for seeing me. Thanks for being so supportive of Jordan's best interests." He turned to Josie and Hoss. "Thanks for your support as well." He started for the door, and then paused as if turning the knife. "Golf Saturday, eight a.m.?"

Kurt and Hammond chortled over weekend plans as Hoss and Josie started to leave.

"Josie, one more thing," Hammond said, waiting for Hoss and Kurt to walk away. "This is a small town. Death is never anonymous as it is on the television newscast."

"I know," Josie sighed. She had heard this speech before.

"And I don't want any animosity you might feel for Kurt to get in the way of sound news judgment,"

"I don't think . . . " Josie paused. There was nothing she could say Hammond would understand. "Of course not!" she said and walked away.

Chapter 16

Duke was waiting at Josie's desk when she emerged from Hammond's office.

"Hey, just the woman I wanted to see. I've got this great story. There was this other fire Tuesday night. I did a brief in yesterday's paper but the two old ladies who died were a couple of piano teachers, and . . . "

"Hammond has other ideas," Josie said, the exasperation obvious in her voice. "He wants you to do an A-one piece for tomorrow about the cooperation between the various fire departments and Union Oil. Give everybody a chance to crow a little."

"Can't Juan or Maggie do that? They've been covering all this."

"Hammond wants the master's touch. Give it a column spin. The whole works."

"Oh-oh. Command performance, eh? Is that what Kurt was here about?"

Josie wished it wasn't so obvious.

"You can do a piece on the piano teachers for Sunday. That would be good. Their former students saying wonderful things about them. Yeah, that could be nice."

Juan came running up from behind Duke. "Hey, there you are. Guess what I got? There was this fissure, see, in the B-forty-seven, that's a connector valve, and one like it blew in California a year ago, but there was only one death in that fire. Anyway, they're launching this big investigation and . . . "

"OK, OK." Josie patted Juan on the back and nudged him toward a terminal. "Let's get it all down in the computer. I think we're clear, aren't we Duke?"

"As mud," Duke said and headed toward his desk.

After Juan was seated at a terminal, Josie placed a hand on his shoulder.

"Before you write the next chapter in this saga, I need to ask you about a call I got this morning from Ambrose."

Juan looked up at her blankly.

"He's the superintendent," Josie continued, seeing no recognition on Juan's face. " From the school board you covered Monday night? He pointed out several inaccuracies in that story. Let's go over your notes and see where you got off track."

Juan shrugged. "It's over. We can't fix it now. Just do a correction."

"Wait a minute. I want to see whether they gave you the information wrong, or you just added it up wrong. I want to keep you from making the same mistake again."

"OK, sure. After I do this story. I'm gonna call the paper in California. See what they know about these valves. Get a copy of their story from last year . . . "

"Fine, but listen to me. This fire is a big story and it may be worth a few more follow stories. But the fire will go out. Then you'll be covering school boards and county fairs, understand? It's not going to be page one all summer long."

"Page Juan," Juan chuckled and reached for his phone.

Josie returned to her desk, feeling totally out of step with the world. Hammond was questioning her news judgment, an intern was too good for board meetings, and her ex-husband pulled more weight in her newsroom than she did. Still, she trusted her instincts enough to make one more phone call that day.

"Sharon? Hey, girl, it's been a while. Let's do lunch."

Chapter 17

Saturday's memorial service packed the high school auditorium. Eight firefighters' hats were lined up across two wooden tables on the stage. A flag was posted at each end, one for the Union Oil fire brigade in which seven of the dead had served and one for the Vollinger Fire Department in which the eighth served. The remaining four -- Kurt was right in anticipating the toll would climb to twelve -- included two maintenance employees, the security chief and a security guard. Names and photos of the twelve fatalities were listed on two large posters to the right of the stage. Behind podium stood Bishop Joseph Rohne and four other ministers representing various faiths. Bishop Rhone spoke.

"These men and one woman were servants of God because they served their fellow man. They died doing their jobs; they died protecting each of us. Surely there can be no greater love than to give up your life for another."

Near the front of the auditorium, Carl and Karen Anderson stood with other members of the Jordan Fire Department and their spouses. Karen was thinking about the female firefighter from Vollinger who had died. She'd had two little children. Why did the thought of a mother dying seem so much sadder than the deaths of all these fathers? Their widows were seated in the first few rows, older children huddled with them, younger ones likely with relatives somewhere. But one stunned-looking widower had a baby over his shoulder. A tear trickled down Karen's cheek, a tear for the baby.

Carl was more concerned about the young woman he had passed on the way in. He peeked over Karen's shoulder and there she was, just a couple of rows behind. Tracy Morton smiled coquettishly and waved. What was *she* doing here? It was his own fault; he had started it and now she was obsessed with him. He would just have to break it off before this foolish girl embarrassed him in public or, worse yet, alerted Karen. He put an arm around Karen, who seemed about to cry. It was a signal to Tracy to back off. But when he glanced over to see if Tracy noticed, she feigned indifference. Carl's heart beat a little faster. He was playing a dangerous game and enjoying it.

Chapter 18

South of the city, in Shabbytown, Duke was at a much smaller memorial service in Messiah Missionary Baptist Church. This service was almost a celebration. A piano had been wheeled to the center of the church and members of the all-black congregation took turns coming forward to play a tune they had learned from Hannah and Zoe Otis. The church's minister of music was a former pupil, and the piano practically danced across the room when he played. The minister's wife was next. As she played, she sang a slow mournful "Shall We Gather at the River." Suddenly she stepped up the tempo, added a jazzy beat and soon all were on their feet, clapping and singing about a joyful gathering at the river. Youngsters came forward, too, with simple, one-hand tunes, and parents proudly clapped.

Perched on the top of the old piano were dozens of photos of Hannah and Zoe with students. One showed Hannah, young and thin, with the deep, wavy hairstyle of the thirties. Another showed Zoe wearing a huge fancy flowered hat that seemed to engulf her. In another they were mere children standing side by side in pale flowered dresses in front of a farmhouse.

At ages seventy-nine and eighty-two they had known long, happy lives, and there seemed more joy than sadness at Messiah Missionary Baptist Church that day. Minister Elijah Stag spoke about the love these women showed for their community, and shouts of "Amen" echoed through the room. It would make the perfect ending for Duke's Sunday piece about the sisters.

But looking around the room, Duke wondered if anger and fear would taint their joy if the fire proved to be due to something other than faulty wiring, as many assumed. The state inspector was investigating, which wasn't unusual in a fatal fire, but the air of secrecy about the fire was a warning bell to Duke. None of the usual reports had been filed. Even Coroner Teasdale hadn't recorded the routine body identifications yet. Maybe it was because the refinery fire had backed up everything. Maybe.

When he left the church, Duke wasn't too surprised to see a sheriff's department van parked a few blocks away at the scene of the fire. These few streets were in Jordan Township, so the county had jurisdiction. Lined with a post-World War II collection of old bungalows, smaller than most of today's homes, the area was primarily a black neighborhood. Most of the two hundred or so houses were covered in appalling brick-patterned asphalt. In this unincorporated area, the roads never got fixed, trash pickup was spotty, and people relied on septic tanks and wells instead of a city water system.

As Duke drove past, he saw his buddy Al Lepalee tramping around in big black rubber boots.

"Hey, Al," Duke called out his car window. "Going fishing?"

"You might say that," Al called back with a wave.

Duke parked and stepped over the yellow tape and into the charred remains of the house. The second story was pretty much gone and a foot of soggy debris filled what appeared to be the old parlor. A piano in the corner was blackened and blistered but still recognizable. Daylight poured through a hole in the kitchen at the back of the structure where firefighters had broken down a wall.

"What's the matter, reporter guy, can't you read?" Al said, pointing to the "Do Not Cross" tape. Duke didn't let it faze him.

"I don't know how you guys can make heads or tails of this mess," Duke said, even though he had been to enough fire scenes to spot some of the signs of arson himself. "So it started upstairs?" Duke surmised aloud because the second floor was most heavily damaged.

"Not necessarily in a house this old," Al said, examining what was left of the front doorjamb. According to the initial report, the door had been standing open when firefighters arrived. Al fished something out of the debris. "Hmmm," he said, twisting his lips to one side and holding up a piece of chain.

"You look like you're all dressed up," Al said, dropping the chain into a plastic bag and bending over to poke through the muck some more. "Goin' to a funeral?"

"Been." Duke responded. "Whatcha got?"

"Huh? Oh sorry, I was just teasing. Who died?"

"I went for the sisters, for a story,"

"Yeah? You doin' a story on this fire?"

"Not the fire really, just the sisters. Why? Should I do a story on the fire?"

Al stood up and looked at Duke, a smirk on his face. "You tell me, reporter guy. Do we give a shit if a couple of old ladies get burned in a low-class neighborhood like this? House was a firetrap anyway. Must be a dozen animal carcasses here, and neighbors said cats howling was what woke them. Cats, everywhere. Crazy old broads."

"Did they get burned?" Duke asked. "Was it arson?"

"Now what do I look like? The state inspector?"

"You're back here for something."

"I tell ya, happens every summer. The temperature goes up and the natives get restless."

"So it is arson?"

"Strictly off the record?"

"Strictly," Duke promised. He wasn't even carrying his notebook.

"This is one sick situation, this one here," Al looked around the debris and shook his head. "Arson definitely. Multiple starting points. But the sweet sisters weren't upstairs in their beds like good little ol' ladies should be at that hour. They were down here." Al walked to the center of the parlor and picked up a piece of bent tubing. It looked like the back of one of the chairs that remained relatively untouched in the kitchen. "Tied up in chairs. Or at least one was tied up."

"Wow, you mean they were killed on purpose?"

"Probably," Al said, tossing the pipe back into the debris. "Teasdale is being tighter than a new pair of shoes. You'll have to get the details from him."

"Elephant excrement!" Duke said, thinking more about how this would affect his story than what to ask next.

"Robbery, I figure," Al said, assuming what Duke's question would be. He walked over to the staircase and picked up a remnant of a photo still tucked under broken glass. He handed it to Duke. It was a signed glossy of Little Richard.

Chapter 19

"Sorry, I'm late," Josie said as she slipped into the booth across from Sharon. "The game took a little longer than usual."

"I thought you said it was Kurt's weekend," Sharon countered, sipping the last of her iced tea and looking around for a waitress.

"Oh, it is, but I always go to Kevin's soccer games anyway. One of these days he's going to score a goal, and I don't want to miss it."

"Glad Jennifer was never into sports -- Hey, excuse me, could I get some more tea?" Sharon said, waving to a waitress. "What do you want?" she asked Josie.

"Oh, I'll have some tea, too, and another menu, please."

There was a stiff moment of silence as the waitress stood over them and Josie began looking over the choices.

"Have you ever had their chicken salad here?"

"It's a green salad with slivers of chicken. Good," Sharon replied.

"Great, I hate those things that are mostly mayonnaise. So, I suppose Duke told you about Kurt's latest."

"No," Sharon said, looking puzzled.

"Well, he decided we should 'downsize' the refinery fire," Josie said, with emphasis on the awkward word. Sharon laughed immediately. A couple of years earlier, when the tractor plant had cut its staff in half, the company refused to call it a layoff but used a catch phrase: It was downsizing. Kurt was the reporter on the story and insisted on making the layoff clear. What a difference three years -- and a new job with a hefty pay increase -- had made.

"I thought Duke would tell you because he had to do this bogus story about interdepartmental cooperation," Josie said.

"Yeah, I saw that story," Sharon replied, her nose buried in the menu. "I think I'll try the Salad Nicoise. That's the one with the raw green beans, isn't it?"

"I think so," Josie responded closing her menu. "Did you get your hair cut?"

"Yeah, I'm planning to go back to teaching this fall, so I wanted something easy."

"Hey, that's great. What does Duke think about you going back to work?"

"It's not up to him."

"Oh, of course not," Josie could tell Sharon was still on the defensive, so she avoided mentioning Duke as they placed their orders and waited for their lunches to come. Finally, Sharon brought up his name.

"Duke said he was going to a memorial service for some piano teachers today. Is that true?"

"Yeah,' Josie said with a laugh. "Did he ever play piano? He's sure got a bug about these teachers who died in a house fire."

In the silence that followed, Sharon's original question echoed in Josie's ears: "Is that true?" Sharon had caught Duke in a lie. That was it. Maybe he was cheating on her.

Josie started slowly. "Sharon, is something wrong?"

"Why do you ask?" Sharon said looking down at her hands. "Has Duke been falling down on the job?"

"Well, no, not really." Josie stuttered, then reached a hand across to touch Sharon's. "Listen, I'm asking as your friend, not as Duke's boss."

Sharon turned away, looking out the window into the parking lot. After a moment of silence, she turned back and looked Josie in the eye.

"You won't hold it against him?"

"Hold what?"

"He's an alcoholic," Sharon said bluntly.

Josie wasn't sure what to say. Duke had been known to drink, sure. In fact, back before Kevin was born, when she and Kurt went to all the office social events, Duke always was the biggest partier. He could put away obnoxious amounts of liquor and never really seem drunk. Sometimes, when he left the office early, Josie knew she could find him tipping back a few at the Trophy Room. But likely as not he would be there with Al Lepalee from the sheriff's department or Carl Anderson from the fire department or one of the guys from the city police and he'd come back to the paper with great tips. It was a long way from that to alcoholism, wasn't it?

"Is he being treated?" Josie asked, as if Sharon had revealed a diagnosis of cancer. Sharon laughed.

"Are you kidding? He doesn't think there's anything wrong with drinking himself to sleep every night. He says I'm a meddling prude. He basically lives in the basement now. Sometimes he'll have dinner with Jennifer and me, if he gets home from the bar in time, but then he'll go down to his office to 'work.' He put our old refrigerator down there, and at first I didn't even catch on. Can you imagine? I thought he was just working on a big story. He's got all kinds of files down there, so I just believed. Then I started realizing how many bottles of bourbon were showing up in the trash. He goes through at least half a bottle every night and that's after having several beers after work. He used to come upstairs and get frisky, but he doesn't even do that anymore. He just falls asleep on the couch downstairs in front of the television. I don't even go down there anymore because I can't stand to see what he's done to himself."

"Wow!" Josie wasn't sure what to say. "He's always okay at work."

"Yeah, sure," Sharon said, turning to look out the window again. "After a few hours sleep and a pot of coffee."

"Maybe it's not as bad as you think," Josie said. "Maybe he's just going through a midlife crisis or something."

"No!" Sharon turned back, her eyes glistening. "It is as bad as I say. Worse. Jennifer is getting old enough that she wants to have friends over and she's embarrassed. I find myself dancing around the issue with her. We both know what's going on but neither of us wants to admit it. It's like the elephant on the table..." She broke off. That was one of Duke's favorite phrases for ignoring the obvious.

Josie reached out a hand again.

"What can I do? I think the insurance program covers alcoholism. I could check it out. Do you want me to talk to him?"

"He'll deny," Sharon said, throwing up her hands. "He'll feel like I betrayed him. He's the only one who can do something. I gave him until the Fourth of July, then I'm out of there. I can't expose Jennifer . . . "

"You're leaving?" Josie was incredulous.

"I won't be an enabler," Sharon said, obviously repeating advice she'd been given.

"But he's your husband, you have a child together," Josie said. "You've gotta see him through this, if you love him."

"No, if I love him I've got to leave so he accepts that this is his problem. Alone. Only he can do something. It is up to him, not me."

"Sharon, I've been through divorce. It isn't worth it. It will be devastating on Jennifer," Josie was panting, the fresh memory of divorce churning her insides. "Look at Kevin; he carries around that old chipped tractor all the time because it used to be his father's when he was little. Kevin is trying to hold on to his father, that's what the psychologist told me, but he won't talk about it. He's so much like his dad."

"Gee, that was sweet of Kurt to pass on a family heirloom. Who would have thought Mr. Downsize could be sentimental?"

"Are you kidding? Kurt didn't give the tractor to Kevin. His father, Pop Walsh did. No, Kurt was never sentimental." Josie said, using a finger to catch a drop of moisture at the corner of her eye.

"I can't believe it," Sharon exclaimed. "You're still soft on the guy."

"I wish we had found a way to work it out, yes." Josie said, looking down at her hands to hide the intensity of her pain.

"You're kidding yourself," Sharon said. "You're in love with a fantasy, a football hero, an eager young reporter. That's not who Kurt is anymore. And that's not who Duke is either. Not anymore."

"See a counselor," Josie pleaded. " I could ask around."

"I've tried. Dottie recommended someone but he wouldn't go. He says there's nothing wrong with him. It's all in my head."

The waitress cleared the empty salad plates and left a slip of yellow paper. Josie grabbed it but Sharon insisted on paying her half.

"No, you can treat next time," Josie said, and then wondered if there would be a next time. She knew how divorces went, everyone dividing up into his friends and her friends. She knew Duke never saw Kurt socially anymore and she always suspected that was out of respect for her. Now if he and Sharon split, where would her loyalties lie?

A few minutes later, Sharon and Josie said goodbye in the parking lot. Sharon was taking Jennifer shopping for a dress to wear in the Independence Day parade in a few days. She was one of the dozen Lady Liberty finalists, an honor Duke hadn't mentioned.

Josie was headed to the ceramics shop as she did each Saturday when Kurt took Kevin. "I lead such an exciting life," Josie laughed. "Instead of margaritas, I make mud pies."

A wedding caravan of cars decked in pink and yellow streamers drove by, honking. Although neither Josie nor Sharon recognized young Scotty Miller and his bride, Brittany, they waved as the car marked "Just Married" passed.

"So young," Josie said, shaking her head.

"So foolish," added Sharon. They parted with heavy hearts.

Chapter 20

Dressing a squirming baby is a snap compared to trying to put a soccer shirt and jeans on a forty-five-pound mutt in the back seat of a car. Josie put it off as long as possible so Chippie wouldn't have a chance to tear the clothes off, but now, wrestling in the back seat, she couldn't imagine what she'd been thinking.

"Hurry up," Kevin called, banging on the car window. "They've called for the second class already."

Second class. That would be elementary school-age children and their pets for the look-alike parade. The preschoolers already had wandered around the ring. Just trying to keep them corralled and somewhat attached to their pets had been so funny that no one really cared if the kids looked like their animals. A poodle and a little girl, each dressed in a tutu, had won.

Now it was time for second class, Chippie and Kevin. The jeans had been fairly easy, really. Some of Kevin's toddler jeans with the seam ripped just enough to accommodate a tail. The elastic waist held them on. But now Chippie was wise to Josie's plan and the golden retriever mix was not about to lift a paw to stick it into the orange soccer shirt. If she opened the car door before he was dressed, he would bolt for sure. Finally, they emerged.

"Here, hold the leash while I tuck in his shirt," Josie said.

"Mom, he doesn't have to be neat," Kevin said in exasperation, his own shirttail sticking out in back. Tucking in the shirt was the piece de resistance. Chippie looked hilarious and more than a little like Kevin, who also was wearing jeans and an orange soccer shirt.

"Here, let me get your shirttail." Josie chased after Kevin.

"Mom, I'm going to be late."

When his turn came, Kevin paraded around the ring with the proudest look on his face. Josie snapped photos and applauded and laughed. Too bad Kurt wasn't here to see. Too bad. Chippie was well behaved and Josie thought they should win the prize, but a pair wearing dragon costumes took first place. The soccer teammates came in second.

On the way home Josie stopped for ice cream to celebrate, Chippie ate his cone off the ground and still got it all over his soccer shirt. "Ah, this is the way the Fourth of July should be," Josie thought. The holiday came at midweek, so there wasn't enough time to travel to her folks' house four hours to the south or to take off for the Lake Michigan beach. Instead, Josie and Kevin enjoyed all the pleasures of small town holidays.

After their ice cream, they had just enough time to drop off the dog and get to the parade. All the soccer teams were marching. Josie parked in the swimming pool lot, walked Kevin across the park to where the parade was lining up and then worked her way back to the street to find a vantage point. Parades are such nonsense, she thought; all these people going nowhere. Yet, it seemed so special. Kevin was beaming as his team walked by and smiled sheepishly when Josie waved and called his name. She could only hope that Kurt was watching somewhere.

Across the street she saw Sharon, waving wildly and cheering as the float with the Miss Liberty candidates approached. "Is that Jennifer?" Josie thought, looking at a thin, dark-haired beauty who seemed to favor Sharon. Suddenly three boys wearing jean jackets that said FFA in big gold letters, pushed past Josie.

"Yo, Natalie," one of the boys hollered, and all three cheered as an auburn-haired girl blushed as pink as her dress.

Chapter 21

Barbecue! The enticing aroma of smoke, grease and spice greeted Becky as she stepped into the sunlight from Leta's basement beauty shop in Shabbytown.

"Ooo-eee, smell them ribs! You better get yo'sef some a them ribs," Leta called after her.

"I just might do that," Becky agreed, walking up the cement steps into the afternoon heat and humidity. Three or four times a year Becky gave up a Saturday or holiday to get her hair plaited into dozens of tiny braids. She had arrived at six thirty in the morning and it was almost three in the afternoon, but as she walked up the stairs her hair bounced over her shoulders, cool and carefree. It felt right for Independence Day.

Becky didn't like Shabbytown. It was noisy and dirty, like the notorious Cabrini-Green in Chicago where she had grown up. Laundry hung on the front porch of the first house she passed. The door was wide open and a Spanish language television program blared. Next door, two old men sat visiting on a threadbare sofa in the middle of a weedy yard. Life spilled out of these faded bungalows like the trash overflowing the barrels at the edge of the street.

A shiny car, stereo system reverberating with so much bass that the words of the rap tune were unintelligible, pulled up alongside Becky.

"Hey, mama! What's happenin'?" the driver called to Becky. He was barely old enough to drive.

"Go home to yo' mama, fool," Becky quipped and kept on walking. The other boys in the car laughed and the driver peeled away from the curb.

Becky was a woman on a mission. She had overheard Duke complaining about not being able to get anyone in Shabbytown to talk about the recent fire that killed two old maid piano teachers. When he knocked on neighbors' doors, no one answered.

"Nothin' good ever comes knocking," Becky recalled her grandmother saying. You had to live with poverty and prejudice to understand.

If Duke had asked for her help, Becky would have been insulted, as though skin color determined what stories she could do. But since he hadn't asked, Becky was free to admit that she might have a better chance getting this neighborhood to open up.

Leta already had told her the sisters had different personalities. Hannah was a strict disciplinarian who tapped her cane on the window if one of the area youngsters took a shortcut through her yard. She often riled residents with complaints about noise or junky yards. Zoe, on the other hand, was loved by everyone, sharing flowers and vegetables from her garden and rewarding piano students with cookies or homemade flavored ices on a hot day.

Becky turned the corner and saw a crowd gathered in a vacant lot around a smoker made from an old oil drum. Beyond, just across the alley, she could see the charcoal skeleton of the sisters' burned out house.

Though the largely black crowd seemed like any weekend gathering of neighbors, the smoker was an informal business, unregulated by the health department and not paying taxes or keeping books. Becky saw several people hand a few bills to the black man standing over the grill and he tucked them into his apron before handing over a plate piled high with the rich burgundy ribs. Many sat around an old wooden picnic table. Some stood in clusters, talking and laughing as they ate ribs and drank beer. Children giggled, piled onto the back of a large man who rode them around like a pony.

Becky fished a five dollar bill from her purse and crossed the street. Conversation seemed to quiet a little as some of the crowd eyed the stranger in their midst. The man with the apron was talking with two well-dressed young black men, but when he saw her coming he smiled broadly and walked forward offering his hand.

"Well, here comes a new customer. Welcome. I'm Eddie Simms," the man said with more than a hint of a Southern accent.

Simms wasn't as tall as Becky, but he held his head and chest high. Even with a few smudges of barbecue sauce on his apron, he was dressed so neatly that Becky correctly pegged him as a retired military man.

"Becky Judd," she said, placing the bill in his hand. "I just had my hair done over at Leta's and smelled your 'cue.'"

"Best barbecue in Illinois," Eddie said, shaking her hand firmly and pocketing the five. "And don't your hair look fine? Don't it boys?"

The two handsome young men, whom Eddie introduced as his sons, Claude and Andy, nodded toward Becky, purring low compliments in a casual, sensual tone that lit a glow in Becky's face. Eddie was as charming as his sons, and Becky followed him as he stepped back to the enormous black smoker and lifted the domed lid. Rows of ribs were lined up like soldiers across the grate, but he used his long-handled fork to snag a couple that had been steeping in sauce near the edge.

"I was hoping you'd be cooking today," Becky said. "You don't cook every day do you?

"No, just weekends and holidays, when the spirit moves. Hardly at all in the winter, except when I gets a hankerin'. Then I come out and start the fire up no matter how cold it is. Y'all be surprised how warm it is tendin' ribs."

As Becky nibbled the rich bones, Eddie basted ribs and talked, rattling on about growing up in Mississippi, his career in the military, marrying a woman with two sons when he got out, and moving to Shabbytown. Even after Becky said she was from the *Jordan Daily News* and wanted to know more about the fire that had killed the sisters, Eddie didn't stop talking.

"Well, I was working security at the tractor plant that night. By the time I got home at two in the morning, the fire engines were already here," he said, turning each of the ribs as snappily as a salute. "It was a shame to lose them. When I married Mae twelve years ago, Miss Zoe played at our little wedding."

"Well, I heard her sister wasn't so well loved. I heard she yelled at the kids and complained about messy yards. Did she ever complain about your smoker?"

Before Eddie could answer, the man crawling through the crowd with three little boys hanging off his back plowed into Becky and almost knocked her over.

"Biggun! Now, stop that horsin' around." Eddie swatted at the man's legs with the meat fork and he reared back, dropping his passengers to the ground. Biggun shot Eddie a look of pure hatred, but the children scrambled up onto his back again and soon he lumbered away with a full load.

"Cretin," Eddie called after the human pony. "Not one ounce of discipline in that boy, but the grandkids love him. I must apologize; are you okay?"

"Oh, I'm fine," Becky replied. "It's good to see a father playing with his sons."

"Oh, Biggun's no father ," Eddie chuckled. "He's a . . . " For the first time, Eddie paused his nonstop banter, searching for the right word. "I guess you'd say he's my wife's half-brother."

" Half-wit half-brother," Andy said, offering Becky a cold beer. "He's not as smart as my six-year-old, Dion, " he said, proudly pointing to the smallest youngster on Biggun's back.

"The other two boys are mine," Claude filled in quickly.

"Well happily married fathers have no business looking so fine," Becky said with a mock pout. Claude and Andy acknowledged Becky's interest with low moans.

"Now here's who you should be writing about in your paper," Eddie said, putting an arm around Andy. "He's the assistant football coach at the high school."

"Sorry, I don't do sports," Becky said teasingly, as though she might if Andy had been single.

"How about drugs, do you do drugs?" Andy quipped. "Claude here deals drugs." Becky was caught off guard by Andy's retort until Claude interjected, "Pharmaceuticals. I'm a drug rep for Chicagoland hospitals."

A tiny, dark-skinned woman with close-cropped hair approached. "Now who's this pretty lady tryin' to steal my men away?"

"Come here, baby," Eddie said, pulling the woman into the crook of his arm. "Miss Judd, this here's my wife, Mae."

The woman, who Becky had noticed hovering around the table like a hostess, seemed as neat and friendly as Eddie. She had none of his Southern accent, though.

"Your husband tells me you're from Chicago," Becky said, pronouncing the word with the proud, long "I" of a native. Mae smiled in recognition.

"I grew up there about twenty years before you, I s'pose," she said.

"Gran'ma had a place on Hudson."

"One of the row houses? I lived in one of the reds," Mae said, using the familiar slang for the brick high-rises of Cabrini-Green.

"Now, don't get talking about the projects like they were heaven instead of hell," Eddie said. "Bet y'all never spoke good of that place when you had no place else to go."

"Jus' home," Mae replied giving her husband a little squeeze. "Come with me, girl, and we'll get you some sides to go with them ribs. D'ja eat at Basil's on Division? Well, my cornbread's way better."

As Mae led the way into a cluster of people, Becky explained she was from the newspaper, hoping to learn a little more about the fire.

"The fire? Is that why you're here? We don't know nothin' about that fire, girl." Mae looked as soft as a kitten, but she could be as snippy as a cornered badger. "What they tryin' to do? Pin that fire on one of our children? This is a good neighborhood, good people. Just 'cause we're poor don't mean we go burning houses with people in'em."

"But if there's an arsonist in the neighborhood, wouldn't you want to know?"

"I tell you that house just caught fire, that's all. Weren't nobody's fault."

"Were you here that night?" Becky asked.

"Of course I was here," Mae said, pointing to the white house next to the vacant lot. "Sleeping right there in the back bedroom. All I know was it was as bright as daylight, that fire. Woke me up even before the fire engines came."

"Daylight almost came before them fire engines got here," interjected a short round woman as she reached for a piece of pie. Mae introduced the woman as Mabel Hastings, who lived next door to the Otis sisters. Her husband, Charlie, had reported the fire.

"He would have been better off trying to put it out hisself," Mabel said, leading Becky to the picnic table. "Those fire engines must have waited a half hour or more."

"Actually, it was only eighteen minutes, but it was way too long," said a tall, long-faced man, whom Mabel introduced as Charlie.

"Do you think the sisters would have gotten out if the firemen had been here sooner?" Becky asked.

Charlie shook his head sadly. "I tried to get to them but the fire was just too hot."

"I heard the front door was open when the firemen got there," Becky said. " Did you break it down?"

"Me? No. I told you the front room was all ablaze. I tried the side door but it was bolted and I couldn't bust it down, no way."

"Did the sisters keep much money? Could robbery have been a motive?"

"Yes, they kept every penny they had in crockery pot in the kitchen. Every kid who ever took lessons there knew that," Mabel said, and then poked Charlie. "I told you that was what they were after."

"Woman! They had ten or twelve kids payin' them five dollars a week. There was barely enough money in that jar for groceries."

Just then, Eddie's voice bellowed over the crowd. "Boy, what y'all doin' with that cake?"

Becky turned to see Biggun at the dessert table stuffing his mouth with handfuls of chocolate cake like a toddler at his first birthday party. Eddie marched from the smoker to the table in a few quick strides, shouting all the way. Biggun huddled protectively over the cake table as though the desserts might escape.

"What y'all think you're doin' there, boy? Look at me when I'm talking to you, boy!" Eddie's sharp drill sergeant voice silenced the crowd. He stood over Biggun, raining a torrent of curses on him. "Look at this mess! Y'all's the stupidest, no-good, free-loading slob. Now, clean it up!"

Eddie punctuated his tirade by whipping Biggun's legs with the meat fork. Becky noticed the subtle prodding and was about to jump to Biggun's defense when suddenly he reared up like a bear, reaching the full import of his nickname. He towered several inches over Eddie and was

58

twice as broad. But Eddie didn't back down; instead he stepped up closer, his chin thrust out defiantly about heart-high on the mammoth man.

Instantly, Mae was there, an outstretched hand on Biggun's chest. "Oh, dear. You've got cake all over your shirt," she said, almost in a whisper. "Go wash your hands," she added, looking up into Biggun's fiery eyes. " That's a good boy."

There was a moment of silence as the two men stared at each other.

"Go on," Mae repeated sternly. Biggun dropped his head and lumbered toward the house, snatching a beer in each hand as he passed a bucket of ice.

"Mae, y'all got to watch what that boy eats, " Eddie said, bending over to pick up the mess on the lawn. "He's ruined your cakes, and with all that sugar he'll probably end up having one of them tantrums."

"Seems to me, whenever you is hollerin' at him is when he has a tantrum," Mae corrected sharply.

"Ooo-eee, she may be little but she's got a bite," said Charlie, handing Eddie a beer.

"Like a pit bull," Eddie agreed.

Chapter 22

The parking lot at the tractor plant was almost empty, but Tracy pulled her rusted Mustang into the spot marked "Herbert Collins, Business Manager," right next to Carl's Bonneville. In less than a minute, she was in his office.

"How did you get away?" Carl exclaimed, extracting himself from Tracy's eager embrace.

"Oh, Johnny's got so much family he'll never even notice I'm gone," Tracy purred and kissed Carl's neck. " They're all at his brother's house, the one with a pool. It's above ground, but they all think it's Hollywood, you know?"

"Mmmm, you smell like coconuts," Carl said immersing himself in her blond hair and holding her lithe body against him.

"Suntan lotion," Tracy breathed.

"I need to be back by dark," Carl said as he reached under her T-shirt, feeling the heat of her bare skin.

"I need you," Tracy echoed, nibbling on his ear.

Carl responded as if charged with electricity. He grabbed her and gobbled up her lips, holding her so tightly she could barely breathe. He tore her T-shirt over her head and buried his head in her breasts, pushing her body back against his desk and charging on top with his hips.

"Wait, wait," Tracy said. "Let's go somewhere else. Somewhere more private. In your car, like that first night,"

"This will work," Carl said, pushing forward. There was no way he could wait.

Tracy seemed equally determined. "No, not here."

"Come on," Carl began fumbling with her jeans.

"Ow, this is hurting me," Tracy whined as Carl insistently pushed her back across his cluttered desk. She reached a hand up to Carl's face and brushed the beads of sweat collecting on his brow. "Come on, it would be so much better in the back of your car," she whispered.

Carl was panting. Look what she had done to him. He had one knee on top of his desk, attacking her like an animal. The power she brought out in him frightened and excited him.

"Of course," he said finally, and backing off he kissed her breasts tenderly. "We'll go for a little drive in the country."

Chapter 23

The *Jordan Daily News* was just across the street from Murray Park, the center of the community's Fourth of July celebration. Employees usually gathered in the parking lot. Hoss was inside doing whatever Hoss did with all his time at the computer, but he was careful not to have any food or cigarettes with so many employees, spouses and kids wandering in and out of the building. Juan was the only reporter on duty. He was over at the park to pick up a little color and would return to input his story while Page processed a fireworks photo.

Kevin was playing with Dottie's two grandchildren in the grassy area surrounding the parking lot while Dottie, a red, white and blue scarf accenting her perfectly coordinated red knit slacks and shirt, passed a tray of spicy chicken wings. Josie swapped tales of holidays gone by with Nick and Becky and their dates.

"I remember three years ago when there was such an awful traffic jam," Nick recalled. "I think it took three hours to empty the place. That's when they decided to have shuttle buses."

"Oh, yeah, I remember that," Becky said. "The Fourth is always the worst. People come early and leave before the fireworks are over to avoid the jam. Crazy people."

Becky's height made her stand out from the crowd like an exclamation point at the end of a sentence. Her long, black hair was plaited into dozens of little braids that bounced saucily at her shoulders as she laughed.

Becky had brought Doc, her beau of late, though Josie had a hard time imagining the two together. A biology professor at the university, Doc was a full head shorter than Becky and at least ten years older. Balding and overweight, he had a swarthy Italian look, and the little hair he had seemed permanently oiled. But he was quick-witted and obviously adored Becky. In return, she seemed to find him amusing.

Nick's blond cheerleader-type companion seemed a likely match for him, though she didn't look much different from a dozen others he had brought to various newspaper functions in recent years. Josie had given up remembering their names and privately thought of them as pompoms, colorful tufts of torn crepe paper that cheered Nick's virility.

"Mom, can I have a snow-cone?" Kevin begged as the vendor's truck made a slow pass.

"Sure," Josie said, reaching for her purse. It was a holiday and all the other kids would have something. Just then, they heard an ambulance coming along Jefferson Avenue and into the main entrance of the park.

"Oh-oh," said Nick. "We didn't hear that."

"Probably a fender bender, or someone passing out from the heat," Becky said. "It's too early for fireworks fatalities."

Duke pulled into the lot, alone. Josie was afraid to ask what that meant, realizing Sharon's deadline had passed.

"Where's that princess daughter of yours?" Nick asked. "I never would have thought somebody as ugly as you could have such a beautiful daughter."

Duke alighted from the car with an open beer in one hand and a small cooler in the other. "Maybe she's not mine," Duke hollered back, downed the beer and tossed the empty through his open car window. He pulled another beer from the cooler and offered it around the group. Nick and Doc each took one.

"You guys are brave," Josie said. "Ham shows up and you're in deep doodoo for drinking on *News* property. Nick looked to Duke for a response.

"He doesn't own us," Duke said. "Not on holidays." He lifted his beer in mock salute. It was ridiculous, of course, but it was enough to satisfy Nick.

"Hey, Peter Pan, I've got Tinkerbell on the line," Hoss hollered from the back door. "Something about a story dropping in his lap."

Josie chuckled. The Page Juan team was at it again.

"Keep an eye on Kevin," she said to Becky and went inside. Within a few minutes she was back, shaking her head.

"The ambulance was for a heart attack," Josie reported.

"Hey, good job. The kid is chasing ambulances." Nick said.

"That kid. Ambulances chase him," Duke said, draining another beer.

"Actually, that's pretty much what happened," Josie chuckled. " He was walking up into the bleachers to interview people and suddenly the guy in front of him keeled over and kinda died in his lap."

The vision seemed so ridiculous that everyone started laughing. A man was dead, probably someone's father, and this group of seemingly heartless people was standing in a parking lot giggling like it was all a joke.

"I can just see him now trying to worm a few words out of the dying man," Nick said.

"And signaling Page to come get a photo," Becky added.

"Oh, I'm sorry," Josie said, doubling over. "I shouldn't be laughing."

"Who started this?" Nick chuckled, unable to catch his breath.

"You people are sick," added Doc, caught up in the contagious cackling.

Suddenly, a burst of fireworks shattered the darkness and a cheer went up from the crowd. At least it interrupted the laughter.

"Kevin?" Josie looked around.

"Over there," Becky pointed.

Josie slid in next to him on the grass. Some things, like fireworks, are meant to be shared with a child. The display was timed to coincide with music, so several in the *News* lot turned up portable radios tuned to the appropriate station. As bombs burst in air to "The Star-Spangled Banner," the chattering crowd rose to its feet in respectful silence. Josie felt moved by a wave of patriotism. She looked over her shoulder to see Duke, standing at attention with his hand over his heart, tears streaming down his cheeks. Perhaps it was because his family was falling apart, or just because he'd had too much beer. Or perhaps, like Josie, he was moved by something greater than all of that.

Chapter 24

Somewhere off a dusty road, Carl Anderson and Tracy Morton lay back on a blanket in the grass, naked as newborns, watching the Fourth of July fireworks explode in the distance and listening to the patriotic music on the radio.

Carl hadn't made it home by dark, as he had promised, and by now, Tracy's husband certainly had noticed her absence. For the past few hours they had been ruled only by their passions with no thought for responsibilities or realities or what tomorrow might bring.

"I like the gold ones," Tracy said, "with those sparkly things."

"Yeah, those are cool," Carl responded. "I like the really big ones that go way up high and then break up into smaller ones. And I like the way the bright light reflects off your breasts," he added stroking his hand across her nipples as if flicking away fairy dust.

Tracy giggled and kissed him.

Northern Illinois is so flat that from this rural spot the couple could see faint explosions of fireworks in every direction, but the most commanding display was a few miles east in Jordan, the largest town in Cade County. Beyond it, lights of the suburbs stretched all the way to Chicago, forty miles away. But to the west were only rare glimmers of light, as the suburbs melded into cornfields.

The lovers hugged as the colorful bursts of the finale climaxed with breathtaking intensity. And then it was over. But out here, away from the city, the sky was dotted with its own little fireworks of stars.

"So, what now?" Tracy asked after a moment of silence.

"Well, I guess we go home and face the music," Carl said stroking her back.

"No, I don't mean tonight," Tracy said, rolling over to search Carl's eyes. "I mean where does our relationship go from here?"

Didn't it always come down to this? Carl was middle-age and married with two teenage sons. Tracy wasn't yet twenty and was way too promiscuous for Carl's taste. Relationship? There wasn't one, as far as he was concerned. He had enjoyed this night of passion and youthful abandon, but already he was regretting the pain it would cause his wife. He didn't want to hurt her. He began thinking of what story he would make up for her, while his hand stroked Tracy's thigh.

Tracy, too, was thinking up fantasies. She knew her husband would be furious. But Carl was so strong and established. He wouldn't let Johnny hurt her. He would take care of her and baby Justin. He couldn't still love his wife, not after the way he had responded to her tonight. She smiled. It was only a matter of time.

Just then, they heard a rustling, an animal maybe, coming over the rise behind them.

Chapter 25

"Where's Duke?"

A voice carried over the deadline din of the newsroom. Josie looked up to see Helen, the receptionist, waving a phone receiver.

"Why doesn't she just transfer the call instead of bellowing like a sick cow?" Josie thought.

She glanced at Duke's desk; it was empty except for his life-size cardboard cutout. Too bad cardboard couldn't answer phones. Josie looked around. Becky was making the morning calls to the area police stations; Nick was still out at the sheriff's department; Maggie had someone at her desk. Every phone was ringing, every keyboard clacking.

"I've got the coroner on the line," Helen hollered, more insistent now.

Teasdale, the coroner, could be calling to brag about a new stethoscope. But Josie knew Duke had been trying to get more information on the old maid sisters who had died in a fire a few weeks ago. Before she could tell Helen she'd take the call, her phone started ringing.

"Hold on to him a minute," Josie shouted to Helen, as she reached for the phone. "Newsroom."

"My brother was killed in a car accident in Tennessee," the caller said in a voice cracked with emotion. "He's a local businessman. We should get something in the paper."

"Oh, I'm sorry to hear that. Let me get a reporter for you." Josie spotted Juan chatting with one of the guys in Sports. She got his attention, transferred the call, then stopped Becky as she was about to make another call

"Teasdale is on the line. Duke called him for more details on those sisters who died in the house fire. See what you can get and schmooze a little."

Josie signaled Helen to transfer Teasdale to Becky. Then, page proof in hand, Josie headed into the photo studio. Mack was arranging a still life of summer fruit for next week's food cover.

"What is this?" Josie said in her angriest voice.

"What?" Mack responded too innocently.

Josie pointed to a photo in the middle of the page three proof, a Norman Rockwell moment of two children pulling a holiday-decorated wagon, complete with dog, in the kids' parade.

"Yeah, great composition, isn't it?" Mack said and turned back to his arrangement, pretending not to notice Josie's tone. Mack loves photos that look like art. He cringes at accident scenes, funerals, angry crowds on the courthouse steps -- life's messy moments. But give him a fireman rescuing a cat, golden flames against a darkened sky or the gap-tooth grin of a six-year-old and he's an award winner. His penchant for perfection, however, goes too far sometimes. In this scene, Josie noticed a squirrel perched on a tree branch just behind the passing parade. Last fall, she overheard the guys in Sports laughing about how Mack had a stuffed squirrel in the trunk of his car that he would place in photos just to improve the ambience. She checked and sure enough, several of his photos included a familiar furry face.

"I thought we talked about this," she said.

"What?" he asked, still innocent. "Oh, that? I didn't even notice him there."

"Mack," Josie admonished in a tone she'd use with her son.

"Honest," Mack responded. "It was just there. I told you I retired little Rocky."

"Are you trying to tell me that is a real squirrel that just happened to be there?"

Mack held up three fingers in a Scout's honor salute.

"He just sat there while this noisy parade was going by?"

"Honest."

"And this dog didn't even notice?"

"Oh, now the dog," Mack responded with a wink. "I didn't say *he* was real."

"Jeez," Josie spun and walked away. Once her back was turned, Mack smiled broadly. Josie was smiling too. It was a lovable charade, but not a game she wanted to play on deadline. After the paper was out, she would demand a tour of his trunk. She tossed the proof onto Hoss's desk.

"Can we crop in a little on this tree?" she asked, pointing to the offending squirrel.

"What's the matter, Peter Pan?" Hoss teased, "Lost Boys taking over Neverland?"

"I have a man who wants to speak to the editor in charge," Helen interrupted. .

"Five-six-oh-four," Josie responded, giving the extension number of her desk. Nick was standing there, flipping pages in his narrow spiral notebook

"I've got a strange one," he said as Josie passed. "Train hit a car about an hour ago."

"Oh, shit. Was someone killed?"

"Nope. The car was empty,"

"They jumped free?" Josie grabbed her ringing phone. "Newsroom, can you hold please?"

"Don't know." Nick replied. "Cops think maybe the car was stolen and just planted on the track out in the country.'

"Dangerous prank. Whose car?"

"They're checking that now. I told them I'd call back."

Josie shrugged and turned to the phone.

"Yes, sir, can I help you?"

"I don't want to speak to the secretary, I want the man in charge," the irate caller sputtered.

"Yes, sir, I'm in charge. Can I help you?" Josie replied.

"Now listen, I've called about this before, and nothing's been done. I want to speak to someone who can fix this."

"What's the problem, sir?"

"Yesterday's crossword . . . "

Josie didn't need to hear any more. An advertisement across the bottom of the puzzle page yesterday had pushed the crossword a few inches higher than usual, meaning it didn't fit exactly in a quadrant of the page, a frequent complaint of puzzlers who like to work on a folded newspaper. Helen had received a few calls; this one made it past her. Josie allowed the man to spout on, calling her names and questioning her ability to edit anything if she couldn't solve such a simple problem.

She had another concern in mind. It wasn't like Duke to miss the morning deadline rush unless he had an important appointment, and then he usually told her. By the time the caller reached his ultimate conclusion of "I'm going to cancel my subscription," Josie had pulled up Duke's home number on her Rolodex.

His phone was on the sixth ring. What had happened to the answering machine that normally cut in after four? Just as Josie was about to hang up, a groggy Duke answered.

"Are you sick?" Josie asked, shocked at his gravely voice.

"No, I just overslept," he said. "What time is it?"

"Late. After nine."

Duke had never overslept before, but Josie remembered he was still downing beers when the fireworks finished last night, and if Sharon had left him . . . .

"We need you to get in right away," she said. "You missed Teasdale's call this morning."

"Turtle turds!" Duke was beginning to sound more like himself. "I'll just head over to his office."

"No," Josie repeated. "Becky talked to him. We need you here."

Chapter 26

When Josie hung up, Hoss waved her over.

"What's this?" he asked, pointing to the story on his computer screen. It was Juan's item on the death in Tennessee. "There's no source."

"Oh, the brother called it in," Josie responded and began surveying the room for Juan. He was telling Helen about the man who had died of a heart attack at the fireworks.

"Juan, did you call the police in Tennessee?"

Juan turned at the mention of his name. "No, I just took what the brother said. The police had called him. He seemed a little upset."

"Exactly," Josie said. "We'll need to quote the brother in this story and confirm with the police in Tennessee."

"But how do we know which police department handled it?" Juan asked.

"Start with the state police, then county, city," Josie said glancing at her watch. "You've got about fifteen minutes." That would leave about twenty minutes for processing by the copy desk. "Get the atlas from Sis in the library to find out what county Murfreesboro is in. If you get a friendly fellow in the state police, he may tell you. "

"It's just a little brief," Juan whined.

"I got a name on the car," Nick said, running up with an excited look. "Carl Anderson."

"Anderson? Isn't he . . . "

"Yep, a volunteer fireman and manager at the tractor plant."

"What's he say?"

"Didn't show up for work this morning. Evidently city cops got a missing person complaint from his wife last night, but they don't act on those until someone's been missing for twenty-four hours."

"Whoa! What's the wife say?"

"No answer at the house."

"Shit, probably not enough time to run over there," Josie looked at the clock. "So is the sheriff's department suspecting foul play?"

"Nah, they're still saying probably a prank."

"But Anderson wouldn't do something like this,"

"Of course not, but he's got teenage sons."

"Call the fire department and the tractor plant. Somebody has to know something."

Josie turned to the library, "Sis . . . " A petite, gray-haired lady met her at the door to the library with an atlas and an envelope containing the most recent clips on Carl Anderson. Inside the envelope was a photo taken the year before, when Anderson was named a lieutenant in Jordan's volunteer fire department. Sometimes it was handy that Josie had a booming voice and Sis had eager ears.

Josie tossed the atlas to Juan and gave Hoss the photo of Anderson.

"So, where do you think, Peter Pan?" Hoss looked up at her with a quizzical expression.

"Let's look at page one."

Hoss and Josie left the newsroom and walked down the hall to the back shop with giant strides. It was almost deadline, time for the pages to be released. In the back shop, men who used to run Linotype machines stood along rows of slant-top easel tables where large, white, poster board dummies of the newspaper pages were lined up. Using tiny scalpels, these surgeons of offset printing cut strips of type to fit exactly into the space available.

Hoss headed to the table that held the front-page mock-up. A large fireworks photo dominated the middle of the page, with Juan's story about the celebration just below. The heart attack death was in a subhead -- it wasn't the most important thing that happened that night, at least to most people. The top story was about the continuing drought; the corn crop was a little behind. Down the side was Maggie's story about the Jacobs trial. An international story about an earthquake in India ran across the bottom, along with a fun piece about a woman who had found a lost wedding ring in her vegetable garden.

"Well, if it becomes a police matter we can replace the wedding ring story, " Josie said. "Your two-karat carrot headline will be just as funny tomorrow. I'll have Mack get a photo of the smashed car and we can move India inside for the final edition. By then we may know what happened to him."

Deadline for the final edition, which was delivered to local homes, was two hours later than the deadline for the first edition, which was delivered to newsstands and corner boxes in time to catch the lunch crowd. Sometimes a front page was completely rewritten in those hours.

"But what if the police are still saying it's nothing?" Hoss asked.

It was a tough call, when your gut says something's really wrong but no officials confirm that queasy feeling. Josie remembered the time a woman reported her husband missing when his sailboat failed to return at the expected hour. The Coast Guard can't afford the luxury of a twenty-four-hour grace period and called out a helicopter to search for the missing sailor. Josie had flown Mack to Lake Michigan to cover the search, and the *Daily News* ran a page one photo before the boat was found bobbing at a dock in Wisconsin, the naughty hubby romancing some sweet young thing below. That wife's humiliation became public knowledge for no good reason. It was not an experience Josie wanted to repeat, but the staff was counting on her to make the call.

"She who hesitates…." Josie could imagine Martin saying.

"If we don't have something pretty solid in ten minutes" -- Josie looked at her watch and realized that would be cutting it close -- "let's keep it a brief, inside, no photo. Right now all we have is an abandoned car smashed to smithereens, barely slowed the train down. No harm done."

Nevertheless, Josie was willing to invest enough in gut feelings to send Mack to Gouch Road to get a photo of one very smashed car.

"And there'd better not be any squirrels perched on the rearview mirror!"

Chapter 27

As ten o'clock approached, Nick had been able to establish that Karen Anderson had shown up at the sheriff's office, quite agitated, after receiving the call about the wrecked car. The business manager at the tractor plant said he did not know of any out-of-town business meetings, "though if something came up yesterday, I wouldn't necessarily know. Mr. Anderson is a very take-charge sort of guy." The volunteer who answered the phone at the firehouse only laughed. "Was it that fancy new Bonneville? Gas hog. He probably ran out of gas and is still walking back to town."

This was sounding less and less like a crime.

"Keep it a news brief on page six, no photo," Josie told Hoss. "I like the quote about the engineer being so shocked at seeing the car on the tracks and glad that it was empty. Yeah, that reads well. Nice job, Nick."

She grabbed a banana from her purse and headed for the break room. Mornings were so hectic that ten o'clock usually was met with a huge sigh of relief, the reporters gathering for a cup of coffee while the copy desk put the final touches on another daily miracle.

After a little small talk about the holiday happenings and some teasing about the beauty on his arm the day before, Josie and Nick reverted to business.

"Give Mrs. Anderson a few minutes to get home and then go visit her," Josie said. "Sounds like she wants to talk about this. You might ask about the teenage sons; that's a good possibility."

" Seems like I remember his oldest boy was the center on West High's basketball team, one of the all-stars," Nick said, making a selection from the candy machine. "Athletes aren't usually troublemakers."

"Oh, yeah? How about what's her name, Rosie Ruiz, the lady who tried to win the Boston Marathon by taking the subway," Becky snapped, as she fed coins into the Coke machine.

"She's a runner. That's not organized sports," Nick countered.

"Not organized, huh? Well, how about tennis and that spoiled brat John McEnroe. He's a troublemaker."

"Trouble? He throws a little tantrum. That's not serious trouble."

Becky and Nick bantered back and forth for several minutes, one-upping each other in a contest of who has more examples to prove a point.

"Lost Boys," Josie thought as she watched the familiar scene. That's what Hoss called the scrappy reporting staff, though several like Becky and Maggie were hardly boys. It was more a generalization of their youthful idealism, their Neverland attitude that refused to grow up and give up on society.

"Hey, where's Duke today?" Becky asked as she pulled out a chair next to Josie.

"Yeah, I think he and Carl Anderson were drinkin' buddies. He might know the family," Nick added, taking a seat across from them.

"Duke had some family stuff this morning," Josie said, looking down as she folded her banana peel so her reporters wouldn't read the lie in her eyes. "He should be in soon. What did our illustrious coroner have to say?"

"He's being very cagey, " Becky said, taking a swig of Coke. "You know the standard runaround: Not at liberty to discuss . . . an ongoing investigation . . . let us know as soon as . . . blah, blah, blah."

"That doesn't sound like our creepy-details coroner," Josie said, taking her banana peel to the trash.

"There's something fishy about this fire," Becky continued. " If the sisters just died in the fire, why doesn't he say so? But he keeps piddling around, so there must be something else."

"That's pretty much what Duke thought," Josie said.

"Black-on-black crime is never a high priority," Becky said. "Who cares if a couple poor ol' black women get robbed and murdered?"

Josie glanced at Nick. They'd heard Becky's racial discrimination tirades before.

"I know, you think I'm being touchy, but it's all around us," Becky continued. "You just turn a blind eye. I got a call this morning from some woman complaining about a guy driving around on the rural roads who looks suspicious to her, and you know what she thought was suspicious? He was black."

Becky mimicked a snooty caller: "'none of the farmers out here are black. What's he doin' driving around out here?'"

"DWB." Nick said, referring to the pseudo crime of "Driving While Black."

"Exactly," Becky exclaimed. "I was over in Shabbytown yesterday getting my hair braided, and those people feel abandoned. They know the sheriff's department is just going to let it slide."

"If neighbors won't talk to them . . . " Nick started to explain, when Hoss burst through the doorway.

"Hey, Josie, you'd better come." He panted the way a heavy smoker does. "Some broad is demanding to see Duke and giving Helen hell."

Josie handed her Coke to Becky.

"Get Bob in security," she said to Nick, as she headed into the newsroom. When she stepped into the lobby, a woman was screaming at Helen, pounding on her desk.

"Then I want to see the managing editor, right now," she bellowed.

"Mr. Reginald is on vacation," Josie said, stepping up from behind her. "Perhaps I can help you."

"I need an investigative reporter," the woman shouted, spinning around. "The police won't do anything. I think they know more than they are saying. He could be hurt somewhere, maybe dying. Something awful . . . "

The woman burst into sobs. Everyone in the newsroom was standing by now, watching. Bob from security was elbowing forward.

"Here, let's step into a quiet room," Josie said, taking the woman's elbow to usher her toward Hammond's office.

"Don't patronize me," the woman snarled, pulling away. "I need a real reporter, right now. I've got a big story and, and . . . " she started sobbing again. Suddenly, Duke appeared from behind her.

"Karen? I just heard," he touched her shoulder and she fell into his arms.

"Oh, Duke, you've got to help me. Something awful has happened, I just know."

"There, there," Duke said in a soothing whisper. "I'm sure there's a logical explanation." Duke's low, melodic voice was almost hypnotic as he guided the woman to a chair in the lobby and offered a tissue from a nearby desk. He spied Nick stepping forward.

"Here's the reporter who's been working on the story. He can tell you what he's found out, and you can tell him what you know. Together we'll alert the public. I'm sure somebody has seen Carl."

Duke stepped back as Nick introduced himself and pulled up a chair.

"Tell her what the business manager had to say," Duke prompted. Nick was soon satisfying Karen's need for knowledge, some word, any word. Then Duke pulled Josie around the corner and whispered, "I don't like this."

"But the police . . . "

"I don't usually question their judgment," Duke said, "But I know Carl. He would never frighten Karen like this."

Josie's gut was turning flip-flops. It was after ten thirty. "Oh, God," she prayed silently. "Help me make the right choice."

"Okay, you've got an hour," she whispered to Duke. "We've got a photo of the car and one of Carl. You and Nick find out what the wife knows, and I'll get Becky to run over to the plant and ask some questions there. And check back with the sheriff's department."

"I'll call Al," Duke said, heading to his desk.

"One hour," Josie repeated, "And, Duke, you'd better be right."

Chapter 28

It was almost 11when Becky crossed the street and walked toward the gate of the tractor plant. The security guard stepped out of his shack.

"Well, if it isn't the braidy lady," the guard said with a big smile. "How ya'll's fancy hair doin'?"

Becky was taken aback by the friendly greeting, but as she got closer she recognized the face under the brimmed hat.

"Oh, Mr. Simms," she responded. "I forgot you said you worked security. You look like a policeman."

"That's the effect I'm trying for," he said, standing just a little taller. "I don't suppose you came here looking for more ribs."

"No, I'm looking for Mr. Anderson."

"He's not here, yet," Eddie said, pointing to the vacant parking spot with the plant manager's name on it.

"Have you seen him today?" Becky asked. "I understand his wife has reported him missing."

"Don't say? Well, I wouldn't know anything about that. She was here earlier and seemed pretty upset, but of course I just waved her through."

"When did you see him last?"

"Last night. Well, I didn't see him, but his car was here. I came in to work six p.m. to two a.m. That's my usual shift. Then the day guy calls in sick and here I am again. I am fifty-three years old and come in here on a holiday after standin' all day over a hot grill, and most of these young kids are too hung over to show up the day after a holiday. No discipline, that's the problem."

A tractor-trailer pulled up to the gate and Becky stepped aside as Eddie waved in the driver and made some notes on a truck log.

"Listen, I'm sorry about that ruckus at the barbecue yesterday," Eddie said. "Biggun came to live with us a couple months ago and Mae still treats him like he was six years old. She lets him watch cartoons all day or play with the boys' old train set down in the basement bedroom she fixed up for him."

"Is he . . . " Becky searched for the right word, until Eddie finished her thought.

"Retarded? No, he's just undisciplined. He's not the sharpest tack in the box, but you should see what joins the army. All manner of slow-witted, lazy bums. And I whipped them into shape. Made responsible soldiers out of 'em. I can straighten Biggun out, too. Andy and Claude were back-talking teens when I married Mae. Now look at 'em. By this time next year Biggun will be running the smoker and bringing me my beer, y'all just wait and see."

Becky smiled. Eddie had such confidence and charisma that it was easy to buy anything he said. But after seeing him in action, Becky was a little afraid to cross him.

"You say Mr. Anderson's car was here last night on the Fourth of July? The plant wasn't running was it?"

"No, but the boss can always find work to do at odd hours. Don't see why anyone would want his job."

"What time did he leave?"

"I can't really say. See, it was really quiet so I was listening to a book on tape. Y'all ever do that? I'm real interested in World War II, and I just got this new tape from the library and I suppose I musta been thinking about my tape and didn't see them leave."

"Them? Was somebody else there?

Eddie smiled, then leaned in closer to Becky and spoke in a whisper. "Some woman arrived not long after I did and said she was here to see Mr. Anderson. She had a plant sticker in the window. I think she works on the line, but I don't know her name."

"Oh-oh. Do you know if she reported to work today?"

"I don't think so," Eddie said with a chuckle. "I suppose those two runned off somewheres."

"Is there someone I could check with, someone who might have her name?"

"Well, you might try Mr. Collins," Eddie said pointing to a rusty Mustang in the spot marked for the business manager. "He was sure mad this morning when he came in and found her car parked in his spot."

Chapter 29

When Johnny Morton pulled in front of the tiny Freeburg police station at eight Friday morning, it was stiflingly hot already. He didn't dare leave little J.D. in the car seat while he stepped inside, even for a moment. It was Johnny's second day of sobriety and he'd had some trouble sleeping the night before, but J.D. was so bright-eyed and curious early in the morning that Johnny wasn't regretting his decision. He was going to be a good parent to J. D. Everything was going to turn out all right.

Johnny nestled J.D., who was wearing nothing but a diaper and undershirt, in the crook of his arm as though he were carrying a football across the goal line, and headed up the three steps of the turquoise stucco building. Freeburg was a small village about six miles west of Jordan where 144th Street crossed County Road 11. Johnny had never been there before but the police station wasn't hard to find.

"It looks like a Mexican whorehouse," the police chief had said when he called Thursday afternoon to tell Johnny about Tracy's purse being turned in. "Used to be a beauty shop. Haven't got the approval yet for some funds to repaint."

The chief's wife served as a clerk in the station three mornings a week. If Johnny wanted to pick up Tracy's purse, he had to come this morning or next Monday. The station wouldn't be open on the weekend.

"One of the kids found it," the clerk said, as she pulled the small red bag out of a cardboard box under the counter. "He was riding his bike just west of town and spotted it down in a ditch."

"Do you need some identification?" Johnny said, reaching for his wallet.

"Nope," laughed the pale woman, her colorless hair pulled into a tight bun at her neck. "I recognize your little fella there from the photo in the wallet."

"Well, my wife's working and . . . "

"Oh, no problem," the clerk said, reaching over the counter to tickle the cooing baby. "There's no money in there. I checked. Do you want to fill out a report?"

Johnny hesitated. "I don't suppose so. What good would it do? Where exactly was it found?"

"Off 144th Street, just before it turns into a gravel road. People dump things out here all the time. Guess they think we don't pay no attention, but we do."

"Well, thank you for calling," Johnny said, juggling the purse and the baby while he reached for the door. Once J.D. was secured in his car seat, Johnny hurriedly went through the contents of the purse. Nothing much. Some lipstick, a hairbrush, the empty wallet with their family photos and identifications. A baby's rattle. Johnny pulled out the toy and jiggled it in front of J.D. who eagerly reached for it.

"Good boy," Johnny said. "That's Daddy's boy."

Before he left town, Johnny drove to the area the clerk had described, but there was nothing to see except a couple of empty beer bottles. Johnny stepped down from his big black pickup truck and picked up one of the bottles, then the other. He looked around, but only the blazing sun was looking back. He wedged the bottles into the space behind his seat. J.D. was whimpering and Johnny realized his stomach was growling, too.

"Yeah, buddy," he said. "I could use a little breakfast myself. I know this great little diner back in Jordan where I can give you a bottle while they cook my eggs. How's that sound?"

Chapter 30

Karen cringed at the sight of the mangled mess that had been Carl's beautiful Bonneville. Even now, bent in half and rolled up on one end like a huge metal cigar, it reminded her of Carl. She knew he hadn't been in the car when it was hit -- sheriff's department deputies had found no traces of blood -- yet she couldn't help but fear that Carl's fate had been just as traumatic.

Thursday's story in the *Daily News* hadn't inspired anyone to call about the missing man, so on Friday morning Duke agreed to take Karen and her sons to see the car at the back of a local towing company's lot and then out to the scene of the accident. City police had begun checking into Carl's disappearance by asking a few questions, but they were not investigating the scene. There was no indication of foul play, they told Karen. What they didn't say was Carl's reputation as a rounder left the distinct possibility he had disappeared on purpose.

Karen and the boys poked around the bent metal, pulling out little things -- a foil-wrapped cough drop, an ink pen -- that reminded them of Carl. Under the remnant of the front seat, one of the boys found a baseball jersey and handed it to his mother, who said it probably was a car-polishing rag. She rubbed the cloth on her cheek and smelled not wax but perfume. It turned her stomach. Duke caught revulsion in her eyes. The boys were at the other end of the car, examining what was left of the engine, when she spoke.

"I'm not afraid," she said. "I want to know. I have to know. Whatever we find. I'm not afraid."

"OK," Duke said. "Let's go out to the scene."

It was a twenty-minute drive from the south side of Jordan to the spot where the old freight line crossed Gouch Road, about a half mile south of 144th Street. On the way they talked about other drives in the country -- the annual search for the perfect pumpkin, target practice at the city dump, the trip to get a Christmas tree. Duke could see this family had done much together, so the unpleasant task before them seemed like just another family adventure.

They crossed the Interstate at 152nd Street and it became a gravel road about a mile later. Then they turned north on the second gravel road, Gouch.

"This is the way to the quarry," fourteen-year-old Travis said. Although the abandoned limestone quarry was probably a half mile away, they could see the huge mound of rock and dirt behind the old pit before they turned the corner. It was the highest spot for miles.

"Dad taught us how to skip stones there, remember Trent?"

His sixteen-year-old brother didn't respond. He just looked out the window at the continuous sea of corn. It was about waist high now, a little taller than the adage of "knee high by the Fourth of July."

"Hey, Mom," Travis said, leaning over the seat. "Maybe Dad was headed to the quarry for something. He told me it's really dangerous to swim there. Maybe he was checking out a complaint or something."

That would be so much like Carl, Karen thought, checking other people's safety on a busy holiday.

"Maybe he did," Karen agreed as they drove past the entrance to the quarry and continued on up Gouch Road toward the railroad tracks. In flat corn country, the tracks were built up and looked like the burrowing of a giant groundhog curving through the fields. They could see the approaching rise in the road from a long way back, but the corn was tall enough to disguise the lay of the tracks. Just across the tracks Duke paused and looked to the east.

"Now if I understand correctly," he told Karen, "the car wasn't right here on the road, it was actually in a little driveway sort of thing. He turned into the right-of-way, a car-width of grass along the tracks. About a hundred yards east he saw the path, not a road actually, that crossed the tracks, built up so a farmer's tractor could get from one side of the tracks to the other.

"This must be where the car was," Duke said and paused his turquoise Pontiac at the top of the rise. "Then the impact carried the car about a quarter of a mile this way," he added, driving over the rise and following the right-of-way. Pieces of the car littered the path -- a plastic lens from a rear light, a side mirror, a piece of chrome. They could see tracks in the grass where the tow truck and police vehicles had followed along the same narrow right-of-way, straying intermittently into the cornfield, leaving clumps of trampled stalks. Finally, they could see a patch of utter chaos, with cornstalks lying every which way. Beyond it the orderly rows resumed.

"This must be where the car came to rest," Duke said, turning around.

"We need to get out and search the fields on foot," Karen said.

"The sheriff's department already has done that," Duke said.

"Not well enough," Karen snapped.

"OK," Duke said. "We'll go back to the point of impact and look around."

They tramped through the cornfields for more than an hour, following the tractor path in each direction. When Duke examined the path closer he realized it was the route of an old siding that probably went to the quarry. The rails and the ties had been removed, but the cinders and gravel of the raised path were just like the railroad bed.

They split up and headed down the cornrows. Karen and Travis were wearing shorts, so the sharp machete-shaped leaves sliced at their legs until they were crisscrossed with red scratches. Duke and Trent paid a higher price in sweat that soaked their shirts and jeans. By noon, when the sun was highest overhead and the temperature nearing one hundred degrees, Duke had convinced Karen it was useless.

They returned to Duke's car and got some sodas out of a cooler in his trunk. Then they all piled into the car, turned up the air conditioner, and pulled back onto Gouch Road. It wasn't even blowing cold air yet when Karen spoke.

"Let's look at the quarry," she said as they approached the entrance.

Duke couldn't believe his ears.

"Maybe Travis is right. Maybe that's where Carl was when somebody took his car. Maybe he was injured at the quarry."

It was a crazy idea, but here they were and, after downing a bottle of soda, Duke no longer felt like he was going to pass out. Maybe this family's quest would turn into a column, he thought, as he pulled into the quarry area. The private property was posted with no trespassing signs, but the old rusted gate was hanging half open and the gravel road into the area showed frequent wear. Sometimes, on hot days, people would swim in the deep, dark waters that filled the old quarry, or lovers would climb the mound behind to view the city lights at night.

Duke drove around, half hoping he would see a pair of legs sticking out of the pile of rubble, an injured man who would put an end to this pointless day. But looking into the inky water, he knew a body could be dumped there and never found.

Far on the other side of the pool, Duke spied the continuation of the tractor path, an old siding, just as he had suspected. He'll never know why, but he pulled in and stopped.

Karen took a deep breath.

"This is as good a place as any. Thanks, Duke"

All four car doors opened, and each person marched into the knee-high weeds that softened the mound of rocky soil behind the quarry.

"I remember coming out here when we were dating," Karen said as she headed up the slope.

"Last one up the hill's a sissy," Travis shouted as he ran toward the crest. His approach scared up a flock of crows on the other side of the hill. A black cloud arose suddenly, the cawing and flapping frightening the boy enough that he stumbled backward and rolled a little way down the hill. The scene was right out of Alfred Hitchcock's "The Birds," Duke thought, and he couldn't suppress a laugh.

Birds circling overhead reminded Duke of his grandparents' blueberry farm in southwest Michigan. Somehow the birds always knew when the berries were just right. One morning they would come and the berries would be gone. But why were all these crows here? The corn was so far from ready, and there was nothing . . . "

Suddenly, Duke knew what had attracted the birds. He started running toward Travis, but he was too late. The boy had disappeared over the crest.

"No!" they could hear Travis shriek. "No!"

Duke was ahead of the others, and when Travis emerged running back over the hill, he ran right into Duke. "Oh, my god. Oh, my god," the boy screamed hysterically.

"Shhh." Duke grabbed him. "Let's just go back to the car."

"No, no!" Travis was screaming and hitting Duke.

"What is it?" Karen shouted, as she and Trent came running from opposite directions. "Oh, Mom," Travis squealed. Karen grabbed her son instinctively to comfort him.

"Just go back to the car," Duke insisted.

Then Karen knew. She backed away a few steps, paused as it dawned on her, and ran around them to the crest of the hill.

"Take Travis back to the car," Duke said to Trent, but the older boy followed his mother. Their wails told him he was right; he had no choice but to follow.

Just over the crest, facing Jordan, was a blanket splattered with red. The two bodies were off to one side, clothed in crimson. Birds and rodents had picked at the faces and wounds, but Duke could guess by the almost black intensity of the chest wounds that they'd been shot. Carl's face was turned toward them, staring with huge, empty eye sockets, as though black magic had claimed his soul. The girl was turned away from them, her blond hair matted with blood and splayed across his shoulder. Even in death Carl's arm circled her waist, his hand resting on her bare buttocks.

In the noonday heat, a stench rose from the bodies like steam. Trent bent over into the tall weeds and retched. Karen fell to her knees whimpering like the mice that scurried from the bodies.

"Mom!" Travis called from behind them, unwilling to return to the horrifying scene.

"Take your brother to the car," Duke commanded, shaking Trent by the shoulders. Trent looked at Duke with dull blue eyes that seemed almost in a trance, but he obeyed. Duke stepped in front of Karen and bent down to look her in the eye.

"We should get the boys out of here," he whispered. He grabbed her in a bear hug and pulled her to her feet. Her cries sputtered in her chest as he took her hand, and they ran as though the horror was chasing them.

Chapter 31

When Josie returned from lunch, Helen was waiting at her desk.

"Mr. McDonald's here to see you," Helen said in an excited whisper. Josie's confused look encouraged Helen to go on. "You know, McDonald. The man who was killed in Tennessee."

"Oh, send him right over," Josie said, clearing a stack of newspapers off the chair next to her desk. The office wasn't set up to accommodate guests, though visitors to the newsroom were a daily occurrence. Inhospitable surroundings encouraged brevity and perhaps that was the point.

"Good afternoon, Mr. McDonald," Josie said and reached out a hand. "Have a seat. We're sorry for your loss."

"Loss? That's a strange attitude," said the young red-haired man, refusing Josie's hand and the chair.

"But he was a relative, wasn't he?" Josie said, puzzled. "I mean the man in the accident?"

"I AM John McDonald," the young man repeated a little louder. "I AM the man your paper says died in Tennessee!"

"Oh." Josie fell into her chair. "Oh, no!" she looked up at the man's face and saw not a trace of amusement.

"My mother called this morning in tears!" he bellowed. "Everyone has been calling her to offer condolences. My mother! You reduced my mother to tears!"

"Oh, I'm so sorry," Josie said, rising again to speak directly to him. "I don't know how . . . "

"Oh, I know how," McDonald said, shaking his head. "My ex-wife, or her brother, or one of her new boyfriends . . . They probably thought it would be funny. She's been wishing I'd die one way or another for a year now! She's probably got that newspaper clipping framed!"

Josie sat down again, shaking her head. "I am so, so sorry."

"Don't you people check things out?" the man shouted and the few reporters and editors looked up from their terminals. The events of the previous morning whirred through Josie's mind. Juan was supposed to check with Tennessee authorities, but did he? There was all the confusion over Carl Anderson. This man could sue them for negligence! Yes, they had failed. Josie jumped to her feet.

"What can we do for you?" she asked in her most conciliatory voice. "How can we make this right? We can do a correction. We can do a feature story on how the mistake occurred. We can . . . "

"No, no," McDonald said, dropping into the chair, his anger fizzling like a leaky balloon. "I just want it to go away." He had his head in his hands, as though he might cry.

"You're probably right," Josie said, putting a hand on his shoulder. Agreeing is always the first step in manipulation. "Perhaps the best thing is to ignore it. It will be forgotten quicker that way."

"Would you call my mother?" McDonald asked, looking up at Josie with defeated eyes.

"Of course, of course" Josie said. "Just give me her phone number," she added, sitting down at her desk and writing the number. "If there's anything else . . . . "

The man sighed. "You think it will just be forgotten?"

"I'm sure of it," Josie said with a smile. "You're wise to just let it fade away."

"Yeah, I think that's the best thing," he said, rising to leave.

"Why don't you give me your phone number, too," Josie said as an afterthought. "In case we get any more prank calls."

McDonald smiled weakly and handed Josie a business card. He was a car salesman.

"Oh, you work at the new Honda dealer," Josie said with after-the-sale enthusiasm. "I've been thinking about one of those. They're rated really well in *Car and Driver.*"

"Yes," McDonald said, his smile brightening considerably. "They're great cars. You should stop over."

"I will, John," Josie said as she walked him toward the front of the office, and waved as he slipped through the door. "Gee," she thought. "I should sell used cars!"

"I've got Duke on the line," Helen said, holding out the receiver. Josie took the phone, and though Helen could only hear half the conversation, she knew something big was happening.

"Oh, my God," Josie kept saying over and over. Finally, she said, "OK, I'll send Page right away. Good job."

As soon as she hung up, Josie rushed to the radio behind her desk to call Page. She had to admit she was feeling more relief than horror at Duke's call. They had been right to gamble with a big story the day before. Of course, there was no way they could keep the television stations from hearing about this before the five o'clock news, but TV wouldn't have the story of how the bodies were found. Yes, she felt a twinge of horror at the scene Duke had described, and a glimmer of compassion for the grieving family who had witnessed it, but these were gripping emotions that the story would elicit in all readers. The very thought charged Josie with excitement.

Chapter 32

Duke had pulled into the first farm he had passed south of the quarry. He left the sobbing Andersons in the car and asked to use the phone, but before he finished his two calls -- first to the newspaper and then to the sheriff -- the farmer and his wife had overheard enough that they were passing out lemonade and hugs to the grieving family by the time Duke stepped out the back door.

"I'll make some lunch," the wife said, hurrying back up the steps to the farmhouse. For some reason, when there's nothing that can be done, women start cooking.

The farmer was trying to console the three, who formed a tight knot leaning against the car. Travis was sobbing openly, cradled in Karen's arms. She repeated quieting phrases, like "It will be all right," though it sounded like she was trying to convince herself as well. Trent was stone-faced, almost angry looking, and had his arm protectively around his mother.

"Come inside where it's cool," the farmer offered.

Karen couldn't move. She felt numb. This couldn't really have happened, could it? But she kept seeing flashes of Carl's demonic stare, his hand on that woman's bare ass, juxtaposed with visions of a bright-eyed younger Carl showing her the city's lights. Then she thought of all the times Carl had dragged bodies out of fires, smelly bodies looking less than human. Somehow in this moment she felt closer to him than at anytime in her life. She needed to talk to him; she needed him to hold her and make the horror go away, and he couldn't. That was the greatest pain of all.

Sirens echoed in the distance. "I told them I would meet them over there," Duke said. "They'll want to talk to you, too."

"I want to go home," Travis whimpered.

"We can't go back there," Karen said, her voice barely audible.

"You're welcome to stay here until the officers finish," the farmer offered. "It's cool inside and Annie is fixing sandwiches."

"I want to go home," Travis cried a little louder.

"We will, dear," Karen brushed his hair back and kissed his forehead.

"I'll call my sister," she said, the decision giving her strength. "If they want to talk to me later, I'll be at home."

"Someone should stay with you," Duke said. "Can your sister?" Karen nodded. "Then I'll tell the deputies to go to your house."

"Come on," the farmer said, corralling the boys up the stairs. "We'll wait inside while your mom makes a call. Let's see what Annie's got to eat."

Duke pulled into the quarry just ahead of the first sheriff's car, so he headed around to the back. He got out and pointed in the general direction; he really didn't want to go back up there. As the deputies rushed up the hill, Duke reached under his car seat and pulled out a narrow notebook. He would put on his reporter's hat and perhaps a feeling of detachment would follow.

Soon there were a half dozen cars, including Al's evidence van and the vehicle of Chief Deputy Don Miller.

"What the hell is the *Daily News* doing sending reporters out to do police investigations?" Miller bellowed when he saw Duke.

"Honest, sir," Duke said shaking his head. "I was just humoring the lady. I never thought . . ."

"Well, this is no place for a woman and kids," Miller said, heading up the hill. "We must be half a mile from the impact site. What made you come here?"

"Evidently Carl came to the quarry sometimes," Duke said and noticed that one of the deputies wrote it down.

"Do you have any idea who the woman is?" Duke asked, his own pen poised.

Miller stopped and smiled. "Well, yes, we have a darn good idea," he said, with a chuckle. "You're about to see some of the best police work in the state. We'll have this murder solved in time to go home for supper."

Duke followed as Miller headed up the mound.

"Since Carl's been missing more than twenty-four hours, the city police started an investigation this morning," Miller continued. "Several people from the tractor plant named a woman who was with Carl on the Fourth of July. Of course, I can't give you that name until we have a positive I.D. and notify the next of kin."

Miller stopped as he reached the crest.

"Oh, jeez," he blurted, and then turned away from the sight. "We're gonna get this bastard," he growled looking right at Duke. "And, I'm gonna let you see it happen. Just stay out of the way, OK?"

"You have a suspect?" Duke asked eagerly.

"I have experience," Miller replied. "Seventy percent of all murders are by someone you know."

Miller turned to confer with the other deputies and Duke stopped Al who was approaching the scene. Gathering evidence was Al's job, but Carl had been his friend.

"Maybe somebody else should do this," Duke said, pulling on his arm.

"You're here, ain't ya?" Al sighed. "Ya do the job and then ya puke."

He pushed past Duke, who had spotted Page heading toward them.

"You'll probably want to shoot from there," Duke said, turning back to survey the scene, a dozen deputies clustered knee-deep in the body-concealing weeds.

Page and Duke had fairly free access to the area for about a half hour, then the first television van arrived. Cameras always make deputies nervous, so Page and Duke knew their access would be reduced. They dutifully pulled back to the parking area where deputies were setting up the yellow tape. Miller came down and talked to the television reporter, but Duke was glad he was vague for the cameras.

"Two bodies, one male, one female. Nude. Probably been dead thirty-six to forty-eight hours. Shot in the chest. It appears to be a large caliber bullet, probably a .357 magnum," Miller said, then added a detail that Duke jotted down. "It appears they were both killed with the same shot. It went through his back and lodged in her."

In response to the inevitable request for names, Miller said he would release them as soon as he had positive identification and had notified the next of kin.

"Who found the bodies?" the reporter asked.

"A private citizen," Miller responded, looking at Duke. "I don't know if I'm at liberty to release that name at this time."

"Do you have any suspects?"

"Well," Miller hedged, "Let's say I have a hunch. I hope to have a statement for you in a day or two."

Chapter 33

The television reporter seemed satisfied and hardly noticed when another sheriff's car pulled up and deputies ushered a short young man of about twenty-five behind the yellow tape. He had long greasy hair and was wearing jeans and a black Metallica T-shirt. He had the beefy arms and deep tan of a construction worker. Page was shooting a general crowd scene and Miller nodded to Duke.

"Your buddy should head home now," Miller said, and followed the new arrivals back up the hill.

"Hey, Page, you'd better go," Duke said, then added more quietly, "I think that last shot you took might have hit a nerve. Save it. "

"Fine with me," Page mumbled. He jumped into his old brown van and drove off. The television crews were packing up, too, as Duke wandered back to the hill.

"Now we're going to have some fun," Al whispered as Duke came up next to him in the cluster of deputies.

"Who's that?" Duke asked his friend.

"The jealous husband," Al replied, a satisfied smirk on his face.

"So, Mr. Morton. John. Can I call you John?" Miller asked as the deputies huddled around the young man, who seemed frightened.

"I suppose," Johnny said, bristling defensively.

"My deputies tell me your wife's been missing a couple of days, John"

"She just hasn't come home," he said, looking at the ground.

"And where do you suppose she went?" Miller asked.

"I . . . I . . . don't know," Johnny stuttered.

"You don't know?" Miller spat. "What do you think we brought you out here to the quarry for?"

"I . . . I . . . don't know," Johnny repeated. "The deputy said he wanted me to look at something, I thought maybe her car . . . ."

"Her car? " Miller was vicious now. He grabbed Johnny and pushed him farther up the hill. "Tell me what does your wife look like, huh?" He pushed Johnny to the crest. When Johnny gasped and tried to turn around, Miller took him by the arm and pulled him over to the bodies, which had been separated and were lying flat on the ground staring up at a stormy sky.

"No, no!" Johnny pulled away.

"I want you to take a real close look," Miller said, shoving the back of Johnny's head down toward Tracy's half-eaten face. "Is this your blushing bride? Huh? See what you've done to her."

"No, no." Johnny ducked away, under Miller' arm and scooted across the ground. Two other deputies moved in to stop him.

"I didn't do this!" Johnny insisted, "I didn't!" He rolled over onto his stomach and puked. Still Miller wouldn't let up. He grabbed Johnny's arm and pulled him around.

"Come on, look at them. Lovers. Out here in front of God and everybody," Miller growled as he forced Johnny to look again. "She was a slut. She deserved . . . "

Johnny pulled free and began slugging Miller.

"You creep," he slurred and struck a few good blows before two deputies pulled him off.

"That's what I expected," Miller said, wiping his jaw. "You've got a short fuse, don't you, hammerhead? You've got a record of barroom brawls. Even your sweet wife here called police a time or two. Record shows she had a black eye when she was seven months pregnant, but by the time the city cops got there she couldn't remember how she got it. Ain't that right, big man?"

The two deputies were holding Johnny so high his feet barely touched the ground, as Miller accented his points by poking a finger into the sobbing man's chest. Finally, Miller curled his lip in distaste.

"Oh, take him to the station. He's making me sick."

A couple of drops of rain fell and the deputies busied themselves clearing the scene as Duke, feeling a bit overwhelmed, headed to his car.

"Hey, Dukakis" Miller yelled, and strode up alongside. "OK, I didn't get a confession on the first try. But before nightfall, I guarantee I will."

"I'm sure you will, Chief," Duke, said, shaking Miller's hand. He admired Miller's no-nonsense approach. He was tough, but this punk deserved it after what he had done to Carl.

Duke stopped back at the farm to thank the couple for their hospitality and then headed to Karen's house to make sure she was OK. When he arrived, deputies were interviewing her on the front porch. They had brought a box of Carl's clothes for her to identify. An almost new pair of Reeboks; could have been anyone's. Same for the navy blue shorts. But the T-shirt. It was from the trip they had taken last summer to Niagara Falls. The Maid of the Mist. Carl had loved that so. He'd said a house would never burn down again if he could figure out how to harness that much water. Suddenly, Karen was overcome. She hugged the shirt tightly, smelled Carl's smell and cried, letting all of the day's emotions pour out like the Niagara River plummeting over the edge.

Chapter 34

By the time they reached the sheriff's department, Johnny Morton was beginning to realize he needed a lawyer and refused to speak without one present. As Miller said, Morton had been arrested a few times for fighting, so he knew an attorney, but it was after five when he called the office, and he feared the message would not be retrieved until morning. Deputies were continuing to question him in the meantime.

"Where's my baby?" Johnny asked, after a while.

"Your baby's fine," one of the deputies said. "We took him to Family Services."

"But it's his feeding time," Johnny said, looking at the clock. "He's on this special formula."

"Family Services will take care of him, don't worry," the deputy repeated, without much interest. "If you want to get home, you've got to answer our questions."

"But I've told you. She left Wednesday to pick up more ice and she never came back."

"Ice? Was that for the case of empty beer bottles we found in your apartment?" the deputy pressed.

"No," Johnny said, shaking his head in exasperation. "I told you. We were at my brother's house. You can call him and see. "

"Oh, we will," the deputy said. "So why didn't you call police when she didn't come back? Weren't you worried?"

"She's late sometimes," Johnny said, looking down at his hands.

"Two days late?"

"Okay, so I figured she had a boyfriend." Johnny looked up, his eyes flashing.

"And it pissed you off, right?"

"Of course it did," Johnny spat. "But I didn't kill her. How could I? I had no idea where she went."

"You knew where she worked," a second deputy interjected.

Johnny seemed confused. "It was a holiday. Why would she go to work?"

"To meet him," one of the deputies said, in a teasing tone.

"She worked with him?"

The deputies were getting frustrated. For a drunken nail-pounder, this kid was good. He wasn't giving them anything to go on. About that time, Chief Miller stepped in with Nate Pigeon, Johnny's attorney. Nate was more accustomed to drunk driving cases than murders, but he knew the best thing to do was to get his client out of here.

"OK, gentlemen, it's getting late. Unless you are filing charges, I'm taking Mr. Morton home."

Johnny was relieved to see the attorney, though he didn't like him very much. Too much of a snooty opera sort for Johnny's taste. Nevertheless, Johnny was glad to see him and followed him out of the questioning room.

"Where can I go to pick up my baby?" he asked, pausing in the doorway.

"Eh, you'll have to check into that in the morning." one of the deputies said. "He's been placed in foster care."

"Foster care?" Johnny plunged forward so that Nate had to grab a hand.

"Easy, Johnny" Nate said. "We'll deal with that tomorrow."

"But I want my baby tonight! He'll be afraid without me. He needs me."

"Tomorrow," Nate repeated.

"But tomorrow is Saturday," Johnny protested, following Nate. "Will they be open?"

"We'll think of something," Nate said, trying to placate him.

When Nate dropped him off, Johnny found his apartment ransacked. Drawers spilled everywhere, the refrigerator open, and food tossed onto the floor. Even his mattress and the baby's mattress were upturned. He checked the top shelf in the bedroom closet and his pistol was gone. The shotgun he kept in the back of the coat closet was gone, too. A bottle of bourbon from the open cabinet over the refrigerator beckoned him. He usually drank beer, but he had purposely run out. The liquor, left over from Christmas eggnog, would have to do.

A full-fledged rainstorm had blown in and drops were pelting the sliding glass door, but Johnny stepped out onto the balcony and let the rain wash the tears off his cheeks as he downed the bourbon, straight from the bottle.

Chapter 35

Huge, dark red drops splattered her arms and legs as if she were a victim of a muddy massacre, but Josie didn't notice. Her attention was fixed on a brick-red mound of clay just in front of her knees.

She preferred working with smooth, white porcelain clay and had fashioned a shelf full of mugs and cereal bowls, glazed in gleaming colors. But now she wanted something taller -- a pitcher or vase -- and every time she tried to pull the soft porcelain clay more than a few inches above the spinning wheel, the shape would crumple right before her eyes.

Su Le, the tiny woman who ran Su Le Ceramics, suggested trying red earthenware. Stiffer and less pliable, the gritty clay was rough on Josie's hands. The stubborn mass held its squat cylindrical shape as Josie drizzled it with water every few turns, her left hand buried in the mound of mud, her right gently riding along the outside. Slowly, patiently she coaxed the walls of the cylinder higher and higher, until most of her lower arm was lost inside.

"That's the way," Su said, as she peeked into the studio from the adjoining kiln room.

Josie looked up, a huge smile beaming through a face freckled with mud splatters.

"Hey, good job," added Barb Denton, who was turning a large white bowl at a neighboring wheel.

Barb spun large porcelain bowls one after the other. Popcorn bowls, punch bowls, salad bowls. She was a paralegal at the county courthouse, and everyone in the building had one of her bowls. She had been taking pottery classes with Su for more than a decade. That first year everyone got a pencil holder, and some desks still sported one. Then there were mugs, cereal bowls, goblets. One year she made three teapots but decided piecing them together was too much like work. Pottery should be easy, relaxing, she told Josie. So, she started making huge bowls that grew out of her wheel as if by magic. She experimented with a variety of finishes: some dipped in deep blue glazes, others painted with intricate designs. She signed them all with a big initial B.

"Well, I just can't believe it," Penny Dunlap said from a nearby table where she and her mother-in-law, Aggie, were painting Santa-shaped cookie jars. "My brother was in Johnny Morton's class. He was over to our house all the time when we were growing up. It just doesn't seem possible that he would kill his wife and her lover."

"I wanted to kill Albert lots of times," Aggie Dunlap said as she painted tiny eyelashes on her Santa face. Aggie was seventy-six, hard-of-hearing, and in the early stages of Alzheimer's. She could be pretty difficult. Penny said Aggie sometimes would lock herself in her room and refuse to come out, or hit them when they tried to give her medicine. But put a paintbrush in Aggie's hands and she was as calm and precise as Michelangelo. Everyone asked Aggie to help with the finest details on their work. Aggie and Penny didn't make pottery; they painted the ready-made greenware that lined the shelves in Su's shop. On many Saturdays the five of them -- Aggie, Penny, Su, Barb and Josie -- gathered at Su Le Ceramics to create and, of course, to gossip.

"Well, today's story in *The News* didn't say he was a suspect," Barb said.

"We try to be careful in the newspaper," Josie said, stepping back to examine the ten-inch-tall jar on her wheel. "I mean we don't print things they only suspect."

"I don't care what people suspect," Penny countered. "I know Johnny Morton and I can't believe he would do this. And I can't believe the police can get away with treating him like a criminal when there hasn't been a trial or anything."

"If you are talking about taking his baby away, that's not the police; that's Family Services," Barb said lifting the thin plastic bat with the huge bowl off the wheel. "They err on the side of caution and remove the child temporarily until the facts can be determined. If there is reason to suspect . . . "

"Now you suspect him, too," Penny blurted. "None of you even knows Johnny Morton, and you all think he is guilty."

"Johnny Morton? I remember Johnny. He played football with my Billy," Aggie said, finishing Santa's eyes and holding the piece at arm's length for inspection. "Nice boy. Nice family too. Always polite."

"Thanks, Mom," Penny said, giving Aggie a hug. "I was beginning to feel a little persecuted."

"Oh, I know," Aggie said, hugging her daughter-in-law back, "but it's all in your head."

A chuckle passed through the room.

"Well, I feel sorry for Mrs. Anderson," Su Le said as she emptied the last of the kiln pieces onto a large table. "After I lost Ling, I had to raise two children by myself in a strange country. It isn't easy."

"And look how well you've done." Barb said, cutting off another chunk of clay. "Andrew is a music professor, now, isn't he?"

"Oh, yes," Su said with a modest smile. "And he plays concerts, too."

"And your daughter, doesn't she do something with computers?" Josie asked, carefully carrying her vase over to the table.

"Oh, yes, at the university. And she has three children." Su smiled more broadly as she moved closer to inspect Josie's vase.

"This is good work, but make the next one thinner," Su advised. "This will be too heavy. You could use this one for a hammer," she said with a laugh.

"The clay is so stiff," Josie complained.

"But you are smarter than the clay," Su chided. "Now you make six more, little thinner each time. Then you will know the secrets of the vase and you can make one out of the porcelain."

Su headed to the front of the shop with two of the delicate, rainbow-hued butterflies she sculpted and sold from a display in the front window.

"No one noticed my new window," she hollered back from the front of the store. The ceramic shop, like many other businesses, had lost its front window from the vibration in the refinery explosion.

"Windows are the kind of things you notice when they're not there," Barb said, following Su past the shelves of greenware to the front of the shop. She rapped on the glass. "Yep, you got a window."

"Did it cost a lot?" Penny asked, coming forward to inspect.

"What's this wire in the glass?" Josie asked, tracing the pattern with her finger.

"Oh, this is burglar arm," Su said, smiling broadly and following the pattern with both hands in a graceful dance.

"Arm? You mean alarm?" Barb said. "Did you have trouble?"

"No, no," said Su, continuing to follow the black wire on her tiptoes. "Is Andrew. He worries for mother here alone at night."

A squeaking sound snatched their attention and the four women turned to see Aggie using a damp rag to wash the alarm mark on the glass.

"That black streak must be on the outside," she said. "Probably birds. They can make an awful mess."

Chapter 36

That afternoon, a long white limousine pulled up in front of Karen's ranch house, carrying the latest in a parade of people paying their respects. Mort Tillman, president of Caterman Tractor Co., had come from the company headquarters in Peoria to take Karen's hand, look into her eyes and try to say what words never can.

Karen had been cradled in a cocoon of caring since she phoned her sister the day before. Her parents, two sisters, and their families all lived in Jordan. At first they all descended on Karen's house, hugging and crying and shaking their heads in disbelief, but soon they decided the crowd was too much for Karen and set up a schedule so one couple would always be there with her.

Carl's family -- his widowed mother, Marie, and one brother -- stopped by too, but by Saturday afternoon Marie Anderson was back at her home, surrounded by sisters and cousins and Andersons Karen had never even met.

Saturday, after the story appeared in the *Daily News,* firefighters' wives and tractor plant employees began showing up with cakes and casseroles until the kitchen counter couldn't hold it all. Karen's sister had taken charge, keeping a list of each donation and packing the food into the freezer. When that was full, she sent her husband with loads of food for every freezer in the family. Her father took over the phone, screening all the calls, giving curt answers to reporters, considerate acknowledgments to friends.

Karen and her sons remained a tight knot. Some of Trent's basketball teammates showed up with a Harlem Globetrotters video and he reluctantly left his mother's side long enough to go outside and shoot a few baskets with his friends. Travis hadn't left her side except to sleep, and then he had slept so soundly that his sheets were wet in the morning.

"Don't worry," his grandmother said. "I'll take care of it."

Karen didn't want to sleep. Even without closing her eyes she kept seeing flashes of the bodies -- Carl's hollow eyes, his hand, that woman's bare ass. Her sister called the family physician, who prescribed a mild sedative, but Karen refused to take it.

When Tillman arrived, he found Karen sitting on the sofa, looking ten years older than at the Christmas party just six months before. Travis was sitting on the floor, his head in her lap.

"Oh, don't get up," Tillman said, rushing forward with his hand outstretched. He held her hand a moment and said nothing.

"I'm so, so sorry," he said, finally. Placing a hand on Travis' head he added. "For all of you. If there is anything, anything at all, please call me." He reached into his pocket and pulled out a business card, which he handed to Karen.

"Please, sit down," Karen said, her voice without expression. "We appreciate you coming."

"Well, I had to go to the plant anyway," Tillman said, taking a small, straight back chair pulled in from the dining room. "We've set up an emergency team to deal with a couple of issues . . . the interim management, grief counselors . . . I'd be happy to have someone stop by here."

"No, we're all right," Karen said, smiling slightly,

"Karey, it might be a good idea," her sister said peeking in from the hallway.

"Maybe in a few days," Karen said. "I don't want to talk. I just . . . " Her voice trailed away.

"The company has set up a fund for the boys' education," Tillman said. "You shouldn't have to worry about that. It's the least we could do. Carl was a good man, a hard-working man, a strong leader. We owe him a lot and we will all miss him."

"Thank you," Karen said, her voice barely audible.

Tillman soon excused himself, pausing in the entryway to talk with Karen's father about a Tuesday memorial service. They couldn't be sure when the county would release Carl's body, but the grief counselor had recommended a service of some kind soon. Tillman decided to close the plant on Tuesday morning for a memorial service, and details were being worked out with the city and the fire departments for a procession of fire trucks and tractors. Karen overheard their talk and appeared in the doorway.

"That woman, she was an employee, too," she said in a hoarse whisper.

"Oh, no," Tillman responded with a hand on Karen's shoulder. "Technically she worked for a temp agency, not an employee at all. There will be no mention made of her."

"Good," Karen said, flushing slightly and then bowing her head as if to hide the fact. She turned silently and walked back to the sofa.

She wrestled with an anger she dared not recognize or express. All these people were honoring Carl the leader, Carl the civil servant, Carl the husband and father. But what about Carl the philanderer? The man who had lied to her, humiliated her and finally abandoned her to deal with all of this alone? No one, not a soul, had expressed shock at his behavior or condemned him for what he had done. Right now, more than casseroles or trust funds, Karen wanted to be given permission to be angry. Just that.

She looked up to see Trent, standing in the doorway, sweat dripping down his cheeks and a basketball under his arm. Standing there, he reminded her of Carl, many years ago, when they met in high school. But in his eyes she saw a reflection of her anger.

Chapter 37

Johnny Morton also was engulfed that Saturday, but not with compassion. He was awakened early by Nate Pigeon's call. The attorney had arranged an eleven o'clock appointment in holiday court to get Morton's baby released from foster care, but a social worker would be making a home visit before then. Johnny had barely hung up when the social worker rang the doorbell. Johnny's bourbon breath didn't help convince the worker that the apartment's disarray had been caused by the police search, especially since the waste can in the corner of the kitchen was overflowing with beer bottles.

Before she left, two sheriff's deputies showed up asking for Tracy's purse. Since they had searched the apartment the day before, Freeburg authorities had reported turning the purse over to Morton's husband.

"Why did you tell the clerk in Freeburg yesterday that your wife was working?" the deputy said in an accusatory tone. "That would have been more than a day after you told us you last saw her at your brother's house."

"Well, yes," Johnny stammered, handing over the small red purse. "But I didn't know where she was, you know?"

The deputy was not amused.

"I've seen enough here," the social worker said, as she stepped toward the door. "I'll just check with a few of the neighbors."

As soon as the worker opened the door, a heavy, noisy woman burst in, with an even bigger, but quieter man, following behind.

"Johnny, why didn't you call me?" the woman almost screamed, and rushed to Johnny. "What happened here? It looks like you've been robbed. Is that why the police are here? Oh, my poor little Johnny. Where's the baby?"

"Ma," Johnny said, "It's Tracy, she's been . . . ." He stopped as though the reality of what had happened had just struck him.

"Killed, I know," the woman bellowed, smothering Johnny in a hug, " But you should have called me. A mother shouldn't have to read these things in a paper. I know it's hard for you dear, but she was no good. I told you that when you married the tramp." Doris Morton looked around. "I still don't understand what happened here. Where's Justin? Next door?"

"No, Ma." Johnny turned to his father for some understanding. "They took J. D. for safe keeping. I'm supposed to go to court in a little while to get him back."

"To court?" Doris exclaimed.

Tom Morton approached the deputy. "Hey, what's going on here?"

The phone was ringing and Johnny answered, but he couldn't believe his ears.

"Why don't you pick on somebody your own size?" came the squeaky voice of an old woman. "You think you are such a big man shooting your wife like that. You should be ashamed."

"I didn't" Johnny said, but the caller had hung up. The deputy handed Johnny a yellow slip of paper.

"What's this?" Johnny asked.

"A receipt." The deputy said. "We're confiscating your truck, too, for evidence." Then he turned to the stunned elder Mortons and tipped his head slightly "Good day."

"Good day?" Doris Morton snapped after the deputies slipped quietly out the door. "Evidence? Good God, Johnny, they act like . . . like . . . ." She couldn't bring herself to say the words. "Well, come on. You're going home with us. When is this court thing? Should you wear a suit? Do you have a suit? Good grief, it's a Saturday in the summer, you'd think a shirt and tie would do just fine."

Doris disappeared into the bedroom and the phone rang again.

"I'll get it, son," Tom Morton said. He picked up the receiver and hung it up after a few seconds. "Wrong number," he said, patting his son on the back.

As the Mortons drove away, they noticed a deputy's car followed them.

"Isn't this harassment?" Doris asked her husband.

The hearing in the courthouse took less than ten minutes. The social worker recommended the state continue emergency protective custody until adequate living arrangements could be assured. The judge set a hearing date for two weeks later.

"Two weeks?" Johnny bolted out of his chair. "I can't see my baby for two weeks?"

"Supervised visits," the judge said, making notes on the record. "Twice a week. You can arrange them through your case manager," he said indicating the dour woman who had just visited Johnny's apartment.

"But he's only six months old," Johnny complained. "He may forget me."

Nate tugged on Johnny's arm and he sat down.

The day didn't get any better. Johnny's brother stopped by his mother's house, and a full-scale shouting match broke out. The brother's wife had never liked Johnny; thought there was evil in his eyes.

"She figured Johnny would fly off the handle like this sooner or later," the brother said.

"Your brother didn't fly off nothin'" Doris spat back. "And I won't listen to no one who says he did, especially not my own son."

"It's not me, Ma" the brother replied, "But, as long as Johnny's here, well, maybe it's better if . . . "

"I don't want to see your snotty face until you apologize for thinkin' those thoughts about your brother," she shouted.

"Now, Doris," Tom said.

"It's OK, Pa, " the brother replied. "Sorry for your trouble," he said to Johnny, who just shrugged, and the brother disappeared.

Doris was on the phone all afternoon, telling her friends how the police and the courts were mistreating her little Johnny, while Tom and Johnny sat in a back room watching a golf match on television and downing beers. By dinnertime Johnny could stand no more. He borrowed the keys to his father's car and drove to the bar Tracy's mother owned. He figured she would be there. The bar was her home; the customers were her family. A marked sheriff's car followed him to Rosie's. He drove extra slow and prayed they wouldn't pull him over. He wasn't drunk but he wasn't sure he could pass one of those breath things.

Rosie's was a corner bar in Lockwood, a small blue-collar town just north of Jordan. The place didn't open until four in the afternoon, and by six, when Johnny arrived, it was packed, mostly with the burly men who worked at the refinery or other construction workers like him. Many had brought Rosie a single rose, as they often did for her birthday or Valentine's Day. Today, it was for Tracy. Roses were strewn on the bar and trampled on the floor. Rosie was behind the bar, crying one minute, laughing the next. She was one of those people who never held anything back, and Johnny liked that about her.

When she spotted Johnny at the door, she fell silent. They walked toward each other slowly.

"What do you want here?" Rosie said.

"I just want to talk to you," Johnny said. "I want you to know that I never…."

"She told me you hit her," Rosie said, sauntering forward.

"Yes, a time or two, but I never meant . . . "

Rosie stepped even closer. " She was afraid of you."

"She didn't have to be," Johnny said, "I would never . . . "

"Did you kill her?"

"No! I swear." Johnny reached for Rosie, but she shunned his touch.

"I don't know if you pulled the trigger," Rosie said, her eyes filling with tears, "but you drove her away from you. She was trusting, innocent, and you drove her away!"

"She was a slut," Johnny responded. "A no-good slut. She was bonking the boss, for God's sake!"

Rosie pulled back a hand to strike Johnny, but he grabbed her wrist and they stared into each other's eyes silently.

"You shouldn't have come here," Rosie said, pulling away.

Who knows who threw the first punch? What difference does it make? Soon fists were flying, bottles were breaking, women were screaming. The deputies outside called for backup and before dark, Johnny was in the county jail.

Chapter 38

Three huge, yellow Caterman tractors moved slowly, mournfully down the street, followed by four red fire engines and an ambulance, lights flashing. Mort Tillman's white limo with the Andersons inside came next, followed by dozens of cars, slowly making their way to a memorial service at the high school.

It isn't exactly on "our" time, Josie thought as she watched out the window behind her desk, but it could be worse. The procession had started at ten thirty, so the *News* couldn't get a picture in the first edition, but it would have the complete story with photos by the final run.

Josie looked around the newsroom. Everyone had stopped working and was standing at the windows. Most didn't even know Carl Anderson, but they couldn't help being impressed by the devotion of those who did.

Helen came up behind Josie and whispered something in her ear. Josie spun around to see two heavyset people standing in the entry.

"Mr. and Mrs. Morton," Josie said, as she came forward holding out her hand. "Perhaps we can talk in Mr. Reginald's office."

Hammond was representing the *News* at the memorial service.

"We appreciate you seeing us," Doris Morton said, following Josie into Ham's office. "We just didn't know where else to turn. Our boy, Johnny, is a good boy. He didn't do this awful thing. A mother knows. Maybe he made some mistakes. He has a temper. But he would never kill Tracy. He would never kill anyone."

Josie knew there was no sense disagreeing with her.

"Mrs. Morton, what would you like me to do?"

"I don't know. You must know something. I mean you've got investigative reporters, don't you? Find out who did this thing."

"Mrs. Morton, the sheriff's department . . . "

"Oh, they don't like my Johnny. They never did."

Josie shook her head. How do you counter a mother's faith?

"We don't investigate crimes," Josie said. "I mean we don't do that kind of investigation."

"But they've taken his son away. He has lost his wife and his son and they are treating him like a criminal. Doesn't he have any rights? He gets in a bar fight with dozens of people and he's the only one who goes to jail. And now that they've got him behind bars, they keep harassing him because they know he will fight back."

"OK, I'll tell you what," Josie said. "If Johnny wants to talk to us, I will have someone go see him in jail. We will check into his side of the story."

"Oh, thank you. Thank you," Doris jumped up and grabbed Josie's hand.

"Now, his lawyer may not want him talking to us, or he may want to be present," Josie cautioned.

Tom Morton spoke for the first time. "Oh, we can handle him. Thank you."

As Josie showed the Mortons to the door, she passed Nick visiting with a young couple in the lobby.

"Gee, you don't look hitched," Nick said, giving his lean friend a playful slug in the arm.

"And what exactly does a hitched man look like?" Scotty Miller asked, his arm firmly planted around his beaming bride.

Nick began poking through Scotty's sandy hair, which was no easy feat since he was a couple of inches taller than Nick, with a thin bony face much like his father, Chief Deputy Don Miller.

"Oh, I don't know," Nick said. "Thought there might be, you know, some sign."

Scotty giggled and pushed Nick away. "What are you looking for? Lice?"

"No, no," Nick repeated in mock seriousness, and started poking through Scotty's hair again. "I'm looking for the hen pecks."

"Oh, get away," Scotty pushed at Nick again.

"Seriously, you both look great," Nick said. "How was the honeymoon?"

"Fabulous," gushed Brittany, the athletic, cheerleader type that Josie would call a pompom. "Eight days in Hawaii."

"And seven nights," Scotty added, elbowing Nick.

"Oh, stop," Brittany pretended to be embarrassed.

Nick noticed the envelope under Brittany's arm and asked to see the wedding photos. Newlyweds had three weeks after the wedding to bring in a photo for a free announcement in the *Daily News*. Nick introduced the pair to Dottie, who gushed over the "lovely" photo, then he excused himself.

"Listen, I have to get to an interview," Nick said, ruffling Scotty's hair again, "but I'll see you at the softball tourney on Saturday, right? That is, if married guys still play softball."

"Are you kidding?" Scotty laughed. "My team plays in the morning and hers plays in the afternoon. This is an all-softball family."

"Just wait till we have kids," Brittany purred and Scotty rolled his eyes.

Chapter 39

Duke had written a story about the memorial service for the first edition, then called from the school to update it with comments from the minister before the noon deadline. Josie took the call.

"The sun peeked out of the clouds for a few moments Tuesday morning as more than 1,000 people gathered at Jordan High School Auditorium to remember Caterman plant manager and volunteer firefighter Carl Anderson."

"Okay, I got that," Josie said, making slight adjustments to Duke's first sentence.

"Now put this paragraph right after the part about how he died," Duke said. He continued dictating and Josie typed.

"Quote, *the sun is always shining,* Close Quote, *said the Rev. Erik Timbers* -- that's Erik with a K, Timbers just like the trees," Duke added and then continued dictating, *"pastor of First Congregational Church.* Period. Quote, *Clouds may get in the way sometimes, so we can't tell it's there. And at night, the whole earth may be in the way. But the sun doesn't go away. The next morning, we will see it again.* Close quote, new paragraph.

"Timbers equated the sun's constant presence with God's love and the lingering love of those who have died. New paragraph, quote.

"Carl hasn't gone away, we just can't see him anymore. But we can feel his warmth. Right now in this room, I feel it, don't you? And we can see his light. There in the faces of his beautiful children. And over there in the eyes of the factory workers who worked with him and the young firefighters who learned from him. Carl is always here. Close quote.

"That should be enough." Duke said, clearing his throat.

"Yeah, that's plenty." Josie agreed. "Everything else stands?"

"Yeah, it's good."

"Are you coming right back? I need to talk to you."

"Yeah, I'll make an appearance at the lunch and then I'll be right in."

Josie sent the story to Hoss at ten minutes before noon. She leaned back in her chair and thought about the morning. The community coming out in full force to honor one of its dead certainly was moving. The procession for one man was greater than the turnout for a dozen refinery workers who had died a few weeks earlier, and certainly the circumstances of death were not as honorable. Yet, none of the Chicago media had been there. They covered the gruesome murder scene but not the community's response.

Could Kurt be right that the media were only interested in the "bad" and not the "good?"

And if the community was so "good," why had there been no procession for Tracy Morton? She had died the same cruel death as Carl. She had worked for the same company, and yet there was not even any mention of her name. There had been a small private service for her. Was Tracy's life worth any less? And what about Johnny Morton? Did he deserve the scorn of the community? Or were Tracy and Johnny already scorned by the community, long before this horrible tragedy brought them into the public eye?

One thing was sure, death certainly was not anonymous. Josie hated it when Hammond was right.

Chapter 40

After lunch, Josie returned to find Duke plunking away on his keyboard under the watchful eye of his smug-looking cardboard cutout. Since that morning last week when he had overslept, there had been no more signs of alcohol problems. Of course, during the intervening weekend, she suspected a few drinks had been tipped in Carl's memory. But Duke had arrived bright and early Monday and again today, and he hadn't mentioned a word about Sharon moving out. Josie wondered if she should bring it up. She rolled up a desk chair.

"So, what are you working on now?" she asked.

"Just making notes," Duke said, stopping his typing. "Wasn't that powerful today? It was so inspiring to see that kind of support. I mean you live your whole life trying to do the right thing and it seems like nobody notices, you know? Well, they noticed Carl. That's got to be some comfort to Karen and her kids."

"Yes, perhaps." Josie looked down at her hands for a while before she went on.

"The Mortons came in today. Johnny Morton's parents."

"Peacock piddle!" Duke exclaimed, pushing back from his desk. "I'll bet they were a couple of scumbags, huh?"

"No, not at all," Josie said. "They seemed like a couple of concerned parents."

"Well, they ought to be. Their kid is gonna be sent away for a long time."

"Duke, I've been rereading our stories, and I think they are a bit biased."

"My stories? Biased?"

"Well, there hasn't been any comment from Morton or his lawyer. There's been no mention of the fact that his son has been taken away. We mentioned that he was arrested for assault the day after the bodies were found, but we didn't really explain that it was a barroom brawl and no one else was arrested."

"The man is scum," Duke said. "He killed his wife and one of this community's leaders because he caught them in a compromising position. End of story."

"Duke, you are too good of a reporter to let your bias show like this."

"Well, excuse me for having feelings!" Duke rose to his feet and punched his cardboard self in the nose so that it bobbed back and forth. After a moment or two he spoke. "So what do you want to do about it?"

"I want you to set up an appointment with Morton, or his attorney. Tell his side of the story."

"Lizard lumps! Can't you have Nick or Becky do that? I don't want to sit down with this guy. You said yourself, I can't be fair."

"I didn't say you couldn't be fair. I said I don't think we have been fair, so far. You are the best reporter we have, Duke. I believe you can set aside any personal feelings and tell Johnny Morton's story. You saw how the cops bullied him to get a confession. No one else has seen that."

"I won't make it look like the sheriff did anything wrong," Duke said. "They have to do things the average person just wouldn't understand."

"I know, I know," Josie agreed. "I'm not asking you to compromise your sources. Just talk to Johnny and give him a fair shake. We'll run it on Sunday."

"OK, OK." Duke sighed and sat back in his chair. "I'll go talk to the kid. But if he hangs himself with some stupid comment . . . ."

"Then he hangs himself."

Chapter 41

Becky was waiting in Zach Teasdale's office when he returned from Carl Anderson's funeral. "Well, this is a pleasant surprise," he said, reaching out to shake Becky's hand. "It's always a pleasure to come home to a beautiful woman."

In Illinois, the coroner is not a medical examiner; he's an elected official. Teasdale owned several local businesses, including the mortuary that handled the arrangements for Anderson's funeral, so he had attended the funeral both as a businessman and a community official.

Teasdale also was rumored to be involved in drugs and was well known for his parties. He was a small man, maybe five foot eight, with dark hair and eyes. He was dressed in a well-cut black suit with a flashy red and gold print tie. To Becky he looked like a mob boss and she wondered why the voters couldn't see it. Everything about him said money, but it was money tinged with evil. She detested him and even shaking his hand seemed slimy. But she wanted his cooperation, so she smiled her prettiest smile and shook his hand.

"I'm hoping you can help me with a story I'm working on," Becky said, forgoing any small talk.

"I thought Duke was handling this Anderson thing," Teasdale said, opening the door to his inner office and standing back so Becky could enter.

"Oh, it's not about Anderson. It's about the Otis sisters, the ones who died in the fire."

"Oh, that's right. I did talk to you about that on the phone the other day. Well, I'm sorry I didn't get back to you sooner. Have a seat."

Becky sat in an oversized Cordovan leather office chair facing Teasdale's expansive mahogany desk. There wasn't a paper on it, just a small brass lamp that reflected in the mirror shine of its surface.

"Well, let's see," Teasdale said as he pulled a file from a matching mahogany filing cabinet behind his desk.

"This is a real sick case, this one," he said laying the file on his desk. "Those people over there don't value life."

"Excuse me," Becky said, holding back none of her ire. "Those people deserve to live in a safe neighborhood and to know whether the neighbors next door were murdered or died in an unfortunate fire."

Teasdale looked startled by Becky's reprimand.

"Of course, I didn't mean to imply otherwise," he said with a smile. He opened the folder, read silently for a few seconds, and then looked up.

"This is an ongoing investigation, so the sheriff's department can't release all the details...."

"For Pete's sake, just spit it out. Were they murdered or not?"

Teasdale sighed and closed the folder.

"You know, murder is a legal definition. A medical examination can't determine murder."

"Listen, I know the state fire inspector's office is investigating it as an arson, so that means if they catch this bastard he'll be tried for murder. I just want to know if the sisters were dead before he lit the match," Becky said, pen poised. "Your medical examiners can tell that can't they?"

"Yes and no," Teasdale said with a smile that showed how much he enjoyed teasing Becky. "Yes, the medical examination has determined the cause of death, and no, they were not dead before the fire. No, not at all. They were immolated, human torches, a pair of witches burned at the stake."

"Oh, my God." Becky cringed and closed her eyes.

"Actually, they were barbecued, doused with charcoal lighter and set on fire, if you want to know how precise our medical examination was. We determined the accelerant was everyday lighter fluid."

Becky scratched Teasdale's words on her pad, though they seemed permanently etched in her mind. "They were tied up in chairs in the living room," Teasdale continued. "Usually when people die in a fire they die of smoke inhalation; they never feel the flames. But these women faced the most horrific death any human being can. Their skin burning. The pain alone would be enough to drive you insane."

Becky looked at Teasdale and saw his eyes were dancing with the joy of winning command of the exchange. At least he wasn't smiling.

"So, if it makes you feel any better, tell your slum friends there's a freak on the loose in their neighborhood. But they already knew that. Half of all the murders in the county happen among the thousand or so people living south of Jordan in Shabbytown. You can say they deserve to live in a safe neighborhood, but they don't. That's a fact. And getting indignant and writing some story about this fire isn't going to change that."

"Maybe it will," Becky said, rising to her feet and heading to the door.

"Aren't you going to ask me what else?"

Becky stopped and looked back at Teasdale.

"There's more?"

"You see, that's what happens when you spend so much energy getting mad. You miss the nuance. Now if Duke had been asking the questions, he would have noticed."

"Noticed what?"

"Noticed that I said some details can't be released to the media. He would have asked what I was holding back that can't be printed."

"You're going to tell me anyway, aren't you?"

"Sure, because it's so gross I know your editors won't let you print it in a family newspaper. But it will give you nightmares, and I figure if I've got to wake up in the middle of the night, I want to know you're awake too."

Becky stood silently waiting for Teasdale's final revelation.

"At least one of the sisters was sexually assaulted," he said with smug satisfaction.

Becky wrote his words on her pad and then stopped.

"Wait a minute, they were old ladies. If they were all burned up, how could you possibly find semen or signs of penetration?"

Teasdale paused this time so the image of his words stood alone.

"We found a flashlight stuffed up inside her."

Chapter 42

When Duke didn't show up by nine Wednesday morning, Josie called his house and accepted his garbled excuse about "a final few for Carl." But when he wasn't there Thursday morning for the deadline rush, Josie was furious and more than a little concerned. She called and woke him, but when she saw him pull into the parking lot about a half hour later, she met him on the sidewalk outside the building.

"Let's go for a walk," she said.

"Well, if we've got time to go walking at nine in the morning, why did you have me rush in here?"

Josie responded a little louder than she intended, "I had you 'rush' in, because it is your job! Or have you forgotten you still work here?"

Josie walked out into the parking lot and Duke followed.

"OK, sorry," Duke said with all the sincerity of a disciplined teen. "I'm going through a bad patch, okay?"

When they were out of sight of the newsroom windows, Josie stopped and leaned against a car.

"Listen, Duke, I know you and Sharon are separated . . . "

Duke seemed a little surprised, but there are never any secrets in a newsroom.

"If you'd like to take a couple of weeks off to work things out, I'm sure I could convince Ham . . . "

"No," Duke said without hesitation. "No, I'd go crazy. I'm doing my job, aren't I? Just 'cause I overslept a couple of times . . . "

"I can't keep calling you. This is not a hotel with wake-up service! Don't you set an alarm?"

"Sure, it's just sometimes I don't hear it."

"Because you've fallen asleep in front of the television?" Josie tried to open the door to the real problem.

"Yeah, something like that," Duke said, squinting at the morning sun. "But I promise I won't do it again. I'll get another alarm clock, two more. I'll put one in every room of the house. OK?"

"OK." Josie smiled weakly. "Just don't do it again!"

After deadline, Duke left for an appointment with Chief Miller. Johnny Morton had been released from county jail that morning -- they couldn't detain him any longer on the assault charge -- and Duke had arranged to accompany Morton that afternoon when he visited his son. But first Duke wanted to arm himself with all the latest facts. He had barely left when Ham came looking for him.

"Well, I wanted to talk to the two of you together," Ham said, when Josie explained Duke's schedule, "But perhaps it is better if you and I meet first." Ham headed back to his office and Josie followed.

"Close the door," Hammond said when Josie stepped into his office, and she knew this wasn't going to be congratulations for all the great coverage of the double homicide at the quarry.

"Sit down." Hammond motioned to a chair as he slipped in behind his desk. "I hate to sit when a lady is standing."

Oh-oh. Courtesy. That was always a bad sign. Hammond's smile was ominous too; only exercising power made Hammond smile.

"I understand that Duke has been late the past two mornings," he said.

"Yes, sir." Josie thought it was better not to say too much.

"And you have called him both days?"

Josie nodded.

"It's not your job to awaken . . . "

"No, sir."

"And what did he have to say for himself?" Hammond leaned back in his chair, narrowing his eyes as though about to swoop in for the kill.

"Some problem with his alarm clock." Josie shrugged and allowed herself a slight smile. "He promised to get a new one. A couple of new ones, in fact."

"Josie, has Duke ever appeared drunk on the job, or hung-over?"

"No, never."

"You know, if he has a problem with alcohol, you are not doing him any favors to cover it up."

"Of course not!" Josie was indignant that Ham would accuse her of lying.

"All right," Hammond sighed. "But I want you to write this up and put a copy on my desk and one in his permanent file. Give the final copy to Duke. Make it clear, in writing, that this is the first warning. The second time he will be suspended for three days without pay – and if we have a third time, he will be dismissed. Is that clear?"

"For being late?" Josie exclaimed. "Anyone can be late. Car trouble, snow, just late. We don't usually . . . "

"Late enough that a supervisor calls and finds someone still at home is too late," Hammond said, reaching into his desk drawer for his nail clipper and starting to trim his nails. "If it happens again, do not call him. Simply type up the second warning and whenever he shows up, hand him a copy and tell him to leave. His three-day suspension will start immediately."

Chapter 43

Duke was surprised by the bigwigs who greeted him at Miller' office
-- Coroner Zach Teasdale, Sheriff Walt Coleman and State's Attorney
Carol Stephens. At first Duke thought he had interrupted another
meeting and expected the others would leave after a few pleasantries.
When the sheriff spoke, Duke realized they had gathered to talk to him.

"Duke, we think your interview could be a big help to us."
Coleman said, his tiny blue eyes twinkling. Short, fat and balding, the
sheriff was an elected official, not a law enforcer. He was the
administrator who made sure the costs decreased, the conviction rate
increased and the county board members lived on safe streets.

"Morton hasn't been as cooperative as we had hoped," he said with
a chuckle, "but I'm sure it's just a matter of waiting until he lets his guard
down."

"Yeah, we thought he might do some talking in jail," said Miller,
seeming much quieter and more businesslike behind a desk than he was at
a crime scene. "I even put a retired deputy in the cell with him, figuring
he'd make a slip up or maybe say something in his sleep. " He finished
with a negative shake of the head.

Across the room, Teasdale had claimed a deep leather chair by the
window. Though it was a warm summer morning, he wore a fine silk suit
and had an air of quiet superiority, even though he was the smallest man
in the room.

"The rain washed away all the evidence at the scene," Teasdale said
quietly, as everyone turned to face him. "And the condition of the bodies
made it hard to get much from them."

Duke looked around the room to see who would speak next, but
there was silence.

"Wait a minute," he said with a little laugh. "Are you tellin' me, you
don't have jack on Morton?"

"Oh, he did it all right," Miller said, leaning forward in his seat. "I'm
sure of that."

Carol Stephens sat primly in a small, straight-back chair next to
Miller's desk. She smiled demurely. "What the gentlemen are trying to say
without sounding like losers is that we haven't got a case, yet."

"Well, I think Carol enjoys catching us with our pants down, so to speak, don't you boys?" Coleman laughed hard and Miller joined in, though Teasdale barely smiled. "What we're saying, Duke, is that we need your help. You tape your interviews don't you?"

"Well, not usually, but I can." Duke said apprehensively.

The men exchanged glances and Stephens made a note in a small memo book.

"We'd like you to tape this one," Coleman continued. "Just in case our boy says something that contradicts what he's told us. We don't need much to crack this one wide open."

"Excuse me," Stephens said, with razor sharpness. "We need a lot. We need a confession. But if we can't get that, we'll settle for motive. Get him to talk about his jealousy. We need opportunity. His truck was all sandy, so we know he'd been out driving on those country roads, but we need something that places him there on Wednesday night. And we need a weapon. The two we got from his house aren't the right caliber and haven't been fired in years. We need a .357 in his possession -- a bill of sale, a shooting range, something."

Her words resounded like a courtroom argument and silence fell over the office when she finished. Teasdale rose, a peaceful smile on his face, and headed toward Duke.

"I've got faith in you," he said, holding out his hand. "You want a good story, and getting a confession would be the best kind of coup, wouldn't it?"

"The best," Duke smiled back and shook Teasdale's hand.

"Then it's settled," Coleman trumpeted, slapping Duke's back.

Chapter 44

By the time Duke arrived at the Family Services office, Johnny was in a conference room cooing with his six-month-old son and Mack was snapping photos from a discreet distance. The caseworker observed from nearby sofa.

After Duke introduced himself and exchanged a few pleasantries, he sat at a table and asked if he could use a tape recorder.

"It's just easier than taking notes at an informal meeting like this, " Duke said. Actually, for this part of the interview, Duke would use his skills of observation more than any words exchanged. He made little notes of how the baby was dressed, the color of Johnny's shirt, the way the beam of sunlight from the window warmed their embrace.

"Sure, no problem," Johnny said, holding J.D. next to his face.

"Don't you think he looks like me? " Johnny said, mimicking the baby's wide-eyed expression. Duke laughed. Nothing could be further from the truth. Johnny's face was scarred from acne; his scraggly, dirty hair stuck out in all directions; his teeth were yellowed from smoking and lack of care. Duke laughed to think that someday this innocent baby would look like this degenerate man.

Johnny held the baby at arm's length, eliciting a heart-melting laugh.

"Oh, you are so cute," Johnny said, bringing J.D. overhead and then shaking his hair in the baby's face. He pulled back abruptly when the infant spit up on him.

"Mr. Morton you must be more careful," the caseworker snapped, jumping to her feet.

"Oh, that's OK," Johnny said, deftly tucking the baby into the crook of his arm and reaching for a tissue. "Babies do that stuff a lot, the doctor told us, especially bottle-fed babies like J.D."

When the caseworker could see that Morton had the situation under control, she returned to her seat, and Duke made notes of it all.

"Tracy wanted to nurse, you know, but it didn't work out," Johnny said, holding a finger up for J.D. to reach. "She got that job when he was only six weeks old, and it was just too hard to do both. Wow, does this kid have a grip!" He reached into his pocket for car keys and jiggled them over J.D., who quickly grabbed at the shiny metal. Mack snapped a few more photos and packed his bag to leave.

"Fine boy you have there, " Mack said, bragging a little about his two grandkids who were now school age. "It doesn't take long."

"Oh, I know," Johnny said. "I can't believe how much he has grown already."

Duke and Johnny talked a little about his life -- how he had played football in high school but never was a starter. Worked construction in summers and then fulltime after graduation. Tracy was a couple of years younger, had gotten pregnant right after she graduated. Her plans for college were scrapped; they'd married and lived with her mom until they could afford an apartment.

"I always liked Tracy's mom," Johnny said. "My mother doesn't think much of her because she never married Tracy's dad and she owns a bar, but hey, she always treated me good, you know? "

J. D. started to fuss and nothing Johnny could do seemed to please him. He tried changing the diaper and feeding him a bottle, but the baby was never quiet for long. Finally the caseworker said it was time to go.

"No," Johnny snarled. "I'm supposed to have an hour visit."

"Surely the visit isn't doing either of you any good when the baby is so tired," the caseworker said and tried to wrest the baby from Johnny's grip. "I'll take him back to his foster mother so he can go to sleep."

"I can put him to sleep," Johnny insisted sharply, pulling the baby away and turning his back to the worker. Duke knew if he hadn't been there, the caseworker would have called a security guard and enforced her edict. Instead, Johnny lay down on the sofa with the baby, who had worked himself into a tizzy. Johnny spoke calmly, rubbing the baby's back while he held the squirming infant on his chest. Before long the wailing had slowed to intermittent snorts.

"I know, buddy. We've had a rough coupla weeks here haven't we?" Johnny said, his patter becoming audible as the baby silenced. "But it's all gonna be better soon. You'll see."

Eventually the baby went to sleep. Johnny had a satisfied smile on his face. "You know, this is the best part of my day. I sure miss this little fella."

The caseworker allowed them to lie there quietly until the hour was up and then Johnny reluctantly tucked the sleeping baby back into his infant seat and waved goodbye.

"I really hate to see him go, you know, but it's only one more week," he said turning to Duke. "I'm gonna have my apartment all spic an' span the next time they come by to inspect, and my ma is going to take care of him while I work. They'll have to give me custody again. "

Duke knew there was practically no chance it would work out the way Johnny planned, but this didn't seem like the time to be discouraging.

"Say, how about we finish this interview over a beer and a burger?" Duke offered. People talk best when they are in a comfortable environment, and something told Duke that Johnny would be most comfortable in a bar.

"You're on," Johnny smiled.

Within a half hour, Johnny was wiping mustard off his lips between bites and telling his tale.

"I'll admit I was pretty pissed when she decides to take this second-shift job, ya know? I mean if I want to get work I gotta be at the union hall before sunup, so if she wasn't comin' home until midnight there weren't no way we was gonna see each other all week."

Johnny paused for a swig of beer.

"But I gotta say, the money sure helped out. I didn't worry near as much about all the bills, and her job was gonna have health insurance for J.D. I got to where I really liked takin' care of the kid, you know? I mean we're really buddies. The first six weeks when she was home all the time, she took care of everything and I'll bet I never held him more than a coupla times. It was kinda hard and awkward, like when I used the nail gun for the first time, you know, and I shot it right into my boot. You just gotta get the hang of it. No, I think she did us both a favor when she went to work, because I got the chance to really take care of my kid."

Johnny stopped and became a little misty eyed as though every now and then reality punched him in the gut.

"Did Tracy ever cheat on you before?" Duke said with a bluntness that made Johnny breathe deeply.

"Hell, we started dating three, maybe four months before she got knocked up," Johnny said. "When did she have time to cheat? I mean she was a little sex kitten even in high school and I'm sure I wasn't the first. But we're both real intense people, you know? When we started dating we were like glued together. She wasn't out of my sight. Then she had a baby in the oven. I don't think she would have exactly been looking for a boyfriend. We had some hard times then because she couldn't drink, and so I just went out without her. It was hard, you know? She was home all the time, watchin' television , gettin' fat, and I was out working my butt off and then when I come home she's bitchin' 'cause I stopped for a few beers with the guys."

"So you hit her."

"A time or two," Johnny said, swilling the last of the beer around in the bottom of the bottle. "I love her, I really do. But she can be so exasperating, you know?"

"I know, I know," Duke confirmed, motioning for the bartender to bring two more.

"I mean she always pushes me over the limit. " Johnny emptied his bottle.

"When did you start to suspect she was having an affair?"

"I didn't really," Johnny said. "I mean I was a little pissed, like I said, about her being gone all the time, but when we were together on the weekends, everything was cool. Like I said, I'm intense. When we're apart my imagination works overtime, but when we're together, she can wrap me around her finger any time she wants."

"So you trusted her and you were really insulted when you found out."

"Yeah, I guess you could say that. I mean we was over at my brother's and she makes some excuse to leave, to go get ice, and I don't think too much about it because she don't get along with my mother too well, you know? So at first when she don't come back, I'm figuring like she's probably gone to the park to see her friends and stuff. Even when the baby wakes up crying and she's not back, I'm not too pissed because I'm still thinking she's trying to steer clear of my family. Ma is going into overload about Tracy being a tramp because she's not there to take care of the baby and, of course, I don't want Ma sayin' those things, so I'm getting more and more angry."

"So what did you do?"

"Well, it didn't really hit me until I went home and she wasn't there -- I kinda thought she was over there pouting -- and I called her mom's and she wasn't there."

"You called Rosie's?" Duke made a quick note. He'd want to check this part of Johnny's story. "What time was that?"

"Oh, I don't know, after the fireworks. I stayed at my mom's until the fireworks were over. Then I went home and put J.D. to bed, and then I started calling around to find her."

"Who else did you call?"

"Her best friend, Angie. I tried the plant, thinking maybe I had misunderstood about the holiday, but it just rang and rang. It didn't even have an answering machine."

"So you decided to go over there and found her car?"

"No." Johnny seemed surprised. "She left her car at the plant?"

"Oh, I don't know," Duke lied, and pushed a second beer in front of Johnny. "So, then you went looking for her?"

"No," Johnny said, shaking his head. "J.D. was sleeping. I couldn't go anywhere."

"My daughter always slept best in the car. You could have taken him with you."

"I guess I could have, but where would I go? No, I just sat up all night stewing. That's when it hit me."

"What?"

"That she was having an affair."

Could Morton really have been this trusting? Duke doubted it.

"So then you went out to find her,"

"No, what could I do?" Johnny sat back in the chair seeming really crushed. "I didn't go to the hall the next morning. I just stayed home with J.D. I told him that I was going to be there for him no matter what, you know? I mean I was really hurt that Tracy would leave us like that, but J.D. is so tiny. So vulnerable. He really needs me."

Duke was getting frustrated. He ordered another beer; Johnny still hadn't touched his second one. "So then you get a call about Tracy's purse."

"Yeah, isn't that the strangest thing? All the way up in Freeburg. I don't think she knows anybody in Freeburg."

"So you go get the purse."

"Not until Friday morning," Johnny said. "The office there is only open in the mornings and they called me Thursday afternoon. It must have been after three because I called the plant right away to tell her."

"You called the plant on Thursday?"

"Sure, I figured she lost it at the park and she would need it."

"I thought you had accepted the fact that she had left you for another man."

"Oh, I thought maybe she had a boyfriend, but I really thought she would still go to work on Thursday. You don't get holiday pay at the tractor plant if you miss the day before or the day after, so I was pretty sure she wouldn't miss that day."

Duke was shaking his head. Either Morton's gullibility was astounding, or he thought Duke was gullible enough to buy this story.

"So what did they tell you at the plant?"

"They said she hadn't shown up. That's when I figured she musta left town with him."

"Do you remember who you talked to?"

"Sure, Caroline. That's the inspector on her line. You got to ask for the inspector because they are the only ones where it is quiet enough to hear the phone."

Duke smiled. "Sounds like you had called there before."

"Oh, sure." Johnny seemed as wistful as any newly married man. "I called her almost every night, because most days I wouldn't be home from work by the time she left, and she would leave J.D. with the neighbor. I would just call her because I missed her, you know?" Johnny batted back a tear and his voice broke.

126

"So this Caroline, she could confirm that you called on Thursday?" Duke was taking notes furiously now.

"Oh, I suppose so." Johnny sniffed and looked away.

"Didn't you worry at anytime that something had happened to Tracy? A car wreck, anything?"

"Sure, I thought about it" Johnny shrugged. "But like I always told Ma, 'No need to worry. If I'm in a car wreck, you'll know soon enough'."

"Did it ever occur to you to report her missing?"

"I thought about it," Johnny said, "but I was afraid they'd take J.D. away, like they have. People just don't trust a father to take care of a baby."

"So you just waltzed in there and got the purse, no questions asked?"

Johnny shrugged again. "Yep, it was easy. I went out where they said it was found, looking for a clue, but there wasn't much there except a couple of beer bottles."

"Beer bottles?"

"Yeah, some odd brand. Red Stripe. Jamaican, I think. I tossed them in the truck."

"You've got the bottles that you found?"

"Well, I had them, but when I picked up my car from the sheriff's department this morning they were gone. Maybe the cops have them."

"Maybe they do," Duke made another note. "Listen, let's play a little pretend game here. Let's pretend you are Chief Miller."

Johnny laughed, "I like this game."

"And you have to solve this crime. Who do you think did it? Who would want to kill Tracy?"

"You know I've actually given this some thought, because when I was sitting in jail there wasn't much else to do. When I first saw the bodies, I thought it was some sort of execution. Like gangs or devil worshipers."

"That's an interesting thought."

"I didn't think of it as some love nest situation until Miller pointed it out. It was just so awful . . . ." Johnny's voice broke, and he shook his head as if shaking the vision from his mind.

"Then I figured it out," Johnny said with complete calm. "Kids. It had to be kids. I mean think about it: who would put that car on the railroad tracks? That had to be a lot of trouble, moving that car and then walking back to get your own car. But if it was a bunch of kids it would make perfect sense. Maybe they were just out there shootin' and drinkin' at the quarry. Maybe they didn't plan to do this and it just happened, you know, and then somebody says, 'Hey, why don't we put the car on the railroad tracks.' That's the only way it makes sense to me."

Duke had to admit that Johnny had a point. Nothing in the sheriff department's case considered the strange placement of the car. But Duke decided to follow another line of Johnny's thought.

"Yeah, that sounds plausible. Some kids just out shootin' at the quarry. You ever do that?"

"No, my brother and I did a little rabbit hunting when I was growing up, and I used to go to the Thanksgiving Turkey Shoot at my dad's lodge and try to get a good pattern in the target, but I never won the turkey. Guess I should have practiced more."

"Nah," Duke said. "Maybe you just needed a better gun. What do you have?"

They talked guns for another five minutes, but try as he would, Duke couldn't get Johnny to mention anything nearly as big as a .357 and when Duke mentioned one, Johnny seemed totally ignorant of that gun's power. Duke downed his third beer before he realized Johnny had never touched his second.

"I'm trying to cut back," Johnny said, as he prepared to leave. "My dad fell asleep on the sofa every night of my life, and he was always in a fog, you know? I love him dearly, and bless him for putting up with my mom, but he just wasn't really there. I realized a couple of weeks ago that I was doing the same thing. Falling into a fog every night. I really wasn't there for Tracy or J.D. I lost Tracy. I don't want to lose my son. Drinking just isn't worth it to me. Understand?"

"Yeah, I think I do," Duke said, as he absently sipped Johnny's abandoned beer.

Chapter 45

At first it looked like Friday the thirteenth would pass without any mishaps. There were no embarrassing typographical errors, no computer crashes on deadline. Duke had even arrived on time.

After Hammond's edict the day before, Josie had feared the unlucky date might jinx everything and Duke would oversleep again. But when she arrived in the office a few minutes before seven, Duke was typing away. He looked up and smiled with a satisfaction that shouted: "See, I can behave."

Josie's superstitious apprehension had eased, so she was taken a little off-guard when she heard raised voices coming from the back of the room. .

"Well, if it isn't Tennessee," Nick chided, as Juan stopped by his mailbox.

"Hey, cut it out," Juan retorted. He was working the evening cop shift but had come in early to pick up his check.

"Kid, you've got to have a little tougher skin," Nick teased back, punching Juan playfully in the shoulder.

"It's not funny," Juan responded and pushed Nick's arm away. The intern had taken no offense at the "Page Juan" nickname; it was a badge of pride. But when Nick and the other reporters started calling him "Tennessee," after the erroneous death report, Juan didn't see the same playful intent.

Josie knew it was time to speak up.

"Hey, Juan, I'm glad you stopped by. I need to talk to you," she said rushing to the back of the room. She handed Juan a county fair booklet opened to the Friday events.

"I need you to cover the diaper derby at three," she said. "Page will be there to take photos. Those little babies are so cute; I wouldn't be surprised if it ended up being a cover story."

"What's a diaper derby?" Juan said with the disgust of someone just asked to change one.

"Don't worry," Josie laughed. "Usually they aren't smelly. It's just a race for crawlers. Parents try to get their six-month-old babies to crawl across the stage. It's funny. Some won't move at all. Some start crying.

Some will go great guns and then stop before they get to the finish line. You'll have fun."

Josie headed back to her desk and Juan followed, protesting.

"But it starts at three, I won't be in until five. You want me to just get the results to go with Page's photo?"

"No, silly," Josie said, surprised she'd been misunderstood. "I want you to go at three. Write a fun story. It probably will be the most exciting thing happening tonight."

"No," Juan protested. "It's a hot night. The natives will be restless."

Josie had never liked that expression.

"This way you can get off early enough to party with your friends or catch a late movie," Josie said. "Start at three, you'll be out of here by eleven. Maybe earlier if Hoss doesn't need you."

"But that's when things start heating up. Anything can happen after eleven," Juan protested even louder.

"Listen, if a big story is breaking, Hoss can authorize overtime," Josie said, returning to the paperwork on her desk. "Otherwise, get outta here. Have fun."

"You're afraid for me to work later into the night because you know that's when the good stories happen and you don't want me to have them. You want to save them for your favorites, like Nick and Duke!" Juan was almost shouting. "You think I'm just a kid, so you send me to fairs and festivals. But I'll show you. I'll find a big story anyway."

Juan stormed out of the room before Josie could catch her breath. Nick and Becky were looking at her, as were Maggie and Dottie. Even Hammond had heard the ruckus and stood in the doorway of his office. Josie's eyes caught Hammond's and she agreed. She couldn't put up with such insolent behavior from an intern. She would come back tonight and have a talk with him about his attitude.

The rhythmic clatter from Duke's keyboard broke the stunned silence in the room. He was typing, engrossed in his story about Johnny Morton and apparently oblivious to the scene that had just taken place. Then a slight upturn at the corners of his mouth gave him away. Insolence always amused him.

Chapter 46

No one answered Becky's repeated knocking, though she could hear the low undercurrent of a radio or television inside Eddie's Shabbytown bungalow.

"Nothing good ever comes knocking," she repeated under her breath. Somewhere she could hear children giggling, so she wandered around the side of the house, following the sound. Suddenly, there was a low roar followed by a chorus of giggles. Three little boys came running past her and another roar greeted her face-to-face as she turned the corner and almost ran into Biggun playing the pursuing monster. As soon as he saw Becky, Biggun lowered his raised arms and seemed to deflate to half his size. His shoulders slumped and his head hung down. He looked like a whipped puppy.

"Oh, hi!" Becky said, holding out her hand. "We met at the barbecue a couple of weeks ago. I'm Becky Judd."

Biggun raised his head and looked at Becky with sad, hound-dog eyes.

"'Lo," he said, in a voice surprisingly quiet for such a huge man. Becky guessed he was about six foot four, at least three hundred pounds, and about thirty years old. There was something about the painful look in his eyes that made her uneasy.

"I'm looking for Mr. Simms," Becky said. "Eddie Simms."

"He goin' to Mississippi," Biggun said, as the trio of laughing boys came running up from behind him. He grabbed the smallest one and lifted him over his head.

"Me next, me next," chorused the other two. Becky watched as Biggun twirled the children one after the other. She was a little startled to hear a voice behind her.

"May I help you?" Mae was standing at the open side door.

"Oh, Mrs. Simms. I was just watching the children playing. You may not remember me, I'm…"

"I remember," Mae said. "Still looking for a fire starter?"

"Mrs. Simms, I'm just looking for justice for those two sisters."

"Justice," Mae snickered, and let the screen door slam as she returned inside. After a second or two, Becky heard Mae calling from inside. "Well, come on in if you want to talk. I've got packing to do."

Becky climbed the few cement steps to the side door, pausing as her eyes adjusted from the bright July glare. She found herself on a landing. A few steps down was a darkened basement room; a few steps up was a narrow kitchen.

"In here," Mae called, and Becky walked through the kitchen into the back bedroom, where Mae was holding up two dresses on hangers.

"Which do you think, the flowered one or the mint green?"

"The mint one is more elegant," Becky said. Mae promptly returned the other to the closet and folded the mint green dress into her suitcase. They were headed to a wedding in Mississippi, she explained. "I don't know what people down there dress like, and it's so hot, they say."

Secure in their common Chicago roots, they shared horror tales of the South as they packed the suitcase. Folding laundry from the basket, Becky asked about Eddie.

"Oh, he's gone looking for a new shirt and tie to go with his new suit. I swear that man is more interested in clothes than ten women. He better get back here soon. Claude's takin' us to the airport at two."

Mae explained that Claude and Andy planned to spend a weekend in Chicago with their wives while the children stayed with Biggun.

"He's been watchin' them for me most days. Eddie says it's good for him to have more responsibility. They won't eat like kings, but they'll all sleep until noon and watch cartoons. They'll have a ball."

"So, you're not afraid for them?" Becky asked. "I mean the police believe the Otis sisters were murdered, tied up, and burned alive. Aren't you afraid there's a madman in the neighborhood?"

Mae shook her head. "A child gets killed by a ricochet bullet, a teenager dies of an overdose, an old man withers away. There are lots of murderers in this neighborhood, girl. You can't live every day in fear. Let those ol' ladies go in peace."

The screen door snapped again and the children came running noisily into the kitchen. Mae quieted them with a raised hand and a stern look. Then she lined up her grandsons and introduced them: ten-year-old Chad and eight-year-old Beau were Claude's sons; six-year-old Dino was Andy's.

"And this is my baby," Mae said, reaching up to drape a hand over Biggun's neck.

"Aw, Mama," Biggun whispered and smiled sheepishly. Becky didn't question his term of affection. Many a sister, grandmother or friendly neighbor has been called Mama in the ghetto. It's a title of daily duties more than biology.

"Biggun is a baby, Biggun is a baby," Chad teased, butting into Biggun's massive bulk with his head.

"Baby, baby," the other two echoed running around in circles. Mae poured Kool-Aid into paper cups and the four retreated to the small, darkened living room where cartoons were playing on the television.

"So, you didn't come to help me pack," Mae said, handing Becky a cup of the purple drink.

"No," Becky admitted. "I was looking for Eddie. I wanted to ask him about Hannah Otis. Did he ever say she complained about the smoker?"

"Hannah Otis complained about everything," Mae said, sipping from her cup.

"The township said she had reported Eddie's smoker," Becky continued. "It's an illegal business. They could shut him down."

Mae crumbled her cup. "Oh, so you didn't come to ask, you come to accuse."

"I'm not accusing anyone," Becky said..

"Why would you call the township if you didn't think Eddie was doing something wrong?" Mae countered.

"Well, technically he is doing something wrong."

"You don't know nothing about my Eddie. He fought in Vietnam. He raised my boys. And you disrespect him with some technicality? Did you forget where you come from, girl?" Mae held open the screen door. "Take your questions and go."

Chapter 47

By early afternoon, Josie was dishing up barbecue pork sandwiches at the annual family rodeo at Ranch Rudy. The children wore exaggerated cowboy hats fashioned from construction paper. Several hours of silly competitions started with a horse race by children riding stick ponies. Then came the jackrabbit jump, a three-legged race with mother-daughter and father-son teams. Josie was glad Kurt had arrived in time, though in his white shirt and tie he seemed hesitant to exert enough effort to get sweaty. Kevin didn't notice though; he was just delighted to share a gunnysack with his hero. Winning wasn't necessary.

Dan Franklin and his seven-year-old, Davy, won the event. A fiftyish black man with muscular arms, Dan wore a T-shirt and jeans and put his all into the race. The duo fell across the finish line, rolling around in the grass laughing as Dan's other children rushed forward to congratulate them. What a wonderful family, Josie thought.

In the mother-daughter event, Dan's oldest daughter, a milk-chocolate beauty of about fourteen, teamed up with his youngest, a shy five-year-old, ebony-skinned like her father with dozens of little braids sticking out in all directions. Dan and his three sons – Davy plus a geeky, bespectacled boy about twelve and a sulky teen almost as big as Dan-- lined up to cheer them on. Their enthusiasm was enough to power a good showing by the girls, though not quite good enough to carry them across the finish line first. Nevertheless, Dan showered them with hugs and kisses; his sons followed his example.

It warmed Josie's heart to watch them. But when she looked around for Kurt she saw him flirting with one of the pretty young day-care workers while Kevin sat quiet and dejected nearby.

Lunch followed the jackrabbit race and Josie volunteered to help with serving the sandwiches, celery and carrot sticks -- ooops, make that "cowboy cactus" and "rattler tails." Kevin and Kurt had been at the front of the line and Josie was pleased to see them chatting, laughing, and even sharing an occasional hug as they lunched on the building's steps.

"Excuse me," a deep voice interrupted Josie's thoughts. "Are you going to serve up that sandwich meat or do I have to wrestle that spoon from you?"

Dan Franklin spoke as little Davy held up his plate with a bun already split and ready for a scoop of pork.

"I'm sorry," Josie said and quickly filled the sandwich. "You have such a nice family," she added.

"Yes, they are nice," Dan said, beaming. "Davy, did you thank the lady?"

"Thank you," Davy mumbled obediently.

"Thank you," echoed his little sister, though her bun was yet to be filled. Josie laughed.

"Have you met my kids?" Dan asked. "This little imp is Bernice. And her big sister here is Nadine, and the boys are Chas and Tre. "Nice to meet you," the youngsters mumbled almost in unison. Josie laughed again.

"And you're Kevin's mom, aren't you?" Dan said, as Josie filled his sandwich.

"Yes, I'm Josie."

"Oh, my wife's name was Josephine. You don't hear that name much anymore," Dan said as the last of his family was served. They found spots along the concrete block wall that separated the play area from the parking lot; the few picnic tables had long since been filled.

When Josie finished serving, she grabbed a handful of cowboy cactus and rattler tails and joined Kurt and Kevin on the steps.

"Dad says we are going swimming tomorrow at a real swimming pool at somebody's house," Kevin blurted excitedly.

"Yeah, " Kurt said. "I wanted to be sure you packed his swimming trunks."

"Well, I didn't put any in," Josie stammered. "But he has several pair of shorts. Just pick one."

"Yeah, that'll work," Kevin said eagerly.

"I don't want him to look like a vagabond," Kurt said, shaking his head. "This is an important affair. The mayor has invited the major manufacturers."

"Well, I suppose you could stop by the house," Josie offered.

"Yeah," Kevin put in enthusiastically, his mind racing with ideas of things in his room to show his father.

"Oh, I'll just buy him a new suit," Kurt sighed, as though Josie was simply too stupid to comprehend. "Maybe even a Speedo," Kurt said, nudging Kevin playfully.

"Yeah," Kevin said and returned Kurt's wink, though Josie was sure he had no idea what a Speedo was. Kevin just wanted to be agreeable, to please his warring parents.

Kurt excused himself to look for a phone, and before Josie could have more than two words with Kevin, Davy rushed over and asked if

Kevin had picked a number for bull riding yet. The two ran off to do so, Bernice tagging behind. Josie joined the rest of the Franklins on the wall.

"The kids sure enjoy this," Josie said. "It was nice of you older ones to come along."

The two older boys were silent, but Nadine spoke up. "We're family," she said. "Davy and Bernice come to basketball games when Tre plays and to the choir things I'm in. Family sticks together."

Dan chuckled. "She sounds just like Fina, that's what we always called my wife. She drummed family into these kids right along with the piano lessons. She was a special woman."

The three kids looked at him in silent admiration.

"Well, I guess I'd better get over to the bronco ring," Dan said. "I'm one of the handlers. You kids, don't dawdle too long."

"Dad, is this all we're gonna eat?" Tre asked.

"That'll hold you until the rodeo is over and we can stop for ice cream later." Dan hollered over his shoulder as he disappeared into a sea of youngsters sporting ten-gallon construction paper hats.

"If you kids are still hungry, I can get you another sandwich," Josie offered. "There was plenty of pork left, and if this lemonade isn't your style, I think I saw some root beer in the kitchen."

The three teens exchanged a look of assent, and soon were following Josie into the kitchen of the day-care building. The boys remained quiet but Nadine talked easily.

"Chas is in a math camp, and I baby-sit for a couple of kids in the neighborhood. Tre has a job at the grocery store stocking shelves. I want to work there next year. You have to be sixteen unless your father signs for you. I think he should sign, don't you? If I had a summer job, I could buy my school clothes. I need more clothes than Tre does. He spends all his money on girls and gas, whenever dad lets him take the truck. "

The trio made fast work of an extra sandwich apiece and gurgled the root beer down almost as fast as Josie filled each glass. She poured each a second glass to take outside, when the sound of laughter alerted them that bull riding had begun.

A huge, black, plastic trash barrel -- stuffed with wadded newspapers and fitted with a head made from the lid turned sideways and set into a groove at the opening -- was suspended between two trees like a bull-shaped hammock. To prevent injuries, an inflated air mattress had been slipped underneath. Rudy helped each hat-wearing cowpoke to sit astride the bull and backed off so they could hang on for dear life while parent handlers yanked the ropes to send the bull lurching and bucking.

"Ride 'em cowboy," the crowd yelled. Kevin's stubbornness paid off and he was the winner in the six to eight age group. Though this meant his friend Davy had lost, Davy and his family gathered around to congratulate Kevin. He held his prize high -- a clanging cowbell. Josie kissed the top of his head but she could see he was trying to get Kurt's attention. His father was chatting with the day-care worker again and didn't seem to notice Kevin's feat.

Suddenly, the owner, Rudy, appeared in his steer costume and all the children gathered round to laugh. Josie couldn't imagine how hot it must be in there, but Rudy was good-natured and seemed to enjoy this part as much as the kids. Once again the event was timed, with four-person teams taking turns trying to wrap a rope around three limbs -- two feet and one hand or two hands and one foot, the teacher explained -- while Rudy tried to wiggle free. The older the team, the more Rudy struggled. Eventually he was tied down 10 times and all kids earned the ultimate reward of the day, ice cream on a stick.

The rodeo finished at about four and parents wiped chocolate off noses, gathered precious pieces of construction paper and waved goodbye to Rudy, his cow head under his arm.

Kevin left with Kurt, riding off in his foreign sports car with the top down. The Franklins, meanwhile, piled into one of those fancy black pickup trucks with an extra long cab and a small back seat, where Davy, Bernice and Chas squeezed in.

"Wow, that's a lot of family to get in there," Josie said to Dan.

"Yeah, I may have to break down and get a van," he said, "But we have an ATV that we like to take out into the country. The boys love to ride on those dirt roads and some of the farmers let us play in their bottomland. I need the truck to haul that."

"Sounds like your family does a lot together," Josie said.

"As much as we can," Dan smiled back. "If my strength will just hold out. I volunteered for the night shift this weekend so I could be here today, but after working until two in the morning, I'll only get four or five hours sleep before they'll want to take the ATV out."

Josie laughed. "Well, Kevin is at his dad's, so I get this weekend off, " she said. "And I need it!"

"Well, good," Dan responded. "Maybe some weekend Kevin would like to go out on the ATV with Davy. I'd ride with him so it would be safe."

Josie smiled. Was Dan trying to make a date or just being nice? She wasn't sure, and it didn't really matter. Being around a close family like this could only be good for Kevin. "That would be really nice," she responded. "I'm sure he'd like that." She watched as Dan got into the truck with his family and drove away.

Chapter 48

About seven, Josie returned to the office to talk with Juan about the morning's outburst. He was apologetic, promised it would never happen again, and begged her to give him another chance. Sometimes he could be so smooth and sometimes so brash. It was almost as if he were two people.

Josie chalked it up to unbridled youth; he would outgrow it. He had great potential as a reporter, and she would hate to lose him for the summer.

Duke was at his desk, putting the finishing touches on his interview with Johnny Morton. Josie hadn't had a chance to read it yet so she read over his shoulder.

"This doesn't sound like a killer," she said. "Have you changed your mind?"

"I've changed my approach," Duke said. "Maybe he did it, maybe he didn't. I don't have to figure that out. That's for the cops and the jury. I just have to figure out what makes him tick."

Josie smiled. This was the Duke she remembered, wise and caring and articulate. This was the reporter she admired, and she certainly didn't want to lose him to some "bad patch."

Duke's story would start on Sunday's page one and continue on the editorial page, where his Sunday column usually ran. That way Duke could be a little freer to analyze the situation.

"You know, I think I'm going to talk to the sons next," he said as he turned off his computer and followed Josie out the door. "Johnny has a good point about the way the car was left on the train tracks. Sheriff's deputies suspected kids in the first place. Maybe Trent thought his dad was having an affair and followed them. Maybe he was avenging his mother's honor. Maybe ..."

Josie laughed. "Maybe you should follow the advice of a very wise man who said that's not your job. That's for the cops and the jury to decide."

Duke stopped and looked at Josie. "You know, I'm sorry I've been giving you a hard time. I don't want to sound like that spoiled kid in there, letting the smell of a good story turn me into an animal."

"Not at all," Josie responded. "The smell of a good story turns you into a really interesting person. You just have a better nose than most."

"Hey, you doing anything tonight?" Duke asked suddenly. "I could use a big plate of fried fish from the Knights of Columbus Hall. Want to join me?"

"Sounds fattening and fun," Josie responded. "Why not?"

Chapter 49

By the time Mae's plane touched down in Mississippi, Biggun was getting hungry. He already had inhaled several cold hot dogs while his little charges left a trail of potato chip crumbs through the living room, kitchen, and down the stairs to Biggun's room. They added a couple of buildings to the colorful village on the table and giggled as Biggun ran the model train around the track, purposely colliding with one of their new creations.

Mae had left twenty dollars on the kitchen table for emergencies so Biggun ordered a pizza. He might be able to drive like an adult and drink and smoke like an adult, but his concept of time and money wasn't much different from little Dion's. And, of course, his appetite was much greater.

By ten, the pizza was gone, as were most of the beers in the refrigerator. Dion and Beau were asleep on the sofa and only ten-year-old Chad remained awake, playing the Donkey Kong video game. Biggun chuckled at the big gorilla tossing barrel after barrel at the funny little man, but Chad was silently intent, his face so close to the television that his breath would have fogged the screen if the room weren't steamy hot already.

Biggun downed the last of the beer, belched, and when the sound didn't elicit a response from Chad, he knew he could slip out unnoticed. He grabbed the few dollars in change left on the kitchen table and stopped by the bathroom linen closet where he knew Mae kept a few twenty dollar bills tucked into an old watch box.

He slipped out the side door and drove the six or seven blocks to the bar where he'd been a few times with Claude. He ordered a beer, but the craps game in the corner was the real attraction. Men were clustered in a circle on the floor, shouting and laughing. It was the only time grownups ever seemed to have fun, Biggun thought. At least, it was the only time he really felt like he fit in with the other men. He loved the feel of the dice in his hand and the excitement of seeing how many spots would come up. In this game, he was the gorilla and the dice were his barrels. He loved tossing them against the wall, and the numbers told whether he had hit the funny little man or not. He played whenever he could get some money. You had to have money or they wouldn't let you play. He hoped the bills in his pocket would be enough, and if not, he knew where he could get some more.

Chapter 50

Richard Angelo pulled his candy apple red Chevy Impala into his usual spot at The Banks, a favorite teen make-out spot overlooking the Jordan River.

"Oh, Richie, it's so adorable and so big," Kathy giggled. The rainbow-colored shell of a huge stuffed turtle filled her lap and its mint green and pink head curled over her shoulder. She peeked around it to catch Richie's eye. At the county fair, Kathy had picked what seemed the most unattainable prize. Richie must have pitched $15 worth of quarters into small glass dishes before he managed to get three to stay in the same dish. When the carnie got out his hook and pulled down the big, green turtle, Kathy was as excited as a maid whose knight had slain a dragon.

"Just rub your cheek against it," she invited. "It's so soft. I just want to stay like this forever."

Richie leaned forward and brushed his cheek against the plush fabric and rubbed his face right into hers. They kissed as passionately as possible with a three-foot turtle wedged between them.

"Tom the Turtle is going to have to take a back seat," Richie whispered.

"Maybe *we* should take the back seat," Kathy responded. They each slipped out their car doors and into the back, leaving all four doors open. No one else was around and it gave them enough room to have their feet hanging over at the end. The back seat was narrow, but at least there wasn't a huge gearshift knob in the middle. Kathy hated that gearshift knob.

They rolled around, trying to get comfortable and somewhat undressed at the same time, with neither willing to let the other get completely out of reach. Richie fell into the space between the seats, the hump in the middle sticking him uncomfortably in the small of his back. Kathy giggled and rolled over on top of him, pulling herself free of her white lace blouse and hanging it by an armhole over the neck of the turtle that still peeked over the seat.

"Oh, no you don't," Richie responded, as he struggled to get his burly body out of the narrow confines between the seats. "I can't move," he mumbled.

"Here, let me help," Kathy laughed, stepping outside the car and pulling him the best she could. He finally emerged and they stood between the two open doors in an embrace. Richie deftly unhooked her bra while she undid his belt buckle. He softly laid her back across the seat and plunged his face in between her breasts.

"Now, that's the softness I want to feel against my cheek forever," Richie murmured.

"Is that a proposal?" Kathy whispered.

Richie pulled back and looked into Kathy's eyes. She didn't like the hesitation she saw.

"Damn it, Angelo." Kathy tried to wiggle out from under him. "Get off of me, you bastard,"

Richie tried to calm her. "Easy, easy. You know I love you . . . and someday we'll get married . . . ."

"Someday!" Kathy continued to struggle, pulling her leg up enough to get some leverage and put her knee into Richie's crotch.

"OK, OK." He jumped back and again was standing between the two open car doors. Kathy sat up in the seat and began crying.

"Aw, babe," Richie said sitting beside her and putting his arms around her bare shoulders.

"I'm twenty-four years old, " she sobbed. "And you're thirty-two. When exactly are you going to be ready?"

"I don't know, honey, I just . . . "

"You still live with your mother, for Christ sakes!" Kathy sputtered, pushing him away.

"Just so I can save more money for us," Richie responded, pulling her back.

Kathy was quiet for a moment, leaning into his chest. "Don't you ever want to make love some place other than a car?" she said finally. "In a real bed? And sleep the whole night in each other's arms and wake up together the next morning?"

"We will, I promise," Richie said holding her closer. As Kathy had said, he still lived with his mother and Kathy lived with three other hairdressers in an apartment upstairs over the shop. It wasn't likely they could find a time to be alone at either place.

They had dated for less than a year. It was too early to be talking marriage, wasn't it? Richie's previous relationships had gone on two or three years before the woman finally got tired of waiting for him to pop the question and left. He hated that perfectly pleasant relationships always came to this juncture.

Richie's thoughts were interrupted by another car pulling into The Banks. He heard the popping of gravel as it turned off the dirt road and headlights lit up the inside of the Impala long enough for him to see the alarm in Kathy's face.

"Oh-oh," she murmured, covering her chest.

"Don't worry," Richie said calmly, reaching up and getting her blouse off the turtle's neck. Just close your door," he said. They each pulled a back door closed. Richie reached up over the seat to pull the front passenger door closed, but Kathy, her blouse dangling open over her breasts, was unable to reach the driver's side door.

"Don't worry about it," Richie repeated, holding her close. "They won't disturb us. They've got their own love to make."

Richie was right. The other car turned off its lights and soon Kathy and Richie were alone with the sound of the crickets and their own heavy breathing. They forgot all about the other car until Kathy looked up and realized someone besides the turtle was peeking over the front seat.

Chapter 51

Deputy Dan Franklin and his young partner, Scotty Miller, left the Tastee Creme doughnut shop at about midnight and got back into their patrol car. Coffee and sugar would keep them alert for a couple more hours, enough to finish their rounds and fill out the obligatory paperwork.

It had been a quiet night. A few traffic stops after the grandstand show at the county fair and a neighborhood squabble over loud music, but nothing too serious. Staying awake at this hour was the hardest part on a slow night.

Dan drove north on the county road, while Scotty radioed the station that they were back in their car.

"So, how does Brittany feel about you working nights?" Dan asked.

"Oh, she's OK with that," Scotty said. "It gives us more time together during the day. We've been looking for a house."

"Already? That's going to take some serious money."

"I know, but you know how women are."

"Ah, yes, I do remember." Dan studied Scotty's young profile in the passing car lights. Finally, he spoke: "You know, if you're looking to make a little extra dough, I might have an idea for you."

"Oh, yeah?"

Dan wasn't sure he should tell him. He didn't want Chief Miller to know.

"I'll tell you what," Dan said. "Let's just leave it for now. You're a young man, busy with a new wife. But if you get to the point where you need a little extra, just remember, I might be able to help you out, OK?"

"What is it? Is it legal?"

"Well, of course it is legal" Dan said. "Would I be talkin' to you about something that was illegal?"

"No, I don't suppose so," Scotty laughed. "So tell me, what is it?"

"Not yet," Dan said with a chuckle. "I'm going to wait until you are really hurting for money, then it might sound good to you. If I tell you tonight, you're gonna be laughin' at me and then . . . "

Dan stopped in mid-sentence.

"Shh, did you hear that?"

"What?"

"Shh, there was another one. Two shots."

"I didn't hear anything," Scotty said as Dan turned the squad car around in the middle of the street. They were just north of 144th Street, a little bit southwest of the Union Oil property.

"It's probably somebody shinin'," Dan said.

"Making moonshine?"

"No, stupid," Dan laughed. "Shinin'. Going huntin' with a spotlight. It's illegal, but we don't usually stop people because it's really DNR. The state's problem.

Dan stopped the car in the middle of the road and listened. Another shot, this time so clear that Scotty heard it, too.

"It came from back this way," Dan said, turning the car east onto a gravel road. They didn't patrol gravel roads; there were too many of them. Dan knew his way around from taking his boys to ride their ATV. He drove slowly down the narrow gravel road just a little north of 144th. That would make this road about 142nd if anybody was numbering them, but Dan had never heard it called by any name. Just ahead was The Banks, a favorite teenage make-out spot that even young Scotty recognized. As they approached, their headlights fell on a car, maybe two, pulled in among the trees.

"We'll ask these kids if they heard anything," Dan said, pulling in behind what looked like some sort of old sixties car. Scotty radioed in to tell the station they were checking possible gunshots in the area of The Banks and Dan reached up and turned on the car's flashing lights.

"We might as well scare these young Romeos while we're at it," he chuckled.

Chapter 52

Natalie Conley feared she would be in big trouble for coming home after her midnight curfew.

"I'm sorry," Leroy Thompson said.

"Oh, it wasn't your fault," Natalie admitted.

After all, it had been her idea to drive up to The Granary, a new dance club in a restored grain elevator in Vollinger. But with one of his headlights burned out and a loud hole in his muffler, Leroy had turned off the Interstate onto the dirt roads to avoid being pulled over by the state police. Even though they knew these dirt roads, it made the trip much slower.

Natalie had been pining for Leroy since they were in grade school together, but he wasn't the type to notice girls. That is, until he saw Natalie in the Fourth of July parade. She was different from other girls, more down to earth. And she thought Leroy was different from other guys. They'd both grown up on farms less than five miles apart. Their parents and grandparents knew each other. It was meant to be, Natalie's mom had teased as she got ready earlier that night. Natalie only hoped her mother felt that way when they arrived home after curfew from their first date.

"Oh, no, what's this?" Leroy said when he saw the police lights flashing up ahead. He briefly considered turning around and taking a different road, but this was the most direct way. He inched the car forward. Natalie and Leroy turned to see what had happened. It didn't appear to be an accident, but there were several cars. Then Natalie saw the deputy approaching.

"Don't stop," she said to Leroy, thinking how the time was slipping away.

"I have to," he said, rolling down his window. "Yes, officer?"

What happened next was a blur. A shot rang out, so loud and deafening that at first Natalie didn't even hear herself scream. Leroy instinctively stepped on the gas and turned the wheel away from the police car. He headed out into the cornfield, the green stalks jutting into the window and some snagging and flapping along the way. Leroy slumped over the wheel but his foot kept pushing down on the gas pedal for a few more minutes.

Then the car stopped, the flapping of the corn stopped and all Natalie could hear was her own hoarse screaming. She grabbed Leroy and felt the hot, wet life oozing from his chest. Her leg was burning, and when she tried to soothe it with her hand, it came away black and sticky.

She opened the car door and fell into the cornfield. All she knew was that the police were chasing them; they would catch her and kill her. She pulled herself along the ground, sobbing and losing a little more life with every move.

Chapter 53

When the clock radio clicked on at eight in the morning, Josie fumbled for the snooze button. It was Saturday, for Pete's sake. Just ten more minutes. But before she found the button, she caught a snatch of the news report:

"Several killed, including one deputy."

She sat up and listened, but the report was sketchy, something about details not being released. What was going on?

She grabbed the phone and dialed the office. Hoss answered.

"Don't you ever go home?" she asked.

"Not if I can help it," he responded.

"So, what's this about a multiple murder?"

"Sounds like it," Hoss said. "Juan's already called in and said he is on the scene."

"Juan? How did he hear about it?"

"Said a buddy called him at home. The kid's pretty smart."

"Yeah, I guess he is," Josie said. "Well, I'll be in and we'll figure out where to put it."

When Josie stepped into the office it sounded like Jamaica. The radio was blaring steel drum music and Hoss was punctuating the melody every now and then with a hearty "Ya, mon . . . Ya, mon." He had the newsroom to himself, a full ashtray and several empty Coke cans lined up on his desk.

"Mornin' Rastamon," Josie said.

"Ya, mon," Hoss said waving across the darkened terminals. No one was scheduled to be in until noon, but on a day like this . . . ."

"Hey, don't you think you'd better go home and catch a few winks? Let the room air out a little?" Josie said. He'd probably been here all night preparing sports scores for the Sunday paper and doing other tasks no one noticed until they weren't done.

"Ya, mon," Hoss responded.

Josie reached over and turned his radio down.

"Seriously, Ham might come in today once he hears the news. He'll probably want to be sure we've made adjustments."

"I know," Hoss said, taking a big puff on his cigarette with a smacking sound as though he were kissing it goodbye.

"So, if you were here all night, tell me what happened."

"Well, about one, after we'd put the Saturday paper to bed, I heard a lot of chatter on the police radio. It's usually pretty quiet by then. So, I turned it up a little. I heard them calling for ambulances and then the coroner."

"Where did this happen?" Josie asked.

"144th and County Road 15."

Josie looked up at the wall map, trying to find that location as Nick came into the newsroom carrying a box of doughnuts.

"Figured I'd find everyone here," he said with enthusiasm. "Nothing like a triple homicide to bring all the journalists out."

"Triple? Are you sure about that?" Josie asked.

He set the doughnuts in front of Hoss and one was gone in a flash.

"Okay, maybe the triple was from the softball game last night," Nick said, "which, by the way, this is really going to screw up our tournament today."

"So what do you know?" Josie asked.

"I know the sheriff's department is buzzing like a hive of bees." Nick said. "They said Coleman would have a statement at noon."

"Coleman? Why not Miller? Is he involved somehow?" Josie asked.

"Don't know," Nick said picking up a doughnut and heading back to his desk.

"Well, find out. Call the cororner's office." Josie also took a doughnut and walked away.

"Hey, don't leave all the evidence on my desk," Hoss said, lifting the box of doughnuts and taking another. "One for the road," he said, as he turned off his computer and started sweeping ashes and pop cans into a grocery sack to be thrown into the Dumpster on his way out. "Try to have this all sorted out by the time I get back at four, OK?"

Josie began looking through the budget of stories planned for Sunday. Duke's piece on Morton would have to go inside. She didn't want an old murder getting mixed in with a new murder. But Duke's fans would find his column anywhere. Maggie's piece about the cathedral restoration would have to be held. It could run midweek.

Josie also made a note on her calendar. "Check murder statistics." She couldn't remember a time before when she had to worry about stories on an old murder and a new murder running in the same edition. There seemed to be an unusually high number of murders this summer, but maybe it was like snowstorms -- a lot may fall on one day, but over the year the average stays pretty much the same.

Just then, Page and Juan came in. Juan was chattering nonstop.

"They got the dogs out, the helicopters, and every cop car in the county." he said, as Josie and Nick gathered around to hear. "This farmer

at the DEA, if he's around on Saturdays, and see if they're investigating this as a drug-related homicide. Juan, write up the color that you have so far and Maggie, why don't you drop in at the hospital and see if anything suspicious is going on there, you know, cops anywhere. See if you can get anyone to open up about the injured."

The reporters scattered in different directions, pastries forgotten for the moment.

Josie called Advertising to see if any funeral homes had called in obituaries. "Died suddenly" was always a good clue. So far, there was only one "after a lingering illness," so Josie asked the clerk to call if any more came in. When Josie looked up, Dottie was at her desk.

"I talked to the manager of the beauty shop. They all room together. She gave me the name of Kathy's boyfriend and his home number. He lives with his mother. Should I call him?"

"No, not yet." Josie said. "We don't know how he's involved. Maybe he was the shooter. Maybe he's been arrested. But keep the name and number for when we find out."

Josie made the rounds to each reporter, starting with Juan.

"So, what did you see at the scene?

"Well, I could only see one civilian car and lots of police vehicles. I think the civilian car might have been the same Chevy I saw out there the night of the refinery fire. And there was something on the other side of the road, off in the cornfield, but I'm not sure what it was."

Juan started to laugh.

"And so much yellow tape you wouldn't believe it. They must have run out, because it was hanging from trees and fence posts like the place had been tee-peed. That's mostly what you'll see in the photos."

Josie smiled. Leave it to a reporter to find humor in a gruesome murder scene.

Josie moved on to Becky. Her tiny black braids were pulled back into a ponytail and giant silver hoops dangled from her ears.

"No answer on Saturday," she said, fidgeting absentmindedly with one earring. "But I left my name, just in case."

Josie turned to Nick. His dimples had disappeared and his eyes had lost their sparkle.

"I'm sorry about your friend."

Nick shook his head.

"You know you've lived someplace too long when you start knowing the people in the obits," he said wryly. "I want to get a job on the *Tribune*, where only strangers die."

"Have you been able to find out anything?"

"I talked to Brittany's dad. She'll see me this afternoon. Scotty's dad will be a little harder. Chief Miller never lets you see him sweat. Grieve?

Entirely out of the question. I'm sure he won't talk to us. But Brittany's dad did give me Scotty's partner's name. He seemed to think he was on the injured list."

"Oh, give me the name," Josie said. "I'll call Maggie and have her check on him."

Nick scratched the name on his pad, ripped out the page and handed it to Josie. She headed back to her desk and was halfway there when she looked down and read the name.

"No," she screamed. "No, this isn't fair!" She turned back to Nick. "Did he say how badly he was injured?"

Nick shrugged. "Do you know Dan Franklin?"

"I just saw him yesterday," Josie responded. "He's the single parent of five kids. Oh, those poor frightened kids!"

Duke's voice came booming from the back door. "Have no fear, kids. Daddy's here. And I have, hot off the presses, the release for Coleman's noon press conference!"

Though it was not quite eleven, Duke had chatted with Coleman's secretary who was put out about being called in on a Saturday to pull together media packets. She couldn't see any harm in giving one to Duke a little ahead of time.

"Wow, a real release?" Becky exclaimed. News from the sheriff's department usually was gleaned from stacks of boring reports and tips from the more cooperative sources. Becky couldn't remember receiving a release from the sheriff's department, except when it wanted the newspaper to run an artist's drawing of a suspect.

"Yep," Duke said. "Coleman wants to make a good impression. The campaign is starting early this year."

Everyone gathered around to read. The names and ages of four dead were listed without ceremony:

Deputy Scott Miller, 22
Richard Angelo, 32
Kathy Woods, 24
Leroy Thompson, 19

And then the injured:
Natalie Conley, 18
Deputy Daniel Franklin, 51

The release included a map showing the location for the Chicago media and a brief explanation.

Deputies Miller and Franklin were investigating possible shots fired in the vicinity of 144th Avenue and Cade County Road 15. Deputy Miller called in their location at 12:21 a.m. A few minutes later, Deputy Franklin called in a request for backup, officer down. At 12:37 a.m. a second car arrived and found Angelo and Woods shot to death in the back seat of a 1962 Chevrolet Impala registered to Angelo. Deputy Miller was found nearby, shot five times, and Deputy Franklin was found on the ground beside his squad car, wounded in the face, hand and hip.

Further investigation revealed a second car, about half-a-mile away, in a cornfield with the lights on and the motor running. The driver, Thompson, was dead of a gunshot wound to the chest and a trail of blood led to Conley, about 100 yards away, with a gunshot wound in the leg.

The deputies' wallets and weapons were missing; no other weapons or wallets were found. Police believe there may have been some altercation between the occupants of the two cars that resulted in gunfire but are still seeking additional suspects and weapons.

"Wow, a shootout at The Banks!" Becky said.

"Well, we have our names now." Josie said, "It's still not clear who the shooter is, so we'll have to be careful how we approach these families. Dottie, you want to go ahead and follow up on the Angelo number that you have and ask for a photo? Becky, you see if you can get a number for the Thompson family. Duke, I need your help tracking down some murder statistics. I think we are way above average this summer."

"How about Franklin and Conley?" Duke asked.

"I'll write up a piece on Franklin and I'll ask Maggie to get some information from Conley's parents. They're bound to be at the hospital," Josie said.

After the reporters dispersed, Josie pulled Nick aside.

"I want you and Juan to go to the press conference anyway. You should be able to get some comments from other deputies for your piece on young Miller. Also pick up photos of the two deputies. I'm sure they have some being made for the television stations. Help Juan with the main story. Go back out to the site with him, if you need to, to clear up any questions you might have."

"But why?" Juan asked, coming up behind. "I've already been to the scene, and now that we have the release, what more do we need?"

"Juan," Josie said, trying to be patient. "You'll learn something at this press conference. Somebody might ask a question you didn't think of. If nothing else you'll see what the television stations will be broadcasting. Work with Nick on this. He's an old pro at dealing with the Chicago folks."

"Yeah, like setting his car on fire," Juan mumbled as he walked away. Josie looked to Nick who simply shrugged and smiled. He was a team player and knew breaking in the young ones made the whole team stronger.

Chapter 54

Becky checked high school yearbooks first -- the newspaper library kept a few on hand just for times like these. She found a Leroy Thompson of about the right age at Cade Consolidated High School. That meant he was a local boy, not an out-of-towner come to buy drugs at some "corner store" as Juan had proposed. When she checked his affiliations in the back of the book she saw that he was a member of the Future Farmers of America. On a hunch, she checked and found Natalie Conley in the same class, also a member of the FFA.

Now she was ready to hit the phone book, looking for a Thompson with a rural address. There were two, possibly related, living on Davis Road. She double checked this against the listing in the city directory -- a cross-referenced book that helps reporters find a phone number if all they know is the address or find a name when all they know is the phone number -- but the rural addresses weren't covered. Calling a family who has lost a loved one is the hardest job a reporter has to do, so Becky tried everything to make it run smoothly.

Finally, Becky took a deep breath and dialed one of the two numbers on Davis Road. After the third ring a woman answered, a little out of breath.

"I'm trying to locate the family of Leroy Thompson," Becky said after identifying herself.

"Yes, he's my son," the woman said without hesitation. Becky was wary because grieving families usually appointed a relative or neighbor to answer the phone. Nervously pulling at the braids in her ponytail, she plunged on.

"I'm sorry for your family's loss," Becky said and paused slightly. "We'd like to write a story about your son and include a photo. I could come out to pick one up."

"A story about Leroy?" the woman seemed a little more hesitant. "Loss? Is this about the county fair calf-roping competition?"

Becky took a big gulp. "I . . . I . . . I must have the wrong number."

The woman chuckled slightly. "No, this is the right place, but my son isn't here. The scamp must have spent the night with friends. He knew we were cutting hay today, but you know how kids are. They have more of a mind for play than for working in the fields. Maybe I can help you."

"No, ma'am. I . . . I . . . was calling about something else. I thought the sheriff's department would have..."

"Is something wrong?" the woman asked.

"Well, maybe it's another Leroy Thompson," Becky said, unconsciously unraveling a braid with her nervous fingers.

"Has something happened to Leroy?" the woman said, her voice wavering a little.

"I . . . just have this release . . . from the sheriff's department," Becky stammered.

"Oh, no, there's been an accident," the woman interrupted. "Delbert, there's been an accident. It's Leroy."

A man's voice suddenly spoke on the phone while a woman's wailing could be heard in the background.

"Where is he?" the man asked. "Are you from the hospital?"

"No" Becky said, "I'm from the *Daily News*. Maybe I have the wrong number. I'm so sorry to have upset you. If this were the right family the sheriff's department would have called you already."

"We've been out in the field since sunup," the man said. "If anybody had been calling, they wouldn't have found us. What do you know about my son?"

"Well, sir, there's been a shooting . . . "

"A shooting?" the man repeated involuntarily and his wife's wailing grew louder.

"Sir, I shouldn't be the one -- perhaps there's been a mistake." Becky said, her nervous hand pulling out another braid.

"Tell me what you know." The man was firm and calm.

"There was a shooting last night at 142nd and County Road 15. Four people were killed and two injured," Becky tried to sound as calm as possible. "Leroy Thompson, nineteen, is listed among the dead."

"Oh, my God," the man said, no longer sounding calm.

"Sir, I'm sorry. I'm so sorry." Becky was starting to cry.

"I need to see to my wife now," the man said and hung up. Becky fell across her desk sobbing.

Chapter 55

The white fog lifted and Natalie could pick out the faces of her mother and father standing on either side of her bed.

"Oh, Mother," she sobbed. "Am I still alive?"

Her mother smiled.

"Oh, yes, darling. You're going to be fine," her mother said, bending over to nuzzle her daughter's cheek.

"Don't worry about a thing, sweetheart," her father said, squeezing her hand.

"Oh, I was afraid I'd never see you again," Natalie sighed.

"Don't think about a thing except getting stronger," Shirley Conley said.

Natalie caught a glimpse, between her parents, of the uniformed deputy standing at her door.

"No, no." She started screaming and turned, trying to get out of the bed. Her parents tried to calm her.

"He's trying to kill me. Don't let him kill me. Please, Daddy, don't let him kill me."

"Darling, you are safe here," her father soothed

"Yes, there's even a guard at the door to protect you." her mother added.

"No! Don't you see? He's the one who is trying to kill me." Natalie whispered, and then screamed when the deputy looked into the room. "Daddy, please, make him go away. Please."

By now the commotion had brought in several nurses and a doctor.

"She thinks someone is trying to hurt her," the father explained.

"Hallucinations," the doctor said. "Some people react to medication that way. I'll try a different sedative, but we need to keep her calm so she doesn't pull out her stitches."

Chapter 56

Josie made her regular Saturday stop at the ceramic shop, just to trim her pieces from the week before.

"Oh, I can trim those for you, " Su Le offered. "I know you must be busy today."

"Please tell us what you know," Barb said. "There's so little detail on the radio. What's happened?"

Josie quickly told her friends as much as she knew, an apparent drug-related shooting right in their own county. Then she told them about Dan.

"He's such a good father and has such a nice family," Josie said. "The kids already have lost their mother. It isn't fair for them to lose their father, too."

"Well, how bad is he?" Barb asked.

"Pretty bad, from what I hear," Josie responded. "The hospital lists him in critical condition, and one of the deputies told our reporter that his whole lower jaw was shot off."

"Oh, my God," Su responded. "Well, at least it isn't his brain or his eyes. They can probably recreate his face. I saw them do amazing things with people who had been shot in Vietnam."

Josie tried to think of amazing medical advances as she took the elevator to the fourth floor west of St. Mary's Hospital. Every floor, every direction looked the same. Josie was glad to feel a little lost; she didn't want to be comfortable in a hospital. She followed the signs for fourth floor west and was just about to approach the nurses' station when little Bernice Franklin grabbed her leg. Davy was right beside her.

"Where's Kevin?" Davy asked.

Josie bent down to look them in the eye. "Oh, hi, kids. Kevin went to, ah, a swimming party," she said, quickly editing out any reference to the word dad. "Where's Nadine?"

Josie looked up and saw the older Franklin kids talking with a doctor. The little ones felt left out, no doubt.

"My daddy's sick," Davy said.

"I know," Josie said. "Is there anything I can get for you? Have you had lunch?"

159

"Yes, the nurses ordered us a tray from the cafeteria," Nadine said, overhearing the question.

Josie stood up and opened her arms. Nadine fell in eagerly. She didn't cry but she held on tightly as though sponging strength from any source she could.

"What can I do to help?" Josie asked.

"Oh, we're okay," Nadine said, stepping back and placing a hand on each of the little ones as though sharing her strength with them. "Aunt Ernestine is coming out from Chicago to stay with us until Daddy can come home."

Suddenly the little ones spied something and took off running down the hall.

"Rudy!" Davy squealed, as he jumped into the man's arms.

"Howdy, pardners," Rudy said. "You'll never guess what I brought in my bag." The kids waited expectantly as Rudy rummaged in a large paper sack. He pulled out a feather, which he handed to Bernice saying, "Here, hold this." He pulled out a ten-gallon construction paper hat, put it on Davy's head, and handed him a whistle. "No, that's not it," he fretted. "Now where did . . . " As he continued searching, a helium balloon emerged and floated up to the ceiling.

"Ah, here they are." Rudy pulled out two huge construction paper smiles. He stuck one on the chest of each of the little ones.

"There, now you're wearing a smile!" he said. "But be careful you don't get them on upside down, like this," he said, making an exaggerated frown by pulling the corners of his mouth down. The children giggled. After a few minutes, Rudy offered to take the little ones for a romp in a nearby park. Josie asked Nadine a few questions to flesh out the family history for her story on Dan Franklin. She got the name of the family's minister and a neighbor and talked to the deputy who was guarding his door. By the time Aunt Ernestine arrived, Josie had all she needed and quietly left the family to their somber vigil.

It was after two in the afternoon and Josie realized she hadn't had anything to eat since that morning doughnut, so she slipped into the hospital cafeteria. There, downing a cup of coffee and a sandwich, was Duke.

"Funny, I didn't think this was one of your favorite watering holes." Josie said.

"Oh, but it is," Duke said, standing up and offering Josie a chair. "What are you doing here?"

"I came to see Dan Franklin's kids. They seem to be doing pretty well." Josie said. "Why are you here?"

"This is where the story is," Duke said with a smile. "Those two people in those beds up there know what happened last night. Chief

Miller himself was over here a little while ago trying to talk to the girl. She's a mess."

"Oh, really? I thought she was listed in fair condition."

"Fair only means she isn't going to die." Duke said, taking a big sip from his coffee. "But she hasn't been too helpful to the deputies, because she insists one of them shot her for no reason. And that's from her parents, because she refuses to speak to a uniformed deputy. Miller came in wearing street clothes, but she didn't trust him much more, from what I hear. And the story she tells is unbelievable."

"What does she say?"

"She says they came upon a police car with lights flashing and a deputy flagged them down. When they stopped, he shot them for no reason. Never said anything. And when they showed her a photo of Dan Franklin, she went into a real panic."

"Well, how about Franklin? Can't he tell them what happened?" Josie asked.

"He can't talk for obvious reasons. They did some temporary surgery to keep his airway open, but from what I understand he has no lower jaw. Plus he lost a couple of fingers. Deputies surmise he must have been shot while he was calling in. The radio was all shot up, too."

"Oh, my God. But he'll be all right, won't he?" Josie said more as a statement than a question. "I mean they can do amazing things with reconstructive surgery."

Duke was too silent. "It will take more than amazing things; it will take a miracle," he said finally. Then seeing Josie's concern, he changed the subject.

"But don't think I'm forgetting your request for some murder statistics. I talked to Miller and he asked one of the secretaries to pull up some reports for me. Cade County averages ten to twelve murders a year. In less than two weeks, six have been killed."

"Wow, that's half a year's worth."

"And if you go back a month you can add two more, the sisters who died in the fire."

"But that's not the same."

"Maybe not, but still it's eight murders in a month."

"How is Chief Deputy Miller doing?"

"The man is a rock. Really. You know he has feelings in there, but you never see them. At least not weakness. You see anger. Boy, is he angry. Maybe he just channels all of his hurt and sadness into anger."

"Well, no wonder the Conley girl was afraid of him if he seems angry." Josie said.

"Maybe that's it," Duke said, "But I think it's just the trauma. Teenage girls are very fragile. Something like this can send them over the edge, I've seen it happen with young female victims before."

Both were silent for a minute.

"I can't imagine if something like this happened to Jennifer," Duke said, switching to thoughts of his teenage daughter.

"Have you seen her lately?" Josie asked.

"Nah. They went to California for the whole month. She and Sharon always have been a little star-struck. They're going to do the Hollywood thing and then the beaches, San Francisco, and Chinatown. "

Josie toyed with her straw, swirling the remaining ice in her empty glass.

"Sounds fun. But you must miss them."

"I miss my youth but that doesn't bring it back," Duke said. "Everything changes. I'm trying to shield Jennifer from this divorce thing."

"Divorce? Has it come to that?"

"It will. Sharon won't change and I won't change. End of story," Duke said. "Sharon wants everybody to choose sides. I won't ask Jennifer to do that. She can be happy in her mother's world and I'll just step out of the picture."

"But she needs you, too," Josie said, "just like Kevin needs his Dad."

"I'll be here when she realizes that. I won't go chasing after her now."

"But she needs to know you care."

"She knows," Duke said making a clean break of the subject. "So, how about your friendship with Franklin? Something romantic there?"

"No," Josie said, blushing. "I just admire him. He's a good father. It isn't easy to be a single parent to one, and he makes fathering five seem like a picnic."

"His wife died, didn't she?"

"Yes, cancer. About a year ago."

"That makes a difference." Duke said. "Losing a mate to death is devastating but it's not a personal attack like divorce. When somebody you love stops loving you and walks away, it's an insult beyond comparison. It's hard to be a parental role model when you question your own worth."

Josie reached across the table to touch Duke's hand and his eyes grabbed hers.

Chapter 57

Even without the name on the mailbox, Becky would have known which house on Davis Road had been hit by tragedy. Several cars lined the driveway and another pulled in just in front of Becky. A couple headed to the porch carrying a casserole, a food offering for an unquenchable hunger. A few hours ago even the occupants hadn't known, but now, after the noon press conference was picked up on the radio, the whole community knew. Still, climbing the stairs to that porch was the hardest thing Becky could imagine.

"Hi, I'm Becky Judd from the *News,*" she said to the white-haired man who answered the door. "I know it's a difficult time, but we'd like to include a photo of Leroy in tomorrow's paper. If you could spare . . . "

The old man looked into the next room and then stepped out onto the porch.

"You're the girl who called here earlier today aren't you?"

Becky hung her head in reply, an errant braid falling from her ponytail and bobbing in front of her face.

"That was hard for them, you know. Really hard," the short, white-haired man mumbled, looking up at the tall dark woman.

"I know," Becky said. "I didn't mean to . . . "

"He was a good boy," the man said. "He was my grandson. He was supposed to take over my farm someday. It wasn't supposed to be like this."

Becky knew that relatives really want to talk. They want to tell the story of their loved one; they want the world to know how special he was. So she didn't ask questions; she just listened while Grandpa Thompson told about childhood pranks and high school achievements, a scattershot of moments that burdened his heart. After a while, Becky asked if it would be okay if she took a few notes. She opened her notebook and only broke into his stories long enough to clarify a spelling or a date. Before long, the front door opened and the couple, minus the casserole, exited the house, pausing long enough to hug the old man. When they were gone, Grandpa Thompson turned back to Becky.

"Come in," he said. "Let's see if we can find a picture."

Becky was hesitant to enter the house; she didn't want to risk the ire of Leroy's parents. She followed the old man into the kitchen, where he whispered to a small gray-haired woman. She turned to Becky with a critical gaze.

"Stay here," she said.

The older couple disappeared into the living room, where a group of guests and family had gathered. After a few minutes, the woman returned carrying a photo in a frame.

"His senior picture," she said, her voice breaking. "Can we get it back?"

Becky promised they could and clutched the photo to her chest.

"I . . . " I'm really sorry," she managed to say. The woman bowed her head and Grandpa Thompson put an arm around her. Becky murmured her thanks and headed for the front door, but when she passed the living room doorway a thin, forty-ish woman with a short, sensible haircut and wearing jeans and a T-shirt, rose to meet her. A fortyish man, also in jeans, joined her. The pain Becky saw in their eyes was unmistakable.

"I'm so sorry," Becky said.

The woman turned away and buried her face in her husband's chest. His red-faced anguish seemed almost too intimate, too private to see. Becky rushed out the door. In the safety of her car, she cried all the way back to town.

Chapter 58

By the time the pizza deliveryman arrived at the back door of The Daily News a little after six, Josie was reading Juan and Nick's story.

"Do you have any details about Angelo's previous drug arrests?" she asked.

Juan whipped through several notebook pages. "Yeah, he was arrested after a routine traffic stop for possession of twenty-seven grams of marijuana in 1975. Let's see, he would have been twenty-three."

Josie shook her head. "Nine years ago? Marijuana? Is that all you have?"

"Well, he tried to buy cocaine from a sting operation in Chicago. That was seven years ago. Nothing lately. "

"Did he do any jail time?" Josie asked.

"Nope," Juan answered. "He got probation both times. But the sheriff's department thinks it's a strong enough link to back up their theory of a drug deal."

"I've got a meal deal," Duke announced, entering the newsroom with three large pizzas. The smell was overwhelming.

"Better take those into the break room," Josie said. "We're about finished here and we'll be right in."

"Come on, Beck," Duke said, trying to entice the still-brooding Becky away from her desk. By now she had unraveled half her normally neat braids and her usual enthusiasm was silenced.

Hoss didn't need an invitation. "Boy, that smells good," he said pulling out his wallet. "What do I owe ya?"

Hoss, Becky, Maggie, Page and Phil, the evening's copy editor, plus Otto, the sports department's blind phone clerk, disappeared down the hall toward the lounge while Josie made some final adjustments to the main story with Nick and Juan looking over her shoulder.

"OK, I think at the very least we need to make it clear the latest arrest was seven years ago and that he never served any jail time, " Josie said, adding a line to the story as she talked. "He's not exactly a kingpin."

She read on in silence.

"Now where does this 'Franklin said' information come from?" she asked. " I thought he couldn't talk."

"Coleman said they used a method of yes/no questions," Nick explained. "Franklin used his good hand to point to one or the other." Josie shivered at the thought, but adjusted the sentence to "confirmed."

"So he confirmed that he saw a black pickup truck there but not the old beat-up brown van that the Conley girl described?"

"Right," Nick and Juan said in unison.

"Then why do the cops say they are seeking a 'white suspect in a light blue pickup with a camper top'? Where does that come from?"

"Oh, that's down here later," Nick said pointing to the story on the computer screen. "Evidently, they had some trouble there last weekend with some peeping tom sneaking around the parked cars, and one of the farmers thought he saw him there early last night. Anyway, he was a white guy in a light blue pickup."

"Wow, that sounds like a really good suspect," Josie said." Maybe we should move that up. Too bad we don't have any comments from people who saw him last weekend."

" Becky said she got a call from somebody, but I didn't get the number," Juan said.

"Well, get it from her and call. That sounds really interesting," Josie said. Nick and Juan gave each other a frustrated glance and Josie sighed. "OK, let's take a break. You two can finish this later. It's looking really good, guys," she added as they started walking down the hall. "You must have scared off the Chicago media. They never stopped by today."

"Yeah, I kept lighting matches and telling them I was a pyro, and I think they believed me," Nick said. When they stepped through the lounge doorway, Duke jumped up and grabbed Josie's purse, which was slung over her shoulder.

"Here's another case in point," he said, opening the purse and spilling the contents onto the table.

"Hey, what the . . . " Josie sputtered.

"Don't worry, he hit all of us," Maggie said.

"I'm considering a sexual harassment suit," Becky mumbled.

Duke grabbed a small wallet from the array of makeup, scraps of paper, pens, checkbook, sunglasses and other paraphernalia on the table.

"Mind?" he asked, and without waiting for a response opened the wallet to reveal six dollar bills and a handful of change. "Eight dollars and fifty-seven cents," he pronounced. "Hey, you're the poorest one yet! Even Maggie had a secret compartment with a ten dollar bill."

"The grownup version of 'always carry a dime to call home.'" Maggie explained.

"Becky, here, is the rich bitch," Hoss said, putting his arm around his still-quiet co-worker. "She had twenty-five bucks."

"Good grief," Josie said, grabbing her wallet and money from Duke. "If my share of the pizza is more than eight dollars, I'll write you a check."

"This isn't about pizza," Duke said. "This is about what women carry in their purses."

"Which is everything but . . . " Hoss said, grabbing a handful of makeup and handing it to Josie.

"This isn't a motive for murder," Duke said, picking up a hairbrush.

"Wanna bet?" Josie said, grabbing the brush and tucking it back into her purse.

"My point is, there's not enough money in most women's purses to be a motive for murder," Duke said, returning Josie's lipstick. "There are really only two motives for murder—sex and money. Somebody didn't shoot six people for what, maybe a hundred and fifty bucks if everybody was carrying twenty-five, like Becky."

"But men carry more," Nick said, pulling out his wallet and spreading a handful of twenties. "I try to keep eighty to a hundred. I hate to feel like I can't buy a round if somebody suggests stopping for a drink."

"OK," Duke said. "I'll give you that. I didn't even look in my wallet before I ordered forty-two dollars worth of pizza. I figured I had enough to cover it."

"So this *is* about the pizza," Josie said, as she reached for a piece of the gooey cheese and pepperoni creation.

"If there's only two motives for murder, why did the sheriff's department say drugs?" Juan asked through a mouthful of pizza.

"Because drugs mean money, real money," Duke said. "Thousands of dollars."

"Not if we're talking twenty-seven grams of marijuana," Josie said. "How about the peeping tom guy? That's some variation on the sex motive, not to mention crazy, which has got to rate at least third place in the motive lineup."

"Peepers are usually harmless," Duke said. "They're too shy to have a life, not confident enough to think they deserve one. They just want to watch. That guy didn't go off the handle and shoot six people, because then he could only watch them bleed."

"But maybe he felt threatened," Maggie said. "Self-defense."

"Six times?" several reporters said in unison.

Everyone laughed but Becky, who looked at her co-workers through misted eyes. She knew they weren't trying to be rude. She had laughed right along with them through many a tragedy, and she knew she would again. But this night she kept remembering that simple living room filled with whispered voices and occasional sobs. And this time she felt responsible. She felt she somehow had been a party to their pain.

Chapter 59

By nine, all the stories had been read, all the questions asked. One by one the pages came together, and one by one the reporters left. Juan, who had worked almost two days straight, finally got so punchy Josie sent him home. Nick rustled up a late date. Becky retrieved the photo of Leroy from the imaging department, where it had been copied, and carefully placed it back in the frame. Then she left, hugging it to her chest.

"Watch where you park that beat-up brown van tonight," Hoss teased Page as he prepared to leave.

"Yeah, you could be a suspect," Duke joined in.

As the reporters disappeared, the sports writers came in, and the talk turned from motives and suspects to batting averages and golf strokes. When Josie finished the last piece and turned off her computer, she looked over her shoulder and saw Duke staring at her.

"Yes?"

Duke smiled and pushed the button to turn off his computer. "Come on. I'll get you a beer and you can try to convince me the peeping tom did it."

"I'm not sure I have enough to buy a round." Josie responded.

"I'm not sure you do, either," Duke laughed. "But you should be more concerned that you don't have enough to make your case for the peeping tom."

"And you do for some drug deal?" Josie said, as they walked out.

By the second beer, Duke was ready to say what was on his mind. "You know, maybe it was Franklin."

"Sure, and he tripped and shot his face off. Then he threw the weapon into the cornfield where it hasn't been found."

Duke laughed. "OK, so he didn't do it alone. But he could have been a dirty cop. He's got five kids to raise, one about to go to college. And didn't you say he drives a brand new truck? Those don't grow on trees."

"A brand new black pickup," Josie corrected. "Maybe he drove two vehicles there."

"Or his son drove it there to pick him up after the deal went down," Duke raised a finger as though that might be the answer.

"Oh, come on now. You're watching way too much television."

169

"Yeah, I guess I am," Duke said, leaning back in his chair. "But he must have shot Leroy Thompson for some reason. Maybe Leroy had a gun."

"Are you crazy? That kid hardly sounds like the guns and drugs type."

"Oh, Becky's being soft on him," Duke said. "She feels to blame because she broke the word to his parents. Tough. But that doesn't make the kid innocent. All farm kids have guns. It's a constitutional requirement.

"Think about it. The farm kids stop by the make-out spot to get a fix from the local connection, Angelo. He stiffs them or something. Leroy blasts him. The cops happen to be close enough to hear. They pull up to see what's going on. Leroy gets off a couple of shots, then the kids jump in his car and try to drive away but Franklin's still got enough strength to blast a couple of shots through the window, so the kids don't get far before Leroy passes out and drives into the cornfield."

Josie leaned back in her chair and laughed.

"I'm glad you weren't writing the main story!" she said.

"No, but I'm going to propose the theory in my next column."

"You will not!"

"No, I won't" Duke laughed. "There had to be at least one more car to get away with all the weapons and wallets."

"I still think the peeping tom is the best suspect. At least there have been complaints about him," Josie said. "Has the sheriff's department ever had any complaints about a drug ring running out of there?"

"No, not that I know of."

"I rest my case."

"You win," Duke said, giving in. "Another beer for the lady," he shouted to the bartender.

"Oh, no, " Josie responded quickly. "Two's my limit. I've got to drive home."

"I'll drive if you get too smashed," Duke said as the bartender placed the third beer in front of each of them.

"Really, I don't like beer that much." Josie said, pushing the bottle away.

"Oh, of course," Duke said. "You want one of the fancy lady drinks with an umbrella, huh?"

"No, really, I've had enough. I should go home."

"To what?" Duke asked. "Kevin's at his dad's. You've put in a rough day. You deserve a break."

"Yeah, I guess I do." Josie said. "Dottie usually orders an amaretto sour, and I've always wondered what that tastes like."

"Sour," Duke said. "An amaretto sour for the lady," he said to the bartender. When the drink came, Josie took a big sip and winced.

"Whoa, that *is* sour," she said, smacking her lips.

Duke leaned over and whispered in her ear. "That's why Dottie always wears a scarf around her neck. She drank so many of these that her neck shriveled up like a prune."

Josie laughed so hard she almost choked. An uncomfortable top-that silence followed. Duke downed his third beer and reached for Josie's unwanted one.

'Before I get too smashed," he said, "I want to tell you that I do plan to investigate Franklin."

"What?" Josie said, smiling and expecting a punch line.

"Seriously," Duke said. "I think I need to look into this, because I don't think we can trust that the sheriff's department will. Miller will be afraid his son will be implicated. They're just going to turn a deaf ear to what that girl says. And Franklin does seem to have a lot of money for a deputy. I'm not saying he's doing anything wrong, but once I check it out, we can be sure.

Josie folded her arms and looked at Duke in silence.

"Okay," she said. "I'm confident you'll find a saint of a man, and as long as he's in the hospital, we'll need more stories on him anyway. He's all yours, on one condition."

"What's that?" Duke asked, downing his fourth beer.

"Don't get smashed tonight."

Duke put down the bottle and looked at Josie for several seconds.

"OK," he said. "A little tipsy, but not smashed."

"It's almost midnight," Josie said. "We're not going to crack this case tonight. And like you said, it's been a rough day."

"I'll follow you home," Duke said, "Just to make sure there's no peeping tom along the way."

When Josie pulled into her driveway, Duke pulled in right behind. She leaned against his car to say a few parting words. Somehow a half-hour passed.

"Listen, the mosquitoes are eating me alive. How about we go inside?" she said finally.

"I thought you'd never ask," Duke said, jumping out of the car and following her into the house.

Josie didn't have any beer, but they found a bottle of bourbon in the cabinet over the refrigerator. Duke mixed the bourbon with Coke for Josie and water for himself. They leaned against the kitchen counter, chatting and nibbling some pretzels Josie had found. The warm comfortable feeling between them was broken now and then by the long awkward silence of something neither seemed able to say.

"Well, I'd better go," Duke said at last and headed for the front door. Josie was right behind him.

"This has been nice. Really nice," she said.

Duke opened the door and turned. Josie was right behind him. A goodnight kiss seemed natural, almost required. As soon as their lips touched, a dam burst. All the emotion of the evening, the joy of the job they both loved, the hunger of their common loneliness and the warmth of mutual respect swirled around them like a whirlpool, sucking them under and pulling their bodies together.

"I'm sorry, I never . . . " Josie breathed between kisses.

"I never either" Duke said.

But it was too late to talk about it. Something more primal had taken over.

Chapter 60

The phone rang several times before Josie realized what it was and picked it up. Her voice was so deep and groggy she hardly recognized herself, but the words she heard woke her immediately.

"There's been another murder," Hoss said.

"Oh, God! Where?"

"Found the guy in a car along the Interstate. Shot twice, right through the window."

"Oh, shit. Are you sure?" Josie struggled to open her eyes. It was six fifteen. She'd only had four hours sleep.

"Yep, I heard a little about it on the cop radio, but Juan just called with more details."

"Juan?"

"Yeah, doesn't it seem like he's just a little bit too lucky?"

"If you want to call that luck."

"Well, I'm gonna go home to bed now. Just thought you'd like to know."

"Thanks, Hoss. I'll get in there sometime today."

Josie lay back and closed her eyes, but she couldn't possibly sleep. Waking to murder two days in a row made her feel a little panicky. Four yesterday, one today. The two on the Fourth of July. That made seven, or nine, if you counted the sisters. My God! Nine people murdered in a month. What was going on? Were the killings related? The story was growing too fast, but Josie's anxiety was more than professional. She was beginning to feel personally threatened, afraid of who would be next. This, she knew in her gut, is what all of Cade County would be feeling when the news broke

Duke rolled over and threw an arm over Josie.

"What is it?" he mumbled.

"Another murder."

"Just one?"

Duke didn't even open his eyes. Soon, he was snoring again, his breath coming in waves like surf crashing on the shore. The rhythm was comforting, and Josie let it wash away her fears. Discussing a story with Duke seemed the most natural thing in the world. Automatic. But seeing him there, naked in her bed, was startling. She looked at his familiar face, the dark hair tousled over his forehead with just a touch of white at the temples, like early morning frost.

She let her eyes wander down his body, the dark, curly hair thick across his nipples, his tummy bare of hair and slightly soft. Below, the dark hair began again, scarce at first and then thicker, darker, more intimate and forbidden. Reflexively, Josie pulled on the sheet until it covered his groin. She clutched the cool cloth to her bare breasts.

Josie hadn't awakened with a man since Kurt had left more than a year ago. Now, suddenly, here was this man she had known for all these years, a man she respected and liked but never once considered a potential lover. She replayed the previous evening in her mind, the kissing, the stroking, the hunger. It had happened so fast, and yet moments flashed into her mind in slow motion.

Josie tried to shake the thoughts. He was married. He was married to Sharon, for Pete's sake. My God, what had they done?

Duke seemed to sense the chill that shook Josie. He grunted and started kissing her neck.

"We shouldn't," Josie whispered.

"Oh, but we should," Duke chuckled and kept kissing her.

"It's not fair to Sharon."

"I told you, that's over," Duke said, prowling her body under the sheet.

"Please, Duke," Josie said more firmly, pushing him away with both hands.

"Please continue or please stop?" Duke challenged, his amber eyes piercing her resolve. She let her hands slip off his shoulders and around his neck, burying her fingers in his thick wavy hair as his lips pressed against hers.

So, again they devoured each other with the enthusiasm of a brand new day. When they were sweaty, panting, and satisfied, Duke wrapped both arms around Josie's tiny, boyish figure and smiled. For now, the murders didn't matter. Neither did Duke's marital status. All that mattered was the two of them, seeing each other for the first time.

"So what happened to you and lover boy?" Duke asked as he outlined her nose and eyebrows with his fingertip.

"You mean Kurt?"

"Yeah, he was always acting like he had the prettiest wife, the smartest kid. You know, like his life was better than anybody else's."

"That's Kurt."

"So, what went wrong?"

"With him it's all image. And when you don't live up to his image of perfection -- when the kid's got colic or the sink's stopped up -- he just can't cope."

"So, breaking up was his idea?"

"Yeah. It was the last straw when Hammond made me acting city editor after Martin died."

"Oh, and Kurt wanted that for himself."

"Of course. It's bad enough to get passed over, but to have the job given to your wife . . . . He could never have worked for me."

"But I thought he got this better offer from the city," Duke said.

"Yeah, and at first I thought that was the perfect solution. But, the damage had been done. All we did was fight that whole last year."

"I know what you mean."

"You and Sharon?"

"I can't do anything to please her anymore."

"Sounds like we're both trying to justify this," Josie said.

"Probably."

Josie nuzzled into Duke's chest, smoothing the curly chest hairs with her hand. She didn't want to think of how this would change her life. Whether she would blush when she saw him at work; whether any of this would last a week or a month or the rest of her life. It was happening now, and she wanted to hide in the refuge of this moment.

"I'd like to tell you I can live on love alone," Duke said suddenly, as he kissed Josie's forehead, "but right now I need coffee."

"Oh, no," Josie said, sitting up. "I don't have any coffee."

"I'll make some," Duke said, slipping out of bed and fishing among the scattered clothes on the floor to find his underwear.

"I mean I don't have any coffee," Josie repeated. "I don't drink it, and Kurt took the coffee maker."

"Caffeine curds! How can you not drink coffee?" Duke exclaimed. His hand absently rubbed the stubble on his chin. "Let me guess. Kevin doesn't shave yet."

"No," Josie smiled.

"Okay," Duke said, stepping into his underwear, then untangling his jeans and pulling them on. "Don't take this the wrong way, but I gotta go."

"I know," Josie said, lying back again. "I think I'll take Kevin to my mother's. It's going to be so hectic here. He'll be better off there for the next week."

"When will you be back?"

"Probably before five."

"Okay, I'll put myself back together and stop by the office. I'll make sure Juan has this covered, and then I'll start looking into Franklin. Maybe they'll even let me visit him. Then I'll meet you at the office."

"Listen," Josie said. "You don't have to account to me. I mean you don't have to just because . . . ."

Duke sat on the side of the bed and ran his fingers through Josie's short, blond hair.

"We didn't *have* to do any of this," he said. "We wanted this to happen. And I want it to happen again. Soon."

He kissed her and then got up, bustling about the room, tucking in his shirttail and using Josie's hairbrush to smooth his hair. Josie watched in silence, clutching the sheet to her chest. Duke started out the door, then stopped abruptly and returned to the bedside.

"I know you want me to say something," he said softly. "But I don't know what this means."

"It's okay," Josie said, looking away. She didn't know what she wanted. A declaration of love would be false. Duke pulled her face back toward him and looked into her eyes.

"Listen, I don't know what makes people start wanting each other any more than I know what makes it stop all of a sudden. I just know that when you lose it once, you'll never take it for granted again."

Chapter 61

After Duke left, Josie called her parents in St. Louis, four hours to the south. As usual, they were getting ready for church but agreed to meet her halfway after services, at about two thirty. Then she did the laundry, dishes and dusting – skimming the surface of her weekend housework. As she pulled the sheets off the bed, she took in Duke's scent and held the pillow close for a few moments. Suddenly she fell to her knees.

Josie had given up pretentious piety in college. She knew God could hear her sentence prayers in a rushed moment at work. Faith mattered more than flourish. But sometimes, such as when she was going through her divorce, praying needed her undivided attention.

"Help me do the right thing, Lord," she breathed, the words slipping from her lips. Then silently she poured out her heart, the strange new relationship with Duke, her fears about the killings, her concern for Dan Franklin and all the victims' families. Over and over, her thoughts returned to Duke, and she discussed it with God as though he was a girlfriend.

"Last night, with Duke, I felt alive for the first time in years. I've just been going through the motions, surviving day by day, but last night and this morning, I felt human again. I didn't have to be strong or make decisions; I could just let go for a change. But I know it's going to hurt Sharon. Help me to know what is right, and then help me do it."

As Josie finished straightening the house, she listened to updates on the radio. State police had discovered a body when checking an abandoned car along the Interstate just south of 168th Street. Although they weren't releasing the name, pending positive identification, he was described as a young white male. The car, an older Ford Taurus, was registered in a rural county more than one hundred miles south. Police surmised he had picked up a hitchhiker or stopped to help another motorist. They were seeking a man on foot in the rural area south of Jordan.

Josie packed a bag with Kevin's clothes and favorite toys and drove to Kurt's townhouse well before the usual noon pickup time. Through the screen door, she saw the two sprawled on the living room floor with the Sunday paper spread all around. Kevin lay on his side, propped up on one elbow, reading the comics, a mirror image of his dad, who was right next to him with the news section. Josie hated to interrupt.

"Hey, you're early," Kurt said, when he looked up and saw her in the doorway.

"Mom, I got a new Star Wars figure from Sylvia!" Kevin squealed running up with the grotesque green and brown figure in his fist. Josie stepped in and gave him a hug, though secretly she winced at the casual mention of Kurt's latest flame. Couldn't he spend one day with his son without having some other woman around?

"Go get your stuff together, honey. We're going to see Grandma Braun, " Josie said.

As Kevin disappeared down the hall, Kurt stepped up, the newspaper in hand.

"So, going to take a few days off, eh, after your big story?"

"Hardly." Josie found herself avoiding Kurt's gaze as though he might see some trace of the previous night's sexual abandon in her satisfied smile. "There's so much going on," she said, looking down at her sandals. " I thought it would be a good time for Kevin to spend a week at Mom's house."

"I should have known," Kurt said, swatting the paper down on a lamp table and bringing Josie to startled attention. "You'll be too busy orchestrating daily doses of blood and guts to take care of your son."

"We're only covering what's happening," Josie responded, matching Kurt's sharp tone. "Do you realize there was another murder last night?"

"Sure, it's all over the radio and television," Kurt snarled, hands on hips. "You media types are all alike."

"Don't you understand?" Josie barked back. "Seven people have been murdered in two weeks. Seven people in three incidents."

"And seven hundred homes are going up in the new Crystal Ridge subdivision just east of here. Seven hundred families   bringing new schools, new customers for our stores, new taxes for our roads," Kurt replied, his voice growing even louder. "That's what you should be writing about on the front page. That's news. That's going to affect Jordan long after we've forgotten the names of a handful of unfortunate victims. I can't believe you insist on wallowing in this sensationalism."

"And I can't believe you insist on spurting whatever development doubletalk they pay you to say," Josie shouted back.

Kevin, standing in the hallway with his faded metal tractor and backpack, started to cry. Josie and Kurt rushed to him with apologies.

"Oh, honey, it's OK," Josie said, kneeling down to embrace him. "Mommy and Daddy aren't mad at each other."

"Why, no, Big Fella," Kurt added, giving him a playful pat on the head. "We're just discussing the news."

"Well, Rudy says you should never raise your voice, cause it hurts people's feelings," Kevin said, rubbing his eyes.

"And, Rudy's right." Josie said, standing up. "Kurt, I'm sorry if I raised my voice," she said and offered her hand.

"And I'm sorry if I hurt your feelings." Kurt parroted, shaking her hand. They both knew the words were just to teach Kevin how such situations should be handled, but somehow they both meant it, too. It was just easier to say when it was mostly for show.

Chapter 62

By noon, Josie and Kevin were on their way, singing their road songs. They were just starting "The Ants Go Marching" about the time they reached the Wilton exit, just past the spot where the Interstate crosses Hickory Creek.

They didn't notice Fred Templeton and his twelve-year-old son Frankie walking along the creek, fishing poles over their shoulders and the morning's catch in a cooler Fred carried. This was the Templetons' Sunday morning ritual, worshiping at the altar of nature. They were headed back to their pickup, parked just off the Wilton exit, where a dirt path led down to the creek. As they made their way on the rocky bank, laughing and talking, Frankie playfully pushed his father so he stepped into the creek about ankle deep.

"Oh, so you want to play rough, huh?" Fred teased. Setting the cooler down in the creek, he scooped up a handful of water and splashed Frankie. The youngster giggled and ran up the bank, under the Interstate overpass, to escape. When his foot fell on something squishy in the knee-high weeds, he assumed it was the carcass of a dead animal. He'd played in weeds all his life and had explored more than one bloated varmint. Even his foot recognized the feel. But when he jumped back, his eyes saw more than a possum or beaver lying there. It was a bloody arm.

"Dad, come quick!" he hollered.

Fred rushed to his son's side. They pulled back the grass to see a young woman, so bruised and bloodied they didn't even realize she was nude.

"Is she dead?" Frankie asked.

"I'm afraid so," Fred answered.

Then, as if in protest to his words, the bloody hand moved.

Chapter 63

Every phone in the newsroom was ringing when Duke arrived in the office just before noon. At first he tried to answer them, but soon he realized it was an impossible task.

"My brother-in-law drives a light blue truck and he's certainly a pervert. I've called the cops but . . . "

"It's a sign of the final days. In Revelation it says . . . "

"The man who rents my apartment drives a brown van. I'm afraid to stay here. I'm all alone."

"It's that nuclear power plant. It gives off radiation that affects people's minds."

Even Bishop Rhone's secretary called about a suspicious man at morning Mass.

Four murders in one night were frightening, but finding another body within twenty-four hours seemed to have pushed the community over the edge. "It's insane out there," Juan said, eager to share tales of their early morning. "We got stopped twice because of Page's van."

"I'm going to paint 'It's not me' in three-foot letters down both sides," Page said with his usual deadpan.

"The cops are stopping cars right and left, and it's really bad if you are walking," Juan said. "One farmer's wife called because she thought somebody was in her barn. They sent a SWAT team with automatic weapons and everything. Turned out to be a frightened doe that had gotten into one of the stalls and couldn't get out."

"I've got pictures of that," Page added. Even he seemed more excited than normal.

The pair had put in a full day already. They were about to go home when Duke arrived. He offered to check Juan's story. Juan certainly had captured the feeling of panic, talking with a man who had been frisked, fingerprinted, and photographed by four state highway patrol vehicles just because he had run out of gas and was walking to the next exit. But Juan's enthusiasm for the dramatic was a bit too strong, using such phrases as "second day of the murder spree" and "dangerous maniac on the loose."

"Just the facts, kid," Duke directed. "We don't want to feed the panic."

Juan's story also implied the two events were related.

"Where did you get that?" Duke asked. "Is that what the sheriff's department said?"

"No, because the state police are handling this one," Juan said, as if Duke were stupid. "But anyone can see they're related."

"Oh, they can, huh?" Duke smiled. "Well, you find a cop – state or county – who says so, and then you can put it in the story."

Of course, there were lots of holes in this early draft. The identification hadn't been released yet. But there was plenty of time before the next edition of the *Daily News* on Monday afternoon. Basically, the intern had done a good job, and Duke was telling him so when something on the police radio caught his attention. He stepped behind Josie's desk to turn it up.

"Body near the Wilton exit, under the overpass" was all he heard. Then over the squeal of an ambulance siren, he made out a question about vital signs.

"Is that an accident or a murder?" Juan asked.

"I'm not sure," Duke said. "But it sounds like the person is alive."

Then they heard the phrase "multiple stab wounds."

"Let's take your car," Page said to Juan.

"I'll follow," Duke said.

Chapter 64

Under the overpass, along the creek bank, one of the dozen or so officers who swarmed to the scene picked up a wallet with a drivers' license for Andrew Howell, age eighteen. The photo resembled the victim from the earlier shooting along the Interstate, and that car was registered in the same name. So, even though the purse that officers found snagged on a tree limb in the creek didn't contain any identification, they surmised that the battered body, which was rushed to St. Mary's Hospital, was Andrew's fiancée, 18-year-old Elizabeth Regent. The good news, if anything in this horrifying discovery could be good, was that the two were together when they were attacked. This was one incidence of violence, not two.

When visited by Aldrich County sheriff's deputies, Andrew's parents explained the young couple had spent the day at Six Flags Great America, an amusement park north of Chicago, and probably were on their way home when they passed through Jordan. Elizabeth's parents were rushing to St. Mary's Hospital from Aldrich County, about a hundred miles south, praying all the way that their daughter would still be alive when they got there.

"This one's a tough one," the Wilton police chief told Duke. "She must have a dozen stab wounds, plus burn marks, and she was beaten so severely that her eyes are swollen shut. I doubt if her parents will be able to recognize her. But I think she's gonna make it. She's tough."

The scene was crawling with media. The Chicago boys had no problem jumping to the conclusion that a serial killer was on the loose in Cade County, though the sheriff's department and state police denied it.

"There's nothing to link these murders but time," Al told Duke as Sheriff Walter Coleman addressed about a dozen media trucks, which had crowded into the field off the Wilton exit.

"One is a shootout and robbery, the other is a rape and lots of slashing," Al explained. "Not the same at all."

"Oh, it's too tempting when you are so positive," Duke laughed. "Let's see, if you're wrong, you guzzle a Guinness standing on your head."

"It's a deal, only if you'll attempt the same when I'm right," Al said holding out his hand.

"Deal."

Chapter 65

Duke thought about the crimes' differences and similarities all the way back to St. Mary's hospital. He would check on Franklin and the Conley girl, and maybe by then Elizabeth's parents would arrive.

All five Franklin children were crowded into his hospital room, along with a hefty woman knitting in a chair in the corner whom they called Aunt Ernestine. As serious as Franklin's condition was, this didn't seem like a sick room. The two youngest children were chasing each other around the foot of the bed, and the two older boys were playing a video game on a hospital television. A pretty teenage girl was reading the newspaper to her father. Duke introduced himself and offered his card.

"Your picture's in the paper," said the girl, who identified herself as Nadine.

Though Franklin was wrapped up like Claude Raines in "The Invisible Man," his brown eyes showed a glimmer of recognition when Duke came over to talk to him

"Afternoon, Dan," Duke said. "You've certainly got the liveliest room in this wing." Dan's eyes blinked.

"Two blinks. That means yes," Nadine said.

"So, Nadine has been reading the paper to you." Two blinks. "Mind if I ask you a few questions?" One blink.

With a flutter of his lashes, the large sheriff's deputy confirmed every step of the story that had run in the paper. He and Scotty had heard three shots and went to investigate. There were a couple of cars at The Banks, a red Chevy Impala and a black pickup. He didn't see a brown van. Scotty was shot first. Dan was shot while trying to call for help. Now, the tough part.

"Did you try to flag down a passing car?" Two blinks.

"Did the driver pull a gun on you?" One blink.

"Did you shoot the driver?" One blink.

"Did somebody else shoot the driver of the passing car?" Nothing. Duke repeated his question and still there was no response.

"I think that means he doesn't know," Nadine said. Two blinks.

"Oh, did you pass out before you could get to the passing car?" Two blinks.

Before Duke could formulate his next question, two nurses came in to check Franklin's bandages and said everyone would have to leave. When they stepped into the hallway, Duke headed for the oldest boy.

"So, do you drive your dad's truck?" he asked.

"Sometimes," Tre said quietly.

Duke tried to sound nonthreatening. "I mean like today. Are you driving your dad's truck today?"

"Yep."

"Well, it must be crowded. How does everybody get in there? I mean Aunt Ernestine is a little, how do you say . . . "

Tre smiled. "Nadine and Bernice rode with Aunt Ernestine in her car, and us menfolk came in the truck."

"Oh, of course," Duke said. "I understand you have an ATV. Have you had a chance to go out since, since . . . "

"No," the boy said, looking down at his shoes.

"Did your dad ever take you to The Banks to ride your ATV?"

"What are you trying to say?" Ernestine interrupted. "Tre is a good boy, Daniel is a good cop. Why do you people keep prying into their lives like they had something to do with this awful thing?"

Duke stepped back apologetically. "I didn't mean to be prying."

"All you people," Ernestine snapped. "You think because Daniel is black that he is a dirty cop. You think Tre is on drugs, You . . . "

"Aunt Ernestine, people are looking," Tre said quietly and put an arm around his aunt. "Let's go get a piece of pie. I hear they got good pie in the cafeteria."

Ernestine snorted but joined her nephew.

"She's just trying to protect us," Nadine chuckled when her aunt was out of earshot.

Duke turned to the friendly girl. "How about money? Do you have enough money?"

"Does anybody have enough money?" Nadine laughed. "We'll do fine. There will be disability checks while Daddy is in the hospital, and then there's the business."

"The business?"

"Dad said not to tell," Chas said, hushing his sister.

"Oh, he's not with the department," Nadine said. "He's with the newspaper. You could join our business. I could set you up as an IBO – that's an independent business operator -- at the newspaper. Do they have rules against soliciting there? Dad didn't want Chief Miller to know he was an Amway distributor, because the department has rules against selling stuff. All the secretaries buy from Daddy, but he's sworn them all to secrecy. Do you want to be a distributor? 'Cause if you do, then I get part of all your sales. Aunt Ernestine is going to become a distributor in

Chicago for me. She likes the shampoo. But they've got almost everything. Want to see a book?"

"You're quite a sales person, " Duke laughed. "Yes, I'd love to see your book."

Chapter 66

After he selected some vitamin supplements from Nadine's Amway catalog, Duke excused himself and headed to the second floor to visit Natalie Conley. He had heard she was doing well enough to be sent home the next day. Duke found her sitting in a chair by the window, the sun giving her soft auburn hair the glow of an earthy halo.

"She still gets confused," her father whispered to Duke. "She talks about going to see Leroy like he's still alive. She knows better, but I guess she forgets. I think she'll do better when we get her home."

Duke pulled up a chair. "Hi, I'm Ormand Dukakis from the *News.*"

"I know," Natalie said. "You're Jennifer's father."

"That's right. How do you know Jennifer?" It startled him to think they might be the same age.

"We were both on the Miss Liberty float," Natalie said, looking back out the window.

"That's right. I forgot," Duke said. "It seems so long ago."

"No, it was just a week . . . " or two," Natalie said with a cautious smile. "Leroy's going to take me to the Liberty Ball. That's next Friday night. Is Jennifer going?"

"No," Duke said with some hesitation. "She and her mother went to California for the month. Natalie, can I ask you a few questions?"

"Why? You won't believe me. Nobody believes me." Natalie sighed and looked out the window again. There wasn't a scratch on her delicate face, yet her injury seemed apparent.

"I believe you," Duke said. "I believe you are a very brave girl who lived through a very bad experience." Natalie didn't say anything but she looked at Duke, her eyes granting permission for him to continue.

"I know it is hard," Duke said, "but if you can just tell me exactly what happened. Exactly."

"We were taking the gravel roads back from Vollinger."

"Yes.' Duke smiled. "And what were you talking about?" He wanted to ease her into remembering every detail.

"Oh, I was afraid I'd be in trouble. I'm supposed to be home by midnight."

"And you were late?"

"Yes, the clock on his dash said 12:15."

"That's good, that's good. So what did you see when you turned onto, what is it, 142nd Street."

"The Banks Road? There was a police car up ahead."

"How did you know it was a police car? It was dark."

" We saw the lights flashing. We should have turned around, but we were late."

"Why didn't you want the police to see you?"

"Because Leroy's car had a headlight out and he's already been stopped once. If he gets stopped again he'll get a ticket."

"Okay." Duke said, patting Natalie's hand.

"We took a chance that the cops would be too busy to notice us."

"But they did notice you," he squeezed her hand a little bit to ease her into this difficult moment.

"Yes," Natalie said, her eyes starting to mist.

"You saw a deputy approaching the car."

"Yes."

"How did you know he was a deputy?" Duke asked.

"He had a uniform."

"Was he a big man? A black man?"

"Yes," Natalie's voice was beginning to shake.

"Now you were heading west on 142nd and The Banks is on the north side, so he must have been approaching the car from your side."

"Yes," Natalie said, involuntarily crouching down in her chair and pulling away from the window.

"So you could see him real well,"

"Yes,"

"Did he have blood on his uniform? Had he been shot?"

"Maybe. It was dark. He was waving his arms. I mostly saw his arms."

"Okay, then he came up to the car on the driver's side."

"That's right."

"Did he cross in front of the car so you could see him in the headlights?"

Natalie looked at Duke as though he was asking an impossible question.

"Or did he walk around behind the car?"

"He must have crossed behind the car." Natalie said with hesitation. "He never crossed in the headlights."

"Okay, so you didn't see him when he crossed behind the car?"

"No . . . " but I saw him at Leroy's window – the same man."

"How did you know it was the same man? What did you see?"

189

"His hand." Natalie started to sob as the vision came into her mind. "When Leroy rolled down the window, he put his hand on the car door like he was going to lean down."

"And was it a black hand? "

"Yes, yes," Natalie was crying loudly now and her father began comforting her.

"But you didn't see his face or his uniform through the window?"

"No, just the gun. Oh, God, it happened so fast." Natalie fell into her father's arms.

"I think you'd better go," Mark Conley said in a voice choked with emotion.

"Yes, I will." Duke said. "You've been very helpful Natalie, and I believe every word you said."

Chapter 67

Duke stepped into the elevator and bumped into Al.

"Are you following me?" Duke asked.

"Probably. You're usually in the middle of every mess." Al replied.

"So, what brings you here?"

" I want to get the Regents to identify this purse we found. A formality before we stash it away in the evidence closet."

"Great. Can I tag along?" Duke asked. "I promise to be quiet. I won't say a word. I just want to soak up the moment."

"You've got lousy taste in moments."

Al exited on the fourth floor. Duke followed as Al walked to a room across the hall from Franklin's. A man and woman stood with their backs to the door, blocking the view of the bed.

"Oh, praise God!" the woman said. "You have spared Elizabeth for your glory."

"Yes, Father, praise be to God," the man said. "We know you can do all things. Give us a miracle. Bring our daughter back to us."

The couple squeezed each other's hands and whispered "Amen" in unison.

"Mr. and Mrs. Regent?" Al asked.

The couple – he in overalls and she in a simple flowered housedress – turned at Al's voice.

"I'm sorry to disturb you," Al said.

"Oh, no officer," the man said coming forward to offer his hand. "We appreciate everything you men have done."

"Yes, you have helped to save our E.B." the woman said, walking to the head of the bed. Her movement gave Duke his first glimpse of Elizabeth. Her face was so grotesquely swollen that she didn't look human. With oxygen tubes in her nostrils and electrodes and IVs attached to every visible swatch of skin, she looked more like something from outer space. But the love and pride in the woman's eyes showed that she could see past the bandages and hospital apparatus.

"I just need you to identify this purse," Al said reaching into his satchel and pulling out a clear plastic bag. Inside the bag was a simple white straw purse, a bit soiled from the creek and missing all money and identification. Al already had examined the contents and found only a hairbrush and some lipstick.

He handed the bag to the man, who in turn handed it to the woman.

"I don't understand," the woman said. "What do you want?"

"I just need you to confirm that this is your daughter's purse," Al said.

"I'm sorry," the woman said, handing it back. "I've never seen this before."

"Oh," Al said, a bit taken aback. "Maybe she bought it at Great America."

"Maybe . . . ." The woman sounded unconvinced. "I think she was carrying a crocheted purse that she made in 4-H. I can't believe she would have given that up, but perhaps. It's always hard to know for sure what your kids will do."

"Yes," Al said.

"And purses seem so unimportant, now," the man said.

"Yes. Of course." Al thanked the Regents for their help. He and Duke stepped out of Elizabeth's room just as Shirley Conley stepped out of Franklin's.

"I just wanted to express my support," Shirley said to Duke. "I wanted his children to know that as much as I want to believe Natalie, I don't blame Deputy Franklin. I don't think he shot my daughter. I think she's just very confused."

"I'm sure that will mean a lot to them," Duke said.

Al had not returned the white straw purse to his leather satchel but carried it in one hand, inside its clear evidence bag. Suddenly the purse caught Shirley's eye.

"Why, that's Natalie's purse. Where did you find it?"

Chapter 68

When Josie arrived at the office Sunday evening she wasn't surprised to find three strangers sitting at the desks. She'd heard on the car radio about the deputies finding the battered female, believed to have been the companion of the most recent shooting victim. She knew the story was developing and the Chicago media would need a local base of operations. A large older man was sitting at her desk when she walked up and set her purse there.

" I'll only be a minute," he said, acting as though he were the one being inconvenienced. Josie visited Hoss's desk.

"They were at the back door when I got here at four. Hoss whispered. "Well, at least two of them. The big guy arrived about twenty minutes ago. He's *Sun-Times.*" Hoss pointed out the others, one from the *Tribune,* one from the Associated Press. "There's supposed to be another press briefing at eight. Maybe they'll go home after that."

It seemed strange to see Hoss working on a weekend without the aid of a cigarette and a can of Coke, but even Hoss knew better than to misbehave in front of guests.

"How about Page?"

"He and Juan took one look at these guys and went home to bed. They'll be back early in the morning after they're gone. Duke told them he would hit the late press briefing."

The mention of Duke's name made Josie smile, and she hoped Hoss couldn't see the change in her face.

"Juan left an early draft of his story in the system and Page has some great photos," Hoss continued. "Sounds like a madhouse out there."

"Yeah, the Interstate looks like Memorial Day weekend with state police everywhere," Josie said. "When there are more cops visible, I just get more scared."

"Maybe I shouldn't say anything, Peter Pan," Hoss said, looking around to be sure no one overheard. "But this Juan kid is starting to give me the creeps. He seems to know what is going to happen before it happens, you know?"

Josie felt an uneasy twinge in her gut. She knew Hoss wasn't joking. Josie put the *Sun-Times* reporter in Becky's desk, which was a little too close to the *Tribune* reporter, who was on the phone at Nick's desk. He automatically turned his back to them and spoke more softly so he wouldn't be overheard. They were all working on the same story with the same information, but each of them wanted to get something no one else had.

The AP reporter, a young man not much older than Juan, was sitting at Dottie's desk, looking somewhat out of place amid her potted plants, cookbooks and array of children's photos. Josie was just starting to read Juan's early draft when her phone rang.

"They're related," Duke said excitedly as soon as he recognized Josie's voice.

"Who?" Josie asked, that smile sneaking back onto her face.

"The murders. Saturday morning and Sunday morning." Duke said. "I've got proof."

"I've got company."

"Then just listen. They found a purse from a Saturday morning victim in Hickory Creek right next to a wallet from the Sunday morning victim. Al's gathering some volunteers and we're going down there to search the creek before dark. It would make a great photo."

"I'll call Mack," Josie said, aware that the *Sun-Times* man and his *Tribune* neighbor were listening to every word. "What about the press briefing?"

"Oh, I forgot about that," Duke said. "It will be pretty routine, I think. I don't know if Al has had a chance to tell Walt about this latest finding."

"I'll find someone to cover it."

Josie returned to reading Juan's story, trying to make the phone call seem unimportant. After a few minutes she went into Ham's office and closed the door. She called Mack and interrupted a family birthday celebration. She told him about the volunteers gathering at the creek. He complained, but she knew he would go.

Josie went to the briefing. After reading Juan's story she felt up-to-date, and she was hoping to steer conversation away from the purse in Hickory Creek. Besides, with the three guests and the AP photographer heading to the briefing, she didn't feel a need to remain behind to oversee the office. Standing with the other media reps waiting for the press briefing, she started chatting with them.

"That's Carol Stephens," Josie whispered, pointing to the shapely state's attorney. "Her father is a judge in Chicago, but you probably know that."

"That's Arnie Stephens' kid?" the *Sun-Times* man said with narrowed brows.

"I've seen him date women younger than her," the *Tribune* man replied, and the two shared a conspiratorial chuckle.

"She's bright and tough," Josie said. "I wouldn't be surprised if she ran for state office in a few years."

"Hmm, attorney general?" the *Sun-Times* man asked.

"Or, lieutenant governor," the *Tribune* man suggested. "The Republicans need a strong woman up front."

Josie was pleased that these two seemed more interested in politics than murder. The representatives of the print media, including the quiet kid from the AP and a couple from smaller dailies like the Morley paper twenty miles south, formed a knot in the center of the lawn in front of the sheriff's department. The television people, with all their cameras, microphones and perfectly coifed hair, sprawled on each side and across the front, jockeying for the right angle, the best shot. Briefings always favored the electronic media, because a minute on the ten o'clock news was worth more points with the voters than a lengthy interview in three newspapers. This disparity, and a feeling among the print media that television was not always mindful of journalistic ethics, created an invisible wall between the two camps that few cared to cross, even for polite chatter.

Sheriff Walt Coleman took the podium first and moved quickly to what he termed "the biggest development of the day." Josie held her breath.

"A man fitting the description of the peeping tom from last weekend has turned himself in," Coleman said, and Josie quickly scribbled notes right along with the rest of the media. "But he was released after questioning. I won't identify the man, because he is not being charged with any crime, but I can tell you he is a pastor in a neighboring county who was trying to minister to the young people at The Banks. He was in an all-night revival prayer meeting with several credible witnesses at the time of the Saturday morning murders."

Darn, Josie thought. There goes that suspect.

"Anyway, we are no longer seeking a blue pickup with a white camper top but are continuing to seek a black or dark-colored pickup and a brown van."

Then Coleman turned the podium over to Teasdale, who gave more gruesome details on the bodies, pointing out that the Saturday victims had been shot three to five times each with a .38 caliber weapon, while the Sunday victim had been shot twice with a .357 magnum. He explained that both slugs could have been fired from the same gun.

Coleman returned to the podium to report on the condition and name of the woman found at Hickory Creek. Elizabeth Regent had been stabbed sixteen times, raped repeatedly, burned with a cigarette and beaten. Her stab wounds, however, were mostly superficial, in her arms and legs. She was in fair condition, heavily sedated and deputies had not been able to complete an interview.

When the conference was thrown open to questions, everyone asked at once about a link between the murders. Coleman turned to Stephens, who took the podium with deliberate slowness.

"I have been informed that we are investigating a possible link between the four deaths Saturday morning off 144th Street and the one death Sunday morning along Interstate 55, near 168th Street," she said with courtroom formality. "However, that investigation is not complete and I am not at liberty to release any details.'

"Yes!" Josie thought with a triumphant clench of her fist. Then she looked to her companions to see if they had noticed.

"Reports in the Chicago media about these deaths being linked in any way to earlier unsolved murders, including the deaths of two elderly women in a fire on June 26, are highly irresponsible and simply wrong." Stephens said. "This is NOT a serial anything. These are two incidents on one weekend that may, I emphasize may, be linked. But we are not investigating any links beyond that. Am I clear?"

Chapter 69

When Josie arrived back at the office she was pleased that none of the other media had followed her, and she was delighted to see Duke's muddy cowboy boots resting beside the back door. He was sitting on top of the desk next to Hoss, his stocking feet dangling over the side, peeking out from rolled up jeans. Hoss was his normal relaxed self, a cigarette in one hand and a Coke in the other.

"So, anything new from the press conference?" Duke asked with a wink.

"A little humble pie," Josie responded. "The peeping tom's been cleared."

Duke gave a hoot. "Well, save a piece of pie for me. Franklin's money comes from selling laundry soap and vitamins, not drugs. I'm convinced Natalie did see him waving his arms, but then he passed out when she wasn't looking and she only assumed the same man shot them."

"So there are no suspects left," Josie said. "What did you find in the creek?"

"Everything," Duke said. "All the wallets and purses. It was a snap. We had about ten guys, and the water's not more than two feet at the deepest part. We just walked side by side and found everything."

"And Mack showed up?" Josie asked, sitting next to Duke on the desktop.

"Showed up but stayed clear of the mud. And look what else I found." Duke picked up a strange beer bottle and held it high.

"A new label for your collection?"

"No. This links it to Carl's murder. Johnny said he found a Red Stripe bottle where they found Tracy's purse."

"Jeez, man" Hoss said. "Those are about as common as black pickup trucks. Anybody could have thrown that there. I'll bet if you look around you'll find a Miller can and a Bud Light."

"Only if the killer is watching his weight," Josie said. "Besides, Stephens was pretty emphatic that these two are not linked to any other murders. One of the papers linked the sisters' deaths to these but didn't say anything about Carl and Tracy."

"That's probably because Coleman told them they had a suspect in that case," Duke said. "They've closed the book on that one. But I think they're wrong."

Duke hopped down from the desk and grabbed a pad of Post-It Notes off Hoss's desk. He scratched a date on one yellow sheet and stuck it on the wall map at the location of the quarry. Then he attached another dated slip to The Banks and a final one at the Interstate and 168th. Although these incidents spanned about four miles, the three slips of paper made a tight cluster on the map of the county.

"Each of these started with a couple in a parked car. Each of these ended in robbery." Duke said. "The details in between may vary a little, but the beginning and the ending are always the same.

"But you're the one who said someone wouldn't shoot six people for the contents of a woman's purse," Josie said.

"He didn't intend to shoot six people. He planned to kill the guy, rape and kill the woman, and take their money. A pretty basic crime," Duke said. "But the cops showed up, and then unlucky Leroy drove by, and our murderer just did what he had to do. Maybe that's why he went looking for a parked car again the next night. He didn't get any sexual satisfaction the first night."

Hoss and Josie shivered at Duke's calculating conclusions.

"And the quarry, ten days before, started the same way. A parked car, easy marks. But wait, it's empty. He goes in search of the couple, intending a simple rape and robbery, but he brought too big a gun. He blasts right through Carl and into Tracy."

"I don't see a yellow piece of paper at Shabbytown," Hoss said.

"I could do that," Duke said, scratching a date on another yellow slip and attaching it to the map not far from the other markers. "But it didn't start out in a parked car. A home invasion requires a lot more balls. And he used fire instead of a weapon. Linking any of these goes against the rules, because he keeps changing weapons."

"A gun for men, a knife for women," Josie said suddenly. "A sexual significance perhaps, or maybe he just feels more threatened by men. He wants to kill them quickly, but he feels certain he can overpower a woman, and the knife is just a little insurance."

Duke shook his head. "You've been reading too many romantic thrillers. Remember, Kathy Woods was shot."

"Yes, I remember," Josie said with a shiver. "Three times. Teasdale reminded us today. But maybe that was when the deputies pulled up. When the murderer realized he wasn't going to get to have his way with her."

A chilling quiet gripped the room as Hoss, Duke and Josie looked at each other and the four innocent scraps of yellow paper clinging to the map of their world.

Chapter 70

Duke and Josie left the office with an unspoken agreement to continue where they had left off that morning. Although neither of them had eaten any dinner, and it was well after nine in the evening, another hunger needed to be satisfied first.

Josie was standing at her front door when Duke pulled into her driveway and headed up her walk with a grocery sack in one arm and a twelve-pack of beer in the other.

"I had to stop for a little pop," Duke said with a self-conscious chuckle. "Mind if I put this in your fridge?"

Josie took the beer and put it in the refrigerator as Duke set his bag on the table. "I hope I'm not being too presumptuous," he said, pulling a coffee maker out of the sack, and then the coffee to go with it. Josie cracked the crooked half-smile that drove Duke crazy. Without another word, he crossed to her, grabbed her in his arms and kissed her passionately. She melted, warm and jelly-like in his arms.

Neither seemed to have the strength to stand another minute, so they slowly sank to the floor. Somehow clothes came off as they tussled, though it was never totally clear who was undressing whom. It seemed they were locked in one long kiss, yet their bodies sought the heat of each other's bare flesh, until they were melded together, warm and one, in the middle of the kitchen floor. Only later, looking up at the glaring kitchen light fixture, did they become aware of the cold hard linoleum beneath them.

Duke started chuckling first, then Josie caught the playful glint in his eye and soon they were laughing so hard they could hardly breathe. Duke picked up Josie's bra and hung it from a kitchen cabinet handle, then draped his underwear over the next knob and her blouse over another.

"Why Mrs. Braun, I love how you've decorated this kitchen," he said in an exaggerated falsetto.

"Stop it." Josie picked up his jeans and threw them at him. He threw them back, which started a free-for-all clothes toss that ended only when they were laughing too hard to go on. Duke leaned back and pulled the refrigerator door open. He tossed Josie a beer and opened one for himself. Josie looked at her watch and jumped up.

200

"We're missing the ten o'clock news," she said, turning on the small television set on the kitchen counter. There, edited for maximum impact, were patrolmen stopping cars and frisking motorists, a SWAT team attacking an empty barn, and close-ups of ordinary citizens expressing their fear.

"I wouldn't stop to help no one, I'll tell you that," one motherly looking lady said with smug satisfaction.

So that is what Jordan had become. Afraid to help.

As the news segment on Jordan ended, Duke dressed, gathering his clothes from various corners of the kitchen. A sock had caught on a push-pin on the bulletin board and when he removed it he couldn't help but notice a list, torn from a yellow legal pad, of all the curse words you could imagine.

"Whoa, what's this? A letter to Kurt?"

"No!" Josie squealed, ripping the paper from the board. "You've heard of television's seven forbidden words? Well, this is the dirty dozen. These are the words not allowed in this house."

"Oh, great! They're not allowed, so you post them for every guest to see?"

"Not every guest, just the nosey ones," Josie said, pushing Duke away from her bulletin board. "I made Kevin a deal. If he says a bad word, he owes me a quarter. If I say a bad word, I owe him a dollar. He's winning."

Duke laughed. "Why don't you try my method? Dingo drizzle isn't on your list."

"Ewwww, that's worse than any word on the list. Don't let Kevin hear your made-up curse words."

They dressed partially and Duke sat at the kitchen table sorting through that morning's Chicago papers, drinking another beer while Josie made tuna sandwiches.

"This *Sun-Times* guy is the one who brings up the sisters as a possible connection," he said, reading the article to her. The reference was vague, without any attribution.

"I met that guy today," Josie said, setting a sandwich and a bag of potato chips in front of Duke. "They must really be taking this story seriously to send such a senior writer."

"Yeah, they like the sensational stories," Duke said. "I'll be interested to see what he has tomorrow."

"Are we any better?" Josie asked. "I have to admit this whole thing gives me a shot of adrenalin."

"It's our job. And it sure beats sewer bond issues and tax anticipation warrants."

They were quiet for a few moments as Josie wrestled with Kurt's comments of earlier that day about seven hundred new homes being more important than seven deaths. Of course, new homes and new sewers and new taxes were important. The newspaper covered all of that. But it was the aberrations, these detours in the orderly procession of their community that seemed to attract attention. Was that the media's fault? Did they create this interest, or was it something deeper, more visceral, this thirst for death?

"You know, I couldn't help but think about that couple from Aldrich County," Josie said, breaking the silence. "They probably drove right through Jordan Saturday morning, maybe even heard the radio reports about the shootings. They might have thought it was part of life so close to the city, but they must not have thought about it much as they went to the park and enjoyed all the rides. Then, on their way home, late at night, maybe too tired to keep on driving, they pulled over to take a nap, never thinking it might be dangerous. Never thinking they would become part of this story."

"We never do," Duke said, opening another beer. "The difference between a routine drive home and a life-changing accident can be just one moment of inattention, just one second of hesitation in hitting the brakes."

"I don't know which is worse," Josie said, "thinking there's one madman doing all of this or having three or four murderers on the loose."

Duke reached across the table for more chips. "Oh, the madman, any day. If we can tell ourselves there's some reason these people died – marital infidelity, drugs, even picking up a hitchhiker or living in a bad neighborhood – then we can feel safe as long as we don't do those things."

"But if there's a madman, then any one of us could be next."

"Yes, exactly, and as long as he's out there, there will be a next." Josie shuddered at the thought.

"Boy, if that Regent gal is in fair condition, I'd hate to see what serious looks like," Duke said, shaking his head. "She didn't even look human. She reminded me of another woman I interviewed in the hospital years ago. Must have been the year Jennifer was born, so like fifteen years ago." Duke looked off into the distance as if trying to picture that day. "She had been beaten, not stabbed, but her face had the same grotesque, misshapen appearance."

"What happened to her?"

"Oh, something sort of like this." Duke knit his eyebrows together as he tried to recall. "Yeah, it was in Lilac Park. She and her boyfriend had been in a parked car. Some kid with a gun. I don't remember, maybe he chased the boyfriend off or something. It doesn't seem there was a murder. Anyway, he beat her up bad and raped her."

"Strange that things haven't changed much in fifteen years."

"That's one of the things about this job. They all run together after a while. Drives a man to drink," Duke said, upending another beer.

"It does?"

Duke paused and looked at Josie.

"No," he said, gathering up the three empty cans on the table in front of him and tossing them into the trash. He headed to the refrigerator for another. "I don't drink to forget or for any Freudian folderol. It just relaxes me. I work hard. I deserve it. And you do, too." He set another beer in front of Josie. She popped open the top and they clanked their cans together.

"She used to call me, but I haven't heard from her in years," Duke said suddenly.

"Who?" .

"The woman who was beaten up in Lilac Park. She called me a couple of times, when he came up for parole, but I haven't heard from her in four or five years. Wonder what happened to her."

"There might be a story there," Josie said, "if her case was similar to these."

"Don't you ever stop working?" Duke said, reaching across the table to kiss her.

A sip or two later, she was reaching back across the table to kiss him. Soon, the table seemed a nuisance.

"Wait a minute," Josie said, as Duke grabbed her and the table leg cut into her thigh. "Before you get too carried away, maybe we should go upstairs."

"Me?" Duke responded, pulling her to her feet. "I thought you were the one getting carried away." Another passionate kiss and he picked her up and carried her laughing up the stairs.

Chapter 71

After midnight, when Josie was purring contentedly, snoring in a reserved, ladylike way, Duke was wide awake. "Ruth, that was her name," he thought, still seeing flashes of a bruised and swollen face that was one minute Elizabeth and the next Ruth from fifteen years ago. The only difference was Ruth had been trying to answer his questions.

Duke tiptoed down the stairs to the shaving kit he had left on the kitchen table next to the coffee maker. He pulled a small flask of bourbon from the kit and took a quick swig, as though medicating a sore throat. It burned, but he didn't care. Then he rummaged in the cabinet for a glass, got some ice from the freezer, and mixed a strong drink with just a little water to finish filling the glass.

He messed with the coffee pot, getting it ready for the next morning. He spilled water all over the counter, his aim affected by the half-dozen beers he had downed. Then he emptied the rest of the flask over the remaining ice in his glass and looked out the window into the night, taking large gulps until he no longer could see Ruth's face.

He must have stumbled up the stairs, because he was in bed, dreaming it was fifteen years ago, when a baby's cry awakened him. He was shocked to turn and see this other woman, not his sweet young Sharon, by his side. A dream, he thought, a crazy dream. There was no baby crying, just a digital clock glowing 4:23. He rolled with his back to Josie, and closed his eyes. Then suddenly he opened them again. Malcolm Jones. That was the name of the man convicted of beating and raping Ruth all those years ago. Malcolm Jones.

Chapter 72

"Tiny Town Terrorized." The *Sun-Times* headline made Jordan seem like some mythical, Lilliputian village where a monstrous evil prowled. It read like an advertisement for a horror flick, not a place with softball tournaments, garage sales, and Fourth of July parades.

But reading the story in the Chicago papers made it official. The terror the townspeople felt was real; the serial killer was real. People tend to believe what they read in newspapers or see on television, even more than they believe their own experience. The bigger the newspaper, the more well known the newscaster, the truer the words must be.

At the grocery store and the fire station, in the nursing home and Su Le's Monday morning ceramic-painting class, they passed around newspapers, read the words aloud, becoming more frightened by the minute. As the Associated Press stories appeared in papers around the country, phones began ringing with relatives from Seattle to Miami expressing their concern. Police had provided a sketch of the suspect, based on Elizabeth's description, and one of the television stations had labeled him the Cornfield Killer, a moniker just catchy enough to stick.

Even at the *Jordan Daily News*, reporters gathered around copies of competing newspapers, searching for inaccuracies, a misspelled name here, a faulty description there. Yet, everyone was eager to read the words. It wasn't that they expected to find out something new; the coverage in the *Daily News* was more thorough. But a story in the *Sun-Times*, teased on the tabloid's cover and spread across the top of an inside page, or a brief mention in the *New York Times* added significance to the work they were doing.

After deadline, Josie called a staff meeting. She'd discussed her plan with Hammond so he leaned in the doorway of his office and listened as the reporters and copy editors clustered around Josie's desk.

"First I want to thank everybody who showed up over the weekend. You did a super job and we can be proud of our coverage. These papers have definite prize potential. But this thing -- whatever it is -- may not be over. If we have a serial killer in Jordan, then it will happen again."

The sobering realization passed through the room like a cloud that darkened every face. Josie took a deep breath and continued.

"I'm passing out a schedule with two reporters on call at all times. We will need to pace ourselves or we'll burn out. This could go on a while."

"Nothing is going to happen until Friday night," Juan said with bravado. "My regular shift. This killer, he likes my work."

A low chuckle passed through the room, but when Josie glanced at Hoss, he wasn't smiling. She continued.

"A development could come at any time, an arrest maybe, or a change in Franklin's condition. That means every one of you must be completely up-to-date on the whole story. I've included a list of home numbers of the major sources so those of you who don't usually cover police can have them with you."

"So, what if nothing happens this week?" Nick asked. "How long do we keep somebody on call?"

"That's a very good question, Nick. Why don't you find the answer?" Josie responded. "Talk to an expert on these things. When can we expect the killer to strike again? And, when can we start to breathe easy? One week? Two? A month? I think our readers would like to know."

"I told you. It won't happen until Friday or Saturday." Juan repeated, but there was no laughter this time. Josie gave him the look of an impatient parent and continued.

"For now, the on-call schedule will continue next week. All vacations are canceled until further notice."

A noisy grumble went through the crowd. Josie raised her hand.

"This is not what any of us would have planned," she said. "But until we know what we are dealing with, I want to be sure we are not understaffed."

"I imagine vacations have been canceled at the sheriff's department," Maggie said.

"That's right," Josie responded enthusiastically. "Good point. That's a story you can follow, Maggie. How is this affecting their workload?"

"I would think there would be an increase in people leaving on vacation, you know, getting the hell out of Dodge," Becky suggested.

"Another good story," Josie responded.

"I know, I know. I'm on it" Becky raised a hand in submission.

They griped, but Josie knew they would absorb the extra load and turn out better stories. Josie made it clear that everyone who came in on Saturday should try to take a day off during the week. She wanted everyone to be rested and ready for the next catastrophe, yet the thought seemed embarrassingly cold and calculating.

Duke came to lunch in the break room with a hot dog in one hand and some newspaper clippings in the other.

"Wait till you hear this story," he said, pulling a yellowed strip of newsprint from a small brown envelope. "I can't believe I forgot this. Malcolm Jones came up to this parked car in Lilac Park with a gun. He made the boyfriend lie down on the floor of the car, and then he beat and raped the girl. When she passed out, he drove her to the hospital and reported he had found her like that. Can you imagine? He was arrested right there in the hospital waiting room!"

"Who in the world is Malcolm Jones?" Josie asked between bites of her salad.

"You remember, the case I told you about last night."

"You mean the one fifteen years ago?"

"Yeah, the one that reminded me of these killings."

"How many were killed then?"

"Well, no one."

"What am I missing?"

"He didn't kill anybody, he just raped and beat the girl. Like Elizabeth."

"Excuse me? I thought Elizabeth was stabbed sixteen times."

"Well, yeah," Duke said, shaking his head. "OK, so it's nothing like these cases. Except it started out the same, in a parked car."

"Isn't there some urban legend about a killer with a hook who attacks couples in parked cars?"

"This isn't some urban legend!" Duke snapped a bite out of his hot dog, and then threw the rest back into its foil wrapper. He took a big swig from his Coke.

"Oh, come on," Josie said, patting his hand. "Don't get your feelings hurt."

"There's a good story here," he said. "A beaver logjam good story. You just don't get it."

"Duke, right now we're up to our armpits in good stories, and most of them are a lot fresher than fifteen years ago. Right now I need you to get an interview with Elizabeth. If anyone can, you can."

"OK, OK," Duke said, slipping the clips back into the envelope but not really putting them out of his thoughts.

Chapter 73

Johnny Morton was up on the peak of a two-story house the crew had just framed in. He was attaching huge plywood sheets with rhythmic bursts of his nail gun. He saw the four sheriff's department cars coming, even before they turned into the expansive Crystal Ridge subdivision. He probably could have slipped down through the frame, monkeylike, and escaped in his truck. But what good would it do? It would only postpone the inevitable. Instead, he finished the piece he was working on, slid his nail gun back into the loop on his belt and walked down the roof with eerie, catlike balance.

When the sheriff's cars pulled up to the house, Johnny was swinging his leg over the side and onto the ladder. He was almost to the ground when a pair of deputies drew their weapons and crouched down in a shooting position.

"Keep both hands where we can see them," one deputy called.

"OK, OK," Johnny said, removing one hand from the ladder and waving it in the air.

When his foot hit the ground, one of the deputies lunged forward and pressed Johnny's face into the ladder, patting his body. Johnny's nail gun offered a bulge the deputy didn't recognize. When he unhooked it, it fell to the ground with a thud and the deputy jumped back in surprise.

Other crewmembers were standing around watching, but no one protested the invasion of their work site or even asked what this was about.

"Am I being arrested?" Johnny asked, as a deputy took him by an elbow and headed to a squad car.

"No, we'd just like you to come with us, to answer some questions," the deputy mumbled.

"And I have a warrant to confiscate your truck," another deputy added, handing Johnny a piece of paper.

"Sure, guys," Johnny said with a laugh that belied the seriousness of the situation. "You really cleaned up the interior nice the last time. This time could you polish the exterior?"

Of the roughly 100,000 vehicles registered in Cade County, more than 20,000 were pickups and probably half of those were black, or some dark hue that could be mistaken for black. Sheriff's deputies couldn't begin to stop all black pickups, so they cross-referenced vehicle registrations with arrest records. Johnny was on the top of the list. In fact, his truck had just been released from the evidence compound on Thursday, the day before the murders at The Banks.

The previous search of Johnny's truck hadn't revealed much to help with the slayings at the quarry. Technicians had swept up some bleached hairs that matched Tracy's, but that only proved she had been in her husband's truck at some point. They had found a few dried smudges of blood on the door handle and steering wheel, but it wasn't Tracy's or Carl's blood type and was presumed to have been left by Johnny after a smashed thumb or some other construction mishap.

Two beer bottles had been slipped into an evidence bag, along with a baby rattle, several cheap pens, nails, and assorted scraps of paper. None of it seemed worth much until beer bottles of the same brand -- Red Stripe -- were found in Hickory Creek with the wallets and purses from the weekend murders. The beer bottles and the black pickup, combined with Johnny's record, were enough to get the deputies excited but not quite enough to press charges.

So, for the second time in as many weeks, deputies obtained a search warrant for Johnny Morton's apartment. Deputies remembered a trash can overflowing with beer bottles on the first search, but when they returned this morning, with the landlord's cooperation, they found the apartment had been swept clean and the dumpster had been emptied.

"So where were you this weekend?" one of the deputies asked once Johnny was seated comfortably at a table at the sheriff's department.

"Listen, fellas, " Johnny responded with a chuckle, "If you are looking for an alibi in the wee hours of Saturday or Sunday morning, I don't have one. I lead a pretty boring life. I was at home, in bed, alone."

"A neighbor, your parents, anybody who can verify that?"

"No, like I tell ya, my life is boring. I worked Friday, had a couple beers with the guys, ate dinner at my folks' and then went home, I don't know, about ten. Got up Saturday morning and started cleaning up the place,"

"So we noticed. Trying to get rid of the evidence?"

Johnny shook his head. "No, just trying to get ready for the Family Services inspection on Wednesday. I'm gonna get my son back on Thursday and I want everything all ready for him."

"So where do you and the construction crew go for a beer after work?"

"Varies," Johnny replied with a shrug. "You mean this week? Friday? We went to Lenny's out on Highway 30. It was close to the job, ya know. But I told ya, I didn't stay long."

The deputy made a note of the bar's name. He would check to see if the bartender could remember if Morton ordered Red Stripe.

Chief Miller was watching the interview through one-way glass in a small adjoining observation room. Although he seemed rock solid to the other deputies, Miller didn't trust his emotions at this point to interrogate a suspect. He listened intently, however, ready to pounce at the first clue that Morton might have killed Scott.

"Did you know any of the people who were killed at The Banks on Saturday morning?" the deputy asked.

"Well, seems like everybody knows somebody," Johnny said with a shrug. "I might have had a run in with Deputy Franklin, I don't remember. But you're probably going to tell me I did. Did he arrest me for something some time?"

"No, it doesn't look like it," the deputy said with a chuckle. "How about Kathy Woods? Did you have a thing for her?"

"A thing?" Johnny asked. "Hell, I didn't even know her."

"You didn't? You both went to Lockwood High School. That's a pretty small school, only seven hundred students."

"Oh, that's why the name sounded familiar. I don't remember her. She must have been older than me. I mean I may have seen her in the halls, but I never spoke to her. She might have been in my brother's class."

"You saying you didn't date Miss Woods; you didn't go there Friday night to snoop on her and her boyfriend, Angelo?"

"Now, wait a minute," Johnny said. "I told ya I didn't know her, or this Angelo character, or the kids from Aldrich County. Or any of it. I'm not your guy."

The questioning continued, even after Johnny's attorney, Nate Pigeon, arrived. State's Attorney Carol Stephens joined them and went through all the questions again. Johnny remained calm, almost jovial, and even agreed to give them a blood sample, supposedly to verify that the smudges in the truck were his. Stephens failed to mention that they also planned to check his blood type against the semen found in the rape victim.

Sheriff Walt Coleman joined Chief Miller in the observation room.

"Well, is he our boy?" Coleman asked. "It would sure help restore confidence in my department if he is. I can't tell you how much we need to wrap this up. The governor was on the phone this morning and I assured him we have it under control. It's not bad enough we have the drug boys sniffing around. I don't need the state police trying to take over."

"I really don't know," Miller mumbled, rubbing his chin thoughtfully. He wanted an arrest even more than Coleman, but his desire was much more personal. Morton didn't seem like the type to go on a rampage, and yet this calm confidence under pressure was a side Miller didn't expect either. He just couldn't trust his gut anymore.

"You shouldn't be here," Coleman said giving Miller a pat on the back. "You should be with your wife. Take the rest of the week off."

"No way," Miller said through gritted teeth. "We're gonna get this guy. I'm gonna work until we do."

Stephens stepped into the tiny observation room.

"We need to release him," she said. "We don't have enough to charge him."

Chapter 74

That evening, Duke fixed mousaka for Josie. He hadn't been successful in his quest to get an interview with Elizabeth, but he had schmoozed with her parents and felt certain that as soon as she was able to talk, she would talk to him. Josie had spent the day on the phone, listening to rumors, accusations, and irrational fears.

"This one lady said she and her husband drove out to inspect the scene and it looked like a space ship had landed in the cornfield across from The Banks," Josie said as she mixed a large salad. "She said she could tell by the pattern of the cornstalks that had been knocked over. She's convinced aliens are killing people."

Duke shook his head as he poured the wine. "With a .38?"

"No, with a phaser that leaves a wound like a .38, complete with the slug. She said she had read a book where aliens had a weapon that could simulate any of our guns or knives."

"Well, then, that explains it." Duke reached for Josie and wrapped his arms around her. "At least you had a few laughs today."

"And now I get this elaborate dinner," she said, eyeing his eggplant, cheese, and tomato creation. "I can't believe you can cook like this."

"Oh, I'm full of surprises," Duke said. "After dinner, I'll let you in on my biggest secret, if you promise not to tell my boss."

"I know. Aliens are writing your stories for you."

"You got me."

When dinner was finished, the dishes washed and the bottle of wine emptied, Duke took Josie down to his office. The unfinished basement room had an unpretentious gray concrete floor and three concrete walls. Cheap wood paneling behind the desk separated the space from the laundry. Furnishings were simple. A hollow door topping two file cabinets served as a desk. An old refrigerator hummed loudly in one corner. Next to it stood a small bar with a sink, running water, and an overhead shelf full of glasses and liquor bottles. A small round table, two chairs, an old couch, and a small television set on a rolling stand were lined up along the far wall.

"Can I fix you a drink?" Duke said, proudly showing off the bar. "I've got bourbon, Scotch, rum, vodka, and maybe a sherry. Oh, here's some Baileys. That's a good after-dinner drink."

Duke pulled an ice cube tray from the freezer compartment of the refrigerator and emptied it into a small yellow ice bucket. Then he clinked a couple of cubes into two glasses, making a bourbon and water for himself and Baileys on the rocks for Josie.

"How do you drink like this every day?" Josie said, accepting the creamy Baileys. "I usually drink just at parties and special occasions."

"Every night can be a special occasion," Duke responded with a twinkle in his eye.

Then Josie noticed the storage area under the stairs. Duke had created a system of deep shelves, filled with cardboard boxes. Each box was marked with a year in black poster paint.

"Great, chronological junk," Josie said. "I've been wondering how to organize all that stuff that ends up in boxes.

"That's not junk," Duke said, "that's my surprise." He pulled a box marked 1969 off the bottom shelf. "It should be in here. That was the year after I started."

He set the box on the table and pulled the string on the overhead light. It illuminated row after row of shiny metal spirals, which Josie recognized immediately as the tops of reporters' notebooks. Index cards with months on them jutted above the rows.

"My God, Duke. What have you got here? Are these your notebooks from 1969?"

"You are so smart, woman," Duke said, downing his drink and stepping to the bar to make another.

"But it's against newspaper policy. You're supposed to get rid of all your notebooks or they can be subpoenaed in court." Josie followed him to the bar, though she had barely touched her drink.

"Think about it," Duke explained as he refilled his glass. "In the sixteen years I've been with the *News*, I've been subpoenaed three times. I've used these files a hundred times."

"But what do you do? Lie to the court?"

"Not at all," Duke said, taking a big sip from a fresh drink. "When they ask about my notes, I tell 'em the same thing I tell Hammond when he asks. I dispose of all notebooks." Gesturing to his store of boxes, he added, "And this is my disposal."

"That's lying!"

"That's my version of the truth. I'm not hurting anybody. It's not like I'm covering up a crime or something. Getting rid of all these notes would be a crime."

"But how can you ever find anything? Notes get cold so fast."

"Well, I wouldn't want to try to recreate a direct quote," Duke said picking up one of the notebooks, "but names and numbers are usually pretty clear. Every time I start a new interview I mark it with the date and name." He flipped pages to show Josie his method. "So, if I know the approximate date, I can usually find what I'm looking for, even several years back. Oh, look at this. I interviewed some of the parents in our Lamaze class. Then, I went back later, after the birth, and compared their expectations with their real experience. It made an interesting story. I'd forgotten about that."

"So, what are we looking for?" Josie asked as she picked up one of the notebooks.

"I've forgotten Ruth's last name, and we didn't use her name in any of the stories because she was a rape victim. Somewhere in these notebooks is her name and phone number. Just look for Ruth something."

They sat at the table, Josie still a bit uncertain about the value of fifteen-year-old notes, let alone the ethics involved. Duke, however, was clearly in his element. Every notebook brought another story. The park district director complaining about how hard it was to keep swings repaired in the poorer neighborhoods because the gang members would steal the chains. A drowning at the quarry. The intricacies of portaging over the dam for the annual canoe relay on the Jordan River. Duke's coverage of the Fourth of July celebration, 1969.

"I think that was the summer that it rained four nights in a row. Every time they rescheduled, it would rain again," Duke said with a laugh. " We ended up having our fireworks in September, I think, with the harvest festival. Yeah, that was the year, because we took Jennifer and she was in a stroller."

As Duke talked and downed one drink after another, he recreated the summer of 1969. There was a youthful cockiness in his stories; he almost sounded like Juan, bungling along, making foolish mistakes and yet never doubting his own ability. The news events of that summer rekindled other memories: Sharon's labor, Jennifer's birth, the proud but frightening moment when he held his child for the first time.

Duke's tales were filled with warmth and humor, but they made Josie uneasy. She felt as if she were intruding in Sharon's house with Sharon's husband. Maybe she should have been ashamed, but what she felt was more akin to anger. Duke seemed so happy recalling another time, one she could never share with him. Josie and Duke had shared only a few nights of lovemaking, hardly enough to call it an affair.

"Here's a Ruth Van Ness," Josie said suddenly, the name popping out of the notebook as she flipped a page.

"That's it," Duke said grabbing the book. "Wow, look, I first interviewed her on July 17, 1969. That's fifteen years ago tomorrow. No wonder she's been calling to me in my sleep."

Duke was soon immersed in the old notebook, trying to make sense of the scribbled words and phrases. Perhaps it was all the bourbon he had consumed or his consuming passion for this story of long ago, but Josie felt as if Duke were no longer there. She felt alone, alone in another woman's house.

"I'm kind of tired," Josie said.

"Really?" Duke spoke without looking up from his reading.

"I think maybe I should head home," she added, expecting a protest.

"Really?"

"You don't need to see me out, I can find my way." Josie headed for the stairs, but still Duke didn't look up. Halfway up the stairs she turned back to see him flipping the page and taking another sip from his drink.

"Good night," she said.

"'Night, Sharon."

Chapter 75

A slow drizzle fell on Tuesday morning for the funerals of the four victims of The Banks shooting. Whether at a little country church or a huge cathedral, the tears and the rain fell just the same.

All of the services were at ten a.m., so reporters were stationed at each, ready to call in a few paragraphs for the final edition. Mack was at Scotty Miller's funeral to get a photo that would be symbolic of all four, snapping discretely from beneath an awning across the street.

As an officer killed in the line of duty and the son of the highest-ranking deputy in the county, Scotty had attracted police representatives from all over the state. Squad cars wound around the block outside Westside Presbyterian, the same modern brick and glass building where Scotty and Brittany had exchanged wedding vows less than a month before.

More than any of the other services, this one attracted people who had no relationship to the victim. Politicians, even would-be candidates, made an appearance along with the concerned and the curious. One deputy pointed out Angela Deline, a University of Chicago researcher who had written *Daddy Made Me Do It*, a book about serial killers.

"Her book says killers like this often attend funerals," a deputy whispered to Nick in the lobby. "That means he could be here right now."

Nick looked around. It seemed half the town was there. He recognized many softball team members and deputies' families. Karen Anderson was there with her sons. Scotty's partner, Deputy Dan Franklin, was still in the hospital, but one of the deputies pointed out his two eldest children attending with Franklin's sister. Nick didn't recognize Johnny Morton dressed in a suit, but one of the deputies did, and soon the buzz had made it to Nick's ears as well.

Chief Don Miller showed little emotion while his wife, a plump woman with a crown of white curls, clutched his arm and buried her head in his chest. Brittany, Scotty's young bride, seemed quiet and strong at the beginning, but as the service came to a close and the uniformed pallbearers started carrying the casket out of the church, she began sobbing loudly and was unable to leave her pew for several minutes.

Across town, a couple of hundred relatives and friends of another victim, Kathy Woods, seemed dwarfed in the immense cathedral. Observing from the balcony, Dottie wrote, "the cavernous space was a metaphor for the towering grief that overwhelmed the stunned family."

The smallest service was for Kathy's beau, Richard Angelo, at the Fulton Avenue Funeral Home. Rumors about his drug involvement may have kept some away, but like so many people in today's world, Richard didn't have a large circle of friends. A couple of neighbors, a few of Richard's co-workers joined his widowed mother, Barbara. She had no relatives really to share her grief. Her son had been her life, and now both of those lives were over. Maggie was there to cover the service. When it ended, she made a quick call to add a paragraph to the combined story, then went back to Barbara's side. The two women cried together for Richard, the other victims, and all women who have outlived their families.

Chapter 76

Richland Baptist Church, a century-old frame building on Davis Road, less than a mile from the Thompson farm, was overflowing with farm families come to mourn the final victim, Leroy Thompson. A sea of umbrellas floated down the steps at the double-wide front door, sheltering those who couldn't fit inside.

Becky knew there was no way she could be inconspicuous in the all-white crowd, but she was used to standing out. She felt called to open doors for black women, even when it was uncomfortable to do so. She had unwound about half her braids during the stressful week, so she tucked her stringy hair into a small black straw hat that gave her bad hair days a neat, dignified appearance.

"You from the paper?" a shriveled little man asked, as Becky tried to blend into a corner of the sanctuary. He was sitting in a folding chair that had been set up at the end of the full pew.

"What was your first clue?" Becky replied , not trying to keep a snide tone out of her voice.

"I know everybody else," the man said with a smile. Becky softened and smiled back.

"I'm Ben Davis. Live down the road a piece," he said, holding out his hand. "Most people call me Old Ben. I don't know why."

"Becky Judd," she replied, reaching for the wrinkled hand and then being surprised at the firm shake she received.

"I know," he said, and Becky realized that her rude call to the Thompson family had become community knowledge. "We sure can use this rain," he added, looking out the window near the corner where she stood.

Becky made no reply. She didn't want to get involved in small talk with this stranger. She was working; she needed to cover the speaker, call in a few paragraphs. But more than that, she wanted to sulk in the corner by herself. She didn't fit in here and there was no sense pretending she did.

"Rain makes a funeral seem sad," Ben said. "It rained at my wife Abby's funeral."

"I'm sorry," Becky mumbled.

"Oh, that was almost forty years ago," Ben said. "I've buried two wives and five children."

"I'm so sorry," Becky repeated.

"Oh, don't be. They've passed over to a better place." Ben went on, talking loud enough that a woman sitting in front of him turned around and gave him a scolding look. The singing was beginning, slow mournful songs with none of the enthusiasm of the Full Gospel Church of Becky's youth. "White people could be so plastic and artificial," she thought, "even in death." Still there was something about this old man. Passed over. He had used that phrase. Becky's grandmother always said passed instead of died.

A man and woman escorted a frail girl to a seat in the second row, and a curious buzz went through the crowd. Becky bent over and whispered in Ben's ear.

"Who's that?"

"Oh, that's Natalie," Ben whispered back.

The pale, weak-looking girl seemed nothing like the robust, smiling photo that had run in the *Daily News*.

"She's taking it really hard," Ben continued. "Having a hard time understanding that Leroy's gone. Shirley—that's her mother—thought coming today might help. Shirley's my cousin. "

Ben was quiet for a few minutes, then pulled on Becky's sleeve until she bent down close to his face.

"It just takes time," he said. "My boy Timothy was Leroy's age when he passed. It took years for me to see it was all in God's plan."

Becky couldn't imagine how a serial killer could be part of God's plan, how any good could come from these deaths. She took a few notes and then slipped into the church office to call in her addition. The umbrellas moved behind the church to the adjacent graveyard and then back toward the church, where lunch would be in the basement.

The rain had stopped and a shaft of sunlight peeked through the trees when Becky looked up and saw Old Ben and a man she recognized as Leroy's grandfather standing on the church steps. It was her chance. She jumped out of her car, a package wrapped in brown paper clutched to her chest.

"Mr. Thompson?" When she handed the grandfather the carefully wrapped package, he knew immediately it was Leroy's photo, but he feigned surprise.

"Come downstairs and have some lunch," he said.

"No, I have to get back." Becky couldn't face that family.

"Come out to the house sometime," Mr. Thompson said. "I think they'd like that."

"Really?" Becky was surprised he'd even offer.

"Yes, I think they feel badly now that you were in that position," he said. "They realize you were trying to do your job."

"Maybe in a week or so," Becky said.

"That would be good." Mr. Thompson turned to enter the church.

"Stop by and see me, too." Old Ben said. "Everything takes time."

Chapter 77

Josie had the office to herself. Most of the reporters were covering funerals, Duke had gone to the hospital to interview Elizabeth, and Juan had the day off. Josie had been waiting for such an opportunity. She opened the desk drawer where she kept personnel records and flipped through the folders until she found Juan's. She was embarrassed to be doing this, ashamed at what she was thinking. But what did they know about Juan, anyway? He had grown up in Chicago and had completed his junior year at the University of Illinois. That's about all Josie could remember. She spread the resume before her, looking for some clue, something that didn't add up. Soon she found it.

A small Catholic high school was listed for three years, but there was no graduation date. Between high school and three years at the university was a gap of two years. What had happened during that time? Though the resume listed several summer employers as references, nothing accounted for those two years. It was as though they had never existed—or as though Juan wanted to ignore what had happened.

Josie made some phone calls. If Juan had a juvenile record, it wouldn't show up. But the state board of education confirmed that Juan had received a General Equivalency Diploma a few months before he entered the university. She asked for a faxed copy of the record, and the form showed that the degree had been granted at Elliot Youth Home, a juvenile detention center.

Chapter 78

At St. Mary's hospital, Elizabeth's mother propped her up with pillows and put a frilly turquoise bed-jacket over her shoulders so she would look as good as her swollen, blackened face would allow. The mother was brushing her hair when Duke arrived.

"Well, you're looking great," Duke said. Elizabeth tried to smile, but it looked more like a crooked grimace.

"I just want to ask a few questions," Duke said. " To make things easier on you, I'll tell you what we think we know so far, and you just say yes or no. OK?"

"Good," Elizabeth said, though only one side of her mouth moved, so it sounded more like "mud."

Duke told the story as it had appeared in the *Daily News*, and every now and then Elizabeth, nodded affirmatively or said something that sounded like "meth." She confirmed her assailant had forced her to crawl to his truck and crouch on the floor with a gun at her head. She confirmed it was a black pickup with "mig mirrors." She even confirmed, tearfully, that her assailant had used various items, including a gun and a kewpie doll to violate her, leaving her vagina torn beyond repair. But when Duke started talking about "the man" who had assaulted her, she became agitated and said "Mo, mo."

"No?" Duke asked. "Is there something you want to tell me about the man?"

"Mew men" Elizabeth said, obviously struggling. Her mother offered a glass of water with a pink plastic straw crooked over the edge. Elizabeth took a sip and continued. . "Mere mas mew of mem."

"Two? There were two men?"

"Meth."

Duke shouldn't have been surprised. Everything about the magnitude of these crimes pointed to more than one perpetrator. But Elizabeth's confirmation meant they weren't looking for one crazy person, one sick rogue with a cockeyed view of the world. She was telling him that two men did this; two men working together, covering for each other, accepting and aiding each other's deranged behavior. Somehow, that was more than twice as frightening.

Chapter 79

Stopping by the sheriff's department that afternoon , Nick recognized Angela Deline coming out of the door.

"Ms. Deline?" Nick queried. "I didn't expect to see you here."

Angela stopped and returned Nick's smile. She was a pale redhead with childlike freckles, almost nonexistent lashes, and eyes as soft as a cloudy sky. She seemed far too innocent to be an expert on killers.

"I'm sorry," she said in an arrogant tone. "Do I know you?"

Nick introduced himself and begged for a few minutes of her time. Then he flashed the dimpled smile that never failed. Angela was smitten. She spied a park bench along the walk and soon they were sitting, chatting like old friends.

"Well, I don't know if I can be any help to the sheriff, but it sure is an interesting case isn't it?" Angela said, crossing her arms and pursing her lips.

"If the murders are related, when can we expect that he will strike again?" Nick asked, pen poised.

"That's what everyone wants to know," she replied. "There is a pattern here, and the pace usually increases. Two related events in one weekend indicate that our killer is about to decompensate."

"De . . . what?"

Angela spelled the word and explained that it was used to describe a mental condition that was deteriorating.

"We can expect another murder any day now," she said. "The fact that there hasn't been one since Sunday may mean we've got a weekend warrior. Maybe he works a regular job. Or whatever sets him off— loneliness, drinking, too much spare time—happens on the weekend or a holiday. The previous incident was on the Fourth of July, remember.

"The fire in June was on a weeknight, but I doubt that is related to these other murders. It's just too different." Angela spoke with enthusiasm, as though she was discussing an elusive Elvis sighting instead of predicting a murder.

"At this point I would say Friday is the night to watch. Unless I miss my guess, he won't be able to hold back any longer. If we make it through the weekend without another murder, well, then I think we need to re-examine the facts. I don't think we have a serial killer—or our man has traveled on."

"Man? Are you sure it's a man?" Nick asked.

"Oh, I would be delighted if it's a woman. That would be a rare case, indeed."

"Are you sure it's just one killer?"

"Well . . . " For the first time Angela seemed hesitant. "There are some indications that more than one person is involved, and that would really be rare. Serial killers are loners. There might be a support person, a lover or a relative, who knows about the crimes and is trying to stop them. There's an indication that something is stopping him."

"What do you mean?"

"Well, this is a murderer who isn't stingy with bullets. He's not afraid to use a weapon big enough to blow a hole through two people. When one or two bullets would probably do the trick, he pumps in five or six. But he loses steam. Two survivors from Saturday, one survivor from Sunday. Another bullet or two and he wouldn't have to worry about witnesses."

Angela elbowed Nick as though telling a delicious piece of gossip. "But he stops. Why?"

"Maybe he ran out of time. The police were coming."

"Of course the police were coming." Angela leaned forward with her eyes flashing. "Yet he took the time to follow those kids into the cornfield just so he could get a wallet and purse. He just as easily could have finished her right then.

"And the rape victim. He stabbed her and beat her, but he never used a gun—except maybe as an object for rape. Why?"

"He thought she would die."

"Why not be sure?" Angela threw up her arms in exasperation. "Something or someone is stopping him."

Chapter 80

On the way home from work, Josie stopped by the hospital to check on Deputy Dan Franklin and take some comic books to his little ones, Davy and Bernice. As soon as she stepped out of the elevator, she knew something was wrong. The waiting area was filled with people chanting, singing, and praying.

Josie and the nurse were the only white people in the room.

Schools and workplaces may have become integrated, and certainly Dan Franklin walked as an equal with all his white co-workers and had the respect and friendship of the entire community. But as his condition worsened and death lurked in the shadows, some stronger more basic bond culled out the superficial friends and left only those who shared his race and his reality.

"What's going on?" Josie asked the nurse.

***

Duke went home alone that night. He knew he had made Josie angry the night before, but he wasn't sure why and he wasn't sure he wanted to know. Women! They are always getting upset about nothing. Life was just simpler without them. He had been foolish, perhaps, to think that he and Josie could love each other. They were too damaged, too hardened by the hurt they had survived. Still, he wanted to talk to her, tell her about Elizabeth. He wanted to talk about Elizabeth's strength and courage. And he wanted to talk about his fear, his complete revulsion that two men could do this thing together.

But he had no one to talk to; he was alone. It had started drizzling again and the rhythm of the drops beating against the windowpane was his only company. Duke sipped a couple of beers, watching the raindrops skitter down the glass. After dark, he downed a couple more beers and a bag of peanuts while watching the news. He was about to go down to his office for a stronger drink when a knock at the door surprised him.

When he turned on the porch light, Josie was standing on his stoop, her tears blending with the rain that soaked her hair and clothes until it looked like the whole flood had come from her heart.

"Dan Franklin's in a coma, Juan has a juvenile record, and I think I'm jealous of Sharon," she blurted without stopping for breath.

Duke stepped out into the rain and held her, the runoff from his roof pelting them like the lapping tongue of a friendly dog. He was so glad to see her, so eager to hold her, so afraid that the magic of a moment like this would evaporate with the morning light.

Chapter 81

Johnny Morton read every notice on the wall of the small room at least three times. He examined the huge aerial photograph of Jordan and found his apartment building. He read the inscription under the mayor's photo and the history of the town's founding. Every now and then he pulled the new squeaky toy out of his pocket, gave it a squeeze and smiled, just imagining the look it would put on J.D.'s face.

Johnny had reported to Family Court at nine and it was almost eleven. This didn't seem like court at all; it wasn't even in the regular courthouse but on the second floor of the city hall. He would have thought he was in the wrong place except his attorney, Nate Pigeon, stepped into the room, smiling and shaking hands with Johnny and his parents as if meeting them for the first time. Then after a while, Nate looked at his watch and excused himself for a few minutes, before returning with a big smile and greetings around.

Nate made comments about "some delays" and talked about other cases and deals that were being discussed in the various rooms along the hall. Johnny thought their little room might have been forgotten, except that once when he stepped out to use the restroom, a blonde in a pantsuit jumped up from behind a desk and asked him where he was going. She insisted that a bailiff must accompany him and summoned a skinny black man named Bill, who Johnny was sure had been washing windows downstairs when they arrived.

Just after eleven that same woman opened the door to their room and said, "They're ready for you."

"Well, it's about time," Doris Morton said closing her magazine. "We're busy people. I don't know what in the world—"

"Hush," Tom Morton admonished softly as he helped the hefty woman from her chair.

"Well, Tom, there's no excuse."

Johnny followed the blonde eagerly, without waiting for his parents. She led him through a pair of double doors into a room furnished more for city council meetings than for court cases. There were nine chairs on a raised platform, behind a huge semicircular counter. In front, looking small and insignificant, were two tables with two chairs each. The social worker was sitting at one table with a man Johnny had never seen before, and Nate was waving to Johnny to join him at the other table. The room was almost dark except for a ring of lights over the raised platform, but Johnny recognized Chief Miller sitting in a darkened corner of the audience.

The blonde took a seat behind a computer placed on the counter. Suddenly she stood up and said, "All rise."

A gray-haired woman in a black robe strode in through the same double doors Johnny had entered and stepped onto the platform, squeezing past the blonde and her computer and choosing a chair in the middle.

"This court is in session," she said, pounding a wooden gavel on a wooden block.

Instantly the man at the next table rose and started spouting something about extenuating circumstances. Johnny didn't understand much of what he said, but soon Nate was on his feet too, voicing objections.

After a brief exchange, Johnny thought he heard the judge say something about July twenty-six then her hammer came down on the wooden block again and she said. "Next case."

Nate started gathering the papers on the table into his briefcase.

"What happened?" Johnny asked.

"They're postponing a week," Nate said without looking up.

"What?" Johnny said, grabbing Nate by the arm.

"Kindly let go of my arm." Nate looked down at Johnny over the tops of his reading glasses. When Johnny released his grip, Nate continued. "Due to the complicated nature—"

"You mean I don't get J.D. today?"

"What's going on?" Doris said as she pushed forward. "We waited all that time for this?"

"It's just a small delay," Nate said, closing his briefcase. "These things are to be expected."

"But you said if I cleaned up my act . . ."

"It's just a week,"

"It's not just a week, it's my baby." Johnny threw his chair back and it clattered against the base of the raised platform. The noise made everyone stop and stare. Johnny stormed out of the room. His parents rushed after him. Nate replaced the chair with an apologetic smile, and two more attorneys and clients moved into position for the next case.

In a quiet corner of the audience, however, Chief Miller smiled. This was the Johnny Morton he had expected to see.

Chapter 82

Duke called the number he had for Ruth Van Ness, but the young man who answered had never heard of her. It wasn't too surprising; the number was fifteen years old and people move an average of every seven years. That had been her parents' number, anyway. Surely she was married and a mother by now.

He called Jordan Township High School. The principal's secretary gave him the numbers of three women who were coordinating the fifteenth reunion of the Class of 1969. On the second try, Duke reached Beth Waggner.

"Why do you want to know?" Beth said when Duke asked about Ruth Van Ness.

"Well, I just thought you might have her number. I was thinking about that incident at Lilac Park many years ago . . . "

"She left town," Beth said curtly. "She was afraid. She knew the day would come when he would be paroled."

"Really? She was afraid after all this time?" Duke no longer felt alone in his obsession with the past.

"Afraid isn't the word for it," Beth said. "She was panicky to be in a car after dark. Never dated, took some classes at the junior college, and got a job at the local library. But she quit after a year. She imagined every customer was a threat. She became a recluse and stayed at home with her parents until her father died."

"Where is she living now?"

"I can't say. She's afraid he'll find her."

"But you know?"

"Yes, we were best friends . . . until it happened. Then Ruth didn't want to do anything."

"Could you arrange for her to call me? I'd love to talk to her."

"About what?"

"About Malcolm Jones. About why she has fought against his parole all these years. I just want to do a little follow-up."

"Isn't it a little late for that? Where were you during the parole hearings?"

"Well, I'll admit we don't have time to follow every guy who goes to jail for rape."

"If you had done a story before, maybe it would have done some good. Why bother now?"

"Now?"

"Don't you know? That bastard was paroled in May."

Chapter 83

At the next desk, Josie's phone was ringing.

"Newsroom," she answered, as she scanned that day's paper with a red pen, marking errors or subjects that would require a follow-up story.

"This is Matthew Billingsly at Holy Family," a distinguished voice replied. "I had a message you called."

Josie's heart jumped, and she looked around to be sure no one was listening. Most of the reporters were out on interviews. Duke was at his desk but engrossed in his own phone conversation.

Cupping the receiver, Josie explained her inquiry.

"We have one of your former students, Juan Hernandez, as our summer intern and he is doing a smashing job."

"He always was a good writer and a thorough researcher."

"You were his English teacher, is that right?"

"Yes, he is a hard worker. Sometimes his imagination gets the best of him, but I suppose at a newspaper you have to stick to the facts."

"Yes, that is the idea," Josie said hesitantly. After an awkward silence, she continued. "As I told you, Juan is doing a great job this summer, but I need to clear up some of this background before I can recommend him for a permanent position."

"Anything I can do," Billingsly said.

"I'm calling to get some information about his senior year." Josie paused, but Billingsly offered nothing. "I know he was expelled but I'm not sure exactly—"

"Why did you call me?" Billingsly said. "I had nothing to do with it."

So, he had been expelled.

"I realize that," Josie said, feeling her way. "But you were his favorite teacher." Billingsly was the only teacher Juan had listed as a reference. "I was hoping you could give me a fair assessment."

"The story he wrote was pure fiction. Strictly imagination, I tell you. There was no threat implied. It was just fiction."

Josie chuckled a little to encourage Billingsly to continue. "Of course. Just imagination."

"The problem was the jocks, the athletes. They don't understand a gentle boy like Juan. They picked on him mercilessly. It was an understandable response. Very healthy, in my view."

"Of course," Josie repeated, not ready to admit she had no idea what Billingsly was talking about.

"Personally, I found it very funny, and I would never have turned it in, but one of the other teachers in the department thought it was frightening."

"So, he was expelled for writing a frightening story?"

"No, no," Billingsly laughed. "It was just a reprimand. He got called into the office. They really made quite a big deal out of it, because he had given the actual names of several students as his victims, and they called the parents in and everything. But once they saw this mousy little boy who had written the story, and it was for a creative writing assignment, and it was creative . . . well, I thought they would let the whole thing drop."

"But, they didn't?"

"No, you know how boys can be. The teasing just got worse. Of course, I don't approve of what he did, but you can understand."

"Sure, it's understandable."

"The gun wasn't even loaded. He wouldn't have hurt anybody. He just wanted to scare them off. Get them to stop teasing him."

"Juan brought a gun to school?" Josie said, understanding at last.

"Actually to gym class. He had it in his gym bag, because that is when they were always teasing him. In the locker room. I wish I could have seen the looks on their faces." Mr. Billingsly allowed himself a small laugh before returning to his very proper demeanor. "Not that I approve of violence, you understand. But Juan paid his price and went on to college, and all that is in the past now.

"He will be a great newspaper reporter. Maybe an editor at the *Tribune*. And those jocks are changing oil at a quick-lube place or working on the factory line. Juan will win in the end. I always told him that, but it's so hard to see when you are young."

"Yes, " Josie agreed. "I was wondering. You wouldn't still have a copy of that fictional story Juan wrote, would you? I'd love to see it."

232

Chapter 84

Eddie Simms was pushing his lawnmower across the little patch of grass in front of his house when the county patrol car pulled in behind his black pickup in the driveway. He was glad to have an excuse to stop, turned off the noisy motor and wiped his brow with a red handkerchief.

"This your truck?" the deputy asked.

"Yes, sir," Simms replied. "Have I forgotten to renew my plates or something?"

"No, sir," the deputy said stepping forward to talk with Eddie while his partner walked around the truck. "You heard about the incident last weekend? We're checking out black trucks."

"Well, I don't envy you boys. Man, there must be thousands of black pickups in this county. Y'all come inside 'n' have a beer."

"No, thank you, sir," the deputy continued. "We've been by here three times this week and the truck was sitting right there, but no one answered the door."

"Oh, me and the missus went to a wedding in Mississippi. My brother's daughter. Didn't get home until late last night. Trying to get this lawn mowed before I go to work at six. I work over at the tractor plant. Security."

"How long you been gone, sir?"

"Flew out Friday. Sure y'all won't come in and have a drink? I could put some ice in a glass of water for y'all."

"No, thank you, sir. So, are you familiar with the murders that happened over the weekend?"

"I heard something about it on the television all the way in Mississippi. So, they think one man is doing all of these?"

"Don't know, sir. I'm wondering if you could identify this," the deputy said, holding out a plastic bag with a scrap of yellow paper inside. The paper was a receipt for $4.75 from Fred's Bait and Tackle. The customer name at the top said "Edward Simms."

"Where'd you find this?" Eddie asked, taking the bag.

"That's your receipt, isn't it, sir?"

"Sure looks like it," Eddie said, handing the bag back to the officer. "What's this about?"

"This receipt was found at The Banks, sir. Do you have any idea how it may have gotten there?

"The Banks? Well, I don't even know what that is. Is that some new megabank consolidation? I been hearing about those. My bank's changed names three times in a year. Hardly know the place anymore." Eddie hoisted himself up to sit on the stoop outside the side door to the bungalow.

"Let's see, it used to be called First National. It's the one at the corner of Sumner and Haynes. Is that this here Banks where y'all found my receipt?"

"No, sir," the young deputy shook his head, unable to comprehend Eddie's frustration with a changing world. "The Banks is what they call this clearing on the Jordan River. It's where four people were murdered in the early hours of Saturday morning."

"Oh, I see," Eddie shook his head. "Well, that's a receipt for getting my reel repaired. Me and my sons like to go fishin' on Sundays, and we've tried all sorts of places on the Jordan River. Maybe we've been to this clearing you're talking about. Where is it?"

"Off a gravel road, up near 144th and County Road 15."

"Oh, yeah, I know where that is. That's where them people were killed? Imagine that! Sure, I've been fishin' there lots of times."

"When was the last time you were there, sir?"

"Oh, I don't know. We usually go on Sundays, so maybe a week, ten days. Sometimes I go in the middle of the week 'cause I usually work nights."

"The receipt is dated May fifteen," the deputy said.

"Yep, that would be about right. Got my stuff out this spring and realized the reel wasn't working good. So I took it in, had the drag washers replaced. Would have been in May sometime."

"And where was the receipt all this time, sir?"

"Hell, I don't know. Never can find the things when I need 'em. I'm not so good about putting things away. Mae tells me that all the time. It coulda been in my shirt pocket, or my tackle box, or just lying loose in the truck. Coulda fallen out anytime."

"And, where was this wedding you say you attended last weekend?"

"Bolivar, Mississippi. It's right on the river. My whole family's from there. Joseph – that's my baby brother – is the only one who lives there anymore."

"And, the service was Saturday?"

"Yep, two p.m. But we got there Friday night so we could celebrate a little ahead of time."

"And family members can testify to that."

"Well, of course."

"Why was your truck here if you were gone?"

"Well, I don't like paying that high parking rate at the airport. My son Claude took me and Mae down there. He has a big Caddy. Thinks he's so much better than his pop, you know. Anyway, plenty of room for all of us and suitcases too."

"And the airline tickets were in your name?"

"Yes, sir, and we showed proper identification, too."

"Yes, I'm sure you did, Mr. Simms, but we need to check it all out."

"Oh, sure. Won't you boys come in for a drink? I surely need one." Eddie stood up and wiped his brow again.

"No, sir, we need to be going. Thank you again for your time, Mr. Simms."

The two deputies got into their squad car.

"That receipt hasn't been out in the weather for a couple of weeks," said the deputy who had been silent. "It was dropped there last weekend."

"I know," mumbled his partner, smiling and waving to Eddie Simms.

"We'll check out this wedding story. But I can't imagine a killer would be mowing the lawn on a day like this, can you?"

Eddie climbed the six steps to the side door of the bungalow.

"What did they want?" Mae asked.

"Oh, I don't know," Eddie said, trying to hide the thoughts that were flashing through his mind. "Just checking things out."

He pulled open the refrigerator door and grabbed a beer, his favorite brand, Red Stripe.

Chapter 85

Johnny sat on the balcony of his apartment, chugging back an Old Milwaukee. It didn't pay to try to do right. He had tried so hard, and where had it gotten him? Where was his little boy? Not here with his father as he should have been by now. He tried to work with the system but it was just stacked against him.

Johnny finished the third beer and threw it across the dining area. It landed perfectly in the kitchen trash can, clanging against the two he had tossed before. It was like riding a bike. He had perfected his shot from this angle and he hadn't forgotten it in a couple of weeks of sobriety.

This is who he was; it was foolish to imagine that he could be something more. Some sort of sober saint. It was crazy to think if he stopped drinking, the world would see him differently. He was stuck like this and he was going to have to claw his way for every scrap of justice.

Johnny reached down next to his chair and pulled another bottle of beer from the carton. He twisted off the cap and held the amber glass up so the setting sun was reflected there. To his surprise, instead of magnifying that glowing orb, the bottle miniaturized its majesty, draining out all the oranges and reds and leaving one tiny ball of yellow. Yellow.

Instead of putting the bottle to his lips, Johnny turned the bottle over and let the golden beer pour out like urine, onto the balcony floor and then drip over the edge to the parking lot below. He opened the next bottle and did the same. "God, it even smells like urine," Johnny thought.

He reached into the next carton and pulled out two beers, twisted the caps off and turned them upside down, the booze gurgling out in two foaming streams. By the time the sun disappeared beyond the horizon, Johnny had emptied all the beers into a smelly puddle at his feet.

But he was smiling. He wasn't going to let that bottle swallow his sun.

Chapter 86

Friday morning, Josie looked up in time to see Juan come in the back door to fish his paycheck out of his mailbox. Suddenly she remembered looking up at a moment just like this the Friday before, when Juan and Nick had exchanged words.

Had it only been a week? So much had happened since then. An hour or so after that mailbox confrontation, she had been laughing with Dan Franklin and his kids at Ranch Rudy, and a few hours after that... Josie shuddered at the recollection. It seemed so long ago.

This Friday, the world was coming to an end. The Associated Press had picked up Nick's interview with Angela Deline predicting that the serial killer would strike again on Friday. Then Deline repeated her doomsday message on a morning television talk show in Chicago.

"Tonight's the night," the charismatic television interviewer said, looking into the camera. He might as well have been predicting the War of the Worlds. Phones in the newsroom had been ringing incessantly ever since. Hammond had recruited a couple of young women from the classified department to help with answering them. Callers were no longer content to report a suspicious person or activity. Now they wanted action.

"I've called three times..."

"I've told the police and they won't do anything..."

"I've got a gun..."

The sheriff's department was receiving a similar flood, so Sheriff Walt Coleman called Hammond.

"You people have created a panic," he said. "This is all the media's fault. It is totally irresponsible."

Hammond made no response. It wouldn't do any good to remind Coleman that the *Daily News* hadn't murdered nine people in less than a month. The *Daily News* hadn't set up press conferences and alerted the Chicago media. The *Daily News* hadn't predicted a repeat occurrence this weekend; Angela Deline had done that.

Finally, when Walt had run out of complaints, Hammond complimented the great way the sheriff's department investigated every possible lead, thanked him for the department's cooperation, and expressed his regret at the loss of young Deputy Miller.

"Thank you," Coleman said, his anger defused. "And now it looks like Franklin won't make it either."

"Oh, is he really that bad?" As soon as Hammond hung up, he headed to Josie's desk.

"We should talk about this Deline person. How did Nick find her? What is her background? And do we have somebody checking on Franklin?"

Hammond forged headlong into a listing of concerns, assuming Josie would drop everything and give him her undivided attention. He was a bit surprised to realize her eyes were focused somewhere behind him. He turned to see what was attracting her attention but there didn't appear to be anything special—some reporters on phones, some empty desks, and was that the intern back at the mailboxes? He turned back to Josie.

"Josie, are you listening to me?"

"What?" she responded. "Oh, yes, sir, what's up?"

At the next desk, Duke answered the phone and then looked up, glad to see that Josie was too busy with Hammond to be paying attention to him. It was Sharon.

"How's the trip?" he asked, excited to hear from her and yet embarrassed to care.

"Fine except the traffic."

"And Jennifer?"

"Fine."

He inquired about Sharon's sister. Heavy sighs said so much more than words.

"When will you be back?"

"Next week sometime. I have a teacher's meeting next Friday."

"Already?"

"New employee orientation."

"I've been hearing about the murders."

"Out in California?"

"Yeah. I'll bet you are right in the middle of it."

"Not really. It's a young man's game."

"I just wanted … I mean, I hope … I mean, Jennifer's worried."

"About me? Oh, that's silly. It's not the Wild West or anything. It's the same ol' Jordan. Let me talk to her."

"She went to the beach."

"Oh."

"Just take care, OK?"

Chapter 87

Friday evening seemed to move in slow motion. Hoss arrived at about four with a plate of Christmas cookies his mother had baked.

"Christmas in July?" Josie asked.

"She was nervous and wanted to do something," Hoss said, shrugging his shoulders. "It's all the anticipation, like something big is going to happen. Almost like Christmas Eve."

"Hardly." Josie's hand went automatically to the blue folder on her desk. Inside was a copy of the fictional story Juan had written as a student at Holy Family Academy in Chicago. The dark comedy about a tortured boy who wreaked havoc on his high school was similar to Stephen King's "Carrie." Juan's story started with the boy, wearing strips of ammunition across his chest like a stereotypical Mexican bandito, accosting a couple in the school parking lot, two guns blazing from his hip. It was just a story, but horrifying.

Juan arrived a few minutes after Hoss, and Josie strained to hear every word he said as he checked his messages and returned phone calls. She'd already asked who called him to the murder scenes in the middle of the night, but he would only say a sheriff's department employee.

Duke thought she was over-reacting. He suggested she simply ask Juan about the fictional story, but she couldn't figure out how to bring it up.

A few minutes after five, Juan took a notebook and headed out to make the rounds of the Jordan City Police and Cade County Sheriff's departments. It was the usual beginning of the Friday night shift, going through stacks of reports looking for something worth reporting. If he found something big—an auto accident or a burglary—he'd have to find a police officer to fill in the blanks and track down the victim for a comment. Then he'd return to the office to write the stories and make calls to the smaller community police stations to see if they had something to report.

Josie watched through the window as Juan got into his compact car and drove away. Then she gathered her things to leave.

"I'll be back around eleven, just to check in."

"OK." Hoss said. He didn't need any explanation. He knew Josie planned to keep an eye on Juan that night. When Josie returned, Hoss wasn't surprised that Duke was with her, or that Duke smelled of bourbon. Hoss knew more than he said.

"So, how's everything been going?" Josie asked.

"All's well, Peter Pan. Haven't heard from Captain Hook tonight," Hoss replied. "Even the phones have stopped ringing."

Juan was at his desk, making calls to track down information on a man who had been injured earlier that day on a riding lawnmower. He seemed caught up in minutia and unaware that Josie had arrived.

"Lots of little stuff," Hoss said, throwing down a page proof of police briefs. "Hasn't been much chatter on the police scanner, either. It's eerie."

"A watched pot never boils," Duke said.

"Yeah, I think all this publicity has scared him off," Juan said, hanging up the phone and quickly catching up to the conversation. Josie watched Juan work, and he seemed like any young reporter dealing with a half dozen minor stories. Always just one more call, check the address, look up a word in the dictionary.

After a half hour, Duke and Josie left and moved her little green Escort into a dark corner of the employee lot. About midnight, after all the night's stories were finished, Juan left. Josie pulled out behind him without turning on the headlights.

"I feel like a high school kid following a girl I have a crush on," Duke said. He was in the passenger seat sipping bourbon and water from a tall, insulated jug.

"I feel terrible," Josie said. "But I would feel a lot worse if there's another murder tonight and Juan just miraculously shows up at the scene. I have to know he's not involved."

Duke and Josie followed as Juan pulled into a fast food drive-through lane. They parked in a darkened area until he had made it through the line and drove away. They followed as he wound through Murray Park, quiet and deserted at this hour. Finally, he headed to the south side of Jordan, parked, and went inside a neighborhood bar neither of them had noticed before. Josie circled the building looking for a good vantage point from which to watch the front door, the side door, and Juan's car.

"Have you been on stakeouts before?" Duke asked, adding more bourbon to his weakening drink.

"No," Josie laughed. "But I had crushes in high school."

"Oh, that reminds me. Malcolm Jones was paroled in May."

"I'm afraid to ask what that has to do with high school."

"Well, I called the high school and they gave me the phone numbers of the people planning the reunion, and ... oh, never mind. I just thought you'd be interested. I checked him out on the Illinois sex offender's list, and it looks like he's living in a halfway house in Chicago."

"That's good."

"It is?"

"Well, Jordan doesn't need any more sex offenders at the moment."

Josie and Duke shared an easy banter for more than an hour, Josie sipping a Coke from the cooler she had brought and Duke polishing off the rest of the bottle of bourbon. His speech was taking on that foggy, not really there quality, and Josie wondered why she had brought him along.

At about one a.m., after Josie was sure Hoss had put the paper to bed, she walked to a nearby phone booth and called him.

"Anything happening?"

"All quiet here. How 'bout there?"

"Boring."

At about one thirty, a rap on the window made Josie jump.

"Hey, ya got any change?" a gangly black man asked. "For the phone."

Josie was too shaken to speak

"Yeah, sure," Duke said reaching into his pocket and handing over four quarters for the dollar the man offered.

"Oh, my gosh," Josie said as she watched the man walk across the street to the pay phone. "I just realized we're sitting here, in a parked car, looking for a guy who kills people in parked cars."

"That's one way to be the first on the scene."

Finally Josie spotted Juan among the patrons who were leaving as the bar was closing at 2. Instead of going to his car, however, he and another patron headed right toward the corner where Josie was parked.

"Oh, shit," Josie said, ducking down and pulling Duke down as well.

"Dingo drizzle!" Duke said a little louder than necessary.

"Shhh, he'll see us."

"I thought we were supposed to see *him*," Duke replied with childlike logic. "How are we going to see where he is from down here?"

Josie could hear Juan talking and laughing as the two walked past their car. Duke sat up slowly, and then said. "Hey, I think I know that guy."

"Of course you know him," Josie whispered. "That's Juan."

"No, I mean the other guy," Duke said. "He works at the sheriff's department. He's a dispatcher, I think."

"The source." Josie sat up quickly. The two men had stopped under a street light behind Josie's car. Peeking over the seat she had a good view of both of them.

"Can you catch what—" Josie stopped in mid-sentence as Juan reached up and kissed the man full on the mouth. They held a long embrace.

"Well, I'll be . . . ." Duke mumbled.

"Oh, no." Josie slid back down in her seat. "Don't look," she said, pulling on Duke.

"What do you mean? It's just getting interesting."

"But we shouldn't be spying on his private life."

"What? I thought this was your idea!"

"Not this. This is his business. It's not our business. We shouldn't know about his private life. I don't want to know. Oh, God, I don't want to know."

After what seemed like forever, but was only a minute or so, an engine started behind them, and Duke sat up in time to see that both men were in the car that drove away.

"Hey, hurry up. Aren't you going to follow them?"

"No! Are you crazy?"

"Well, maybe he's going to kill him. Or maybe they are in it together or—"

"Just shut up, OK?" Josie said. "This was a bad idea."

All the way back to her house, Josie chastised herself.

"Why am I so suspicious? What would make me spy on one of my reporters?" Duke chuckled. Josie was still blaming herself when she pulled into her driveway, but Duke hadn't commented for several miles. He was sound asleep.

"That's just like a man," Josie mumbled, giving Duke's arm a shake. "Listen, I really need you tonight. I need somebody to tell me I'm not as stupid as I think I am. Come on, Dukakis!"

When Duke barely stirred, Josie continued talking out loud to no one. "What was I thinking? So he was the first on the scene twice last weekend. He didn't cover the quarry murder at all; that was Nick and you. And Juan was busy covering the refinery explosion on the night the sisters died." Josie shook Duke's arm again, but he slept on.

"Damn you, Duke! Why do you drink so much? Is there some awful secret you are trying to forget? You don't have to hide your call from Sharon, you know. I heard you talking to her. I have ears in the back of my head. It comes with motherhood."

Josie noticed how sweet and innocent Duke looked as he slept. She brushed his tousled hair out of his eyes.

"Our week is almost up, you know. I'm going to pick up Kevin on Sunday, and Sharon will be back soon, too. What's going to happen to us? Is there any 'us'? Damn it, Dukakis. How dare you drink yourself into a stupor and leave me with all these tough problems!"

Josie reached across Duke and unlatched his door, then began pushing on him with both hands.

"Come on, you crazy Greek. There's a parked-car-killer out there somewhere tonight, and we need to get out of this one before we have to write our own obits!"

Chapter 88

Josie awakened with a start and realized it was almost nine a.m. She spotted the note taped to her mirror in Duke's even hand. "See you tonight." She called the office, but there was no answer. Hoss had gone home, and it was too early for the Saturday shift. After the hectic week, it seemed way too quiet.

Unable to sit back and enjoy the calm, Josie threw on a T-shirt and shorts and headed to the ceramic studio. There she could lose herself in the revolutions of the wheel and forget the world spinning outside.

Downtown Jordan always was quiet on Saturdays. Shopping had moved to the mall long ago, and industry had built up near the Interstate. Mostly offices and bars remained downtown. On weekends, however, the office buildings were silent monuments to red tape.

The ceramics studio was about two blocks south of Main Street on South River Avenue, which ran along the Jordan River. Buildings along this narrow street seemed to be down in a hole. The natural slope at the riverbank was accentuated by the huge drawbridges that spanned the Jordan River. When open, they stood like soldiers at attention, for the barges that passed through on the waterway to or from Chicago.

On weekdays South River Avenue was in the shadow of the traffic bustling over the bridge, but on Saturdays it was forgotten. The huge flat parking lots along the river were empty; the storefront insurance and accounting offices were closed. The bar on the corner never opened until after four in the afternoon, though sometimes when Josie arrived on Saturday mornings, she could hear voices, as though some of the previous evening's revelers had been trapped inside.

Su Le was opening the ceramic shop when Josie arrived at ten.

"Oh, you are so early," Su said, when she unlocked the front door and turned over the red "closed" sign in favor of the green "open" side.

At first glance, the studio had an unwelcoming, sterile appearance. All that could be seen from the entry were row after row of gray steel shelves filled with even paler greenware, lifeless shapes waiting for customers to paint them and give them personality. The top of a cash register peeked over a counter on one side, surrounded by a display of small jars of glazes, their colorful contents muted in opaque plastic.

Chattering away, Su and Josie disappeared between the maze of shelves, bound for the brightly lighted studio behind.

"Is no murders?" Su asked, flitting like a hummingbird from door to counter to shelf, picking up out-of-place items and straightening things as she went.

"No more murders," Josie responded, trying to keep up with Su's quick steps.

"Is mistake to try to understand evil," Su said, turning to catch Josie's eye. "Evil speak its own language."

With those words of wisdom, Su disappeared into the kiln room on the far side of the studio and left Josie alone in the workroom. A long table, surrounded by six chairs, sat in the center of the room. Two pottery wheels stood in the corner. A higher, standing-height table had been created out of plywood, with cardboard boxes of clay stashed beneath. Over by the kiln room, on rolling carts, were the studio's treasures, shelf after shelf of works in progress. One cart held unfired works, a plastic tarp covering it so they would dry more slowly. Another cart was filled with chalk white jars and bowls, works that had been fired once and were awaiting glaze. The final cart held colorful finished pieces.

It was almost like Christmas to open a kiln and see how the pieces turned out. But Josie had been neglecting her hobby in recent weeks, so she knew there were no finished pieces on the shelf with her initials.

It was just as well. Today was a good day to begin anew with a fresh chunk of clay. Josie opened one of the boxes under the plywood table and pulled out a plastic bag of reddish earthen clay. Using a wire strung between two wooden handles, she sliced off a three-inch slab and then quartered the square slab into four Rubik's Cube-size chunks.

Kneading each cube to remove any air bubbles, she pushed and pulled the chunks with a rhythmic motion until each curled into a wedge shape. The work didn't require much concentration and yet the repetition erased all thoughts from Josie's mind.

Three pieces were lined up like a family of clay cones and she was working on the fourth when a voice startled her out of her daze.

"Josie! Why, I wasn't expecting to see you here today."

Josie jumped and turned to see Barb Denton at the bottom of the stairs.

Barb had parked at the back of the building, which was several feet higher than the street side. A half flight of stairs, tucked behind the kiln room, led up to the back parking lot. Su Le often kept that door open to let in a breeze

"Sorry," Barb said with a laugh. "People are so on edge this weekend. I'm surprised you didn't slap me in the kisser with that wad of clay."

"I could have," Josie agreed.

"So what's going on out there?" Barb asked, getting out a box of porcelain clay. "Did they evacuate the town and not tell me?"

"I know, it's really deserted, like Super Bowl Sunday," Josie said, taking her armload of clay mounds to one of the wheels.

"Well, it's still early. Everybody probably stayed up late last night waiting to see if they would be the next victim."

"I know," Josie laughed. " Isn't it insane? I think even the crooks stayed home last night. There were hardly any police reports."

"I thought it was just my imagination."

The bell on the back of the front door rang, announcing a customer. Josie and Barb paused their conversation. Su stuck her head out of the kiln room, but none of them could see beyond the towering greenware.

"It's just us," came the call from the other side, and in a few seconds Penny Dunlap appeared, carrying a large cardboard box with her latest creations: a lamp base shaped like a teddy bear and a pair of salt and pepper shakers that looked like a cat and dog. Aggie, Penny's aging mother-in-law, followed close behind with a small, pink plastic case filled with brushes and glazes.

"Josie!" Penny exclaimed. "Well, now maybe we can get some news. What's going on? There's nothing on the radio, and I didn't see anything much in the paper."

Josie shrugged. "Nothing's happening, I guess."

"That's unbelievable."

"Hello, Aggie," Barb said, talking extra loud for the hard-of-hearing lady. "How are you today?"

"I don't need any clay," the woman responded. "I just paint."

The misunderstanding was ignored as the women examined the darling lamp base and Penny checked the shelves for finished works.

"Well, they are still treating Johnny Morton like a criminal," she said finding a brightly colored gnome and a pair of mushroom-shaped salt and pepper shakers. "He still doesn't have his baby back. Can they do that?"

"Well, maybe he is guilty." Barb said. "There may be things you don't know."

"I know if they can take away Johnny Morton's baby, then my two aren't safe, either. I think we have more to fear from the police than some serial killer. What would you do, Josie, if they decided you weren't a fit mother?"

"Well, I'm probably not a fit mother," Josie responded. "It's just that Family Services doesn't want to pick up Kevin's messes."

"Ain't that the truth," Barb added, laughing. "I never had to worry about anybody taking away my boys. They would've driven the social workers crazy."

Chapter 89

Duke pulled into the driveway at Beth Waggner's house. He hadn't told Josie about his appointment because he knew she wouldn't approve. Going up the walk of the stylish condo, Duke could see a white poodle standing on the back of the sofa, looking out the window and yapping. As soon as he touched the doorbell, the dog disappeared. Seconds later Beth answered the door, impeccably dressed, the still-yapping poodle under her arm.

"Oh, hush, Bitsy," Beth said in a soft, cultured voice. "You'll have to excuse her, Mr. Dukakis. She'll settle down in a minute or two. She just wants to be sure you know who's in charge."

"Oh, I know," Duke said with a smile. He raised a hand to pet the dog, then thought better of it.

"I have everything set up in the dining room," Beth said, leading the way through a sparkling white living room – white sofas, white carpet, white walls, white drapes and glass tables on shiny gold-toned legs. A vase full of multicolored fresh flowers sat alone on the coffee table.

Two telephones, one portable and the other hastily plugged into the wall sat on the polished, wooden dining room table. A slight breeze wafted through the open sliding glass door, bringing a scent of roses.

"Can I get you some iced tea or lemonade?" Beth asked.

"Oh, no, nothing for me," Duke replied. "I really want to thank you for doing this."

"Oh, it's no trouble. Honestly, I only wish Ruth could find some peace." Beth looked at her watch. "She should be calling in a few minutes. Are there any questions I can answer for you first?"

"Well, when did Ruth leave town?"

"About six, seven years ago. Right after the first parole hearing. Her father had died a few months before, and she just couldn't take it."

"And she has protested at all the parole hearings?"

"Well, not her personally. She's way too timid for that. But she writes letters, and her mother and I make phone calls. I talked to you personally, Mr. Dukakis, four or five years ago, and you showed no interest at all."

"I'm sorry. You must realize that there are hundreds of old cases, hundreds of parole hearings. We can't follow—"

The ringing phone interrupted him. Beth grabbed the portable and slammed her other hand down on the second phone so Duke couldn't pick it up.

"Yes, dear. He's here. Oh, he's very nice and . . . well, you don't have to answer anything you don't want to. I'll be right here on the other line." Beth released her grip on the second phone and motioned for Duke to pick it up. "Here, he is dear," she said, nodding to Duke.

"Hello," Duke said with exaggerated enthusiasm. "I want to thank you so much for calling like this. Is it as hot there as it is here?"

"I don't want to talk about where I live, Mr. Dukakis," Ruth replied curtly. "You can't trick me like that."

"Oh, I wasn't trying to trick you," Duke responded. "I was just trying to make small talk, to be friendly." There was a moment of awkward silence.

"Ruth," Beth began gingerly. "Mr. Dukakis would like to talk about Malcolm Jones. Can you help him?"

"What would you like to know?" Ruth spoke without emotion. "I see him every night . . . in my nightmares."

"Well, I know it was a long time ago," Duke said, "but if you could just describe what happened . . . ."

Ruth told the story of that night, speaking with calm detachment as though it had happened to someone else.

"Arnie—my boyfriend at the time—was forced to lie in the front seat while this beast raped me in the back seat. He held a knife to my throat and told me to describe everything that was happening so Arnie would know. He laughed at me, a deep, ugly laugh. I'll never forget that sound.

"Sometimes I didn't know the words to say what was happening, so he would hit me and order me to 'Say it, say it.' He put things in there. I'm not even sure what things. The gun, the knife, I don't know. I was in so much pain and bleeding so much.

"I was a virgin, you know. I'd never had sex before, and after that night there were so many scars . . . . I'm thirty-three years old and I've never had sex. Sometimes I wonder what other people . . . ."

Ruth's voice faded away.

"But then he took you to the hospital," Duke said.

Ruth suddenly came to life again. "That was the worst part! He . . . he was talking the whole time. Mumbling mostly, except when he was yelling at me or laughing. After my face started swelling and I couldn't see, I imagined there were two of them. It sounded like two or more of them talking about me, prodding, poking, punching me.

"He kept saying the strangest things. Like 'good boy, good boy,' like he was cheering himself on. Arnie told me later—oh, it was years before

Arnie would even face me again—but he said there was a point where he looked up from the front seat and the creep seemed to be having a conversation with himself, an argument.

"Eventually that monster pulled me out of the car and onto the ground. That's when Arnie got away. Sometime after that, he stopped, just lay there on me like a dead man. I was barely conscious and my eyes were totally swollen shut by then. Suddenly he started talking to me in this really sweet, young voice. Like a little boy. He said 'You're hurt. We need to get you to a doctor.'

"And then he carried me back to the car and drove me to the hospital. Arnie had found a policeman by then, and when they heard on the police radio about me being brought to the hospital, they took Arnie there and he identified Malcolm Jones, sitting right there in the waiting room."

Duke had been taking notes as fast as he could write and hadn't asked a single question until Ruth paused.

"You say he was talking to himself in different voices? You mean like multiple personalities?"

"MPD," Ruth said, matter-of-factly. "That's what one report I read said."

"My God," Duke said. "Why didn't any of that come out in court?"

"The state isn't stupid. If he had pleaded insanity, he would've been sent to some expensive hospital. He'd still be locked away. But it was just a rape charge, twenty years max. He served almost fifteen. Saved the state some money, I guess."

Chapter 90

By nine that night, Duke and Josie were curled in her bed, flushed with the afterglow of lovemaking. They knew this would be their last night together for a while. Josie would pick up Kevin the next day, and she would never have an overnight guest with Kevin in the house. Sharon and Jennifer would return soon, and Duke was anxious to see them.

But like a dieter who gobbles up chocolate chip cookies without counting the calories, Duke and Josie were enjoying these moments together without talking about tomorrow.

"She was a cheerleader, an honor student," Duke said, recalling his interview with Ruth Van Ness. "She could have been a doctor or anything. Instead she's trapped by fear for the rest of her life."

Josie smiled. She loved the way Duke cared about people. She didn't understand his obsession with this fifteen-year-old crime, but she couldn't help being caught up in his passion for these people.

"What will you do with this story?"

"Oh, I don't know. Maybe when this serial killer thing blows over . ."

"You think it will blow over?"

"If that phone doesn't ring tonight . . . then, baby, it's gone with the wind."

"What do you mean?"

"I mean some gang members will confess to that Shabbytown home invasion. Johnny Morton will get ten years for justifiable homicide. And someplace south, Springfield or maybe St. Louis, they'll arrest some drifter and he'll brag to his cellmate about his two-day murder spree in Jordan. End of story."

Josie curled into Duke's chest.

"You're right, of course. But what if that phone rings?"

"Then you and I, greedy newshounds that we are, will jump up— even if it rings during the good part—and chase that perverse thrill of another big headline, another shocking story. We'll shake our heads that it excites us so, but we will give up sleep, food, and love for the story."

Duke began kissing her breasts.

"Are you looking for more, Mr. Dukakis?"

"Well, we do have to stay awake all night just in case the phone rings, so we might as well have some fun."

Chapter 91

Monday dawned cool and sunny. Birds singing welcomed the townsfolk as they returned to their weekday routines like squirrels venturing out of their burrows after a summer storm.

They had made it through the weekend without so much as a traffic death. The phones were oddly silent, and as Josie looked up and saw Juan working at his desk, she imagined lots of suspicious people were feeling just like her. Ashamed.

There seemed to be plenty of little stories—second-quarter unemployment figures, an EPA air quality warning, a local community theater bankruptcy—so Josie had plenty on her mind when Nick approached her desk with a pretty young blonde. Just his type.

"Josie, I don't know if you've met Brittany Miller. Her husband, Scotty, was one of the people killed a week ago," Nick said.

"Why, of course," Josie said looking up. "I'm so sorry for your loss."

"Thank you," the girl said, her eyes filled with a sadness beyond her years. "I want to talk to you about a community tournament."

Josie looked to Nick for an explanation and then back to Brittany.

"The softball tournament was canceled after the murders a week ago, and there's been some talk of not having it at all," Brittany said, youthful enthusiasm softening her sad eyes. "I think that's a mistake. I think we could use the tournament to bring the community together now, perhaps raise some money for the victims' families. Not me, of course, but some of the others, like Richard Angelo. His mother is all alone now. I hear she may not be able to keep her house on just Social Security. And, of course, all of Dan's medical bills.

"I just think we need a big community event that says we're in this together. I think we can pull it off for this Saturday. This is a good town, and some madman isn't going to turn us into scaredy-cats living behind locked doors."

Brittany's enthusiasm was the jolt of energy Josie's morning needed. Nick was beaming.

"I think it's a great idea," Josie said. "Nick, do an announcement for today's paper and then a full feature for tomorrow enumerating the financial needs. We can probably come up with a story every day this week. It's been a pleasure to meet you, Brittany. Good luck, and just let Nick know if there is anything we can do to help."

After Brittany and Nick had returned to his desk, Josie glanced at the clock to see how much time they had before deadline at ten. That's when it hit her like a bullet. It was almost nine and Duke had not come in.

Her heart pounded in her ears as she tried to think if there was something she'd forgotten, some explanation. She was afraid to ask around; she didn't want Ham to know. But when she looked up, she saw Hammond gazing at her from his glassed-in office. He knew.

Josie looked around to see if any of the reporters had noticed Duke's absence, but all were conspicuously busy. It felt like a Wild West showdown, she and Hammond staring at each other across the bustling room, each waiting for the other to make a move.

On her computer, Josie called up the warning letter she had written the last time Duke was late. She made the necessary adjustments and sent the letter to the printer. She went and stood by the printer, over by Helen's desk, afraid someone would see the letter before she could retrieve it. All the while, she kept hoping Duke would come in chattering about some story he'd been working on.

Instead, the printer spat out three copies of the letter, just as she had requested. The clock on the wall seemed to be audibly ticking away the minutes—9:04, 9:05, 9:06. Josie closed her eyes and leaned against the wall. There must be some explanation.

She didn't realize Hammond was standing beside her until he spoke. "What are you waiting for?"

"What's the rush?" Josie responded, with a sigh of resignation. She handed Hammond the three letters and followed him into his office. He signed the letters and handed her the pen for her signature. Without a word, she left his office and headed across the room to place a copy on Duke's desk. Now everyone seemed to be watching. Somehow they all knew.

After deadline, when Josie was in the break room, Ron Greene from Composing stuck his head through the doorway. "Duke's here."

Did the whole building know?

Everybody in the break room rushed to the newsroom and stood in the doorway as Duke finished reading the letter. He turned to look at Hammond first, then Josie, and burst into laughter.

"Three days? Three days, huh? Well, great. The rest of you sit around and play deadline tag. I'm going fishing."

He strode across the room toward the knot of co-workers in the doorway, his head held high and a big smile on his face.

"Too bad you can't join me, pal," he said, slapping Nick on the back as he passed. When he strode out the door, even Bob, the security guard, was shaking his head.

Josie rushed after him. She waited until they were in the parking lot, a good distance from the door, before she spoke. But it didn't matter. Her voice was so loud and angry it was easily heard inside.

"Damn it, Duke, why did you do that? Why the hell did you do that to me?"

"To you?" Duke shouted back. "Why, the eternal inferno did you do this to *me?*"

"What choice did you leave me?"

"You have lots of choices, babe, but you let Hammond do your thinking for you. Do you think that idiot can put the paper out without you and me?"

"Yes, I'm sure he could."

"Canary crap!" Duke said, and jumped into his turquoise Pontiac, squealing the tires as he pulled out of the parking lot.

Chapter 92

Without thinking, Duke turned onto the Interstate and headed south. He wasn't sure where he was going, just away. Away from those shortsighted people. He talked out loud as he drove, listing every stupid thing Hammond had ever done, from letting the local tractor plant get away with calling a layoff "downsizing" to giving front-page play to every community development scheme that came along.

He never said anything about his own mistakes. Never said, "Maybe I shouldn't have drunk so much last night, maybe I should have set two alarms." Those thoughts were somewhere in the back of his mind, but he never said them aloud.

Finally, he started reading road signs. Where was he? He needed a drink. But it wasn't noon yet and he had a rule against drinking before noon. If he didn't have rules, he'd become a lush. Everyone knew that.

He saw a sign for Emory, the county seat of Aldrich County, and suddenly Duke knew where he had to go. He exited onto Illinois Highway 109 and followed it into town. He remembered the Regents were farmers, so he stopped at a grain elevator, just outside of town, and asked directions. Before long he was winding his way down a gravel road, pulling into a rocky driveway, and fending off a big, enthusiastic black Lab.

Mrs. Regent came to the back door in the same flowered dress she'd been wearing the night Duke saw her at St. Mary's Hospital. She was wiping her hands on a dish towel.

"Well, I'll be. Aren't you a bit out of your area Mr., ah, Du . . . Du . . ."

"Dukakis," Duke said, reaching out a hand as he approached the door. "Man, this is a friendly dog. He could lick you to death."

"Oh, yes he could. Down, Blackie," Mrs. Regent said. "What brings you to Aldrich County?"

"Oh, a little fishing trip. Just thought I'd stop by and see how Elizabeth is doing."

"Well, isn't that kind of you. Come in." Mrs. Regent held the screen door open. "She's in the front room. You'll have to excuse the mess in the kitchen. I'm making jelly and it takes up every pot I've got."

She led through an old cluttered kitchen and into a simple living room with an odd assortment of Victorian and modern furniture. Elizabeth was propped up on a sheet-swathed sofa reading a magazine.

"She can't climb the stairs, so we just turned this into our hospital room," Mrs. Regent said. "Look who's here, E.B.—that nice Mr. Dukakis from the newspaper. You can have a seat there, Mr. Dukakis. Can I get you anything to drink?"

Duke paused. He didn't trust himself to answer the question.

Elizabeth spoke. "Yes, mom, could you bring me more ice water?" Her face was an ugly blue and yellow, but the swelling had gone down and her speech was clear.

"Of course, dear. And for you?"

"The same," Duke said. "Thank you."

"Is something wrong?" Elizabeth asked when her mother had left the room.

"No. Why?"

"I thought maybe there had been another murder and they didn't want to tell me. You would tell me, wouldn't you?"

"Of course! You seem strong enough to handle it," Duke said with a wink.

Elizabeth smiled. Mrs. Regent brought in two glasses of ice water and a small bowl of blueberries.

"Help yourself, Mr. Dukakis. I've got more than I need."

Elizabeth reached out a hand slowly, painfully, and picked up a few berries. She awkwardly brought them to her lips. It hurt to watch her move.

"I was talking to somebody the other day who went through something similar to your experience many years ago," Duke said. "She said something that got me thinking. Do you mind a few more questions?"

Elizabeth looked to her mother and then answered with a wink. "I can handle it."

Duke smiled. "Well, you said there were two men, but you only described one for the police sketch artist. What did the other man look like?"

"I don't know, I never got a good look at him. I guess my eyes were swollen shut by then."

"So, how did you know there were two of them?"

"They were talking, arguing. I think the one thought the other was too rough."

"So you heard two voices. Can you describe the voices?"

"Yes. One was pure evil. Very deep with a hateful laugh. The other was younger, softer. He seemed a little afraid, I think."

256

"Elizabeth, have you ever read 'Dr. Jekyll and Mr. Hyde?' It's a book by Robert—"

"Louis Stevenson. Yes, I know. We have schools in Aldrich County, you know!"

Duke laughed. "Well, that's the story of two personalities in one man. Is it possible that both the voices you heard came from one man?"

"Is that what the police think?" Elizabeth's mother asked.

"To be honest with you, Mrs. Regent, I don't know what the police think. I just want to know what Elizabeth thinks."

He turned to Elizabeth, who had dropped her magazine and was hugging herself with both hands. Her eyes were wide with terror.

"Yes," she said finally. "Yes, it could have been."

Chapter 93

Duke awoke on the sofa in his own house. He didn't look at the clock. It didn't matter what time it was. He drank three cups of coffee and started making a list. First, he would call Everett Winter, a psychologist who had examined Malcolm Jones and testified against his release before the parole board. Winter might be able to provide some background. The reports of the parole board hearings Duke had obtained were sketchy, basically just a list of who had served on the board, who had testified and the decision. Jones had been up for parole every year since 1975, and it always had been denied until this time. The obvious difference was that Winter had not testified this time.

"I'm afraid I can't be any help to you," Winter said, when Duke finally tracked him down shortly after noon. "Any conversations between Mr. Jones and myself are protected."

"I realize that," Duke said, "but I was wondering why you didn't testify this year."

"Oh, that. I've changed jobs. Opened a new practice. I don't deal with state patients anymore. He has a new psychologist."

"But you were already familiar with his case. Could he have changed that much in one year?"

"I told you," Winter said with an edge creeping into his voice. "I can't talk about Jones. I'm not saying he has changed, I'm only saying he isn't my case anymore."

"I know, I know," Duke repeated, "But I'm assuming that for eight years your testimony kept this man in jail. Is that right?"

"Well, it was more than my evaluation."

"But you did not favor his parole?"

"Of course not!"

"And if you had been at that hearing this year, would you still have been opposed to his parole?"

"Absolutely."

"Why? What is it you know about this man? Is he still a danger to society?"

"Yes, in my opinion he is criminally insane. There, I've said more than I should."

"That's OK, Dr. Winter. I won't quote you. I just wanted some background before I interview him."

"Well, I can't discuss his case, but, you might look up Simpson . . . Bernard Simpson, I think, in your newspaper's morgue. It was in all the papers in 1956. That's all I can say."

Chapter 94

Wednesday morning Duke went to the morgue, but not the one at the *Jordan Daily News*. He wouldn't do them the favor. No, Duke could get by just fine without the *Daily News,* much better than it could get by without him.

Duke was in the *Chicago Tribune* morgue after pulling a few strings with reporter friends there. Trying several variations on the name Bernard Simpson, Duke finally found a story about a Bernie Simonson who was killed in 1956.

Simonson had been beaten to death by a six-year-old boy. Duke unfolded clipping after clipping, trying to piece together the horrific tale. Simonson, it seems, had gotten a little rough with a prostitute. Her son, who weighed nearly one hundred pounds, and his infant brother, had been locked in the closet, the prostitute's regular practice whenever she brought home a john. The six-year-old had spent a lot of his life locked in that closet, listening to his mother do her business. This time, he broke down the closet door and proceeded to beat the john with a closet rod.

Evidently, no charges had been filed against the boy, who was placed in a foster home. The mother retained custody of her infant son and promised never to lock him in a closet again.

The boy was never named in the story, but the prostitute's name was Eula Jones. Duke did some quick figuring in his head. Malcolm Jones was born April 1, 1950. He would have been six years old in 1956.

Chapter 95

After a quick lunch with his *Tribune* reporter friend, Duke headed to the next stop on his list, the McCleary-Evans House, on Roosevelt Road, on the city's south side. This was a halfway house of some repute. It had been around for many years, even back when Duke was growing up in Greek Town. Parolees lived there for six months or so to get adjusted to life on the outside.

Duke circled the block three times looking for the address. Finally, he pulled into a parking lot and walked the block. He remembered a sign in front of one of these old brick buildings, but when he found the sign on foot, it had been so heavily vandalized, spray-painted, and beaten with a bat, it was impossible to read what it had once said.

Duke looked up at the old brick Victorian house with the gargoyles on the top. The windows and door were boarded up and decorated with colorful spray paint. He surveyed the area. Several buildings on this block were boarded up. Only one, a small grocery, appeared to be open. He stepped out of the glaring sun into the dark store.

"Can I help you?" came an Indian-accented voice.

Duke looked around but couldn't find the source of the voice. Finally, his eyes focused on a short man, almost hidden by the high counter.

"Yes, perhaps you can," Duke said, and self-consciously bent to talk more directly to the man. "I'm looking for the McCleary-Evans House. It's a halfway house for parolees."

"That one." The man nodded, indicating the boarded up Victorian with the gargoyles.

"But it looks closed," Duke said, not comprehending.

"Oh, yes, it is. It's been closed maybe six months."

"But I'm looking for a man who lives there," Duke said, holding up the report on Illinois sex offenders.

The little man shrugged.

Duke stepped outside, and a frightening realization hit him as harshly as the blazing July sun.

Chapter 96

While Kevin brushed his teeth, Josie grabbed the kitchen phone. Then she stood there, just holding the receiver, thinking.

It was Thursday. Duke was due back at work today, and she was afraid he might not show up. She thought about giving him a wake-up call, even though it wasn't her job. But this was serious. If he were late again, he would be fired.

"Who's on the phone?" Kevin asked.

"Huh? Oh, no one," Josie replied. "I was going to make a call but I changed my mind. Ready?"

After Josie dropped Kevin off at Ranch Rudy, she drove to Duke's house and rang the doorbell. There was no answer and no car in the driveway, so she went around and peeked in the sliding glass door to see if he was asleep on the sofa. A pizza box was open on the coffee table, but the sofa was empty.

Josie glanced at her watch. Now, she was going to be late if she didn't hurry. Duke probably had gone in extra early, just to make a point, she thought.

Josie approached the back door of the office a few minutes after seven.

"Oh, you just missed Duke," Nick said, rushing out the door. "He was heading out to talk with Sheriff Coleman, something about that case from the past he was interested in. I'm headed over to try to grab Judge Small before court this morning. I should be back a little after eight."

Before Josie could get a word in edgewise, Nick disappeared into the parking lot.

"Duke just left," Becky repeated as Josie passed her desk. "He said if you need him, call Coleman's office."

Josie shook her head. Why was Duke so caught up in this case from the past?

As soon as she signed on to her computer, a message popped up from Duke, basically repeating what Becky and Nick had said. When she looked up, Juan was at her desk with a question and Maggie was right behind him, so Josie didn't have much time to think about Duke's choice of stories on his first day back. When Hammond pulled her aside, however, she tried to sound enthusiastic.

"He's out talking with Coleman about the long-term trauma some crime victims experience. He's got some great sources. It will be his column for Sunday."

Meanwhile, Becky was rapidly unraveling her remaining braids. She had called the county's evidence tech, Al Lepalee, and several favorite breakfast joints trying to track down Duke—who, contrary to the tale she and Nick had told Josie, had not shown up for work that morning. Now, Nick was calling in with bad news from Duke's place.

"OK, I broke in, but he's not here. I checked the basement and the garage, too. His car isn't even here."

"Maybe he did go fishing," Becky whispered while keeping one eye fixed on Josie across the room.

"No, I told you. I saw him Tuesday night. We had a couple of drinks. All he wanted to talk about was this story from fifteen years ago. Sometimes I think maybe he's losing it."

"Well, if his car isn't there, I'm going to assume he's in a ditch somewhere. I'm calling the state police."

"You know, he might have headed to Chicago. He wanted to check out some halfway house there."

"Okay, so I'll try Cook County hospitals, too."

"I'll be in to help."

Nick was back in the office by eight as he had promised, but he and Becky seemed to be working on something together. Josie figured it must be a story about the tournament. Becky had done a wonderful piece for Thursday's paper about the impact on the Thompson and Conley families and how fellow farmers were helping them. Brittany had been in three or four times this week talking to Nick about plans for the tournament. It was turning into quite a community event. Josie didn't need any help on deadline this morning, so she ignored their project.

She did try calling Coleman's office, just to warn Duke that she had promised a Sunday column out of this interview, but Coleman's secretary said Duke and Coleman had gone to breakfast without saying where.

"I'll have him call you when he comes in," the secretary promised. As soon as she hung up, the secretary called Becky to report.

"Thanks, Jane," Becky whispered, giving Josie a cautious look. "No, we haven't tracked him down yet, but I'll call you as soon as we do."

Becky looked up to see Maggie standing at her desk with a big smile.

"I've got him," Maggie whispered. Nick and Becky leaned in closer to hear. "Cook County Jail. He got into a barroom brawl in Greek Town last night!"

Becky and Nick breathed a sigh of relief.

"OK, I'll go bail him out," Nick said.

"Done," Maggie said, placing her hands on her hips. "I called one of his cousins, the one with the restaurant. I told him to have Duke call Becky before he talks to anyone else."

"Yes, that would be good," Josie said, walking up behind them. "We want to be sure he gets his story straight."

Then twirling her banana, Josie passed by, bound for the break room. Suddenly she turned back with a broad smile. "Oh, and be sure he knows I expect a Sunday column on that 'interview' he had this morning."

Chapter 97

By early afternoon, Becky was repeating the story of that morning's subterfuge to a round of laughter at the Thompson dinner table. Dinner on a farm, is a midday meal, a break during the heat of the day when the farmer and his helpers can eat hearty before returning to the field to work nonstop until dark. Today the Thompsons were eating at a pair of picnic tables under a shade tree.

Earlier in the week, Becky had visited with the Thompsons and Conleys to write a feature in advance of Saturday's tournament. Both families had moved past the shock stage and into the "can't shut them up" stage. Beverly Thompson wanted to talk about her only son, pull out the photo albums, relive the memories. Becky wanted to listen. Before the story was written, Becky had made some new friends.

The story appeared in Thursday's paper, so Becky took the Thompsons several copies of the paper and gratefully agreed to stay for dinner. The grandparents were there, as well as Old Ben and a couple of Leroy's friends who'd been hired to help. Everyone was devouring squash and tomatoes and the first of the corn.

The Thompsons were doing better than the Conleys. Natalie was too frightened to be left alone, so Shirley Conley had taken leave from her job to care for her. Twice a week they drove into Chicago to take Natalie to a psychologist who specialized in crime trauma, an expense not covered by insurance.

"A softball tournament sounds like a great idea," Old Ben said. "I might even take my fastball out of retirement."

Everyone chuckled, especially the two teens.

"Don't laugh," Grandpa Thompson said, "Ben here was on the state champion team from Jordan, back in 1923. That was when baseball really meant something. When a baseball player was a hero."

"What are you talking about, Albert? You were only a kid in '23."

"Yeah, but I remember, Ben. I was nine or ten, and you were my hero."

"Yeah, well, that was before I knew about bursitis."

Everyone chuckled again and Becky overheard one of the teens ask the other in a whisper, "Is Bursitis a famous baseball player?"

Chapter 98

By the time Johnny Morton's name was called, everyone in Family Court knew something was up. The seventy-five chairs in the audience were filled and one of the janitors was setting up extras in the aisles.

Doris Morton had been calling people, telling them how her Johnny had been mistreated, complaining about the court snubbing her rights as a grandmother. After all, the baby had been removed only because Johnny was being questioned in the death of his wife, and no charges were ever filed. The state hadn't presented any evidence that Justin had been mistreated. A happy family had been disrupted by bureaucratic red tape. Rosie, Tracy's mom, came up with the idea of inviting a lot of people to observe the court in action.

"A little gentle pressure of the people," Rosie called it.

So they came, mostly people from the blue collar Lockwood neighborhoods: construction workers, refinery workers, waitresses still in uniform, a mechanic with his first name embroidered on his dark green shirt.

The grandmothers, Rosie and Doris, sat side by side in the front row. The two women never had been friends, but they were united on this issue. Neither of them had seen their grandson since he had gone into foster care almost a month ago.

Johnny was prepared for another setback. He didn't expect to understand a thing the attorneys said, but after brief speeches by each, the judge launched into a soliloquy. Johnny wasn't sure if she was saying good things or bad things, because she looked so stern. When she finished with "petition denied" and the clap of her gavel, his heart sank. But then the back doors of the courtroom swung open and the same social worker who had visited his home came in with J.D. in her arms. The state's petition for protective custody had been denied. J. D. was to be returned, immediately, to his father.

When the social worker approached Johnny's table, the baby fairly leaped out of her arms into Johnny's eager embrace. The seven-month-old had no words yet, but a happy "ga-ga" seemed to suffice. Johnny pressed the baby to his neck, trying to hide the tears that welled up in his eyes; the room erupted in applause and cheers.

Rosie, Doris, and Tom clustered around, smothering the baby with kisses. There was so much laughing and talking that no one heard the judge's gavel at first. When they did, a hush fell over the room, and Johnny was relieved to see a smile on the judge's face.

"Please celebrate elsewhere, Mr. Morton," she said. "And good luck."

"Everyone's invited to Rosie's," Rosie said loudly. "Even you, Judge."

The crowd dispersed fairly quickly, but from a seat in the back row, Chief Don Miller silently watched. Johnny stopped by the doorway on his way out and made a honking sound as the baby squeezed his father's nose.

Even after the room was quiet and the bailiff and judge had left, Miller remained in his seat. He pulled out his wallet and began flipping through the photos: Scotty's wedding picture, Scotty in uniform, Scotty's senior picture, Scotty in Little League. Then Miller pulled out a small faded photo, tucked behind the Little League picture, a snapshot of a baby tweaking a man's nose. His hands began to shake and a pitiful, wounded cry exploded from his lips.

Chapter 99

J. D. Morton was the star attraction at Saturday's softball tournament. Maggie wrote a story for Friday's *Daily News* about the Family Court decision to return the boy to his father. It ran with Mack's prize-worthy photo of father and son leaving the courthouse. Even before Johnny pushed J.D.'s stroller up to the bleacher section reserved for "special guests," several people stopped to congratulate him.

"What a beautiful boy," one elderly woman exclaimed, looking from J.D. to Johnny. "He's got your eyes."

" Here, I knitted you a pair of booties," another said, bending over to tie the pale blue coverings onto J.D.'s bare feet.

"Oh, you're that boy from the paper," a young mother said. "I'll bet you're glad to be back with your father."

"Here's my card," a distinguished-looking man said to Johnny. "I was touched by all you've been through. If there's anything my church can do, don't hesitate to call."

This was the kind of community outpouring Brittany had envisioned. She wouldn't be so gauche as to introduce the victims and their families, but she had reserved a section of bleachers for them and after the week's stories in the *Daily News,* most were easily recognized. Community people felt free to introduce themselves and offer support.

The fundraising event and the *Daily News* stories covered all the families touched by the summer's murders, without regard to whether the cases were related.

Brittany had recruited community participation to expand the usual tournament. After the morning round of softball games, the high school marching band gave an early demonstration of its new football halftime show. The director dedicated the display to the band's fallen trumpet player, Leroy Thompson, and among those marching were Tre and Nadine Franklin and Trent Anderson.

Then the choir from Missionary Baptist Church sang a few songs, and everyone stood in a moment of silence for Hannah and Zoe Otis, a pair of piano teachers most of the community had never heard of until a week ago. The tragedies had crossed economic and racial lines and attracted a mixed group to the stands, from the Thompsons and other white farm families to blue-collar workers from Lockwood to the mayor and city council to clusters from Shabbytown. Eddie and Mae Simms were there with Claude and Andy, their wives and children, though Biggun didn't like crowds and had stayed home.

The Jaycees opened a hot dog stand and the Knights of Columbus had their fish-fry vats going. Proceeds would benefit the newly established victims' fund. The PTA set up some carnival games and face-painting booths. The 4-H members ran a petting zoo and led horses around the ring to give two-dollar rides to city kids.

The sheriff's department had a dunk tank, where people eagerly stood in line to toss softballs at the red metal lever that would drop a uniformed deputy into a pool of water. Proceeds from this event were earmarked for Deputy Dan Franklin's mounting medical bills. The line of deputies willing to be dunked was almost as long as the laughing crowd paying their dollars.

By the time Josie arrived, after Kevin's morning soccer game and a short visit to the ceramic studio, the second round of softball games had begun. She grabbed a couple of hot dogs and climbed into the stands for the Media Moguls versus the Tractor Tyrants—*Daily News* employees and a few ringers from the local radio station against a team of Caterman Tractor workers.

Josie spotted Karen Anderson and her sons sitting with Duke, Sharon and Jennifer. Trent, Karen's eldest, was leaning back to catch the eye of Jennifer at the other end of the row. Jennifer smiled demurely but pretended not to notice.

"Who's that, who's that?" Kevin asked, pulling on Josie's sleeve.

"Oh, just someone from work," Josie responded absently.

"Duh! Of course, he's someone from work," Kevin said, shaking his head. "He's a Media Mogul."

Only then did Josie realize Kevin was asking about Nick, who was up to bat.

"Oh, that's Nick, our best player," Josie whispered to Kevin, and then hollered "Sock it to 'em, Nick!"

She realized belatedly that her outburst had caused several rows to look her way, including Duke, but plying an instinct as natural as Jennifer's, she gave Kevin a hug and pretended not to notice.

"Hey, look! There's Dad!" Kevin shouted. Before Josie could stop him, Kevin was on his feet shouting and waving both arms. "Daaaaaaad, over here!"

Kurt, shaking hands like a politician running for office, looked up and waved. To Josie's surprise, he was alone and slowly worked his way up the bleachers until he was hugging Kevin and asking pertinent questions like, "Who are we rooting for here?"

Kurt sat down and Kevin snuggled up to him, pointing out Nick and other players Kurt already knew, but he allowed his son to be the expert for once. After a few minutes he leaned over his son and spoke to Josie.

"Now, this is really a great thing you've done here. This is the power of the press."

"We didn't do this," Josie said with a shrug. "It was all Brittany's doing. Brittany Miller."

"Oh, it took some leadership, but most of these people are here because of the stories in the *Daily News*. This is the best thing to happen to this town all summer, and on behalf of Jordan, I want to thank you."

"Oh, now you speak for the whole town!" Josie said.

"Jeez, babe, can't you take a compliment?"

Josie blushed. Kurt was sincerely being nice and she was ruining it. She smiled and whispered an embarrassed "Thank you."

"Hey, Dad, you're missing it!" Kevin said pulling on his father's arm. "He's stealing third!"

Josie and Kurt turned in time to see Nick dance between second and third as the basemen trapped him in a rundown. When the third baseman dropped the ball, Nick darted all the way to home plate and the crowd went wild.

Chapter 100

Over at the hot dog stand, Becky ran into Old Ben having a little trouble squeezing mustard onto his purchase.

"Here let me help you," Becky said. "Beautiful day, isn't it?"

"Gorgeous, and the day isn't too bad either," Ben said with a playful chuckle.

"Oh, I'll bet you were a case when you were younger," Becky said, shaking her head.

"I'm still a handful," Ben said in a conspiratorial whisper. "Want to join me for lunch?"

"Sounds dangerous," Becky said with a smile, "but what the heck?"

When the two were seated at a picnic table under a shade tree, close enough to hear the crowds cheer as Nick ran home, Becky asked about Ben's background.

"Did you really play baseball?"

"Oh, yeah, a little community league. Everybody played then. But I was gooooood."

"You told me once that you had buried two wives and what was it, five children?"

"Yes, I've outlived them all."

"How sad that must be."

"Oh, no," Ben replied, mustard dribbling down his chin. Becky quickly blotted his chin with her napkin. "Thank you, dear. No, life has been so good to me, because I had two wonderful wives, five beautiful babies, and eighty-five years to watch the corn grow. So far."

"But to lose them all . . . ."

"Did you ever lose someone, dear?"

"Well, just my grandmother. My grandfather died before I was born. I never knew my dad's family."

"Ah, now there's a greater loss. Tell me about this grandmother. Do you remember her?"

"Of course. She was a lot like you, actually."

"Well, then she lives forever, in your memory. She's become a part of you, and everyone who knows you will see a little bit of her. What a legacy!"

Becky smiled. "But loss can be so devastating," she said. "Like your cousin Natalie. She seems to be taking this the hardest."

"She feels guilty, probably, because she survived," Ben said, polishing off his hotdog and leaning back against the tree trunk. "I was in a car wreck when my first wife and the two youngest died. That was the hardest loss, because I survived. Natalie needs to know there's a purpose to it. I didn't at first. But after I met Opal, my second wife, I knew why I had survived."

"So, you think Natalie will come out of this?" Becky said.

"In time." Ben smiled.

"She seems so . . . " Becky struggled for a word that wouldn't be too pejorative. "Fragile," she said finally. "I mean, her mother said she's afraid of everything: cars, dirt roads, anyone in a uniform."

"Ah, yes, well, sometimes I think the uniforms try to instill fear, especially in young people," Ben said. "Sometimes the police should listen to people."

"What are you talking about?"

"Well, earlier this summer, back when the fields were being planted, there was a strange man driving around the farm roads. I know people reported it to the police, but they wouldn't listen."

"What was so strange about him?"

"Well, for one thing he was black."

"Ben! I can't believe you can be so bigoted! Do you think I'm strange because I'm black?"

"I think you are angry because you are black," Ben said, pausing long enough for Becky to consider his words.

"The stranger stood out on the country roads because he was black. No one who lives on those roads is black."

"Well, maybe he was looking for a farm to buy, did you ever think about that?" Becky said, her irritation showing.

"I don't think so. I think he was looking for a place to practice shooting his gun. One of the farmers found him shooting holes in a stop sign. Just shooting holes in a stop sign in the middle of the night. That's strange."

"Okay, now I'm listening. Did you tell the cops he had a gun?"

"I'm getting to that. One evening, he was following Natalie home in this dirty black pickup. She pulled in at my place to get away from him. She said he fired the gun at her car. Imagine that. Her father reported it to the county, but we never heard no more about it. The police should listen to people."

"Wait a minute, you say he was driving a black pickup? What did the man look like?"

"He was black, I told you."

"Young? Old? Short? Tall? Skinny? Fat?"

"Young . . . everybody seems young when you are my age, but not too young. Not a teenager. Big. I never saw him standing up, but he filled up that truck cab. And it was a good-sized truck, not those little pretend trucks that haven't got room in back for a cord of wood."

"Okay, what kind of truck?"

"I don't know, but check with Mark Conley. I think Natalie got a license number."

Chapter 101

The sun set on a beautiful day. Kevin was finally asleep, a dragon face-painting from the PTA carnival booth curled on his cheek. Josie poured a glass of wine over ice and went out on the front porch to sit in her wicker rocker and think. It wasn't long before the object of her thoughts appeared.

"Mind if I join you?" Duke said, stepping up onto the porch.

"Oh, you startled me," she said. "Where's your car?"

"In the next block," Duke said, plopping down in the second rocker. "I felt like a walk."

"Sounds like you felt guilty about coming to see me and you don't want Sharon to find out."

"That, too, though I don't think she cares, really."

"Of course, she cares. I saw you two together today."

"That was for Jennifer. Sharon is still keeping me at arm's length."

There was a long, awkward silence. Duke wasn't carrying his usual sidearm drink, and though Josie was sure he'd had a few beers, he didn't have that fuzzy, not-quite-there glaze in his eyes. They smiled at each other and rocked silently for several minutes before Duke spoke again. "That was a great tournament today, wasn't it? I mean not just the softball but all the people, all the camaraderie, all the money raised."

"Yes, that's the real Jordan. Too bad the Chicago media didn't see that. You know, Nick said he ran into Angela Deline there, and she said an event like that would infuriate a deranged killer. Camaraderie is just the opposite of the effect he wants to create. She predicted another murder tonight to wrest the attention back to him."

"Oh, I'm sick of her predictions," Duke said. "I liked it better when murder was an unwelcome surprise."

"Speaking of which, what are you doing here?" Josie said.

"Oh, come on. I've stayed out of your hair all week. I thought tonight, maybe . . . ."

"No way, not with Kevin in the house. Besides, I think we should cool it for a while, let you get your bearings with Sharon. And with the way things are at work . . . ."

"OK, I'm sorry if I put you in a bad position, but I thought we had something . . . ."

"Duke, you know I hate to agree with Hammond, but he has the right to expect a reliable employee. If the reporters hadn't covered for you on Thursday, you'd be out on your ear. Is that what you want?"

"The old man is being unfair, inflexible. So, I overslept a few days. Look at all the nights and Saturdays I never turn in. He gets his money's worth from me. He always has.

"And how about Sharon and Jennifer, are you willing to lose them, too?"

"That's her choice, not mine."

"But it is your choice, don't you see, Duke? You're choosing alcohol over your job, your family, your—"

"Oh, now you sound just like Sharon. Why is it women think a little sex gives them the right to control every part of a man? Women want to be liberated, wear the pants in the family. When do men get liberated? When do we get the chance to drink as much as we want without some self-righteous bitch trying to tell us—"

"Duke, admit it, you need help. The company will pay for treatment, but not if you continue to flout—"

"I don't need treatment, and I certainly don't need you telling me how to live my life."

Duke rose and strode off the porch into the night. Josie watched him go, knowing she had done the right thing and regretting it already.

A few hours later, not five miles from The Banks, a gunshot and a woman's screams pierced the peaceful night.

Chapter 102

Josie was on the way home from the Lake Michigan beach when she heard the radio announcer say something about "the Cornfield Killer." She didn't catch it all, but it sounded like there had been another murder. Ignoring the sand in her hair and the sunburn on her nose, she stopped by the office as soon as she reached Jordan. Hoss was the only one there.

"Yeah, there's a story on the wire," he said. Holding up his jeans with one hand, Hoss rose to the wall map and reached up to point to the location.

"It's really only about five miles from The Banks, but it's over the border into Cook County. And it wasn't in a cornfield. It was in one of those new apartment complexes that sort of abut the cornfield. The AP story doesn't say anything about a connection to the Cade County murders."

"Well, maybe, since it is so close," Josie said, shaking her head. "A murderer doesn't know when he's crossing the county line. Did any of the reporters phone in? Who's on call today?"

"I called Nick, it's his day," Hoss responded. "We don't usually cover Cook County, cases but I thought maybe on this one . . . ."

"Hoss, you're a lifesaver."

"And how's this little Indian?" Hoss said, ruffling Kevin's hair.

"I'm not an Indian," Kevin giggled.

"Why, you've got red skin!" Hoss replied.

Nick's story in Monday's paper had all the basic details—a young married couple killed in their bed, he with one gunshot to the head, she shot several times. Though both were nude, Cook County police did not suspect a sex crime. It was a marital bed, after all. Nor did they see any link to the Cade County crimes. Cade County officials seemed to agree.

"Of course we are working with Cook County," Sheriff Coleman said in an official statement, "but there is no evidence at this time to link this murder to any of the recent, unsolved murders in Cade County."

Off the record, Coleman complained to Nick that Cook County was uncooperative and unwilling to share any information about its investigation. "The killer could have left a note confessing to the Cade County crimes and they wouldn't tell us," Coleman said with disgust.

But the media—especially the Chicago television stations—had no trouble linking the murders. "Cornfield Killer strikes again" was the top story on Monday's five p.m. and ten p.m. newscasts on all three stations. Instead of using the reserved comments of the Cook County Sheriff's department, they filled their screens with panicked neighbors and pseudo-experts like Angela Deline.

Media attention was focused on the latest victims, so the television vans were circling in the little suburb of Park Forest. Jordan was forgotten as yesterday's news, which was fine with everyone living there. They liked their lives getting back to normal.

Chapter 103

"Listen, Mr. Dukakis, I don't need some punk reporter to tell me how to do my job," bespectacled Roger Gregory said from behind his desk. Gregory was in charge of the parole division in Cade County. "We have three hundred parolees in Cade County, and every one of them is being interviewed in connection with these unsolved murders. Every one of them. Do you have any idea how many man hours—"

"I'm sure your people are doing a wonderful job," Duke said, trying to smooth the ruffled feathers. "But I'm only trying to check on one parolee, Malcolm Jones."

"Well, with a name like Jones, he could be anyplace," Gregory said as he thumbed through a long card file.

"I found him on the sex offenders report," Duke said, "except he wasn't where the list said he was."

"Useless," Gregory muttered. "That report comes out once a year, and it's already out of date by the time they get around to typing—well, look here. Your Mr. Jones *is* in Cade County, and he's already been interviewed," Gregory said, pulling out a yellow card.

"Yessir, deputies Blake and Cummings. " Gregory scratched the deputies' names on a bright orange index card along with Jones' address in Jordan township. "Interviewed him on July twenty-five. No suspicions noted here, but you may want to talk with the deputies," Gregory said, handing over the orange card. Duke slipped it into his shirt pocket.

"Let's see, his parole officer reports that he attends his weekly parole visits, only problem seems to be getting him a job. Don't know what that's about. Hey, you're in luck, if he's as punctual as this report says, he's probably upstairs right now. One p.m., Tuesdays. Stop by Martha Bailey's cubicle, third floor."

"Right now? Hey great, thanks," Duke said, heading for the elevator.

The parole officers' cubicles surrounded an open reception area lined with chairs. Duke took one close to the opening marked "Martha Bailey."

"But that's no reason to walk off the job," the stocky, white-haired woman was saying to a large black man. The man sat with his back to the open doorway and spoke so softly that Duke couldn't understand him.

"Well, here's another one to try. A warehouse. You should be good at that," the woman continued. "It's on the bus line, but the hours start pretty early, six a.m. I doubt you can get a bus that early. You may need to borrow a car. Don't you have a relative who could drop you off?"

The man made some reply, but again Duke couldn't be sure what it was.

"Well, you need to come up with some accommodation on your own. You need a job if you are going to stay out of jail. Do you understand the connection?"

After a pause for the man's reply, the woman continued.

"I don't want to hear excuses. The buses are running today. Take one over there right now. This afternoon. I'll call Mr. Ravel to tell him to expect you. Don't put it off. Get a bus schedule from the driver. Show it to Mr. Ravel. Tell him you can be there on the first bus. There's probably one by six thirty or seven. Show him you are willing to do the best you can. I think he'll give you a chance. I'll talk to him a little. Get this job, save your money, and in no time you can buy a car, and then you can work whatever hours they want."

The man rose, but Duke still couldn't understand what he said. The woman followed the man through the doorway, "Now, next week when I see you, I want you to have a job—and the week after that, I want to see your paycheck. You understand?" Then she gestured into the reception room, pointing toward a tattooed young man with long greasy hair and watery eyes.

"Marty, come on in," she said.

The big man lumbered for the door and Duke followed. Once they were in the hallway, Duke spoke.

"Excuse me, are you Malcolm Jones?"

The black man turned slowly, and Duke tried to hide his surprise. This was not the face he was expecting. Though he'd never said so, Duke was expecting to see the Cornfield Killer, the square-jawed, muscular face from the artists' sketches. The face Elizabeth described that they had been running in the newspaper. The face that was flashed on television screens and tacked onto bulletin boards all over town.

Instead, he saw a rounder, softer face and something he hadn't expected at all—a goatee. None of the witnesses—Franklin, Natalie, Elizabeth—had said anything about facial hair of any kind. It was too obvious to miss. Duke's heart sank.

"Yep," the man replied, softly. "Do I know you?"

Duke introduced himself and offered to give Malcolm a ride to his appointment.

"Now, why would you want to do that?" Malcolm said, continuing down the hall. "We can pick up a sandwich on the way," Duke said. "You look like you could use a little something to eat."

"What you want from me?" Malcolm asked as they stepped into the elevator. There Duke seemed to shrivel next to the huge, linebacker of a man who wasn't much taller but was so much broader.

"Oh, just some talk. I'm from the newspaper, and I want to talk to you about Ruth Van Ness," Duke said, looking for some reaction on the expressionless face.

"I don't know no Ruth," Malcolm said, shrugging his shoulders.

"She's the one who . . . " Duke struggled for the right words. "You took her to the hospital many years ago."

"Oh, yeah," Malcolm said, exiting as the elevator door opened. "I never knew her name."

Malcolm walked in quick, long strides and it was all Duke could do to keep up with him.

"I won't take much of your time," Duke said, tagging behind as they went outside and turned the corner of the building. "I can drop you wherever—"

Suddenly Malcolm turned and shoved Duke up against the wall.

"Look, Cocky or whatever your name is, I don't have nuthin' to say to you." Malcolm spoke in a low voice, almost a whisper, but his eyes were shouting.

"Ah, sure," Duke said, "you don't have to talk. I'll just give you a ride, then maybe later—"Malcolm pressed him harder into the rough concrete.

"I don't need a ride, neither."

"Listen, I heard what Mrs. Bailey said about the warehouse," Duke said smoothly as his confidence returned. "I know you need to go there about a job. I can give you a lift. No questions, I promise."

"You don't hear so good, do you?" Malcolm repeated calmly. "I ain't goin' to no warehouse. I ain't gettin' no job. I don't need no ride."

"But Mrs. Bailey . . . "

"You don't get it do you?" Malcolm said, his voice tightly controlled. " The bitch don't tell me what to do."

"But she's your parole officer."

Malcolm started laughing, turned and strode away.

"So, what's she gonna do to me, huh? Send me back to jail? " Malcolm stopped at the corner waiting for traffic to clear, and Duke caught up to him. "This is worse than prison. This freedom you like so much," Malcolm mumbled, looking straight ahead. Then he looked down at Duke with an icy stare. "I get respect inside. No fidgety little lady constantly harping on me. Little pissant like you wouldn't last a day."

As a bus stopped at the corner, Malcolm stuffed the warehouse address into Duke's face, shoved him down to the sidewalk and boarded. By the time Duke was back on his feet, the bus had pulled away.

Chapter 104

In a press conference Thursday morning, the Cook County Sheriff's Department announced the arrest of Gary Pfeiffer for the murder of the Park Forest couple, Don and Susan Harlow. Pfeiffer was Harlow's ex-husband, and a restraining order had been issued against him because he had threatened her life. He left his fingerprints on the sliding glass door, where he entered their bedroom, and a splotch of her blood was found on his shoes.

The *Jordan Daily News* rushed to make over for Thursday's paper.

"Sounds like they've got this case sewn up," Hoss said, as soon as the edition was released.

"Yeah, that's good, I guess. I mean, that it's not another unsolved murder," Josie said as they walked to the break room.

"But . . . ?" Hoss said, waiting for Josie to finish her thought.

"Oh, I don't know. I guess I'm glad the 'Cornfield Killer' hasn't struck again," Josie said, giving a television announcer's melodramatic emphasis to her words. Hoss laughed.

"But now," she said, " I'm beginning to worry they will never catch him. It's been almost three weeks now. Without any new clues . . . ."

Eddie Simms was thinking the same thing as he opened the paper and sat down to read it at his kitchen table. He took a long pull on his beer as he read about Gary Pfeiffer and the "crime of passion," as Cook County officials were calling it.

He shook his head as he read. Any fool could have seen this wasn't like the Cade County murders. Those television announcers had been wrong, as always. There wasn't even a mention of the unsolved Cade County murders on the front page, so Eddie opened the paper to page four, where the story was continued, to see if there would be any mention there. He paused for another swig of beer as Mae came marching into the room.

"Edward Albert Simms," she said as loud as her little voice would go. Then she thrust a dark revolver onto the newspaper in front of Eddie. "What do you have to say for yourself?"

"What's this?" Eddie asked, a bit surprised.

"That's the latest toy!" Mae stood with hands on her hips. "Dion and Beau were playing with it this morning in the back yard, chasing each other around. A black boy finds guns soon enough without you bringing one home to them."

Eddie said nothing but grabbed the gun. He flipped open the chamber. It was empty.

"I know you have to carry one on your job, but you must keep it locked up from the kids. Can't you just store it at work? Why do you have to bring that in here?"

"I'll take care of it," Eddie said, reaching out his large hand to caress Mae's cheek.

"You're not going to sweet talk your way out of this," Mae said indignantly. "My babies could have been killed."

"The gun wasn't loaded," he said and rubbed his thumb softly across her cheek. "I'll take care of it."

Mae huffed and left the room as quickly as she had entered. Eddie stared at the pistol. It was a Smith & Wesson .38, the same kind the sheriff's deputies carried. He took a hefty swig of beer, and stared again at the gun. He had thought putting the truck away would be enough. After the deputies had stopped by that day, asking questions, he'd moved the truck to his friend's body shop. He told Mae he was getting a camper top added to the back and would be using her car to go to work. With the truck hidden, Eddie had felt safe.

Now he knew he would have to do something with the guns as well. He wrapped the sides of the newspaper over the pistol and left with it under his arm.

Chapter 105

Tre found Nadine sitting on a windowsill at the end of a long, sterile hall. St. Mary's six-story hospital was the tallest structure in Cade County, and Nadine could look beyond the glistening lights of Jordan to the blackness of the farm fields, melting into the vastness of the starless sky.

Nadine was the family chatterbox, but she hadn't spoken a word since the doctors told the family that morning that Dan Franklin's brain activity had stopped. Fever and infection had finished the job that bullets had begun. Franklin was less than a vegetable, the doctor had said. There was no chance of recovery.

Tre was the silent one in the family, but looking over Nadine's head into the emptiness of the darkened sky, he knew it was up to him to speak.

"Remember when Mama went in for that last operation, and she made Daddy promise that he would never make her live hooked up to machines?"

Nadine said nothing.

"Daddy cried. That was the only time I saw him cry. But he did what had to be done. I know now how hard it was for him."

A tear drizzled down Nadine's cheek but she didn't say a word.

"Remember he told us that the angels had come for Mama? He said those machines were like leaving the lights on in an empty room. Mama was already gone."

"Do you think Daddy's gone?" Nadine said.

"I think he went to be with Mama 'cause he loved her so much."

"Then, I guess we'd better turn out the lights," Nadine said, looking up into her brother's face. The two embraced and sobbed loudly, but there was no one in the abandoned hospital corridor at that hour to complain.

***

"It must be so hard on those children," Penny said as she painted broad strokes of green on a ceramic Christmas tree during the regular Saturday morning gathering in Su Le's ceramic studio. "What are they going to do?"

"I understand they are going to live with an aunt in Chicago," Josie said, kneading a clump of rich red clay. "Or maybe the aunt is going to come here to live in their house. I'm not sure of the logistics."

"Well, I know he was a friend of yours, Josie," Barb said, the muscles of both arms bulging as she wrestled with a large mound of white porcelain clay on the whirling wheel. With firm pressure on the clay, Barb tamed the wobbling mass until it rode smoothly in the center of the wheel. "But for me there's a sense of closure. We knew Franklin had to die eventually. Now it's over."

"Is so hard for children to lose both parents," Su said as she passed by with the latest pieces from the kiln.

"Oh, yes," Josie agreed. "Children have a hard time understanding death. When I told Kevin that Davy's father had died, he showed no reaction at first, but then last night I found him crying in bed. He said he was worried his father would die, too."

"Oh, no," a murmur of sad acknowledgement passed through the room.

"Of course, I called Kurt right away to have him reassure Kevin, but he wasn't home."

"Isn't he with his father this weekend?" Barb asked.

"Yes, but by the time Kurt picked him up this morning, Kevin seemed to have forgotten the whole thing."

"Isn't that just like a child?" Penny said. "They recover so quickly."

"Well, I may not color as quickly as you, but I'm getting there," Aggie said, looking up from a detailed bouquet of flowers she was painting on a vase.

"Oh, silly," Penny said, dabbing a wide stroke of green paint on her mother-in-law's forehead to the delight of everyone in the room. "We weren't talking about you."

Chapter 106

Duke was at the copy machine when Becky stepped into the darkened newspaper office Saturday morning.

"What are you doing here?" she asked.

"I might ask you the same," Duke said.

"Oh, I thought I'd look through that database of phone tips Helen keeps to see if there are any license numbers in there. It's the craziest thing. In order to look up a report in the Sheriff's Department's traffic division, you have to know the license number. And the license number is what I'm trying to find."

"I hear ya," Duke said. "I'm running into the same Catch-22. We publish these composite drawings to help people recognize the suspect, but when the suspect doesn't match the drawing, I say it's time to change the drawing!"

Becky went to her desk and was silently perusing the database while Duke made some adjustments to an enlarged copy of the police artist's sketch. After a few minutes, he got up from his desk and took his drawing to Becky.

"Okay, you're a woman," he said.

"Glad you noticed."

"I mean, you use makeup to accent and define, right?" he continued. "I mean, I've read how models can create the appearance of high cheek bones by the way they apply blush."

"I've read that too. Ends up looking like a lot of blush, if you ask me."

"Well, I'm wondering if facial hair might do the same thing for a man. I mean, could a goatee make a man with a round face seem to have a square jaw?"

"Sure, that's why a mustache or a beard is such a good disguise. It changes the whole face."

"But is it possible that you would notice the effects without noticing the hair? I mean at night, dark hair on a dark face." He threw two sketches onto Becky's desk. One was the untouched sketch of the Cornfield Killer that they had been running in the paper. Next to it was Duke's modified version, a rounder face, all shaded gray with a pencil and then a goatee shape shaded just a bit darker. Becky twisted her head from side to side examining the sketch.

"Well," she said. "You're a better writer than artist."

"I'm going to send a copy to Elizabeth," Duke said, picking up the sketches. "It's worth a try."

"So what makes you think the guy has a goatee?" Becky asked.

"Oh, it's a long story. It's just that this guy, Malcolm Jones—"

"Oh, yeah. I've heard you talk about him."

"Well, I met him the other day."

"And he seems suspicious?"

"No, not really. He seems, I don't know, hardened from prison, but strangely detached. Like nothing's real to him."

"Maybe he was on drugs."

"Maybe . . . ." Anyway, what's this license number you are looking for?"

"Well, it seems Natalie Conley was harassed months ago by a guy in a black pickup who had been hassling folks out on Davis Road. She reported it to police, with a license number, but they never did anything."

"And she doesn't still have the number?"

"No, it got pitched. I mean this was way back in June. The night of the refinery explosion, actually."

"The night the sisters were killed," Duke added.

"Well, yeah, I guess that's right."

"So you can't get the number from the police report?"

"It was called in, so the information was transferred to a traffic report, filed under the license number."

"But it was on the phone log?"

"Just the incident report, not the license number."

"Wait, a minute. I covered cops the next morning." Duke turned and ran across the room. He moved the cardboard cutout of himself to one side so he could open a file drawer in the credenza behind his desk.

Becky rushed to his side and looked over his shoulder as he opened a drawer full of reporter's notebooks.

"Alter Ego here guards my stash," Duke said, as he fell to his knees and began rifling through the notebooks.

"But you're not allowed to keep those."

"I'm not allowed to do a lot of things," Duke said, snatching a couple of books from the drawer. "These are from that week. Let's see, I remember starting a new book for the cops beat because I didn't want it to get mixed up with some other stuff . . . yep, this is the one. OK, what did you say was the report number?"

Becky ran back to her desk for her copy of the phone log.

"I can't believe you write down every report. We wouldn't have used a harassment complaint like that."

"I know, but names, addresses, phone numbers, license numbers . . . I always make a note of them. Never know when—here it is!" He held out the notebook for Becky to see.

"MBL 376. That's the license number?"

"Yeah, and now to get that number translated into a name and address." Duke turned to his phone and began punching numbers. He schmoozed one person after another, talking baseball scores and weather, until finally he was transferred to someone he called George.

"Just a little favor, George," he said, and then waited on hold for a few minutes. "Uh-huh, uh-huh," Duke mumbled as he made notes on a fresh page in his notebook. "Bingo!"

"Listen, George, transfer me to Coleman—he's going to want to hear this. Well, call him at home. I'm telling ya, this is it. Call Stephens, too. You're going to want an arrest warrant. I'll be there in ten minutes with all the particulars. Just do it, George, believe me. This is it!"

Duke turned to Becky with a huge smile.

"What is it?" she asked.

"Your black truck is registered to somebody named Edward Simms," Duke said.

"Eddie Simms?" Becky exclaimed.

"You know him?"

"Well, sorta, but he doesn't seem like—"

"Well, he's probably not, " Duke said, pulling a bright orange index card from his pocket and tossing it on the notebook. "The address George gave me for that truck is the same as the one the parole office gave me for Malcolm Jones."

Chapter 107

The world spins at a different pace when you're lost in a potter's wheel.

Josie was trying to perfect a pitcher shape, flared a little in the middle then collared in with a narrow neck and a rounded lip. She was on her third try of the morning and this one was looking very good, but she kept shaping it just a little more. She loved the smooth feel of the clay slipping through her hands, the turn of the lip in her fingers.

"Don't overwork the clay," Su said as she walked past.

Josie looked up from her trance. It was the first anyone had spoken in half an hour.

"Oh-oh, look at the time," Josie said. It was ten minutes before noon, Kevin's game time. Josie used her trimming tool around the base of her pitcher, then stopped the wheel and pulled a wire under the clay to release the pitcher from the plastic bat.

"That's a nice shape," Barb said. Josie lifted the plastic bat and carried the pitcher to the table, which was fast filling with her red earthenware pitchers and Barb's large, white porcelain bowls. Josie used one finger to pull a little spout into the rim of the pitcher and smiled to herself at how perfectly the clay stretched into a rounded hollow.

"There," she said, hands on her hips and a smile of satisfaction on her face.

"Nice," said Penny from the other end of the table, where she was painting a second large Christmas tree. Aggie didn't even look up. She was lost in the delicate flower design she was making.

"Now I gotta run," Josie said, pulling an oversized T-shirt over her head to reveal her unsplattered short set beneath. At the sink she washed her hands and ran a washcloth along her legs to wipe up the red splatters. "I'll be back in an hour to clean up my wheel," she said.

"We'll be here," Barb said, turning her head slightly to examine the shape of the bowl on her wheel.

"We'll be cheering for Kevin to make a goal," Su added, peeking around the corner from the kiln room.

"I'll be in the little girl's room," Aggie whispered loudly, as she stood slowly and started her painstakingly slow journey to the small restroom in the corner of the studio.

Josie disappeared into the maze of greenware and out the front door into the almost deserted street, where she had parked her car. As she slipped behind the wheel she noticed a black man coming from the bar on the corner. So, she hadn't been imagining voices; there really were people inside that darkened bar at this hour.

As her car turned the corner and sped out of sight, the man opened the door to the ceramic shop and stepped in, the bell over the door announcing him.

"What did you forget?" Barb hollered from the studio, and the women looked at each other in silence as they waited for a response.

Chapter 108

At the same time four sheriff's department cars pulled up in front of the Simms house on Logan Street. One car threaded its way down the alley behind the house. Deputies alighted from the cars and surrounded the small bungalow.

Mae dropped a plate and screamed when she happened to glance out the window.

"Is it a mouse?" asked Beau, jumping up from the kitchen table.

"Where?" echoed Dion.

"Yes, a mouse," Mae said. "Now, you boys go hide in Grandma's bedroom. Go on now. Close the door and don't come out no matter what you hear. Go on." Mae clapped her hands.

"Did I hear someone say—" Eddie rose from his chair in the living room in time to see a deputy rush by the window, gun raised. The two little children ran giggling and screaming into the bedroom as Mae and Eddie exchanged a fearful glance. Then came the pounding on the front door, Mae wincing a little with each thunderous blow.

"Police, open—"

Eddie threw back the door before the speaker could finish his command, and several officers rushed into the room.

"I have a warrant for Malcolm Jones," a plainclothes detective said, handing a paper to Eddie.

"No," Mae wailed, stretching her body across the kitchen doorway. "He's my baby. He's sleeping."

The officers pushed into the tiny kitchen and then down the stairs to the basement.

"No, no!" Mae protested, pounding on a deputy's back until Eddie pulled her away. Two other officers bolted into the bedroom, and the squealing children came running to their grandparents, standing dumfounded in the entry.

"There's no one in the basement," an officer announced, coming up the stairs.

"But he's always down there!" Mae said. Eddie gently put a hand to her mouth.

Two officers scurried up the stairs to the attic room, another examined the side door. Duke and Becky were outside the house talking to the neighbors who gathered on the sidewalk.

The detectives and evidence techs crowded into the basement bedroom, but it hardly seemed a killer's lair. A train set and dozens of colorful Lego houses filled an old Ping-Pong table. A narrow bed stretched along one wall. A huge, mint-green stuffed turtle with a pink head occupied one end of the bed.

A deputy opened the small refrigerator next to the bed to reveal several bottles of Red Stripe beer. He pulled out two boxes from underneath the bed, filled with plastic building blocks and odds and ends.

"Look at this, " Al Laepple said, pulling a bullet from among the colorful pieces of plastic.

"Take the whole box," the detective said. He bent down and noticed a brown stain that looked like blood on the foot of the turtle. "Take this, too."

Al set the turtle on top of the box. With a gloved hand, he lifted some signs that were hanging over the bed. He headed out the side door to put the box in his van. Duke and Becky were waiting for him.

"What did you find?" Duke asked. "Any guns?"

"Hey, give us a minute, will you guys? This is a police investigation." Al opened the back door of his van and set the box inside.

"What's that sign say?" Becky said, reaching a hand toward the box.

"Don't touch anything," Al admonished. "Just some stupid sampler sentiment."

"Every Good Boy Does Fine." Becky said, turning her head sideways to read without touching.

"What's it mean?" Duke asked.

"Piano class. That's how kids remember the musical staff," Becky responded.

Eddie and Mae had retreated to the vacant lot by the smoker and were sitting at the picnic table watching their two grandsons run around the yard when the detective found them a few minutes later.

"Are you Jones's parents?" the detective asked.

"He's her half-brother," Eddie said quietly.

"He's my son," Mae corrected, sitting up proudly. "I won't deny him; I'm not ashamed. He's my son, and he's a good boy."

"Yeah," the detective said. "Is that why he spent fifteen years in jail for rape?"

"He didn't do that," Mae said. "He never did any of the things they said. It was all a mistake."

"So, where is he now?" the detective continued.

Mae was silent.

"Listen, if he is innocent like you say, he's better off talking to us."

"I don't know," Mae mumbled. "I thought he was downstairs asleep. He never goes anywhere. Just sleeps and eats, builds his houses and watches cartoons. He's a child, really. If you knew him . . . ."

"How about you, Mr. Simms? Do you know where Jones is?"

Eddie shook his head silently.

"Are you going to take my grandpa away, mister?" Dion asked, pulling on the detective's pant leg.

"No, son," the detective said, keeping his eyes on Eddie.

"Baby, why don't you take the boys inside and give them some lunch," Eddie said.

The youngsters followed Mae into the house. Eddie glanced about, saw his neighbors gathered on the sidewalk and police cars everywhere he looked.

"In the guard shed, behind the tractor plant," he said almost in a whisper. "I found some guns under his bed and I took them to the guard shed. They're in a grocery sack, up on the top shelf. Three of them."

"Did you have any idea what your wife's son—"

"Not until the damage was done. Not until the police came here asking about the truck. Then I got to thinking about the time he had borrowed it and stayed out all night."

Eddie dropped his face into his hands and was silent for several minutes. Finally, he looked up.

"I thought I could control him, y'all see? I took the truck away. I took the guns away. I thought I could stop it. I mean, what's done is done. The best anyone can do is to keep it from happening again, and I thought I could do that. But if he slips out the door in the middle of the night . . . ."

"You don't know where he is?"

"Well, there is a place he goes sometimes. A bar. They play craps all night long. He likes to play craps. I've caught him taking money out of my jeans. And I suspect he takes money from Eula Mae, too, though she'd never admit it.

"She thinks it's all her fault, but she's a good woman. She loves her boys. She cried herself to sleep every night he was in prison. Every night for fifteen years.

"She was so proud to have him home, safe, where she could feed him and dote on him. I think, sometimes, she loves Biggun the best just because he is a little hard to figure out."

The detective scrunched up his face and squinted one eye.

"The bar, Mr. Simms. What bar?"

Chapter 109

Inside the house, Dion was refusing to eat the sandwich his grandmother placed in front of him. He wanted to return to the back yard to retrieve his *Star Wars* character.

"Is this what he wants?" Becky said, standing at the screen door and holding up and tiny black-robed figure. Eula Mae Jones came to the door, opened it a little and took in the figure. She handed the toy to Dion and then turned back to the screen door, her lip quivering.

"My baby," Mae started sobbing. "They've come to take my baby."

Becky placed a comforting hand on her shoulder. She'd seen the report on Malcolm Jones. She knew he was thirty-four. But Mae didn't look like she could be fifty. Could he really be this woman's son?

"The man they are looking for, Malcolm Jones. That's Biggun isn't it?" Becky asked, and Mae's eyes confirmed it. "I heard you tell them he was your son. So, is he your son or your brother?"

Mae turned away, looking out at the men gathered at the table. "Both," she said. Slowly she turned and looked at Becky. "Don't act so surprised. These things happen. I was 12. My father took advantage."

"Oh, my God."

"My mother said I was an evil child, said it was my fault. She kicked me out because in the ghetto men are harder to come by than children. I hated that baby, blamed him. But I loved him, too. Fiercely. He was the only family I had left. We had to learn to survive on the streets together."

Mae clutched Becky's arm, digging her fingernails into the flesh. Her words came choked, desperate. "Sometimes I locked him up to keep him safe. I had to so I could work. But I wasn't a bad mother. I think he liked being closed up. I think he still likes small, dark places. It's the world out there he doesn't like."

Mae covered her face with her hands and Becky hugged her. After a few sobs she pulled back and looked at Becky again.

"It really wasn't my fault. They took him away from me, shuttled him to foster homes where who knows what they did to my baby. By the time I got him back, he was a teenager. I thought he was just moody the way teens are. Sometimes he was my little boy and sometimes . . . ."

Mae sighed deeply and closed her eyes. "I thought if we got away from the projects. . . . With three kids, I got enough ADC to move out of the city, rent this place. But still, he just didn't fit in with the other kids. He'd have those tantrums."

Mae clutched Becky's arm again, and hissed her words, desperate for someone to know. "But he didn't do the stuff they say. They put him in jail all those years when he was just trying to help that lady he found. He's not the one who hurt her.

"When he came home on parole in May, Eddie said we should say he was my half-brother so it wouldn't reflect bad on Andy and Claude." Mae looked back at her grandchildren, then searched Becky's face for understanding.

" I know he's not done anything wrong since he's been back. He's a good boy."

Chapter 110

When no one answered Barb's question, Su Le went to investigate. Perhaps she had a customer. Barb and Penny turned their attention to their projects and Aggie closed the door on the restroom.

Suddenly, Malcolm burst into the studio, his big arm wrapped around Su so her upper body almost disappeared in his grip. In the other hand, he held a small gun.

"Oh, my God," Penny said.

"What the—" Barb jumped to her feet.

"Sit down and shut up!" Malcolm said in a gruff voice.

"No way, you bum." Barb lunged across the table. Malcolm tightened his grip on Su and met Barb's forehead with his gun.

"No, please, no!" Su said. "Just take the money and go."

"You! Take that tape over there and tape that bitch's mouth shut." Malcolm pushed Su in the direction of a roll of duct tape sitting atop the boxes of clay. Barb locked eyes with the determined man and saw a spark of madness that made her step back.

"I'll be quiet," she said.

"Tape her mouth," Malcolm repeated. "And her arms, too. Over here, sit over here." He tapped the back of one of the metal folding chairs with his gun.

Su pulled a little bit of tape off the roll, then told Malcolm she needed to get the scissors. She walked to the cabinet by the back door and Malcolm followed her. When she opened the drawer a little, he yanked it from her hand and sent the contents spilling across the floor. She screamed and jumped away from him.

"Pick up the scissors," he said pointing to a pair in the middle of the floor. "Just don't try anything stupid."

"No, no," Su said, holding her hands up. "We not do anything stupid. You take the money now. You go."

"Tape up your friends first," Malcolm said motioning with his gun.

Su did as she was told, first Barb and then Penny, a strip of tape across the mouth, a couple of bands around the arms and the back of the chair. Penny was whimpering.

"We mothers," Su said. "She has little ones. You no hurt mothers."

"No one's going to get hurt if you do as I say," Malcolm said, his voice rising. "Now bring me the purses."

Su picked up the two purses on the floor by Penny. Suddenly she remembered Aggie in the restroom. Her eyes caught Penny's.

"Bring 'em here, and that one, too." Malcolm indicated Barb's small purse hanging on the back of the chair. Su took the three purses to Malcolm. Hers was in the front room, under the cash register, but maybe he wasn't counting.

Malcolm hung the small purse over his neck and opened up one of the bigger ones.

"Okay, let's empty that cash register into here," he said, handing the purse to Su. She was walking forward hesitantly to take the outstretched purse when the restroom door opened.

Lightning fast, Malcolm spun and shot toward the unexpected sound. The bullet hit Aggie smack in the middle of the splotch of green paint on her forehead. The force blew her body back into the tiny restroom.

'Now, look what you made me do," he grumbled.

What happened next seemed in slow motion, each reaction, each movement seeming separate and yet somehow all happening at once.

Penny jumped up with so much adrenalin that she fell, chair and all, across the table, sending a half-painted Christmas tree crashing to the floor. Su took advantage of the distraction to lurch into the aisles of greenware.

"Damn bitches," Malcolm shouted, turning to chase after Su. His big arm reached out and grabbed her long ponytail. She screamed as he pulled her to the ground.

"Stupid, stupid," he said with an evil chuckle. He yanked Su up until her face was just under his goatee and looked her in the eye. Pulling a switchblade from his pocket, he slashed her throat with such force that he almost severed her head.

Violence seemed to feed him like stoking a flame, and he roared with delight. Penny was rolling helplessly about amid the soft clay pieces on the table and couldn't see what had happened to Su, but Barb could see and started pushing herself backward in the chair, trying to get away.

Malcolm grabbed Penny by the hair.

"Look at the mess you're making," he chided, and slit her throat, too.

"Now, who's going to clean this up?" he said, as he headed toward Barb.

Chapter 111

Josie was so excited as she pulled into the parking lot behind the ceramic shop that she started shouting as soon as she entered the open back door.

"He did it! Kevin made a goal!"

But when she stepped from the bright sunlight into the dim stairwell leading down six steps to the studio, she saw something that silenced her enthusiasm.

"Barb?"

She could make out a figure crumpled at the bottom of the stairs.

"Su, help me," she hollered as she rushed to Barb's body. "Something has—"

As she rolled her friend over, horror grabbed the voice from her throat. Barb's head lolled back like a rag doll that has lost some of its stuffing and blood gushed from the grotesque red smile just below her chin. Barb's eyes were open wide in disbelief.

Josie wanted to scream but no sound would come. Her mouth moved as if trying to pump up words from deep inside. She turned and saw blood and broken pieces of half-finished pottery everywhere. Penny lay awkwardly over the table, her head surrounded by the puddle of blood that oozed from her throat.

A moan pulled Josie's attention to the right and she could see a pair of feet sticking out of the bathroom. Josie stumbled over Barb and the chunks of shattered Christmas tree and fairly fell on Aggie in the bathroom. There was hardly any blood on her, no seeping streak of red across her neck, just a perfectly round hole in the middle of her forehead.

"Aggie! Aggie, can you hear me?"

The old woman was unconscious but moaned again.

"I'll get help." Josie headed for the phone at the front counter. As she started through the shelves of greenware, she passed Su's body, bent in half, looking perfectly delicate except for the circle of red that surrounded her. Josie didn't slow to check her but stumbled on to the phone, looking back in horror to see her footprints tracking through the blood. Her footprints and someone else's.

She ran right into him, a mountain of a man standing at the register, one purse dangling from his neck, one at his elbow, and his hands stuffing dollars from the register into the third purse.

Josie squealed in surprise and Malcolm chuckled with macabre satisfaction. Josie turned and ran, past Su slumped against the greenware, around Penny teetering on the table. She was just about to leap over Barb at the base of the stairs when a huge arm encircled her waist and yanked her into the air.

"No! Put me down," Josie screamed, finding her voice at last. She flailed her arms and legs wildly as Malcolm whirled her around, laughing as though playing with a squirming child. In her fight to break free, one of Josie's jerking feet found its mark in the big man's groin, and he threw her to the floor as he bent in pain.

Josie crawled a few feet to the base of one of the rolling pottery shelves. Without thinking, she grabbed one of Barb's gigantic porcelain bowls, whipped around and hit the still bent Malcolm Jones in the head. He stumbled backward a few steps, enough that Josie probably could have made it up the nearby stairs, but an odd rage possessed her. Unaccustomed power heightened her senses and a strange feeling of invincibility vanquished any fear.

"That's for Barb," she thought as the bowl shattered. Then she turned and grabbed one of Penny's gnome cookie jars, so big that it took two hands for Josie to pick it up.

"And that's for Penny," she screamed as she threw the heavy piece. It glanced off the madman's back.

Malcolm shot up to full height and growled like an angry bear. No longer was he having fun. His switchblade glinted in his right hand and he lunged at Josie, barely nicking her leg as she ran around behind the shelf, grabbing pieces of pottery and slinging them as she went. Even Su's dainty butterflies, which could sting no more than a mosquito bite, sailed toward his advancing hulk. Aggie's delicate designs bounced off his shoulder and exploded on the floor.

In the rage that gripped her, it seemed that each of her dead friends was placing weapons in her hands. The china shop was avenging itself on the bull.

Amid the pelting of pottery, Malcolm slashed at Josie, pushing her back to the wall by the shelves of heavy greenware until she was trapped in a corner. She had nothing more to throw and no outlet for escape. Malcolm paused to laugh at his triumph.

"Father, help me," Josie breathed, looking into the madman's eyes. Pressed against the concrete block wall, she reached an arm behind the shelves of greenware. She felt something solid, a water pipe, and pulled. Just as Malcolm stabbed toward her with all his weight, Josie disappeared, slipping into the imperceptible space between the shelf and the wall as miraculously as a newborn emerges from a ten-centimeter opening.

Frustrated, Malcolm poked at her behind the shelf but his beefy arms were too big to reach her as she slithered up the backs of the metal shelves.

Through the shadowy greenware, Josie could see Malcolm straining like Hercules to pull the shelf away from the wall. Feeling the shelf start to move, Josie grabbed a water pipe overhead and straightened her legs, pushing against the top shelf with all her strength. The unit wavered and then toppled forward with a thunderous crash.

Dangling from the water pipe like a kid on monkey bars, Josie saw a streak of movement through the torrent of ceramic shards. Malcolm Jones had escaped.

No longer thinking of her own safety, Josie dropped to the floor and started after him. Beyond the register she could see that the front door was open. Had it been standing ajar before? She couldn't remember.

She ran to the door and looked both ways but could see no one. She was turning back into the room to call police when Malcolm slammed her head into the doorframe, practically knocking her out.

"Where you goin', bitch?" he whispered with eerie calm. He pulled her back into the room, closed the door, and bolted it.

"It's my turn," he said pushing her up against the counter. Her face was bloodied now, one side swelling where she had hit the doorframe. His lips curled into a hideous grin, but his dark eyes lacked the fire of madness Josie had seen before. Instead, as he lifted the knife to her throat, she saw sadness in his brown eyes . . . and hesitation. Two words flashed into her mind, words Duke had said when she wasn't listening but that somehow had stuck with her for their incongruity.

"Good boy," she choked out. "Good boy."

Startled, Malcolm lessened his grip enough that she slipped under his arm and tried to run back into the studio. He grabbed her wrist. She whirled around and threw one last piece of pottery, the heavy earthenware vase that Su had said could be a hammer.

Perhaps it was her aim, or the way Malcolm jerked to one side, or maybe it was a guardian angel's doing, but the vase missed Malcolm entirely and sailed like a vandal's brick through the plate glass window at the front of the store. The lights seemed to flicker as the glass shattered in slow motion, the break creeping in all directions with a crackling noise as it painted a spider web on the pane.

The shock seemed to stop Malcolm and Josie for a split second. Then Malcolm's fist exploded into Josie's face, and everything went black.

Chapter 112

"What bar?" the detective repeated to Eddie Simms.

"I don't want to get them in trouble," Eddie said.

"You're already in a hell of a lot of trouble." The detective grabbed Eddie's shirt and pulled his face across the table until the two were nose to nose. "It's your truck. Your beer, your house. If the guns are where you say they are, what's to say you didn't do all these murders?"

"Eddie?" Mae called from the side door.

"Listen, if I thought I could make this all go away, I would confess." Eddie pulled free of the detective's grip and rose to his feet. "Don't think I haven't thought of doing that very thing. I would go to jail in a heartbeat if that would mean Mae could have her son back. But you and I know that won't stop this killing."

Eddie turned his back on the picnic table, looked at Mae standing at the door, and turned back to the deputies.

"Joe's. Joe's Tap Room. On the corner of Second Street and South River Avenue. Let me call someone to stay with Mae and I'll go with you. If he's there, maybe he'll come to me without any trouble."

The sheriff's department radioed the city for backup. But two squads were en route to a burglary in progress at Su Le Ceramics, two doors down from Joe's Tap Room. The call had come in when a broken window activated the burglar alarm system.

The city police pulled up in front of the ceramic shop, and one officer caught a glimpse of a man inside with a possible hostage. Soon, sheriff's deputies arrived, and the block was surrounded. A couple of officers tried to sneak in the back door, but shots rang out and caught one officer in the shoulder, the second in the knee. The injured policemen retreated, and everyone ran for cover. The officers reported seeing a body at the bottom of the stairs.

"Let me talk to him," Eddie said. "Maybe he'll listen to me."

In a matter of minutes, Chief Miller handed a bullhorn to Eddie.

"Biggun, son. It's me, Eddie."

"I'm not your son," came the thunderous reply from inside the building. "Did you turn me in?"

"They came to the house, boy. Frightened Mae. She needs you to come home now."

There was a brief silence and then a voice that sounded like a young boy called, "Mama?"

"I'm not going nowhere until those pigs leave," interrupted Malcolm's deep, gruff voice.

"Jones, put down your gun, and come out with your hands up," Miller said, grabbing the bullhorn.

"Is Mama here?" the boy's voice called again.

"Biggun, you know how Mae hates it when you make a mess," Eddie called, taking the horn back. "Come out, and we'll get the mess all cleaned up before she gets here."

"You're just another pig!" came the gruff reply. "Get those cops out of here or I'm gonna to kill this bitch."

Miller grabbed the horn. "Jones, how many hostages do you have?"

"Hostages? I ain't got no hostages, just one bitch who's still breathing. But she won't be for long!"

"Okay," Miller said. "Don't get excited. Send the woman out and we can talk."

"No way, man," Malcolm said. "She's going with me."

The officers could hear a conversation inside the building, and then a woman's scream.

"Send the woman out," Miller repeated into the bullhorn. "We have to see that she's okay."

There was no reply. After a few silent minutes the officers could see movement in the doorway, a bloodied face emerging, and behind her, a giant, dark shadow.

"OK," Malcolm said as he stopped Josie in the doorway, holding her by one hand twisted behind her back and pressing a gun to her head. One of her eyes was wide with fear, the other was swollen shut. She whimpered softly.

"Here's your woman. We're going to get in that car over there and drive away as soon as all you pigs get back in the pig pen."

From one of the purses, Malcolm had selected keys with a Cadillac logo and headed toward Barb's large yellow Caddy parked in the lot behind the ceramic shop.

"We can negotiate," Miller shouted.

Malcolm cut him off. "Tell your officers to disappear. If I see one pig, she gets it in the head."

Miller turned to the squads that ringed the parking lot and waved for them to leave. The officers got into their cars and slowly pulled away. Becky climbed into Page's brown van, and they backed slowly down the alley.

Holding Josie like a shield across his chest, Malcolm backed toward the Caddy.

"Get out of here," Malcolm repeated. "And take that pig in father's clothing with you. He's just another stupid cop."

"Biggun," Eddie said, "Your mother would not approve—"

"Shut up! Just shut up!" Malcolm fired a round in Eddie's direction. Miller shoved Eddie toward the squad car, and the remaining deputies scattered.

Malcolm pressed the hot barrel to Josie's temple and pulled her closer to the yellow car, as Mae came running through the gangway between the buildings. When she saw her son holding the gun to a woman's head she gasped, then she pulled her shoulders back, raised her head and spoke in a controlled, reproachful tone.

"Biggun, put that gun down before somebody gets hurt."

"Mama?" Malcolm said in a voice so small that Miller opened his mouth in disbelief.

Just then the door of the Cadillac opened with full force into Malcolm's back, sending him sprawling to the ground. He lost his grip on Josie, who crumpled before the open car door. Malcolm's pistol skittered across the pavement.

Duke tumbled out of the car, where he had sought refuge, and threw his body over Josie's. He expected a shootout, when a dozen officers lunged out of hiding, guns drawn on Malcolm. But the monster was gone. Only a big boy remained, curled in the fetal position and whimpering, "Mama."

Eddie held Mae back as she tried to run to her son.

"Don't hurt him. Please don't hurt him," she screamed as the officers rushed forward, cuffed Malcolm and dragged him to his feet. Malcolm seemed deflated and limp as the officers shoved him into a squad car.

Josie moaned and squirmed beneath Duke's weight.

"Are you OK?" Duke said, pulling back and seeing Josie's swollen face for the first time. "Jeez, you look like, like . . . "

"Peacock piddle," Josie croaked in a voice he could barely hear.

Chapter 113

Becky leaned against the fence, watching as a trio of corn pickers sucked in the brittle brown stalks and spewed golden grain into the open trucks behind. Like an army of bright green tanks, they devoured everything in their path, mowing down Mark Conley's vast fields in a matter of hours.

The October ritual had been played out in these fields every year for more than a century, but it was the first harvest for Becky. She was amazed at the speed with which the fruit of the fields was neatly condensed into trucks. The Conleys weren't even here to enjoy it.

Three months had passed since Natalie Conley was wounded during the summer's murder spree, but she still was unable to cope with reality. Her paranoia and depression had become so severe that she had attempted suicide twice. Shirley had moved with her daughter to a friend's beach house in South Carolina, hoping the total change of scenery—and a mental health expert in Charleston—would heal her unseen wounds.

Neighboring farmers had offered to take care of the harvest so Mark could join his wife and daughter. Becky was here to chronicle this act of charity for a Sunday story in the *Jordan Daily News*.

She had finished her interviews with Delbert Thompson and the other farmers who were helping. Mack had taken his photos and left, but Becky remained, trying to absorb the rhythm and grandeur of the whole operation.

Watching the transformation of the cornfield made her think of an old joke about not being able to tell a secret in a field because the corn has ears. Oh, the secrets and sadness this corn had heard! Last spring, when Mark planted it, he couldn't have imagined the death, fear, and ultimate unity that a "Cornfield Killer" could create.

Malcolm Jones still was making headlines in the *Daily News*. Just the day before, his attorney's petition for a change of venue was resolved and a court date had been set for early December in Peoria, one hundred miles to the southwest. Already jokes had started about "playing Peoria," though Becky doubted the trial could move to any city in the state that hadn't heard of the Cornfield Killer.

The summer's events had left a mark on the *Daily News* as well. Josie had taken a month off after her ordeal in the ceramic shop. She and Kevin had spent two weeks at a cottage in the Ozarks simply treasuring life. The experience had transformed Josie into a tiger, with a strength and determination she'd never had before.

Becky smiled, thinking of the day Josie had burst into the office, a full week before her leave was scheduled to end, and marched into Ham's office to demand that Nick be made her assistant to allow her more time at home with her son. She'd also demanded that Hoss be named news editor. Hammond argued that Hoss's failure to follow basic rules made him unfit for management. Josie countered, loud enough for the whole newsroom to overhear, that the rules about not eating or drinking in the newsroom were stupid and punitive and had been broken by virtually everyone. She pointed out that even Hammond had a roll of Life Savers in his desk drawer.

She offered a compromise: No eating at desks during regular business hours but no prohibition against snacking at the desk after hours. That brought the rules into compliance with practice, and was something even Hoss could accept. Of course, there was the little matter of smoking in the newsroom, and Josie assured Hammond that rule would not be broken by Hoss or any of the late-night sportswriters. Then, somehow, she convinced Hoss that his new title and hefty pay increase were worth his compliance.

The air had seemed fresher in the newsroom in the last month or so, and the reporters had a pool on how long it would be before the determined Josie convinced Hoss to give up the vile habit altogether.

After all, she had convinced Duke to enter a dry-out clinic for six weeks, at the newspaper's expense. Though Sharon and Jennifer had not moved back into the house officially, the family was together every weekend. Duke had been out of treatment for less than a month and seemed strong in his sobriety so far, writing more poignantly than ever.

Yes, so much had happened since this corn was planted. "Do that many changes happen every season?" Becky wondered. These events had been more dramatic perhaps, and closer to home, but as Becky watched the last corn picker finish the last row, she thought how change is all around us all the time. Some of it makes it into the newspaper, some of it doesn't, and the events that never make print are sometimes the most significant.

Becky weighed these thoughts as she pulled out of the Conley driveway and headed down the gravel road to Old Ben's. He would have some wise words to share. Becky had visited with Old Ben regularly during the past few months, hungering for the rural simplicity that she never had known and feeling an acceptance there she never had expected.

Becky could see him in the porch rocker as she pulled up, but he didn't rise to greet her or wave as he usually did. He must be asleep.

"Hey, Ben," she called as she came up the walk. She bounded up the two steps onto the porch, expecting the creak of the old step to awaken him with a start. When he didn't jump, her smile melted into concern.

"Ben?" Becky said tentatively, then reached out her hand and gently shook his shoulder. "Ben!" she said louder and touched his cheek. The cool stiffness of his body made her jump back.

"Oh, no! Ben! Ben! Can you hear me?" When there was no response, Becky ran into the house and quickly dialed the Thompson place. She knew it was too late for an ambulance, but she had to do something. Grandpa Thompson said he would be right there, but Becky still was shaking as she went to the kitchen sink and filled a glass of water from the tap. The well water had a strong metallic taste, but Becky noticed only the coolness that seemed to ease the burning in her chest.

She walked back to the porch and sat down in the rocker next to Ben. The contentment on his face conveyed a calmness that made her smile.

"Oh, Ben, how lucky you are," she said aloud. "You've never been to college or around the world, but you learned all about life watching corn grow. Watching sunsets and rainstorms, tilling the soil, planting seeds, harvesting grain. I wish I had half your wisdom, half your faith!"

Becky was silent for a few minutes, the porch creaking as she rocked. She could almost hear Ben's reassuring chuckle.

"Time" he would say. She would have her wisdom and faith in time. She smiled again, tears seeming out of place. Ben's passing was an occasion for celebration. His season had ended, his harvest had come.

A "V" formation of geese passed overhead honking loudly, but to Becky it seemed like a chorus of angels trumpeting a soul's arrival in heaven. She felt at peace, rocking and watching the cloud of dust from Grandpa Thompson's car wending ever closer on the old dirt road.